"Veteran writer Poyer tr... derdog hero fighting aga... strong, supple prose that ... captures the revolutionar... near-slave-labor conditions for workers—many of them immigrants—in a giant oil consortium in western Pennsylvania during the bitter winter of 1936. . . . Using stark detail, Poyer depicts the conditions of employees with no security or safety protection, subject to wage cuts to subsistence-level pay when profits were threatened. . . . The terrifying denouement further illuminates the complexities of the workers' plight, yet there's not one scene of gratuitous violence in a novel full of violent death. Poyer's pitch-perfect dialogue and explosive imagery capture both sides of the bloody battle that gave birth to the unions. This is a stunning period tale in which the oft-forgotten essence of the American dream is visible in every chapter."

—*Publishers Weekly* (starred review)

"Poyer's chilling look into the heart of the early union movement is dramatic and suspenseful, full of despair and hope."
—*Booklist* (starred review)

"Richly entertaining . . . reminiscent of both early Steinbeck and John Sayles's *Union Dues* . . . Graced by consistently vivid writing and knowingly detailed descriptions of such relevant manly pursuits as boxing and deer hunting along with (really first-rate) explications of the oil refining process . . . A rousing good read, and one that ought to make a nifty miniseries."

—*Kirkus Reviews*

"A rosy-eyed earnestness and clear-headed attention to detail illuminate David Poyer's ambitious historical novel, *Thunder on the Mountain*. . . . Poyer strives mightily to paint the complexity of the key characters and their motivations. . . . The pages are sprinkled with some keenly realized portraits of place, and some memorably drawn lesser characters."

—*Pittsburgh* magazine

David Poyer

THUNDER ON THE MOUNTAIN

FORGE®

A TOM DOHERTY ASSOCIATES BOOK
NEW YORK

This is a work of fiction. All the characters and events portrayed in this book are either products of the author's imagination or are used fictitiously.

THUNDER ON THE MOUNTAIN

Edited by David G. Hartwell

A Forge Book
Published by Tom Doherty Associates, LLC
175 Fifth Avenue
New York, NY 10010

www.tor.com

Forge® is a registered trademark of Tom Doherty Associates, LLC.

ISBN: 0-812-54004-2
Library of Congress Catalog Card Number: 98-43454

First edition: March 1999
First mass market edition: August 2000

Printed in the United States of America

0 9 8 7 6 5 4 3 2 1

Acknowledgments

Ex nihilo nihil fit. For this book I owe thanks to James Allen, Jim Bryner, Steve Burnett, Tommy "D'Arcy" Cardamone, John Cummiskey, Tom Doherty, Justin D. Dyrwal, Doris and Noel Galen, Fran and Vince Goodrich, David Hartwell, Helen Handley, Jim Haupt, Mary Ann and Rosanne Johnston, Bill Kaschube, Ronald Kent, Emma Knapp, Don Lambert, Stephanie Lane, Paula Mills, Trisha Morris, Dolores and Roberta Myers, Dave Myers, J. Craig Nannos, Jerome R. and Alan Pier, Lenore Hart Poyer, Alan Poyer, Hank Pruch, Walter Pudlowski, Eileen Reddy, Karen P. Thompson, Elizabeth Brady Upshur, John Vanjonak, Tom Weaver, and others who preferred anonymity. Thanks also to the National Women's Hall of Fame, the State Museum of Pennsylvania, the Penn-Brad Oil Museum, the Bradford Area Public Library, the National Guard Association of the United States, the T. Edward and Tullah Hanley Library, the Bradford Landmark Society, the Eastern Shore Public Library, the Slovak Institute of St. Andrew Abbey, the Arkansas Museum of Natural Resources, and the International Labor History Association. As always, all errors and deficiencies are my own.

"Union Maid" words and music by Woodie Guthrie. TRO © Copyright 1961 (renewed) 1963 (renewed) Ludlow Music, Inc., New York, NY. Used by permission.

History's not their story. All the books in the world
can't tell what really happened back then.
Each winter was a death,
Frost thick as bitter icing on cheap glass,
Snow weighing down the derricks like a
rent payment due Friday.
"You just got to stick," they told each other. They baked
sugarless cakes, stuffed newspapers in the cracks,
did what they had to do,
looking over their shoulders into the face of hunger.
Let this be to remember them.

Prologue

They came at the coldest hour of the night. She woke to a sudden splintering thud and the shriek of door-latch screws ripping out of the wood. Then shouting men filled her room. They kicked over the bureau and smashed the chairs with axes. They hurled the lamp across the room, shattering it in a burst of glass and kerosene-reek. She huddled, cradling her head, but they yanked off her covers with a whoop and a howl, dragging her from her warm bed into the freezing air of the unheated cabin.

She stared up at white facelessness penetrated by two holes.

"This the one?" The voice was casual, but with a chill undertone.

"Yeah, that's her," somebody else said, that voice, too, muffled by the hoods they wore. "Cabin fifteen, cabin sixteen. Two men, one woman. One of 'em's a smoke."

They dragged her outside, onto the porch. Instead of screaming as pine splinters ice-picked her bare feet, she clenched her teeth, locking her throat. She wasn't going to cry, or plead.

A cold silver mist rivered past the headlights of the automobiles outside the tourist cabins where she and Keim and Hendricks had moved after the relief office and strike headquarters had been burned. The men who stood waiting wore dark suits and fedoras and heavy brogans caked with the yellow clay of the county. They carried rifles and shotguns in the crooks of their arms. Her eyes rose to the smoky flames that swayed from their torches; then lifted again, to the lofty cross that burned high on the bluff above the hollow.

She tried to twist free, but the gloved hands were like iron shackles. "Let me get dressed, please," she said. "Let me go back for my robe." But no one answered. Someone was lashing her wrists behind her back. Other hands groped up beneath her nightdress. She stopped struggling and concentrated on trying to breathe.

Yells and the crash of more breaking furniture came from the adjoining cabin. Then Hendricks staggered out, face oiled black with blood in the golden firelight. He wavered, hands stretched out like a blind man. Then a rifle-butt swung, and he slammed to the muddy ground.

"Look what we found under his mattress. A thirty-eight."

"Haw, haw. Whoopee! Okay, let's let these good citizens get some sleep."

She tried to fight free again as they carried her down the steps, but they were too strong and her body was so weak. She smelled shaving lotion and sweat and coal-smoky night, the sweet rotten-peach smell of whiskey.

Behind the glare purred a black touring car. As they folded her into the rear seat she realized suddenly that they were being watched. Hollow-cheeked men, gaunt women with spindly arms folded over the bodices of their nightgowns, hawkeyed kids in ragged shifts or torn men's shirts. They stood immobile as carvings on their shadowed porches, or on the bare earth in front of the paintless, decaying houses. Gathering her strength, she screamed, "Don't just stand there. Get the police. Get the sheriff!" But they only watched, gazes motionless and resigned, even the children, looking on in the windguttering torchlight; as if they had known and foreseen forever this inevitable end to all their dreams.

This was her third campaign. She'd worked textiles, mostly, Carolina and farther south. The coal strike had started in May, in the Atlasburgh-MacDonald mines, when the owners dropped the wage to twenty-six cents a ton. By late June, 42,000 miners were out in western Pennsylvania, eastern Ohio, and northern West Virginia. The union was new and weak, and the league had mobilized every organizer to give it a fighting chance.

She was appalled at what they found. The miners' families lived in tents or shacks, thrown out of the ramshackle company houses the day they struck. They had no food, no clothing, no soap, no newspapers, no milk, no shoes. Their thin, sickly children picked coal from slag heaps for fuel. But they were filled with hate, and they trusted nobody. They were ripe for organizing, and she'd thrown herself into it. Talking, exhorting, walking the line. Serving out weak coffee and bean soup. And always, always, pounding in again and again the one simple message they had to carry stamped on their hearts:

If we all stick together, we can win.

Now she shivered in the rayon slip as the open machine rushed through the dark hills and down winding forest-roofed roads. It passed coal-tipples sparkling with tiers of electric lights. It rushed past rail crossings, crossroads hamlets, roared across cast-iron bridges below which the silver mist glowed like pale radium above hidden rocktumbling creeks. The taillights of another automobile bobbed and jerked ahead of them. The tall man and another, squat-bodied fellow sat flanking her in their white robes in the rear seat. The squat man had a rifle propped between his legs, the butt resting on the floorboard. The tall man's hand rested on her thigh, as if restraining her from leaping out. Her eyes fastened slowly to the cuff of a white shirt. Traveled down the long tapering fingers. As they passed a crossroads store with a single bulb burning above the gas pumps, she made out a gold ring, a complex symbol inlaid on a red stone.

"Are you from Pinkerton's?" she asked him. He didn't answer.

"I'm cold," she said. "This rope is hurting my hands."

"It won't hurt much longer," said the one with the rifle.

The driver chuckled, glancing back over his shoulder. He'd taken off his mask, but she still couldn't see his face in the rushing dark. "That's rich," he said. "Ain't it? She's a sheba, ain't she? For a Jew girl. Hey, you. You done it with the nigger?"

"Shut up," said the man with the ring. He had taken out a handkerchief and was dabbing at his face with it under the hood, the motion strangely delicate, the way a woman might correct her lipstick.

"Are you from the Mineowners' Association? Where are you taking us?" she asked them. "You realize this is kidnapping. You'll answer to the law for this."

"The law?" The man with the handkerchief chuckled. "Don't worry about that. We own that, too."

And a little while later the driver began singing "Yes Sir, That's My Baby" to himself. Just the first two lines, over and over: "Yes, sir, that's my baby; no, sir, don't mean maybe."

At last their velocity ebbed. The automobile passed through another sleeping hamlet, and she saw a sign that read BEECH WOODS. Shortly after that the lights ahead bobbed and flickered, then suddenly vanished. Their driver slowed even more. They crept along for a few hundred feet, then turned, lurching and creaking, down off the road and out onto an open field. The headlights traced a dark line ahead. The automobiles sagged and swayed over the uneven turf. The men with her stirred. The cars ground their way up to the black line, headlights transforming humped shapes into individual trees, till finally hand brakes ratcheted on.

The tall man said, "You can get out here."

She stumbled getting down from the running board, unable to use her bound hands, and he grabbed her hair as she slipped and dragged her back upright. The grass felt icy under her bare feet.

The other vehicles' engines died, becoming mere blocks of blackness in the murmuring night. Theirs left its engine idling, headlights aimed at a stand of beech.

Someone pushed Keim and Hendricks into the light, and she caught her breath. Their heads rolled. Clotting blood streaked the fronts of their nightshirts. Then she saw that the men around them, smoking cigarettes, carried whips and coils of rope.

Beside her the tall man raised his voice. "Listen up, Reds! Take a message back to your friends in New York. We don't need you here stirring up trouble. This is an American town. We don't want your kind here, and the next time, nobody'll ever hear what happened to you."

She started to protest but they pulled her bound arms upward till she heard something tear in her back. They pushed her after the others, toward a rushing murmur she thought was in her own ears before she recognized the song of one of the swift creeks that in the day roared and tumbled golden with the sulfur mine-drainage down from the deep hollows between the folded hills.

The rope soared into the treetops, then rattled down; soared again, and dropped over a stout branch. Keim stood with knees shaking, staring into the headlights. "Stinkin' finks," he said. He lisped, and she saw that his front teeth were gone.

"Haul away, there. Get 'em up in the air." Men bent to the ropes, and two bodies straightened, hauled upward by their extended arms till their toes left the grass.

The horsewhips cracked and sang. She flinched at each blow, no longer feeling the cold as cold but as part of the numb, disbelieving horror that would never fully leave her after this night. It went on until the organizers' backs were a mass of blood, and they dangled unconscious, heads sunk on their breasts.

The squat man jerked the ropes free from around her wrists. He forced her hands around to her belly, and retied them so tightly she gasped. Then pushed her toward where the others swung, turning slowly in the focused light. They tossed a third rope up for her, and hauled her up between them. She danced in the dark air for a moment, bare feet grazing the sharp, painful grass, then was pulled aloft with a great heave.

Swinging free of the earth, she clenched her eyes shut, waiting for the lash. But the breathless silence was broken only by the creak of the rope above her, squeaking as it rubbed tree bark. The clatter of the motor and the sigh of the wind through the naked trees.

"Let her down, boys," said the casual voice at last. "We don't want to scar up that pretty white skin, do we?"

Instead, they dragged her to the hood of a Ford. Gloved hands pulled her nightdress up around her waist. Others pinioned her arms.

Much later, it seemed to her, a locomotive whistle screamed not far away. Gradually the engine chuffed slowly closer through the darkness, panting and hissing like a harsh hurried breath in her ear. She lay staring up at where a few stars gleamed through scattered blacknesses of clouds. The heavy animal snuffing came nearer, closer, and behind it the hollow musical clack and jingle of railcars.

She couldn't walk then, couldn't move or respond, so they picked her up and carried her down to the tracks. She landed facedown on cold, gritty iron. Two other bundles lay there. Only when one stirred did she recognize the wet mass as a human body.

The icy iron hardness shuddered under her. Steam hissed. Slowly, with a clank and a squeal and a prolonged sigh, it began to move. It clacked over the uneven line of the spur, then gathered speed, rocking and swaying faster and faster through the night.

Fighting the blackness pulsing in her head, she raised herself on her elbows, to see that they were coupled into an endless snake of coal cars. When the train came to a curve, Hendricks and Keim slid toward the edge of the open flatcar. She threw her arms out, and her fingers sank into their slack, unresisting flesh like steel claws.

They rode westward all that night, along the winding ridges, above the black hollows, through the sleeping unknowing towns. And in those endless, clattering hours a bitter knowledge grew within her.

When light finally came again she was still awake, but cold now, a cold rigid and unyielding as ice sheathing and protecting her inmost heart. She lay stretched out on the rusty jolting iron, still holding the two unmoving bodies as her unseeing eyes traveled over hillsides and hollows outlined as if new-created by the first rays of dawn; beholding with that tearless unflinching gaze a world emerging from darkness into the light of a new day, when all injustice would be smashed, everything corrupt would be cleansed, and the forms of all things would melt away in the penetrating glare of a new and merciless sun.

One

―――――――――

Chilly morning, W. T. Halvorsen thought, even for the high Alleghenies; kind of an early taste of winter, though he hadn't seen any snow yet. He was pushing twenty miles an hour, coming down off the ridge into Fees Hollow in the brand-new bright-red Dodge Power Wagon, when he glimpsed the crown block of Favorite Number Fourteen looming above the brass and scarlet of the treetops. He didn't want to go any faster, not with a hundred and forty quarts of nitroglycerin packed in behind him and a ravine dropping away from the rutted, rock-littered lease road.

Halvorsen was twenty, lanky and blond. He had on green work pants with red suspenders and a red-barred hunting jacket. Worn black-rubber bighole boots rode the clutch and brake. The headlines of the paper on the seat beside him read: AIR ATTACKS SPREAD DESTRUCTION THROUGH ETHIOPIA. LEAGUE VOTES SANCTIONS AGAINST ITALY. LEWIS PLEDGES

MINE WORKERS FOR ROOSEVELT. He drove with one leather-gloved hand, elbow sticking out the window, the mountain air ruffling the cowlick that stuck up from behind his work cap. Every once in a while, when the road came to a switchback, he leaned out to spit dark juice toward the hillside.

When the derrick loomed out of the woods, seventy-two feet of bolted-together hemlock and iron, the foreman and the tool dresser were standing by the engine house. Halvorsen locked the brakes and skidded the last few yards, then stuck his head out and yelled, "Bryner Torpedo. You fellas call in a shot?"

The older man nodded. Halvorsen wheeled the truck around so that the back, where the nitro was, was right up against the derrick walk. He cut the engine and got down, stretched, then walked around to the rig.

"Ike Keller," said the foreman. "This here's Karl Grau, my tool dresser."

"Bill Halvorsen."

They shook hands. Grau was big, callus-handed, and he bore down harder than he had to. "Halvorsen. Didn't you use to work for Evans Cresson?"

"Uh-huh. Roustabout, then tool dresser."

"Know a guy called Len Brinton?"

"Sure, I know Brinton. Big-mouth champ of the oil field. Potzed most of the time, to boot." Halvorsen shook his hand loose. He asked Keller, "She on the bottom?"

"Oh yeah. Karl bailed her dry, she's all ready for you."

The derrick rose above them into a charred gray sky, massive black timbers climbing in a narrowing taper high as a man could loft a baseball. The wind moaned through the upperworks, making the drilling cable clang as it swayed. The big old Buffalo engine banged in the engine house. Six inches of rough-cast pipe stuck up above the drilling floor. When he bent, Halvorsen heard a gurgle deep in the ground. The air shimmered above the pipe. He smelled methane wet with natural gasoline.

He straightened. "Who you like for the Series?"

"I been watching Derringer and the Reds."

"American League?"

"I like Detroit. Greenberg and Gehringer in the field. Schoolboy Rowe and Mickey Cochrane, a great battery."

"This kind of a wild well?"

"She's making a lot of salt water."

A shovel leaned in the corner, coated with muck and bits of dead grass. Halvorsen picked it up and went to the forge. He got a bladeful of cinders and shook them out across the drill floor, out to the derrick walk. He searched around, found a plank, and laid it slanting down to the ground. Jumped on it a couple of times, making sure it wouldn't turn under his boots. Then carried over another shovelful and ashed the board too, making a gritty path all the way from the truck to the wellhead.

He asked Grau, "How about shuttin' down your engine there, toolie?"

But the dresser just stood there with his arms folded till the foreman said, "Karl, you heard the man. Shake a leg."

Halvorsen went back to the Dodge. He took off his Burley Bears and left them on the seat. He got a sheave out of his kit and a line off the power-driven reel on the back. He walked the line over beneath the derrick and tied the block off to the drill bit, which was set down on the drill floor, with a length of soft manila.

"Last time they shot, they brung the wagon out with those roans," Keller said. "Those sure were a spanking team of horses."

Halvorsen didn't answer. He gathered juice in his cheek and spat into the mud, thinking about the shot.

Grau came back from the engine house while Halvorsen was running the bobber down. He ran it all the way and read off eighteen hundred and fifty-six feet.

Halvorsen and Keller squatted over the samples laid out in one corner of the drill floor. The foreman said the hole went down ten feet past the bottom of the sand. The "sand" was a narrow sandwich-filling of chocolate-colored sandstone oozing-rich with crude. The shot would fracture it, letting the oil flow into the well.

The dresser went back to the truck with him, standing right beside him as he sawed the pipe for the anchor. Halvorsen asked him to give him room to work, but Grau didn't move.

"Len Brinton's a shirttail relative a mine."

"Yeah, you sort of take after him."

"How long you been shooting wells?"

"Not that long. Two, three months."

"Couldn't make it doin' man's work, huh?"

"A couple mugs blew themselves up out near Myrtle," Halvorsen told him. "Horses, wagon, and all, nothing left but the crater. That's what opened up the position."

"Guys get hurt out here, too," Grau said. "Like that rig collapsed in August, pullin' pipe down in the Kinnimahot'ny. Crippled one of the guys on the floor."

"I didn't say they don't. All I was sayin' was, fella sees a chance to advance himself, he ought to get stirring."

He pushed past Grau and carried the anchor up to the derrick floor, then went back and got the shooter's hook. He hung this on the end of his line and started making up the string. He got an empty shell, a sheet-tin cylinder sealed at the bottom, and hung that from the hook. He hung the anchor off that, then ran the assembly down into the well till all that showed was the open top of the shell.

He said to Keller and Grau, "You boys might want to give me a little room here."

"Call us if you need anything," said the foreman. The dresser lingered for a moment, scowling; then sauntered off after his boss.

When he opened the back of the truck there was the soup, two dozen cans of it, each nestled into its rubber boot. He took a couple of deep breaths, then reached in and very smoothly pulled out two by their soldered tin handles, drawing both up at once, one in each hand. Balancing them like milk pails, he walked their weight slowly and carefully up the cindered board, along the derrick walk, and set them down gently on the rig floor on either side of the shell.

He remembered what Pete Riddick had told him when he

was breaking him in on the shooting game. Ain't no point being scared around nitro, Riddick had said. Screw up and you'll never know. So just take your time and make goddamn sure you don't never let anything slip.

Each can was closed with two corks. Removing an awl from a loop on his belt, he carefully pried them out and set them aside on the rig floor. That glisten on their ends was nitroglycerin. Step on one by mistake, you could blow your foot off.

His bare hands were getting numb now, and he took a break, sticking them under his armpits to warm while he looked out across the valley. Under the cold sky the long hills, all exactly the same height, walked away to the end of the world. Hills, and the fiery-colored solidity of the forest, and down in the valley, the dry ginger tan of farmers' fields. Here and there rose the peaked roof of a farmhouse, or the skyclimbing tower of another rig. He listened to the wind, and gradually another sound seeped into his consciousness. A sound that was always there, in this country, so that after a while you couldn't hear it. But now he listened, tuning in like the Magic Brain in the new Zenith. And heard the whole wide valley, the earth itself, resounding with a slow pulse and creak: the thudding of engines, off among the hills; the creak of rod-lines working the pumping jacks.

They were bringing up what God or Geology had hidden deep beneath these woods, these ancient hills, worn down like an old nag's teeth. Millions of barrels of the finest oil in the world. Pennsylvania crude. You smelled it everywhere, in the fields, along the creeks, seeping up from the ground itself, rich and strong as Monongahela whiskey. He'd always liked that smell, from the day he'd started working in the fields.

With a grunt, he picked up one of the cans and tilted it over the shell.

The nitro came out clear but with a purple tint to it, thicker than water because it was cold. He held it steady, gradually tilting it up, till the can dripped empty. When it was safely set down he stretched, shaking the tension out of his shoulders. Then he reached for the next one.

When the shell was brim-full he corked the empties and carried them back to the truck. Then he ran the shot down into the well. He took it slow, running the winch at a creep. From the corner of his eye he noticed that the drillers had come back. They stood a few yards away, watching the line go down.

At five hundred feet the winch threw slack. He cut power, then threw it into reverse. "Somethin' wrong?" Keller called.

"She's hung up. You guys must of been pushing it pretty fast. Got a crooked hole here."

"You sayin' we don't know our jobs?" said Grau.

"Hey, I know how it is. The lease super's on your ass to push that tool, you run that bit too long, it gets out of gauge—"

"You little smart-ass son of a bitch. Yeah, Len told me about you. Only crooked hole around here's that Hunky hoor you been shagging."

"Karl, I told you about that mouth," said the foreman.

Halvorsen studied the wire, pale blue eyes narrowed. From the sound and the smell, it could be making fluid down there, spewing oil or conate water into the well hole. Old seawater, trapped for who knew how many million years. A wild well could float the shell right back up on that and the gas-flow. Then it was either run like hell or try to catch it in your arms before it hit the drill floor. He watched it for a second more, then set the winch and walked up to where Grau was standing.

His right jab snapped the toolie's head against the Samson post. The bigger man lunged back, snarling, to find the foreman between them. "Not now. Break it up! Get this shot done, then you two can go settle it in the woods."

Halvorsen waited. Grau rubbed his jaw, glaring down at him. "I'm gonna fit you for a wooden kimono, you little bastard," he said. "I'll clean you and give you carfare home."

Halvorsen turned away and went back down to the winch. He gave it a little power. He played with it, pulling the string up a few feet, then running it back down, feeling his way through the tight spot. Finally he was through and the winch hummed again. He breathed out, and the white smoke of his breath flew away with the chill wind that came down the hollow, cold as the close and stony sky.

When he eased it into the bottom, the Z in the hook unlatched. He ran the line back up, leaving the shell in the hole, and went to get another.

He did this five more times, till he had six full shells sitting on top of each other down there. A hundred and twenty quarts. He checked the shot card to make sure that was right, then told the foreman he could go ahead and water-tamp it down.

Keller said to Grau, "Run about three barrels down in there. And don't give this guy any more lip, or you'll be back on relief."

While they were running drilling water down into the hole, he started on his squib.

Rigging the detonator was an art. You started with a piece of tin pipe, like stovepipe, a little larger in diameter than the anchor and about three feet long, with one pointed end.

Taking two sticks of straight dynamite out of the box in the truck, he shoved one heavy wax-coated cylinder down into the tin pipe. He used his awl on the second one, pressing a slanting hole into one end. He trimmed the end of the Clover Brand Safety Fuse square across with his Case knife, making sure the gunpowder core showed, and inserted it gently into the cap. He crimped it with the tool, using slow, even pressure, all the way around. Then pushed it deep into the dynamite.

When he had the fuse timed he dropped the second stick in on top of the first and filled up the squib with sand, making it nice and heavy. Then he bent the top over and sealed it with pliers, leaving two feet of fuse sticking out.

The drilling crew retreated again as he carried the go-devil up the plank, down the derrick way, to the hole. He set the tip down on the floor, a foot from where the casing came up through it.

This was the tricky part, as tricky as pouring the nitro. Nerve, that was what a shooter had to have. That and a steady hand, even after you'd taken on a load at an all-night poker game the night before.

Squatting over the well hole, he hoisted the squib with his left hand and slid the tip into the pipe. Slanting the fuse to the right, out of the upward rush of flammable gas, he pulled his new lighter out of his jacket.

Holding the squib tight with his left hand, he flicked flame from the Zippo and held it wind-whipped but still burning against the bare stripped end of the fuse. Suddenly it caught, sputtering, spitting fire. Moving very deliberately, he dropped the lighter back in his pocket.

With his right hand, he pinched the yellow waxed-cotton casing. When he felt the hidden heat, the fire etching its way down into it, he picked up the heavy tube with both hands, and with a flourish like a man releasing a homing pigeon, dropped it down away into the hole. A rapid muffled rattling echoed back.

He rose slowly to his feet and strolled away, toward the woods.

He was fifty yards off when the shock kicked the soles of his boots. The ground began rumbling. He kept walking, knowing it would take a little while for everything to come up eighteen hundred feet through a six-inch hole. He got to where the others were standing, and turned.

A chocolate-dark cylinder suddenly extruded itself from the earth. It came up from the casing-head looking solid for the first fifteen or twenty feet, though it wasn't; it was oil, water, rock, and pay sand. Then it blew apart and up and out through the top of the derrick with a deep-throated roaring *whoosh* and he saw the amber glow deep in it, shining through it like a dirty-golden rainbow. Yeah, she was gonna be a producer. He could smell the scratch from here.

"Guess we'll get to work," Keller said when the last wavering veil of spray drifted away downwind. "Karl, you start and wash down, I'll get her ready to clean out."

"Give her a couple of minutes," Halvorsen told them. "Let those fumes blow away."

"That's about how long I'll need to take you down a peg," said the tool dresser. He spat on Halvorsen's boots. "Ready for a little go-around?"

"I got another shot to do today."

"Uh-huh. You ain't got the time, that right?"

Halvorsen looked him over again. The tool dresser was bull-muscled from hammering out white-hot drill bits with a fourteen-pound sledge. Grau looked to be four, five years older than he was, and heavier by about forty pounds. He had a cruel-looking smile. He moved edgy, like he was getting ready to dance.

"Oh, I can make some time for you," Halvorsen told him.

Two

The tall man in whipcords and riding breeches was flipping through lease contracts in the back seat of the black Chrysler when he felt the thud. It was faint, attenuated by distance and the tires and undercarriage of the heavy car. Another might not have noticed it. But Daniel Thunner lifted his head. He stared out at the passing woods at, a tin-roofed power shack.

"Take a right past this bridge," he told the driver.

Daniel was the third man to own Thunder Oil. The first had been the legendary Beacham Berwick Thunner, who had hand-drilled the first producing well in the Seneca Sand in 1869. Back then it was the Sinnemahoning Seneca Oil Company. After his hunchbacked partner Napoleon O'Connor was killed in a boiler explosion, it had become Thunner Sinnemahoning; then Thunder Sinnemahoning; then, and for the last fifty years, just the Thunder Oil Company. After Beacham had come his son, "Colonel" Charles, and now Dan. One son and heir per generation. He had only one child so far, a daughter. But there was still time. He was no longer quite young, but Leola was only twenty-eight.

When the derrick rose from the trees he saw the shooting truck but no crew. "Honk the goddamned horn," he said. "Where the hell is everybody?"

The foreman came out of the engine house, wiping his hands on a bright red rag. "Oh! Morning, Mr. Thunner," he said, peering in at him.

"Ike, did I just hear a shot?"

"Yessir." Keller seemed uneasy; his eyes kept sliding toward the woods.

Thunner glanced that way but didn't see anything. "Well, how'd it go?"

"Oh, fine. I was just running a bailer, cleaning her out. Good flow down there. We'll get her tubed up, nail her onto the line—"

Thunner snapped out suddenly, "Where's your toolie? Where's the goddamned shooter?"

Keller said reluctantly, "Off in the woods."

"Doing what?"

"Fightin'," said the foreman, looking apprehensive.

"Goddammit, Ikey, I don't pay you to run a fight card. I hire you to drill a goddamned well."

"I been pushing her, Mr. Thunner! Made eighteen hundred feet in thirty days. I didn't want 'em goin' at it on the drill site. Told 'em if they didn't like each other's looks, to take it out back."

"Keep the motor running, Harry," Thunner told the chauffeur. He reached for a pair of riding gloves, jerked the door open, and swung a boot down. Then he hesitated, and reached back behind the seat.

Slipping the Colt into his pocket, Thunner slammed the door behind him. He told Keller, "Okay, let's go see how they're doing."

With a long stride—he was six feet three, tall and lean—he followed the foreman off into the woods.

Rollling up his sleeves after they got to the clearing, Halvorsen recalled from out of nowhere the first fight he'd ever had. He must have been seven, and it was with Fatso De-Santis, that first day after school. A scuffle, that was all, wild overhand punches followed by a twisting on the dusty ground; he didn't even remember now who'd won. But after that they'd played Two Old Cat with the rest of the gang till night came.

A few feet away, Grau threw his coat over an autumn-scorched bush. The ground was carpeted with dry, dead leaves, and around them crouched the thick scrub second growth, all that was left after the loggers had come through years ago. Scarlet flags still fluttered on the maples. As he turned his head to shoot his chaw he noticed two men standing at the edge of the clearing. Keller and somebody else, a rangy fella in lace-up boots, gloves, a tweed jacket like they wore in English movies. For a second he thought he knew him. Then his face was masked, covered by his hat brim as he lit a cigarette.

He pulled his mind back as Grau stepped in. Put his fists up, warily, and was in the fight.

Thunner lit an Old Gold, snapped the case shut, and slipped it back into his jacket. Squinting through the smoke, he sized them up as the opponents circled. He knew Grau. The other, though, was new to him. A spare, loose way of moving. Not a big man, but large hands on sinewy arms. A fine, long Nordic head, and a clear eye; Thunner liked the look of him at once. They were fighting with bare fists, their breaths puffing out white in the cold clear air.

The smaller fellow suddenly attacked, landing a left jab, then a right. He wasn't schooled, you could see that, but he was fast. Grau shook his head and kept moving in. The smaller fighter stood his ground, parried a swing, then danced away.

"Want me to stop 'em, Mr. Thunner? Get 'em back to work?"

"No, let 'em have it out," he said softly. He took another drag off the cig and held it deep in his damaged lungs, head

back, hands on his hips, watching the circling men as narrowly and coldly as if they were a pair of fighting cocks.

Keller stood beside the Big Boss, not knowing what the hell
he should do now. He should have sent Grau off on some
chore when he saw the two of them getting on each other's
nerves. He'd figured, What the hell, let them get it off their
chests. But then Thunner had showed up, out of the blue . . .
he needed this job. He'd taken two cuts since '29 but you
didn't squawk about that. Thank God he hadn't bought the
house like his wife wanted.

- Squaring his shoulders, he caught his breath as Grau
lunged forward, and Halvorsen, moving back, tripped over
some unevenness or buried root. The toolie lashed out, and
the younger man spun around and went down, into the
leaves.

Halvorsen had figured to just spar around; he'd paste the
Kraut son of a bitch one, take a shot himself, then kiss and
make up. But he'd landed a couple by now, one in the eye,
and Grau had just shook his head and snorted like some kind
of bull. He hadn't been trying to hurt him, just get the damn
thing over. He wasn't into scrapping for scrapping's sake.
But Grau had put his dirty mouth on Jennie.

Remembering that, he head-faked, waited till the other had
his haymaker on the rails, and ducked under it and hammered
him in the face, left, left, right to the ribs. Hard, because he
wasn't going to let anybody get away with that kind of talk
about his girl.

He was moving back, sucking him in for another dose,
when he stepped into some kind of groundhog hole or something. He was fighting for balance when Grau's fist came out
of the sky and bango, he was on the ground with the dirt
cold against his cheek, looking at the pretty lights.

Thunner had been thinking the kid wasn't doing so bad. The
older fellow had to have thirty-five pounds on him, though

there wasn't much difference in their reach. "What's his name?" he asked Keller.

"That's Karl Grau."

"I mean the Scandahoovian lad. The shooter."

"Name's Halvorsen. Used to work for Evans Cresson, he said."

"Like how he handles himself. Up on his toes. Always moving, you never know what's coming next."

"Yeah, he's doin' swell. But Karl keeps going in."

"He's stupid," Thunner told him. "The kid's making him chase him around. He's landing more punches than your boy is. Grau's logy and slow, and he keeps leavin' himself open."

Then Halvorsen stumbled and took the haymaker. The sound of bone on bone came to the watchers. Keller flinched and grunted. Thunner started to turn away, thinking it was over, but after staying down for a second or two, Halvorsen bounced back up, leaving his boots behind in the mud. The bigger man tried to knock him down again on the come-up, but he weaved and faked and left Grau standing flat, like a puzzled bear.

Thunner stopped, taking another draw on the cigarette, narrowing his eyes against the flat cold light.

Grau was wheezing. Couldn't get enough air. The trampled mud was deep and sticky, grabbing at his boots. His eye hurt where the son of a bitch had pasted him, not once but about four times. This mug punched so fast he couldn't see them coming. But he'd landed that last one so hard and solid he thought for a second he'd broken his mitt. Would have put out most guys he'd fought. But the kid had jumped up so fast he'd missed when he tried to club him again.

He knew the tall man beside Ikey Keller. Everybody knew Thunner liked a scrap. But he was on company time now. Time to finish up. Blowing hard, he moved in, faked a left, and started his fight-ending uppercut up from the ground again.

*　　*　　*

Halvorsen watched Grau telegraphing his right from about a hundred miles away. He waited for it, jerked his head aside to let it graze off his skull, and went in. He popped the guy hard on his big nose, feeling something break, cartilage or bone, then hammered in a second right, then a left to the ribs. He slipped free and turned, fists up, to find himself facing the bigger man's back as Grau stood half-bent, turned away from him, blowing a string of blood and snot out onto the trampled mud.

Thunner kept adding up points. He liked the way the kid moved. He'd taken one on the kisser, and gone down. But he kept his head and used it, took a rest on the count and then bounced up gay as a red rubber ball.

"Hully gee," said Keller, beside him. "Get an eyeful a that! Hey! You guys! Ain't that enough?"

Grau stood still, holding his face like a cracked teacup. His eyes were shocked white. "He broke my goddamn nose," he said. Behind him Halvorsen stood with fists cocked, blue eyes alert.

"All right, that's enough. You're the one wanted to fight, Karl."

"He had enough?" said Halvorsen.

"Oh yeah. He's done."

The kid dropped his guard, and bent to pull his boots out of the churned-up soil. He'd fought the last minute in his stocking feet, and they were coated with mud like thick brown wool stockings.

He was walking past the bleeding man when Grau suddenly lashed out. Halvorsen folded, the air coming out of him with an explosive "*puh*." Thunner tensed, but then Keller was there. Had his arms around the toolie, who was yelling "You ain't seen the last of me, you little shit." Was leading him away, looking warningly back toward where Halvorsen stood bent over, gasping and holding himself. Jerking his head, mouthing silently: *Get him out of here.*

"Better learn to guard yourself, son," Thunner told him.

"Even when you think everything's over. Still, that was a pretty little tussle."

Halvorsen grunted "Thanks." He was still clutching his groin, and his face was white.

"You okay? He bust anything?"

"Nah. Just gimme a minute." He breathed hard, then tried to straighten.

"I was watching you mix it up. You're a cool fighter."

"I'm a well shooter, mister. Got to stay cold, handling the nitro."

"My name's Dan Thunner," he said, holding out his hand. Halvorsen looked at him for a second, then took it.

He felt weak—Grau had nailed him good, with that last below-the-belt shot—but when the swell said his name, he snapped to attention inside. Now he knew why that mug looked familiar. He'd seen it lots of times, on the front page of the Raymondsville *Century*.

"Bill Halvorsen," he said, shaking hands.

"See you're drivin' one of Jim Bryner's trucks. Been with him long?"

"Not long. Coupla months."

"Who'd you work for before that?"

"Vic O'Kennedy. Before that, slush boy for Don Ekdahl."

"I know O'Kennedy. Why'd you leave him? You ain't a troublemaker, are you? A Bolshevik, or anything like that?"

"No, I ain't. Ask Vic, he'll tell you. Bryner was offerin' more, that was all. If a guy don't look out for himself, who will?"

Thunner half smiled. "I'd say you've got that right. What do you pull down out there?"

"How much? Fifteen per. I last a year, he'll up it to sixteen."

"I'll give you seventeen a week, startin' today. That's a foreman's pay with Thunder."

"I got another shot card to do right now," Halvorsen said, stalling while he tried to figure this out.

"Finish your day's work, then tell Jim you're coming to work for me."

"Doing what? Shooting wells?"

"I don't have company shooters," Thunner told him. "Cheaper to hire it out, let somebody else assume the risk. But if you worked for O'Kennedy, you ought to know how to dress tools."

"I been a toolie already."

Thunner grinned. "Oh, you want to be a driller? Okay . . . I got a man can't seem to whip his crew into line. We'll see how you do with 'em."

He held out his hand. Halvorsen hesitated, looking at it. He was tempted. On the other hand, he liked shooting wells. And Thunner's assumption that he could walk in and buy him didn't sit right. Silly to get his back up about it. Still, it was how he felt.

He said slowly, "That the whole deal, mister? Or is there something you ain't telling me?"

"There is one string to it. Like I said, I like the way you fight. What do you weigh?"

"Uh . . . I ain't exactly sure. About a hundred fifty-six, maybe fifty-eight, I guess."

"Middleweight. Might grow into a light heavyweight. That'd work."

"What you got in mind?"

"I want you to go into training with Father Guertin. Take you two, three months. You can do it after work, and on weekends." Halvorsen waited. Thunner took the cigarette from his mouth, examined it, then ground it into the mud with a polished boot. After a moment he added, "Things work out, there's a fella I might want to match you up against. He's good, but I think with the right training you could beat him. How about her? Interested?"

"I'll shake your hand again, Mr. Thunner, but I think I'll pass on the deal."

Thunner seemed to take it all right; he just said "Pity," and turned away. Halvorsen glanced toward the engine house—no sign of Grau or Keller—and then followed him back toward the truck.

Three

Jennie Washko was standing at the front window when her mother came out of the kitchen. "Jennie," she said in Slovak. "Don't look out on the road."

"*Preco nie, Mamicka?* Why not, Ma?"

"You look like one of those ladies from River Street, that's why."

She sighed and let the curtain drop, looking around the dark little front room.

It was painted the color of bitter baking chocolate, with cream trim over the archway that led into the dining room. Saint Anthony gazed toward heaven on one wall, with a framed color rotogravure of FDR only a little lower. A sepia-toned Gramma and Gramps Yanick stared grimly from an oval frame. A Philco stood in the corner, beside a horsehair easy chair with its seat worn the color of sand, and a high-backed sofa squatted against the far wall. From the kitchen came a clatter of pans, the familiar rattling slam as the oven closed.

She turned back to the curtain, hearing a popping noise,

swiftly growing louder till he coasted into view, the wheels of the motorcycle bumping up onto the brick sidewalk. When he came up the steps she flew to the door.

"Billy. Hi!"

"Hi, Jennie." He stood twisting his cap, glancing past her into the depths of the house. She waited for him to take her hand, but he didn't. He brought a smell of gasoline and tobacco and something sweet, hair oil probably, into the closed air of the parlor. "Your dad home?"

"Probably not till later."

"Your mom?"

"Yes, she's here. You gonna have supper with us?"

He patted his hair, slicked down flat and gleaming except for in back, where a cowlick stuck up stubbornly. "Supper? I guess so. After that, I thought we could go out."

"Maybe for a while. Noplace fancy, I'm not dressed for it."

"You look fine," he said, looking her up and down. She was glad she had the new dress on. It was the first thing she'd bought with her paycheck from the stocking factory. "But—what'd you do to your hair, Jen?"

"Put it up. Do you like it?"

"Oh, sure. Makes you look . . . swell. Like Claudette Colbert."

She told him to take his jacket off and stay awhile, and he grinned and perched on a couple of inches of sofa.

Her mother was bent over the kitchen table, rolling out tomorrow's noodles on damp cloths under a bare dangling bulb. The stove sizzled. The hot air seethed with the smells of pork and hot bread, onions and garlic and ground spices. Jennie lifted a cloth on the sideboard to reveal a pie made of home-canned cherries. The flour-dusted fat under her mother's arms swayed as she bore down on the rolling pin. The screams and grunts of her littlest brothers fighting bounced down the narrow, steep staircase. The kitchen, not the stuffy front parlor, had always been the focus of the family. Seven kids in this cramped little house, but there was always room around the big white-enameled table. Seven kids living, and two small stones in the cemetery on the hill. They hadn't gotten to grow up, but they were still part of the family.

"Is *he* here again?" Anna grunted.

"Is it all right if he has supper with us? Ma?"

"We got food. Then what? You go out?"

"For a little while."

"Where?"

"I don't know yet. A movie or something."

"You don't drink, go to pool halls. You don't go to his room at that boardinghouse. You don't ride on that *hlupy* motorcycle either."

"No, Ma. I know what Pa said. We're takin' the trolley."

"What time you be back?"

"Nine."

"You be back at eight-thirty, get your sleep so you can work tomorrow. Don't let him get fresh with you, feel under your skirt."

"Ma, I'm seventeen. I'm makin' my own money. And besides, Bill's a gentleman."

"He's Protestant. He don't believe in God, what's to stop him doing anything he wants."

Viola, the youngest, came down the stairs. She was singing, "Mellon pulled the whistle, Hoover rang the bell, Wall Street gave the signal, and the country went to . . . heck," she finished, glancing at her mother and sister.

"I'll set the table. Will Pa be here?"

"Not till later." Her mother dusted her hands off and reached for the sideboard, for a pottery jar in the shape of a fat black mammy. "Here's twenty cents, carfare. In case you have to come back by yourself. A lady always takes the carfare."

When she came back she found Bill on his feet, looking at the pictures on the walls. "Who's that?"

"Saint Anthony. Those over there are my mother's parents, Mary and John."

He stood with his arms hanging, and she saw that his small talk was exhausted. She started getting dishes out of the cupboard, setting the table in the little dining room.

Her brothers came in as they were about to sit down. As Bill joked and fooled with them, she felt better. Johnny, the oldest, had left school to help out with the bills. He'd just started working down at the refinery. Bernard was still going to St. Bartholomew's; he was going to be an electrician, maybe a radio operator in an airplane. He was aeroplane crazy. They started talking about the new airport the WPA was building north of town. She went back and forth, bringing out bread and Warsaw pickles and beet soup. Her mother stayed in the kitchen. "Aren't you coming out, Mrs. Washko?" Bill called.

"You young people eat. I wait for my husband to come home."

"Your dad's working late."

"He works hard."

"You do okay here," he said, but as he looked around the crowded room with its dark walls and heavy old furniture, everything clean but old, worn, she wondered what he was thinking. Sometimes she was ashamed of her parents, and the smallness of the house, and sometimes . . . she prayed every morning and night to Jesus and Mary like the Sisters had taught her, but sometimes she even felt funny about the pictures of the saints and the Sacred Heart, when she saw him looking at them. Then the food came, pork chops and gravy, pirogies, beets and string beans canned from the garden in back of the house, and the good-smelling hard-crusted soft-inside Italian bread they got at the corner store. And for a while everything was quiet except for asking for things to be passed, and the youngest boys kicking each other and fighting, till she told them they'd get the strap when Pa came home.

She got up after a while and brought out the pie. It was thick-crusted and heavy, and she watched Bill eat two pieces. "This made with lard?" he said. "It's good."

"I think Ma uses Crisco. It ain't gone up at all."

She thought about having a slice but didn't. At last he used his napkin and said, "You about ready to go?"

"Just let me get my coat."

"Be home at eight-thirty. Your father will be here," said her mother again as she went through the kitchen, and she didn't answer, just brushed by her, wanting more than anything else right then just to go, out of this tight dark little house, this clamor of family that she loved so much and yet hated at one and the same time.

The woods skated smoothly by the open windows of the trolley. The air was cool and the trees were a million tones of orange and ocher, blood and gold. "It's gonna be cold soon," she said, shivering a little.

He put his arm around her. "Yeah, winter'll be here before you know it. Too bad, I ain't lookin' forward to it."

"I don't mind it. At least we don't have to worry about the polio for a while."

Halvorsen leaned back, happy to have his arm around the prettiest girl on the car. That's what had drawn his eye first: dark, smooth, straight chestnut hair, and a sweet smile that somehow looked knowing at the same time, and trim ankles. She wasn't stuck up or snooty. He never felt he had to be anyone else, or any different, than just the way he was. And she was straight; she didn't smoke or use lipstick or rouge. Then a shadow crossed his mind. Trouble was, she was Catholic.

"You never took me to the park before. I thought we were going to the show."

"You never been to Hecla Park?"

"Oh, to swim, when we were little. But not at night."

"You'll like it; it's classy. There's dancing and stuff, and they show a movie, too."

Halvorsen looked at her face again, happy and young, and had to look away. Part of him wanted to be with her. Part wanted to be alone, back in the boardinghouse, reading an Edgar Rice Burroughs book about Mars or listening to the radio in the parlor. "How's it goin' at work?"

"Okay, I guess. Some of the girls are sick, it's goin' around. Hope I don't get it, we need the sand."

"A funny thing happened to me today. Out at one of the rigs."

A shadow crossed her face, and he knew why. "With the nitro?"

"No, this was after the shot. This big Hun was giving me a hard time, and we were out back going at it."

"Going at it. Fighting?"

"Just mixing it up a little. Just a little scrap."

"What about?"

"Oh, nothin'; that ain't important. But guess who showed up?"

"The police?"

"No, no, they don't care, that kind of stuff. No, it was Dan Thunner."

"The one who owns Thunder Oil?"

"That's right. Anyway, he watches us, see, and after it's over, he offers me a job."

"What kind of a job?"

"Foreman. And two simoleons more'n I'm makin' at Bryner's."

Her eyes got big and round. "Bill, that's great! Why, that'd be seventeen a week—that's more'n my pa gets, since the cuts, and he's got sixteen years with Thunder!"

"Well, wait a minute. I didn't take it. There's a catch. He wanted me to box for him. See some Father Ger—Gerdon—"

"Father Guertin?"

"That's him. You know who that is?"

"He teaches the boys, at Saint Bartholomew's."

"Well, he must coach boxing too. Mr. Thunner wanted me to train with him, then fight somebody for him."

She looked out the window, lip caught between her teeth. Finally she said, so low he almost didn't catch it over the clack of the wheels and the sputter of sparks overhead, "Why didn't you take it, Billy?"

"I don't know. I don't mind shootin' wells."

"But it's so dangerous. Isn't that how you got the job? People blowing themselves up?"

"Yeah, but I won't. Look at old Bryner, in the business since 'ninety-eight and he's still drinking a quart a day."

"But you wanted to be a driller. That's why you quit out at Gasport. They said you were too young and had to wait. It sounds great to me, Bill," she said, and looked up at him with a look so infinitely wistful he could only hold her brown eyes for a moment before he had to look away and clear his throat.

"Well . . . this here's our stop. Let's talk about it later."

Hecla Park was miles out of town, out past where the smoke from the refinery and the oil-smell reached, although there were pump-jacks there too, hobbyhorsing away right in the middle of the grounds. The dark was coming as they walked down a dirt-worn path through the woods and then suddenly there it was, hundreds of electric lights sparkling through the trees, and the bingo caller yelling and the rides going around and the people screaming and laughing, and past and beyond it the already shadowy mass of Cherry Hill. He reached out for her hand, and suddenly he was happy, there in the evening with a dollar in his pocket and the lights and the band starting up in the dance pavilion and pop and ice cream and the whole evening ahead. And later on they were sitting together at the top of the Ferris wheel, waiting for the ride to start, and she took his hand suddenly and said, "It's scary up here. Isn't it?"

"Naw. This thing's built solid. The engineers, they figure the stresses an' everything so nothin' can go wrong . . . hey, what's wrong with your hand?"

She tried to take it back, but he held it firm, lifting it to the light to examine the tiny red cicatrices.

"It's the carding machine. You got to put the cards on, fast, so it can put the socks over them. And sometimes the paper, it's so sharp it cuts. Some of the women—they've been there a long time, their hands look just like they have gloves on. Only they don't."

"Jennie, what are they payin' you there?"

"Thirteen cent an hour."

"Darn. We got to get you out of there." He put his arm around her, suddenly feeling frightened, he didn't know of what. She nestled under it, and he smelled her hair. She looked up then, quick and shy and surprised.

Their kiss seemed to last forever, as they whirled through the air and the hurdy-gurdy loud brassy music played, and all the hill and the light and the night wheeled around them.

He whispered, holding her close, "What do you want, Jennie?"

"What do I want?"

"Yeah. You know. What you dream about—when you lay awake at night—or when you're working, and your mind wanders a little . . ."

"I don't want that much," she said. "A little house; not a big one—they're too hard to keep ret up. Just a little place, with wood floors, and some throw rugs; and a picture window; and a garden, I want a garden so. A nice kitchen, and a washing machine and a good vacuum and like that, so I don't have to work as hard as Ma does. And I want one little room that's all my own, where I can read, or study—just big enough for a desk and a bookcase, and a what-not for my pictures and things from when I was a kid. And in the bedroom I want wardrobes, nice big ones, one for me and one for—my husband. Deep brown and dark yellow, I think. And a linen closet, painted with that lavender-scented paint I read about."

"Gee, you've got it all planned out, don't you."

"Well, you asked me." Her eyes flashed, then she bent her head.

And a while later she whispered, "Billy, all I really want is to make you happy. I think we could be happy together. Don't you?"

He looked at her shining hair, her quivering lips. "I think we could, Jennie," he said softly. "I hope we can."

A shadowy figure was sitting on the porch glider when they came back up the walk. The window was open, even though it was cool, and the host of the *Firestone Hour* on the radio inside was introducing Jussi Bjoerling, singing "Celeste Aida." By the flickering light of two gas-flares down the street Halvorsen saw that it was her father. He gave her his arm up the steps, then tipped his cap. "Evening, Mr. Washko."

Her father didn't answer and he stood there awkwardly, facing Jennie. He'd planned to kiss her, but that was out of the question with her old man watching. Finally he said, "Well, good night."

"Good night, Bill." She squeezed his hand, glanced at her dad, then slipped inside.

On the radio, the Swedish tenor launched into Verdi. Halvorsen was going down the steps when the rough foreign voice said over the music, "Wait minute." It sounded like "Vwait' minnit."

"Yessir?"

"Come around the back wit' me." Washko got up slowly, the glider creaking and rocking, and stuck his head inside to holler, "Bring us milk, out back."

Halvorsen followed him around the house, past the hollyhocks, past a little garden and the little lean-to shed that smelled of cow manure, back to a little grape arbor. Everything was small, but well kept. Their accents were strange, their customs were different, but underneath that sometimes he felt the Washkos weren't that different from his family. His dad Thorvald had come over with nothing and ended up just about that way, too, the farm worn out before he died in '19 of the flu, gasping and choking as he drowned, the red foam coming out of his mouth till the bedsheets were wringing with it. . . . Past the arbor he heard the chuckle of the little creek. In the daytime you could see how it was covered inches deep in oil sludge and refinery scum and sand-pumpings from the leases up on the hill. The summer before it had caught fire and burned down their garage. The cracked cement square still showed the scorch marks.

The back door opened and Mrs. Washko set two glasses of milk on the stoop. Washko led him silently over to a couple of rickety kitchen chairs set under the grapevines. It

was dark there, the window-light didn't reach very far. He
heard the old man groping up in the vine leaves. Then a cork
popped. He understood then, and held the glass out while
Washko tilted the bottle.

"Better for your stomach, with the milk."

"Yes, sir, I heard that."

"You like the hootch?"

"I take a little bit."

"How old you, Billy?"

"Twenty, sir."

"How much you make, shooting the wells?"

He told him. Washko rocked back in his chair, and he saw
for a moment the old man's leathery face, the jutting jaw,
the dark, weathered skin. He had a puckered scar across his
forehead. Jennie said he used to work in steel, down in Pittsburgh. She said Joseph Washko wasn't his real name, but
he'd never told anybody what it used to be.

"You got feelings for Jennie?" Washko asked him.

"Yes sir, I do."

"You gonna marry her?"

"I was hopin' to, Mr. Washko."

"Suppose you did. She keep working, down at the mill?"

"No, sir. I can support her."

Washko snorted. "How? You gonna blow yourself up with
that damn hell stuff."

Halvorsen considered telling him what he'd planned: to
save his pay, go back and finish school; study to be an en-
gineeer, something that would let him keep on working out-
doors. But Washko would think he was daydreaming, or
bragging. So instead he said, "I got offered a foreman job
today."

He saw the shadowy head come up. Old as he was,
Washko was still a roustabout, doing the heavy work around
a rig: dragging in casing and sucker rods, laying pipe, hauling coal and cement and sand. With his bad English he'd
probably never do any better. "Foreman? Sonofabitch . . .
who make you foreman?"

"Thunder Oil."

"Sonofa*bitch*. Where they got you working?"

"I ain't took it yet." He felt in his pockets, said to the old man: "Want a chew a Mail Pouch?"

"What you mean, you ain't take it yet?"

"I'm thinkin' it over."

"So you ain't a foreman yet."

"Didn't say I was. You want any of this?" He bit off a jawful, held the plug out.

"Jennie a good girl. She cook good. Go to church. Who the hell are you? You, I don't know nothing. Ride motorcycle. A Protestant." The old man spat into the dark. "What kind bastards the kids gonna be?"

"I told Jennie we can raise 'em Catholic. But suppose I take this job. You gonna let me marry her if I do?"

"There's more to keeping family than making seventeen a week," Washko said, and Halvorsen for a moment heard something not unlike sorrow or regret in the rough voice; something ominous and frightening, like a premonition of the way life was, would be, instead of the dreams he and Jennie had, probably everybody had, when they were young. A shiver ran up his back in the creek-chuckling dark.

"What do you mean?" he said.

"Sometimes a man talks big. Then he gets family. Pretty soon, he don't talk so big anymore. Maybe he got dreams, got to forget them, they're shit. I raise seven kids. They never hungry, like I was in old country. America good, sure, but I work hard."

"I work hard too."

"But you no like the job, you walk out. Like you walk out on Vic O'Kennedy. Jennie tell me. You gonna do that, you got family, kids? Then I say, hell with you. Take your foreman money down to whores on River Street."

Halvorsen sat rigid. He put the milk and whiskey down. "If you wasn't Jennie's dad I'd take you on for that, Mr. Washko."

"Go ahead, hit me. I beat plenty men bigger than you." But he didn't sound angry; just tired. "Goddamn, I don't want to talk no more. I got to be at work at five. You work tomorrow?"

"What's tomorrow? Oh, Saturday. Half a day."

"You take foreman job with Thunder. That's good offer. See how good the boss like you. Then I think about you and Jennie." The shadow got up, and he heard the sad heavy sound of a fart. Washko climbed slowly up the back steps, and let himself into the house.

Halvorsen stood watching the kitchen window, hoping for one last glimpse of her. He'd always found it strange that they painted their kitchen bright blue. He could see the walls, like a part of the sky still in there, still glowing like day. But he didn't see Jennie; didn't see anybody. When the kitchen light went out, he stood there still.

Four

The great house emerged slowly from the darkness, like a majestic liner steaming from night into day.

The Sands crouched among massive blackened oaks, on what had once been a forest bench. It was built of an intricately carved local stone, turned lightless by soot and time. A turret needled to four stories, and triple columns framed an enormous porch. Beveled windows flashed ruby and gold in the rising sun. Behind a wall topped with iron spikes lay an arbor, brick-paved walks. On a marble fountain, cherubs and naiads entwined in polished sensuousness beneath the cold, lascivious smile of an aging centaur. Beyond and above the garden rose the hill, first as lawn, then, suddenly, as forest. From the high woods came an eerie thudding and creaking, as if of hundreds of doors slowly opening, then slamming closed.

Behind tasseled damask curtains, Dan Thunner lay motionless in an upstairs room, head back, eyes closed, listening to water running. He was enjoying the heat of the soaked towel on his freshly shaven skin.

He started to rise, then lay back. He gave himself five more seconds, then raised his arm and pointed to the towel. Hurrying steps approached. When the cloth was lifted Thunner sighed and sat up. Vincenzo's fingers glided lightly over his cheek, checking for stubble. Thunner rose, patting his cheeks dry with a linen cloth, and went into the bedroom to finish dressing.

His wife was an irregular lump under the bedclothes. He debated waking her, then decided he had to get moving. He had to talk to Pretrick about the fire stills. They were monsters, they were obsolete, and he needed to decide soon what to do about them. A thousand details to attend to, then the organizational meeting at noon. He dressed rapidly, riding boots, jodhpurs, a gray suit coat. He spent half the day in the field and the other half at the office, and chose his dress accordingly.

Eggs and bacon were laid in the kitchen, with the *Times*, the Buffalo *Evening News*, and the Petroleum City *Deputy-Republican* set neatly beside his plate. He ate quickly, scanning the headlines. The Hauptmann trial. War in Ethiopia. The sanctions might include an oil embargo. He'd have to check what percentage of Thunder exports went to Italy. . . . A London doctor was killing people with incurable diseases, and said he would keep on until a "right to die" was acknowledged. A seven-year-old girl had been found hanged with a man's handkerchief in a Seattle garage. She'd been the victim of a criminal assault. . . . Gunfire exchanged between strikers and police at a cotton mill in South Carolina, fifteen wounded, one woman dead. The sports page, Baer and Lewis were set to fight. That might be worth a trip to New York. But Leola wanted to go to St. Augustine; she loathed the cold. He turned to the business page, calling to the cook for another cup of French coffee. Penn Grade fields production was still dropping. The price was down, too— not a good sign. Drilling reports: a dry gas well in Tioga County, shut down at 5,635 feet. Allegany lost a string of tools in John Higley Number Two. Tiona Refining was shutting down, going out of business. The tanks, pipes, pumps, and tools would be sold at auction.

As he pursed his lips over this last he heard the Chrysler starting. He wiped his mouth and ran down the stone steps, shrugging on the overcoat Vincenzo had ready at the door. Feeling the cold air against his cheeks like another razor, he glanced at the sky. A few tiny flakes spiraled out of the gray. Then he looked down, at the city that lay below.

The great edifice reached to the sky like a tower, like a mountain: eight full stories sheathed in brownish yellow brick baked from the clay of these hills. The exterior was nearly complete, except for where, high up, men labored on scaffolds where diamond-shaped inlays of milky and jet-black glass would proclaim to the world, THE THUNDER BUILDING.

Late morning. He'd just come from the railroad station, where the last few luncheon guests had stepped off the 11:10. Others had driven in, and one had landed in a brand-new Taylor Cub. Now he was leading them on a tour of the new headquarters. He gave them a few moments, till the suited, topcoated men in felt hats and homburgs had time to appreciate its size, the quality of its materials, to realize it was being built to last a century. Then said, "Shall we take a look inside? Follow me, and please, watch your step."

The lobby was huge, a third of the entire ground-to-third-floor square footage. He'd designed it to overwhelm and overawe, and it did. Even now, only half finished, still filled with workers and noise and dust. Overalled men were fitting the mirrors along the walls. Others were gilding the stars on the vaulted expanse of Krupp Enduro K-2 stainless steel that formed the mighty arch of ceiling. A team from Otis was rigging the elevators. An old man with a white beard knelt in the middle of it all, alone, rapt, tapping gently at the floor. Kristin Kohors, the world-famous Swedish muralist.

Thunner paused again there, admiring it. The great mosaic floor portrayed the Progress of Energy. Sturdy peasants illustrated muscle power, sweeping scythes through acres of yellow grain. Then came high-stepping horses, then sail-power, then coal and steam. And finally, the new world brought to Man by electricity and oil. Streamlined trains and egg-shaped automobiles sped along rails and roads; high-winged aircraft and airships soared above a city that stretched to the sky. Then he led them on, crossing the sections that were still hardening on bridges of planks. He liked this smell, of drying lime, new concrete, new brick, fresh paint. It was the smell of creation, of building.

But then beneath it all, faint but there, there, welled up the deadly residue of gas that lingered at the bottom of shell-craters, and rotting man-meat and explosive. He drew a breath and stopped, balancing himself on the narrow walk-way, suddenly looking past and through what lay around him into another landscape, shrouded by mist and blowing smoke, littered not with building debris but with shattered trees, dismembered horses, cratered earth, and rusty wire.

Second Lieutenant Thunner had joined the Keystone Division, 109th Infantry, Company D, for the last big push through the Hindenburg Line, tramping on day after day behind an army that had suddenly melted away, leaving only a murderous rearguard of Spandau gunners; and in the last week of the war had been gassed, wounded, and buried alive for almost an hour at the Étang de Lachaussée before his men succeeded in digging him out of a collapsed trench. Even now, he couldn't stand enclosed spaces. He cleared his throat, forcing himself somehow to act despite the paralyzing fear, and said, turning to the suited, topcoated men, "This way, gentlemen. Sorry the lifts aren't running yet; we'll have to hoof it."

They stood on the topmost floor, in the center of an enormous empty space that was not yet a room. Plasterers and electricians glanced at him apprehensively. Thunner had inspected their work, insisted on rip-out and rework, shouted at them; but this time he ignored them. He said to his puffing guests, "This will be the boardroom. It looks out and down on Number One, as you see." And turned toward the huge sheet of glass that was the eastern wall.

This block of land had been the location of the old Harriman Supply Rig, Reel and Boiler Works. Harriman had been rolled flat in October of '29, and he'd been able to buy cheaply. So that now this building would stand like a colossus, dominating the west end of the city as the Thunder works did the east. And now as he led them forward, some of them hanging back, fearing the height, he looked down on it all from far above.

A pall of smoke and steam and flame sheeted off the horizon, cutting off all sight of the hills beyond. Beneath it lay the true heart of Hemlock County. Refinery Number One covered nearly five hundred acres of once-fertile river bottom with pipe stills and cracking towers, storage tanks, furnaces, pumping sheds, and railway spurs. By day it was a pillar of steam and smoke, boiling with workmen and railcars. By night it was a twinkling carnival of lights, capped by fire. Three hundred feet above the valley the waste gases made a roaring yellow-orange flare so bright you could read a newspaper by it anywhere in town.

From eight thousand wells scattered through these hills the raw Pennsylvania crude, finest in the world, throbbed down to Number One; and fully a third of it was from Thunder's own lease lands. Its refined products flowed out in black Erie Railroad tank cars to lubricate, fuel, and light the world. Everyone in America had heard of Thunder Gasoline, Lightning Kerosene, Thunderbolt Triple-Filtered Lubricating Oil, Sinnemahoning Pure Lubricating Grease, Cure-O-Line Petroleum Jelly.

A low, hoarse rumble behind him became the voice of Derleth E. Burrows, president of Pennzoil, a shaggy-browed old man who leaned on a gold-headed cane. "Impressive, Daniel. Tasteful. Overwhelming. Most impressive!"

"Thank you, Mr. Burrows. Coming from you, that is indeed a compliment."

"But is it a wise use of your capital? Would your father

have approved? The Colonel believed in making every nickel do its work. As do I."

Past Burrows Thunner saw the others listening, and knew he had to respond. Pennzoil was as large as Thunder, and its market reputation just as good. Where Burrows led, others would follow. He raised his voice. "I believe, sir, that every cent I have in this building will pay for itself many times over. We must plan now for the future. And oil *is* the future. For lubrication, for fuel, for peace—and for war. Thunder, and its sister refiners, must build now for that destiny, or it will pass us by."

"Brave words, Daniel. But I do not believe this is the time for business expansion. Not yet. I have insisted upon re-trenchment."

"I agree that there is danger, Mr. Burrows. But I believe this is also the time of our greatest opportunity."

The old duffer remained silent, biding his time, Thunner saw. Very well; he would be prepared. He turned, to meet their leveled, unsmiling gazes. "That's about all I have, gentlemen," he said, aware that they saw him against the backdrop of steam and smoke and fire as its owner and master. As he was; and as he would someday pass it on, all that he and his father and his father's father had built. "Thanks for indulging me. I know it was a climb, but I wanted you to see the future. Because, in a way, I'm going to be asking all of you to throw in with my vision of it, this afternoon. Are there any questions? Then let's go to lunch, shall we?"

If the Thunder Building was the future, then the Petroleum Club was the past.

It had been built toward the end of the great oil rush, fifty years before. Crystal chandeliers lit a great oaken bar carved with nude caryatidi and overflowing bowls of fruit. In the etchings that leaned out above walnut wainscoting, hundreds of timber derricks porcupined the hills, Governor Hoyt clipped the ribbon to the Jenny Lind Opera House, Adah Isaacs Menken posed nude on a white stallion, and Company

I, Sixteenth Regiment, marched in puttees and slouch caps down Main Street toward the invasion of Cuba. In a recent photograph Daniel Thunner himself, straight and spare in frock coat and wing collar, shook hands with Herbert Hoover. He led them past the bar into the dining room, where a party of prominent county businessmen waited. Waiters in tails and ties stood at attention as they all, outsiders and Petroleum City men, sat down together.

Luncheon was light. Pâté, Waldorf salad, leg of lamb, a modest selection of light wines. He wanted their minds clear for the business session. The executives talked about Section 9-C, and "hot" crude, and told the latest Eleanor jokes. Thunner moved around the table, exchanging a few words with each guest. When he dropped his hand on the shoulder of a slim, mustached man in a sack suit, he said, "Elisha, I think I've finally got a man to match against Gigliotta."

Elisha Denton Gerroy leaned back. "Against Louis? Haven't you learned your lesson?"

"You're the one ought to learn. Remember how McKee laid Mooney out?"

"You've got more depth in your stable, I admit it, but Louis is the devil with his fists these days. Who is it this time?"

"A Swede I found out in the fields. He's green as grass. You'll have to allow him a couple months under the good monsignor's tutelage. But I believe he'll give your middleweight a run for his money."

"How are you backing your boy?"

"How's a thousand sound?"

"Odds?"

"Two to one."

"Sight unseen? On your description? Hell, you could have gone to Brooklyn, gotten a pro."

Thunner affected hurt. "Ellie, Ellie. We've been friends a long time."

"Friends, Daniel?" Gerroy smiled faintly. "Acquaintances, yes. There is respect between us, certainly. But can our sort of man afford to give way to real friendship?"

Thunner studied him, then nodded. "I'll send word around when he's up to snuff," he said.

When the last diner had finished and shoved back his chair, Thunner flicked his eyes toward the maître d'. That worthy clapped his hands, and the waiters refilled the coffee cups, set out humidors and ashtrays, and filed out, easing the heavy door shut behind them.

He stood for a moment at the podium, looking down at the membership list Rudy Weyandt had typed up for him. Then he lifted his eyes. To the impassive, heavy gazes of D. E. Burrows, Pennzoil; K. T. Edbert, Quaker State; T. T. Schoenfield, Wolverine-Empire; R. W. Carrier, United Refining; J. L. Winterbotham, Kendall Refining; M. P. Haeberle, Tidewater Oil; C. E. McKinney, Freedom Oil; O. S. Ruffenach, Crystal Oil. And the local men: Gerroy, George White, Conrad Kleiner, Keith Colley. They were independent producers, owners of the crude fields that fed Number One. Not, strictly speaking, the peers of the refinery executives. But that wasn't why he'd invited them here. They were oil men too; but they were his, and they'd vote according to instruction.

For this was no gathering of boon companions, though he knew most all of them personally. These men had forgathered and drunk together more than once, and the older men, such as Burrows, had known his father in his day. These dark-suited, heavy-jowled businessmen who leaned back now to clip cigars or light cigarettes were his adversaries as truly as if they stood face to face in the ring. Strong, ruthless men who had fought, plotted, and gambled their way to the top. Anglo-Saxons, most of them; no longer young but still virile, still aggressive; cunning, hard, efficient businessmen to whom risk and battle were a way of life. Men who would destroy him if they scented any weakness.

And knowing this, seeing it in their eyes, just for a moment his hands trembled faintly on the podium.

Because he *was* weak. Terribly weak.

Despite its robust appearance, Thunder was a shell.

He'd started speculating in '26, and done well, until he

was making more from speculation than the family did from their oil holdings. He'd plunged deeper, in '28, and made even more with Insull and RCA. But he'd hung on too long, believed what the brokers said: that the Great Bull Market would just keep on going up and up, forever. And when it crashed he'd been in it up to his neck. Not just with his own resources, either, though God knew he'd dropped far too much of that. He'd put the pension fund in, too. Who could have believed it could all just melt away, that half the wealth Americans had accumulated in three hundred years could vanish into thin air like mist on the hills?

But the men facing him could not know that. And seeing him leading them would make it impossible to believe any rumors that reached their ears. Which was one reason, though not the only one, he had determined on this meeting. If he could keep that secret—and somehow endure . . . he clutched the wood and dismissed doubt from his mind. Giving them a fierce grin, he began.

"Gentlemen, welcome. To what I hope will go down in our histories as a date of considerable benefit to us all. For those of you who can stay the night, let me invite you to a game dinner at the Sands this evening. Shall we say seven o'clock? Please leave your card with Mr. Weyandt if you can honor me. I would be delighted to welcome you to my home.

"This is indeed an august gathering. The thirteen of us here hold votes or proxies for nineteen leading refiners of the finest crude oil in the world. Lubricants made from Pennsylvania Grade Crude are free from thinning under heat and thickening under cold, making them invaluable for motorcars and irreplaceable for modern aircraft engines. You may be aware that in the most recent coast-to-coast Air Derby, twenty-five out of the forty finishers used Thunderbolt Aviation Engine Super Oil. And together, we in this room today control the production of eighty-four percent of this superior oil, by my reckoning.

"If you will indulge me, I would like to look back for a moment at crises we have met together in the past. Not many years ago, people were using words like 'played out' about the Pennsylvania oil fields. We were facing shutdown; there wasn't enough yield to make continuing operation profitable.

"Then a few men attempted a new method of recovery. They proposed resurveying our lease lands into two-hundred-foot squares and drilling wells at each corner. Water would be pumped down those injection wells under hydrostatic pressure. This pressure would force the oil inward, through the intervening sands, toward a fifth well in the center of the square.

"Water flooding has worked so well the Hemlock field has increased its output five-hundred-fold since its introduction.

"Again, the Crash. Not long ago lines of tank cars stood idle on our spurs, full of finished product no one had the wherewithal to buy. Wage cuts, reduction in work hours . . . I'm proud to say I never had to lay a man off at Thunder, but I came close. Maybe some of you did, too." Grim chuckles came from around the room, from behind a thickening curtain of smoke. "But now our spurs are emptying. Prices are still at rock bottom, but demand is rising. We may have come through the worst. Especially if this war scare increases stockpile buying in Europe.

"So we've surmounted crisis before. But there are common problems in sight for us as producers and refiners right now. What are some of them?"

"Fuller's earth," said Carrier.

"The gentleman from United Refining has put his finger on one. Not the most glamorous, but of interest to us all. We all use fuller's earth and other basic chemicals and supplies— sulfuric acid, caustic soda, tetraethyl lead, absorbents, reagents—in enormous quantities, but we buy separately and transport separately. What if we united our buying power? Allow me to point out another. Mr. Edbert: What does Quaker State pay for shipping on a Group B rate to the northern Pacific Coast, through the Oregon gateway?"

"I know, but I won't tell you."

"Of course you won't; and neither would I tell you my rate; and the Central Freight Association lines use our lack of cooperation against us. Whereas, if every shipper here held the line on a Class Thirty-two and a half basis, I estimate we would gain a seven percent decrease on freight rates for our finished products."

For the first time, he saw thoughtful nods around the room. A point scored; move on. "What other issues could best be met acting together? I'll name several. Combined marketing campaigns. A common policy concerning organizing activity and collective bargaining. Separate legal representation within the national petroleum association. Establishing a single, central research facility for the improvement of refinery processes and research into new products made from Pennsylvania grade crude."

He paused, letting them turn it over in their minds. You didn't force men like this into association. You had to let them smell the oats, and urge themselves into the harness. Someone asked whether dues and expenses would be prorated, say according to a refiner's output. He said mildly he didn't see why not, that would be for a subcommittee to look into.

"Now, I'm not proposing a monopoly, or any restraint of trade. You men remember when Standard Oil was smashed back in 'eleven, and nobody rejoiced more than we did. We'll still be out there competing with each other in the marketplace. However, the additional advantages should—"

A low, hoarse voice. "I'm sorry, I don't see those advantages as clearly as you do, Mr. Thunner."

Men turned in their chairs as Burrows spoke on, sprawled in his chair, the old man outlining again his idea that the market was due for a renewed downturn, that they faced an inevitable shakeout and struggle that would end with only two or at most three of the largest Pennsylvania refiners standing. Given that, he said, he saw little advantage in any local association; and the costs involved, travel, stationery, postage, doubtless an office, would form an additional layer of overhead without any corresponding return. Thunner waited until he paused for breath, then cut in. "Mr. Burrows.

Are you speaking for your company at the moment, sir, or yourself?"

"Those were my personal observations, Dan."

"I am glad to hear that; for if such an association were established, of course, it would be crippled from the outset without participation of all the Big Four—Pennzoil, Quaker State, Kendall, and Thunder. Your observations about overhead are well taken. The strictest economies will be called for. But if you do not care to participate personally, sir, perhaps you might prevail upon one of your vice presidents to attend."

Burrows looked taken aback; reluctant, just as Thunner had anticipated, not to be left behind while younger men forged ahead. "Well, if we were necessary for its success . . ."

"It would of course be best to have the principal officer attend, instead of a deputy," Thunner said. Burrows nodded, caught himself, frowned. He locked his hands over the head of his cane and fell silent.

Another palm lifted. "You mentioned combating organizing activity, Mr. Thunner?"

He turned his voice sober. "I did, Mr. Eberle. It's on its way just as sure as I'm standing here. It's happened in rubber, and steel, it's going on right now in the cotton mills down South. A dangerous element's taking advantage of hard times.

"But those are only a few of the concerns we have in common. Even more will occur to us as we ponder a dangerous trend of events. I refer now to what may be the most serious menace of all: the threat, in an already weakened market, of government interference, government regulation, government meddling—and most particularly, the current administration's socialistic effort to nationalize the oil industry. I believe the time has come for the American industrial community to act together to defend our legitimate interests."

For the first time, applause rose. Before it could fade he rode it, raising his voice. "Yes, I'll say the word aloud: Cooperation. And why not? Our enemies believe in it. They are working together, night and day, to bring our country low. I believe we can turn back the tide, and restore prosperity, if *we* determine to work together as closely as they do. To put it the way we used to when I was in France: We've all got to fall in together for this fight."

A second burst of clapping, the delegates attentive now, hanging on his words. *That* was what they'd wanted to hear. It was time to close, and ask for the sale. "Therefore," he said, and let the word hang for a moment.

"Therefore, I hereby propose that we band ourselves together today, to work for our mutual benefit, and that of all America, in a group to be called the Pennsylvania Grade Crude Oil Refiners Industrial Association."

He knew from the applause and shouts as he stepped down that he'd struck the mark, that they were his and the association was a reality. When the motion to constitute had been moved and passed, Kit Edbert opened the floor for nominations for officers. Thunner was elected president, Edbert vice president, Terrence Schoenfield secretary, and Randolph Carrier treasurer. When he took the podium again, Thunner appointed five committees: Bylaws, Purchasing, Transport, Labor, and Research, making sure each refinery president in the room was either an Association officer or head of one of the committees. He concluded, "Our next meeting will be on the twentieth of next month, to vote on the bylaws and hold our first working sessions. Feel free to send a representative, but make sure he has your confidence and the ability to vote. I believe that ends our business today, and thank you for attending."

Thunner stood in the lobby for some time after they adjourned, young Weyandt hovering unobtrusively behind him, permitting the departing businessmen to slap his back and shake his hand, meeting each hearty phrase of praise and congratulation with a bland curve of his lips that could be interpreted as a courteous smile. He had not only brought them together, they had entrusted him with leadership. An hour of glory, and he allowed himself to savor it. Yet even in the moment of his triumph he seemed to hear the cautionary voice behind him in the chariot. He could not give way to illusion. He could neither trust nor go unarmed. These men were still his competitors. They would still destroy him if they could. They knew he'd do the same to them.

But all the same, they'd taken the first step on his road.

Five

While the crew was setting up on the spudding gear, Halvorsen stepped back from the drill rig to spit. He lifted his new green cap with the Thunder Oil lightning bolt, wiped his hand through his hair, and found himself looking through the kitchen window at Mrs. Christen standing at her sink.

The well he was drilling was twenty feet from the side of the house, so close he could make out the twined-roses pattern on the dish she was washing. The company owned the rights under all this land, deep beneath everything, hills and fields and even the cemeteries, and though they couldn't actually move your house, you couldn't stop them from drilling in your kitchen garden. He'd had to nail iron sheet on that side of the rig so he wouldn't splash mud on the siding when he pulled his tools. But old Mr. Christen hadn't minded; when he'd handed him his hundred-dollar damage-and-inconvenience check he'd grinned so you could see he'd said good-bye to his last tooth a long time ago. He was watching them now, sitting in a broken-backed rocker on the porch. Behind and above him the hill ran upward fold on fold, covered with beech and birch and blackberry hells in the clearings. Halvorsen wished he was walking up through there right now, his .30-30 heavy in his hand. There'd be deer in those tangles. He spat again, and looked up into the sky, noticing for the first time white specks slanting down against the blue-gray backdrop of the hill. The first snowfall, and overdue. The woolly worms had long stripes on them this year; there'd be two, three inches on the ground by morning.

A motion under the porch caught his eye; a hound was lying there, watching him, too, and the old dog under the porch and the old man on top looked so much alike he had to grin. Then a roustabout yelled and he jerked his gaze around to the bull wheel, and ducked under the tug rope to get back to it.

The rig was a cable-tool, not the new rotaries they used out in Oklahoma or Texas, where the earth was softer than it was in the Allegheny Mountains. A standard rig didn't auger, it smashed, pounding its way down like a giant chisel. The bit worked like a whip, the walking-beam nodding up and down, the spring in the line cracking it against the rock. At first you could hear it down there, smashing through the shale and sand and limestone, but gradually the impact grew fainter. Though when you put your hand on the line you could still feel it, if you knew what you were feeling for.

Which he guessed he did. Halvorsen had caught the look on his toolie's face, a dirt-mouthed bigbellied Polack named Steve Popovich, when he'd told him, "I'm the new driller." But he knew what he had to, to get a hole dug. Like he'd told the guy out at Favorite's that day he'd met Thunner, he'd started when he was fourteen, working slush boy, tool boy at the lease on Portage Creek.

He stood in the falling snow, hands thrust into his red-barred hunting coat, and remembered. At Ekdahl's you were on the job at seven, sunup or not, whether you had to ride or walk or crawl. His first job had been building the fire under the storage tank. It wasn't exactly Boy Scout stuff; you always had plenty of oil-soaked rags, and the long plugs of paraffin the pumpers left lying around after they pulled the tubings to clean the wax out of the wells. Or you just skimmed some fresh crude off the top of the tank. And then it was work, work, thawing out the rod-lines with torches made out of rags wrapped on sticks and dipped in crude, shoveling snow, clearing brush with billhooks, mowing out the rod-lines, shoveling bottom sludge and raw paraffin out of the settling tanks and dumping it into the creek. That's how he'd learned to run a rig, learned it on the job, watching the old fellas who'd done it all their lives.

It had taken them a week to set up here at Christen's. He had a bulldozer come in to grade while the Cletracs dragged the disassembled rig in on sledges. The big dozer had scraped off Christen's orchard, leveled the site, and dug a pond for the sand pumpings. When the sledge train came in the guys unloaded the mud sills, heavy rough timbers to be the foundation for the engine house and derrick. Popovich had got the engine house up and the derrick put together in one day, working a five-man crew from dawn to dark to beat the snow. You could throw a rig up in the snow, but it was miserable work, and everybody knew that and worked like dogs except an Italian who kept complaining until Halvorsen fired him on the spot. He hadn't had a bit of trouble with the men since then.

He was in shoulder to shoulder with the crew, wrestling the spudding bit into position so they could start the hole, when Popovich yelled above the engine noise, "Somebody here to talk to ya, Bill."

"What?"

The toolie pointed. A blue Chevy coupe was pulled up by the house, frost-smoke put-putting from the tailpipe. A kid in a bow tie and a soft fedora stood beside it, hands rammed into the pockets of a black overcoat. He was looking up, at the snow.

"Get her set up, Steve. Remember she's gonna go soft at first." Popovich nodded and Halvorsen jumped down to the muddy ground, feeling the crackle and give of frost already in the earth, and trotted over the yellow churned-up clay. "Lookin' for me?" he yelled.

"You Halvorsen? I'm Mr. Thunner's secretary, Rudolf Weyandt."

"What can I do for you?"

"Father Guertin says you haven't shown yet. Mr. Thunner told me to call you, get you in there toot sweet, but they don't have a phone out here."

"No, old Christen ain't got one. Should tell him to, now he's a oil millionaire."

Weyandt didn't crack a smile, just said, "Well, now you know. Get over to the gym."

"Look, see this big piece a shit behind me? That there's an oil rig. I don't push it, that tool don't go anyplace."

"That's Popovich's job, push the rig. Your job's to get over to the gym."

"Bull shit."

"No, Mr. Thunner's orders," said Weyandt, and the eyes, young as they were, turned so icy Halvorsen was intimidated despite himself. "Maybe you don't know how things work at Thunder Oil yet. Get your ass over there and damn smart, or I'll write your pink slip myself."

Halvorsen was about to tell him to go abuse himself behind a tree when he remembered his little talk with Mr. Washko in the back garden. He swallowed and said, "Where you say he wants me?"

"He told you already and you better learn to listen. Doherty's gym, down on Kane Street."

"Okay, soon's I get this spudding started—"

"Now," said Weyandt. "Get in the car."

Halvorsen felt like punching him in his snotty face, but restrained himself again. He glanced back toward the rig. Popovich had the right bit; they were lowering it into the set-in pipe.

"Get in the *car*," Weyandt said again.

He squelched his boots back across the muddy patch and yelled to Popovich, "Gotta go into town. Be back as soon as I can. Spud her to thirty feet, then start drilling."

Popovich nodded, patient as a saint, and then bent; straightened, holding something in his hand; tossed him down his lunch box. Halvorsen got the picture. He sighed. Yelled to Weyandt "I got a motorcycle," and went around the other side of Christen's house. The old man watched from the porch as he kicked the engine to life and pulled out of the yard.

The Indian was a bone-shaker, but it went like blazes once he was off the dirt and back on asphalt. He took it along Todds Creek and then along the river, murky and scum-foaming amid jagged rocks that shone the metallic blues and greens of beetle-cases, through the little town of Raymonds-ville and then west. Now that it was snowing he kept his eyes on the road, watching for the dark patches where out-flow from the springs above the road froze into a black treacherous sheet. Then another six or seven miles, the black ridge-lines accompanying him as he roared on, to the out-skirts of Petroleum City. In Gasport he slowed behind a truck loaded with jouncing springy lengths of sucker rod sticking out the back, and started looking for Kane Street.

They said that back in the old days Gasport had been the Tombstone Territory of Hemlock County. Before his time, but he'd worked with men who remembered, and they passed on tales of the nymphs du pavé who thronged the free-and-easies, the gambling hells, the fights between the bulls and the wild bears the mountain men brought down out of the hills. He remembered coming in here in the buckboard with his dad when he was little, getting fodder and farm supplies at Kaefer's Hardware, which was closed now. Then he'd worked out of a shed over under Knaller Hill for Evans Cres-son and the Foster Run Company. Between the road and the tracks were the machine shops and sheds of the Gasport Mo-tor Works, smoky iron-clanging blocks of long tin-roofed sheds where they made everything you needed to drill and pump a well. Beyond it was a tank farm, an outlier of the big refinery, and then the old Evans Street bridge across the brown roiling flood of the river.

And beyond and above that too rose Irish Hill, solid with basementless shacks, hanging out over the hillside with steep wooden stairs leading up between them. His first payday, the men on the crew had taken him up there to a house with a Liberty Bond poster in the window. He remembered the crucifix on the board wall, and the girl in the flowered wrap who'd curled her legs up against her white belly and let him do anything he wanted. The memory gave him a hard-on. There were still a couple houses left where you could get your ashes hauled. Maybe he could make a quick stop after seeing this Guertin.

The truck slowed suddenly and so did he—he didn't want to get punctured by those iron rods—and there was Kane Street and a sign, Doherty's Boxing Club. Some tough-looking birds in cloth caps were standing around in the lot with their mitts in their pockets, smoking. He parked the bike and went in past them. They gave him the eye and he gave it back, but no one said anything. He passed a deserted counter, a towel room, a door that read SHOWERS. On down a green-painted corridor roofed with steam pipes, and through another door, grimed black with decades of handprints, from the far side of which came shouts and grunts and the thud of blows.

The heat hit him first, so steamy hot that sweat prickled instantly on his scalp. Then the smells, gas heat and old sweat and leather, sawdust and carbolic and the sting of liniment, with a one-two punch that made it hard to breathe at first. He took his hat off, looking around the enormous space that narrowed off and up into the distance into smoky obscurity and inchoate light.

Doherty's had been a factory once. You could see that from the iron-beamed roof and brick walls painted green to head height and here and there the jutting I-beams that had been crane rails. The concrete floor was covered with cigarette butts and discarded newspapers and moving shadows that seemed darker somehow than they ought to be. An elevated running track ran around the building twenty feet up from the floor. Above it the smoky light slanted down from high dirty windows. At the west end guys in shorts and underwear tops were working on speed-bags and sandbags and wall weights, tossing medicine balls, or shadowboxing in front of full-length mirrors. The far ring was set up with bleacher seats on three sides. Gas heaters roared along the walls, old men in gartered shirtsleeves crouched toward them on folding chairs. Grunting, yells, the slap and thud of gloves hitting leather or flesh floated back down from a ceiling as far away as Heaven.

"What you need, buddy?" A bent gnome with a seamed monkey face, a stack of yellowed towels under his arm.

"Got a Father Guertin here?"

"First ring, over there by the water can."

He kicked his way through the sawdust and trash toward the man in the black suit, clerical collar, and black sneakers. "Pastor?" he said, uncertain how you addressed a Roman.

The massive close-cropped white-haired skull turned slowly from its contemplation of the dance in the ring.

Jules Guertin's face and chest were so flat and broad he looked like a much bigger man compacted and flattened by some enormous pressure. Tormented-looking small blue eyes were ringed by deep-slashed wrinkles, as if he had squinted for years into a blast furnace. Halvorsen thought he looked like pictures of Hindenburg. Thick blunt fingers extracted a cigar from between immobile lips as the priest looked him up and down.

"Mister Thunner sent me, uh, sir. Name's Bill Halvorsen."

"I was expectin' you a week ago."

"I was settin' up a rig."

"Bring your gear?"

"Boxing gear? No, sir, I don't have any—"

"See Angie Picciacchia. Get dressed out."

"Who?" The priest pointed with the cigar, and Halvorsen saw he meant the monkey-faced dwarf.

He got a pair of Everlast shorts, gray baseball-style cotton sweats, a pair of light shoes, an aluminum groin cup, a leather headpiece, two sets of handwraps, and sixteen-ounce training gloves. Nothing else smelled like new leather. Pic-

ciacchia took him back into the locker room and gave him
number 48, a lock, a towel, and a bar of raw-smelling bright
red soap. He said to use the padlock if he wanted to keep
any of it. The trainer also told him some interesting things
about the priest. The pain Halvorsen had glimpsed in his face
was real. Guertin had been hit so hard and so often during
his ring career that the base of his skull had detached from
the top of his spinal column. He was seldom free of an ex-
cruciating headache. Halvorsen dressed quickly. His gut was
tight and his fingers felt like bugs were crawling around inside their tips. He went back out and found Guertin again
and said, "Okay, I'm dressed."

The priest led him over to a corner and Halvorsen followed, wondering if he was going to ask him if he had any
sins on his soul. Mining his fingers into his own eye sockets,
Guertin said, "So, you're thinking of getting into the boxing
game. Ever fight before, son?"

"Just scraps."

"Win?"

"Most of 'em."

"Let's see your form."

He took a stance. The priest circled him, shadowing his
eyes against the light from the high windows. "Turn your
left foot in a little. That gets you closer to your opponent.
Pull your elbow in. Cover your ribs." He was shifting his
feet when Guertin tossed one, low and hard and sudden, no
telegraph at all. Taken aback, he damn near didn't block fast
enough.

"Good, never take one you can dodge. But not everybody's gonna be as slow as I'm getting these days. What
we're gonna do with you, get you set up to do a little fighting, see if you like it, if it likes you. You the boy used to
handle the nitro?"

"That's right, Father."

"You might have the heart. It's a manly sport. Sure it's
rough sometimes, so's life. How you feel about that?"

"Okay."

"Scared?"

"No."

"Excited?"

"Sort of. Sure."

"Okay, good. Now I want to see you go over and play with that bag over there. Just go on and work up a sweat for a while."

Guertin let him hammer the body bag for nearly an hour, till he was soaked and dizzy and his shoulders and arms flamed with pain. Then he sent him to the speed bag. Finally Halvorsen figured it out. He dropped his gloves and went over and said, hardly able to get the words out, "I'm beat."

"You got good wind. You don't smoke, do you?"

He said he didn't, not mentioning chewing tobacco. Guertin gave him a little pep talk about taking care of himself. No booze, no fags, get plenty of sleep, eat plenty of steak. "You married?" the priest finished. Halvorsen said he wasn't. "Got a girlfriend?"

"Yeah."

"Good girl? Or a little bit easy?"

"Yeah, she's a good girl. Catholic, matter a fact."

"That's fine; but still you might want to put her on the shelf for a while. Tell her you're still sweet on her, but you got a couple fish to fry, got to be at your best. That goes for anything you might do on your own, too. You know what I'm talkin' about."

"I guess so. Yeah."

"Okay. Now I got somebody I want you to see."

Halvorsen trailed him through the sawdust to the far end of the gym. Guys made room on the lowest row of the bleacher, and he sat beside the priest, looking up as somebody switched on the lights. Beyond them darkness lay behind the high windows. Shoot, was it night already?

When the trainer took the fighter's blanket off, Halvorsen went quiet inside seeing the hard, well-defined chest. The head that looked like it had been machined out of tool steel. The coarse slicked-back blond-streaked hair. McKee's nose had been broken, probably more than once. A tattoo of a sailing ship covered his chest. He looked as hard and tough as the business end of a casing cutter.

"Jack McKee," said Guertin. "Ex–Pacific Fleet boxer. Used to work for the Gerroy outfit. Now he's a mechanic for Thunder. Mr. Thunner's favorite heavyweight."

They sat watching as McKee sparred a couple of rounds. He was strong and fast, outpointing his partner, a colored fighter Guertin said was named "Dandy" Nix. At the end of the last round he attacked, and put the Negro on the canvas with a flurry of blows too fast to follow.

As McKee swung his body through the ropes Halvorsen saw that aside from a gleam of sweat he didn't even look tired. As a trainer threw a blanket over his shoulders, Guertin murmured, "Well done, Jack."

"Thanks, Father," said the fighter, but the way he jerked his words out, hard and angry, made it sound like a curse. Cold eyes clamped themselves on Halvorsen for a second. Then the trainer tugged at his arm, and McKee turned away and followed him back toward the locker room.

"Okay, Nitro, get your headgear on," said the priest. "Let's see how you do in there."

He sparred a couple of rounds with Nix, the colored man McKee had been dancing with. He couldn't seem to get past the guy's guard. He could see he had a lot to learn. He also wasn't in as good shape as he thought. When the bell clanged to end the second round he staggered to his corner and threw up into the water bucket. Guertin watched from ringside, cigar stuck in his jaw.

He went two more rounds, taking a lot of punches but at least staying on his feet, before the priest pulled him out. Guertin told him to go up to the track, run forty laps, then he could get a shower; and to show up tomorrow at three, whether or not he was done at the drill site.

Climbing the stairs to the track, hardly able to lift one foot after the other, W.T. Halvorsen realized it was going to be a long winter.

Six

The trouble started two months later, at Thunder Number One.

The five men on the maintenance shift that early November morning couldn't see the hills, though dawn had come an hour before. The snow was falling too hard, dropping from a turbulent sky to join the drifts already piled deep on the hills, on the dead fields, on the raw earth embankments around the storage tanks. All they could see was the whirling flakes, the low clouds, heavy and dark as old pipe-solder, and the rough iron to which they clung, gloved fingers cramping stiff from the cold. It was near the end of a ten-hour night shift, and they were all exhausted. Not that it probably made any difference, as far as who lived and who died. They'd have had to move very fast, and been very lucky. But it didn't help any of them to be dead tired and frozen through when it happened.

Donnie Rapisczek was checking and tightening the collars at the top of the bubble tower, an eighty-foot-high rolled-steel structure that led the product pipes off to the various cooler towers and dewaxer units, when he heard the first explosion. It wasn't a loud noise, or especially startling. Just a dull reverberation that made him think for a second that a sheet of iron had fallen, down in the steel yard, or that two railcars had collided on the spur. Then the echo rolling back from the hills told him it wasn't. That, and the rapid-fire succession of cracks and bangs that followed, jarring the I-beam he clung to so that powder rust and paint flakes surrounded him in a sudden, skin-stinging, blood-colored cloud.

The straw boss, thirty feet away and almost invisible in the whirling snow, yelled, "Get the hell off the iron!"

He didn't wait to figure out what was going on. There was only one ladder down, and five men working up here. He threw his tool belt over a valve wheel and ran, heavy brogans hammering, along the vibrating, icy, railingless beam that was supposed to be a catwalk. Then stopped dead, struck by a flash and a pulse of heat that made him fling up his hands to shield his face.

Mark Shaughnessey was a few feet ahead of him, out over the gas-oil pipe heater, when he saw a yellow phosphorous glow like a struck match suddenly ignite below him. A moment later a fireball of blazing gas shouldered its way up through the spindly network of beams and pipes and guy wires that caged the snow-laden air. He spun around, pressing his face to the steel, covering the exposed skin at the back of his neck with cold-stiffened work gloves. The force of the blast pressed him into the iron lace so hard that when he pulled his face away from it bits of skin and flesh stuck to the icy metal.

T. O. Callahan was the oldest man on the iron that day. His father had worked for Thunder, and his grandfather's brothers. He was the lead man, the one who'd yelled to get the hell off the iron. Now as they scrambled toward him, explosions rattling and quivering the steel structure they stood on, he hesitated.

At the far end, closest to the hundred-foot shaft of the tower, the youngest man, Washko, stood staring down. Unmoving, probably unable to; he'd only been working on the high iron for a week.

Callahan swung aside to let Rapisczek go past, sliding down the single ladder. Pecora was next, still holding the oilcan he'd been lubricating the valve stems with. Callahan struck it out of his hand and pushed him toward the ladder. Shaughnessey reached him. His face was horrible, raw skinless patches streaked with soot. But he was moving, eyes blasted wide with fear amid what looked like bloody ground round. He hesitated at the top of the ladder, and Callahan shouldered him forward, pushing him down it. He saw the red glow spreading below them. They didn't have long. From the bubble tower, the fractionated crude went off through condensers and into the satellite processes: heavy bottoms, lubricating oils, fuel oils, kerosene. The tank directly below them held fifty thousand gallons of raw gasoline.

There wasn't going to be any way around it. Pulling his cap as low as it would go—his ears were already scorching—he started along the beam, back toward the motionless Washko.

Rapisczek and, above him, Pecora and then Shaughnessey were half climbing, half sliding as fast they could down the ladder when they heard a noise like a pistol shot. It was a rusty, fume-corroded rivet holding the ladder to the framework. Then another went, and another, popping out under their weight.

Shaughnessey and Pecora began screaming as it toppled backward.

Rapisczek made a last, despairing lunge off the ladder as it came free, and managed to seize a cross-brace as the two other workers fell past him, running in the air. He caught a horrifying glimpse of Pecora going by, his open mouth screaming soundlessly in the immense all-obliterating roar as tanks of acid and caustic exploded, as gasoline and propane and hot liquid paraffin sprayed out of split pipes and hit the air and burst instantly into flame. Then they were gone.

Thirty feet above, Callahan reached Washko. The kid was frozen to the iron, staring down. It wasn't any good yelling, not in that din. It was getting hard to breathe, too. The hot choking smoke seared his throat. Callahan slapped the kid and got his attention. The snow danced around them, melting in the turbulent zone of heated air, then flashing into invisible steam. Below them another tank let go with a rumbling boom, its contents rolling outward, erupting into a rolling halo of leaping orange fire as the iron shell collapsed.

If he stayed there much longer, they were both going to cook. He slapped the kid again, then tried to uncrimp his fingers from the iron. The boy winced.

Frantic, gasping, Callahan slapped him a third time, and jerked his thumb over his shoulder. The kid nodded and—God be praised!—found his nerve, and scrambled after him as he retreated toward the ladder.

He got to where it had been and looked around, squinting as if into a blast furnace at full charge. The smoke roared up toward them like an upside-down Niagara, laced with long twisting ribbons of white-hearted flame. Then he looked down and saw that there was no ladder anymore. Saw Rapisczek hanging there from a pipe-brace, clothes smoking, outlined by the flames beneath his kicking feet.

Callahan shook his head, sadly, but also with a sense of triumph as he knelt on the hot iron. Breathing the air that now scorched and shriveled his lungs, he could feel them crisping but it was all miraculously painless, he crossed himself deliberately. Father, Son, and Holy Ghost. Thinking: I'm all right. I'm all right. I still got time for a Act of Contrition.

Below them, Rapisczek hung by his hands, staring in helpless fascination into the inferno beneath his scorching, dangling boots. Now the whole area around the cooling tower was a lake of fire, licking and swirling around the foundations of holding tanks, of the pipe stills, of the tower itself. He craned around desperately, body jerking, dangling by his blistered, bloody fingers. But there was no other way down. And the iron he gripped was getting too hot to hold.

In the city, men and women came out from houses and offices into the street when they heard the explosions, then the scream of the whistle. Standing in the snow, they stared at the pall of inky, greasy smoke that billowed above the plant. Every one of them had friends or relatives who worked there. They listened to the rumbling in the earth, and stared at the firelight that grew, reflected down again into the narrow valley by the overcast sky. They listened to the frantic clang of alarm bells, to the rising chorus of sirens as fire engines headed in from surrounding towns.

Then they began running.

Seven

Lew Pearson brought the news out to the Christen lease, driving up in a Thunder field-service truck that afternoon. By then the snow had stopped falling, and Halvorsen's crew had the rig shoveled off and the stove roaring red-hot full of soft cheesy bituminous, and it was damn near almost livable, at least where the wind didn't get to you. Which it did on the driller's bench, where he spent most of his shift.

He grabbed the drill cable as the crank dropped, and felt the shock come up from far below even through the double gloves. Despite the cold, he liked running a rig. He liked the smells of coal-smoke and grease and mud, the groaning of ropes and timbers as the string came up, like the way he figured a sailing ship must sound, coming back up after a heavy sea knocked her down. Then the band wheel speeding up again as the string dropped. Drilling down into Mother Earth . . . he checked the temper screw. Just about time to pull her.

Pearson parked a respectful distance from the rig, and came trudging up to it as he threw in the clutch to stop the band wheel, then nudged it over a couple of inches at a time till he figured the bit was on the bottom. Popovich took the pitman off the crank and pulled it down, till the walking beam was clear. He redraped the rope on the bull wheel and stepped back as Halvorsen popped the clutch, starting the wheel going around again. He reached behind him and kicked the throttle up a couple notches. The Buffalo coughed and clattered, and the rope started winding back and forth onto the drum as it brought up the string. Pearson waved and Halvorsen yelled, over the racket of the engine and the grind of the wheels and high steel singing of the cables, "Be right with ya, Lew."

"Take your time, I'm done for the day," Pearson yelled back.

He nodded, watching the cable. He had twine markers on it, to tell him when the bit was getting near the top of the hole. You didn't want the son of a bitch to come up too fast. If it hit the crown block you'd wreck the rig.

As the tool-string came out, dripping muddy water and sand, he eased off the throttle and disengaged the clutch. The string—rope socket, jars, auger stem, and the bit itself, the whole thing about thirty feet long—swaying and tolling dolefully in the wind above them, Popovich braked the bull wheel and disengaged the belt. Halvorsen powered it around a couple of inches to help him get it off. They eased off the brake band and Popovich and Foley pushed the string off to the side of the platform as it eased down.

He helped them throw on the brakes and chains and then stepped over to where Pearson was standing.

His hunting buddy was lean and bent and going bald early under the floppy-eared cap. He was from down South and had a drawl that took getting used to. "How's things going?" Halvorsen asked him. "We goin' to get out in the woods this season, get us a couple buck?"

"Oh yeah, yeah, we'll do some huntin'." Pearson was interrupted by a spell of coughing that left him bent even more than usual. He blew his nose into his fingers and slung it away into the snow and mud. "Guess I got a touch a lung trouble. Been fightin' this for a week now."

"Somethin's going around, all right. Couple guys in my crew had it."

"Heard you were with the company now. Thought you liked working with the nitro."

"Fella's got to better himself, if he can."

"Hear you tooken up boxing, too. Couple fellas said they seen you fight, down at Doherty's. Said you done real well, fancy footwork like Jimmy Slattery."

"That was just a sparrin' exhibition. Not a real fight."

"When we gonna see you mix 'er up with Louie Gigliotta?"

Shit, did everybody in the goddamn county know his business? He said crankily, "A while yet. I'm still gettin' inta shape. What brings you out here, Lew?"

Pearson said to his crew, and to him, too, "Wish it was better news. You boys hear about the big blowup over at Number One? Five fellas killed. Roasted to death. They couldn't get off the iron."

"Jesus," said Popovich, turning from setting up the bailer. The other men stopped working too, looking at the driver anxiously.

"Who was it got killed?" said Foley. "I got family works there."

"Heard it on the radio. Wrote 'em down . . . here they are . . . Rapisczek, Callahan, Pecora, Washko, Shaughnessey."

Halvorsen went still. Popovich was asking, "That Tommy Callahan?"

"Dunno, just a T. Callahan. A lot of the guys there walked off the job once the fire was out, just downed tools and walked out."

"Shit, I don't blame 'em. Least out here, you can light out for the woods, you get a gas flare or something. Those poor sonsabitches, they got a million gallons a gasoline wallin' 'em in."

Halvorsen said, "That Washko. That the old man? Or the kid?"

"That'd be Johnny Washko, it was at the refinery," Foley told him. "The old man, he works over at Lee's Camp."

Popovich said, "My sister's husband works at Number One. He was always sayin' there wasn't no way to get off that iron if anything went wrong."

"They oughta done something about that."

"No shit. That ain't the first time people been killed 'cause Dan Thunner won't spend a dime."

"They're callin' a meeting tonight, at the Jenny Lind," Pearson said. "All Thunder employees."

Halvorsen stood irresolute, wondering if he should go into town and see if it was Johnny. If they'd downed tools at the refinery, they weren't going to need this well anytime soon. But they were behind schedule; they'd had a bit jam the week before and lost five days fishing it. He saw the others watching him then, and snapped himself out of it. "Yeah . . . thanks for telling us that, Lew. Okay, let's get that new bit on there," he said, and they swung into action again.

As he came into Gasport, head hunched into the icy wind and trying not to skid off the road, he saw something odd in the center of town. Or rather, noticed something missing; blinked at an unsettling emptiness, as if some great building had been suddenly destroyed, bombed from the air perhaps; leaving a void, a vacuity where the eye was accustomed to . . . what? Then he understood. No accustomed pall of smoke, no shroud of steam hovered over the valley. A knot of men stood in front of Tracy's Hudson, gazing in silence toward the smokestacks and flare-offs of Number One. The clear air above them struck him as obscene, vacant, and disturbing.

It was getting dark now, and he suddenly realized, shivering, that he wanted a car. He loved the bike, but it just wasn't what you needed in a Hemlock County winter. Maybe he'd ask around, see if anybody had a used jalopy. Jennie could ride with him then, too. Her parents had made her promise she wouldn't ride on the Indian, but if he had an automobile . . . he daydreamed about that for a couple of minutes, about what they could do if he had a car, when he remembered where he was going and that her brother had just died, and felt ashamed of what he was thinking, and turned his mind away from it. He was slowing down, almost to Main, when he saw a face he knew from the old days at Evans Cresson. He hadn't seen "Teabag" Salada for years, but when he pulled over, all Salada wanted to talk about was the fire. "You goin' to the meeting tonight?" he asked Halvorsen.

"The one at the opera house? I figured it was just the plant people."

"Everybody Thunder, 's what I heard. You're working for them now, ain't you?"

Halvorsen said yeah, he was. Salada looked worried as they came abreast of a streetlight, Halvorsen pushing the Indian through the slushy snow. "What's eatin' you, Teabag?"

"They're talking wild, that's what."

"What do you care? You're still with E-C, ain't you?"

"Yeah, but you mugs buy all our production. Anything ever happens to Thunder, it's gonna sink everybody in the county."

"Well, I guess I'll go and see, then."

He swung back up on the bike and rode down Main Street, waiting at the crossing while the gate came down and the red lights pulsed as a freight rumbled through. A murky yellow fog of smoke and steam blew across where he sat on the idling machine, and the taste of the coal smoke on his tongue and the damp close smell of steam and the slow click and bow of the rails as the big shining wheels rolled past brought back suddenly to him the days when he'd dreamed like every other boy in America of growing up to be an engineer, like Casey Jones. He smiled to himself, quick and faint, then when the caboose swayed past went on again through a renewed light dusting of snow past Kreinerson's and the Odd Fellows and the Onuffer Block, Rogalsky's Jewelers and the old Oil Exchange and the Petroleum City Bank and Trust, heading toward the Washkos'.

*   *   *

The porch light was on. People in dark clothes sat on the steps and stood about in the snow in the front yard. A plume of smoke streamed up from the chimney, glowing palely in the light of the gas flares. As he came up the walk he heard women wailing inside the house. Round Slavic faces turned as he passed; that strange rapid language, the women in their clumsy boots and long coats and bright patterned babushkas, made him feel different and tall and American. He stamped his boots off on the porch, not wanting to go in, but knowing he had to.

Viola opened the door. The little girl looked frightened, and her face was swollen. "Hi, Billy," she said. He patted her head and went in, leaving his boots on the slush mat and padding on in his stocking feet.

Washko was sitting in front of the Philco, a bottle of liquor and a glass in front of him. The radio was on, but it wasn't tuned to a station. It was just on, humming and glowing in the darkened parlor. Another shadow, just as motionless, turned out to be Bernard.

Halvorsen looked into the darkness beyond them. "Jennie?"

Washko opened his eyes. He stared dully at Halvorsen, then motioned to the bottle. "Billy. Billy Hal-wor-son. Take drink viskey," he said.

"No, thanks, Mr. Washko. I heard the news out on the lease. I'm sorry about Johnny."

"Johnny all right. Johnny home tonight. Take drink, I said." Washko struggled up and with glassy eyes poured him the tumbler full of rye. They watched him as he took a slug, coughing as the raw spirit seared his throat. The old man picked up the bottle and tilted it above stubbled jaws. Halvorsen looked back into the darkness again. He said, "Bernard, how are you doing?"

"I can take it," said the kid.

When he set the tumbler down Washko lurched forward and grabbed it again. Liquor gurgled. "Sir, that's enough."

"Naw, plenty viskey. Maybe better dis vay. Johnny probably die in next war anyway."

The cheap Monongahela burned in his gut. Jennie's face took shape out of the dim. He got up and went toward her, carrying the glass. She stood immobile as he hugged her, then her arm came up; as if she had just remembered who he was; but it didn't stay; just pressed his back, then let go.

"I'm real glad you came," she said. "He's back here."

The coffin was set up on the dining room table, almost filling the cramped dark room. The lid was nailed down. Votive candles sputtered on the buffet. A dozen women in dark clothes were weeping and talking loudly in Slovak and eating store cookies out of a tin. To his horror, Halvorsen slowly became aware of the smell of roasted meat. He wanted to leave again, but got a grip and kept on, following Jennie. She turned once, to ask him if he wanted to see her ma; he nodded.

Mrs. Washko lay in the back bedroom, swathed in an ancient black taffeta dress. A rusty shawl covered her face. The room smelled of damp and mold and old clothes. The smaller children huddled against her recumbent form like lifeboats against the side of some great foundering liner. Halvorsen didn't think she saw him when she opened her eyes. He said he was sorry to hear about Johnny; he was a good boy. She said something; Jennie spoke to her in the same language, stroking her hair as the children stared at him.

"What did she say?"

"She said, thank you for coming."

"Is that all? She said a lot more than that."

"Come on, Bill. This is my aunt Margaret—Uncle Jim— these are the Yanik girls—they're our cousins, from Brandy Camp. This is Sister Cecilia, Margaret's girl, she teaches at the convent in Ridgeway. This is Bill Halvorsen, he works drilling wells for Thunder."

He shook hands with the men and bowed awkwardly to the women. Finally he got her alone behind the kitchen door. "Is there anything I can do for your ma, or for the family?" he muttered. "Anything I can go get?"

"I don't think so. But I'm glad you came, Bill."

"Are they gonna need anything for the funeral?"

"No, Ma has burial policies on all us kids from the First Catholic Slovak Ladies' Union. A hundred dollars each. Are you coming to the funeral?" She searched his face anxiously.

"When is it?"

"Tomorrow at ten. At Saint Denis's. I really need you to be there, Bill."

He took his watch out and looked at it, not to see what time it was, just to look somewhere else than at the grieving faces. "Yeah. Yeah, I'll be there. Look, I got to go now, there's a meeting downtown."

"There's not gonna be any trouble, is there?"

"What do you mean?"

"I don't know. Just be careful," she said. Her nose wrinkled. "You smell like whiskey."

"Your dad made me drink it. Here, take the glass." He patted her shoulder, then went out past the humming radio and the silent pair in the parlor and down the steps, back into the freezing darkness between the wavering, crazy dance of the gas flares.

Hovering above the descending tiers of satin-upholstered seats, blond Muses scattered armfuls of roses. Naked cherubs peered down from the pendentives. Bearded Pan-heads projected grotesque tongues. Looking up at them, Halvorsen figured whoever painted this place had to have been bad drunk.

The Lind was a movie house these days, and not in good repair. The rose satin was faded and torn, the frescos faded and water-spotted. The balconies had been roped off since one collapsed in 1914 during Buffalo Bill Cody's Wild West Show. But the floor was standing room only tonight. Enterprising kids were hawking packs of Wings and Hershey Bars in the aisles. Smoke and cursing rose toward the enormous electrolier. He pushed his way down through men in working clothes, denims and worn twill pants, bundled in heavy jackets, toward the front. There was Popovich, wiping his nose with a snot rag, pointing with the other hand at the seats he'd saved.

"Steve. What's this all about tonight?"

"Company's gonna try to get us back to work, most likely."

"How many guys walked out?"

A beefy middle-aged man in suspenders and a high-button undershirt twisted round in his seat. "Just about everybody at Number One."

"That where you work?" Halvorsen asked him.

"Uh-huh, in the foundry. Guys been stewing about this a long time. You know, like they charge you for safety shoes, right? But when we pulled the hoses today, try to put that fire out, what we find? Just that they're goddamn rotten through, that's what."

"Is that right? You mean they never—"

"Okay, men, let's quiet down." A stocky, fiftyish fellow had come out onstage, followed by two other men and a blond woman. Whistles and shouts rose from the audience. The men set up a folding table and chairs. Halvorsen saw one of them was the kid who'd come out to the rig to tell him to get his tail in to the gym. The blonde ignored her admirers. She sat down, flipped open a steno pad, lit a cigarette, jerked a pencil from her bun, and jotted a couple of lines as if to warm up.

"All right, you kids, the ones selling stuff, clear out of here, we got business to discuss. Close those doors, you fellows in back.

"Those of you don't know me, I'm Earl Vansittart, manager of Number One. These gentlemen are Otis Goerdeler, senior foreman, and Mr. Rudolf Weyandt, special assistant to the president. I've got some news, some good, some bad. So let's have your attention." He waited and the men muttered and then quieted. "Otis," said Vansittart, and sat down.

The senior foreman had long arms and a long jaw and a shaggy gray Bismarck mustache. He said, "We still don't know what happened, exactly, but the pipe fitters think it might have been a failed gasket on the Dubbs cracker. Anyway, we got the last of the fires out about three thirty. Had help from the fire departments of Gasport, Raymondsville, Rich Falls. Plus the city department, they were right on the spot. The cleanup people are still down there. They're going to need a lot of additional hands tomorrow.

"The good news is, we got process shut down in time. Hell of a mess, but most of the equipment's salvageable. Bubbles one and three are still operational. We can shunt the product stream around the damaged sections while we repair. We'll be at around sixty percent capacity for the next two weeks, then back up to eighty, and have all our repairs completed around the first of April. That means we're not gonna have to lay anybody off."

He paused, but there was no overt reaction from the men lolling in the patched satin seats. "What's the bad news?" somebody yelled from the floor.

Vansittart said, "The bad news is, since we're not going to be shipping as much product, we have to cut back somewhere. So effective Friday, everybody at the plant's taking a ten percent cut. Nobody likes it that way. But the company's committed to keeping everybody on payroll, and that's the only way we can."

The hall buzzed. The manager waited it out, then when no one spoke up nodded shortly and looked back toward Goerdeler. But just then the red-faced guy in front of Halvorsen stood up and yelled, "Why are *we* payin' for the accident? We been complaining about how the plant ain't safe for years. And that cut—is that just the plant personnel that's taking it?"

Vansittart: "That's right, plant personnel only."

"That ain't right. We take the goddamn risks, working in that hellhole. I don't see why the field boys don't take a piece of that."

The murmur swelled, turning angry. Halvorsen listened, taking it all in as they went back and forth about it, Goerdeler trying to mediate. He was getting kind of mad himself. Five workers had burned to death, and all they could find to argue about was who was going to get it took out of his pay envelope. The whiskey Mr. Washko had forced him to drink didn't help; it just seemed to make him angrier. Finally Vansittart said, "Well, you might have a point about including the field people in the cut. That might be a way we could make it lighter, spread the load more. I'll take that to Mr. Thunner—"

Halvorsen yelled from his seat, not knowing the second before he did it that he was going to, "To hell with spreadin' the load. It's somebody's fault those guys died. What are we gonna do about it? Just troop on back to work like nothin' happened?"

Men turned in their seats, looking back toward him. Popovich cleared his throat, looking worried. "Take it easy, Bill. This ain't your lookout."

"Damn it, Steve, I work for this company. And I knew one of them boys cooked to death today. It ain't my lookout, who in hell's is it?"

Goerdeler said, "Whoever said that, a work stoppage ain't gonna change anything. Just hurt a lot of people for no reason. The plant engineer's down there tonight, figuring how to fix things so there's no more blowouts."

Halvorsen jumped to his feet. Popovich tugged at his sleeve, but he yanked it out of his hand and yelled up, "Hey, I'm one of the foremen in this outfit. I just come from where Johnny Washko's laid out. I want to know, what are we gonna do about it?"

"The company extends its condolences. There's not much more we can do than say we're sorry."

Now others were on their feet throughout the hall. One shouted that Thunder didn't care how many of them were maimed or hurt. The company didn't care how many of their kids got sick from the smoky air and lousy poisoned water, either. Then Halvorsen heard a familiar slow drawl. He twisted in his chair. It was Lew Pearson. His hunting buddy was saying, "Back where I come from, we had this out with the coal comp'ny, about how to keep the mines from caving in. We had to strike to get it, but we got us a safety committee with teeth in it."

No one said anything for a moment. The word just hung there under the big chandelier. Then an older man stood up. He said he didn't like to hear people talking strike. He'd tried striking Thunder in the nineties, again in the teens. They always lost.

"That don't mean it don't do no good. We got to have some say over safety at the plant. We got to have some kind of committee set up."

"Now, let's all calm down," Vansittart said, pushing his hands down as if he could smooth them all back down into their seats again. "You men know the company's trying to do the best it can for everybody. It hasn't been easy keeping the plant going. TioPenn and Tiona both went bust this fall. And there's already a safety committee."

That was an unwise remark, because five or six voices immediately yelled, "And you don't listen to it," "Ya, ya, and you see how good it works," "I told my foreman there wasn't no way off that iron if things went to shit," and similiar remarks. Weyandt rose abruptly. He stood for a moment facing the throng, head cocked as if listening; then went offstage, disappearing behind the curtain. Somebody threw a half-eaten potato after him.

Goerdeler took the floor back, and began explaining how safety precautions cost money and cut production. The men listened patiently for ten minutes, then someone threw more food. Others remonstrated with the throwers, and shoving matches broke out. The senior foreman concluded, raising his voice over the growing tumult, "Anyway, it ain't the workers' business, working conditions. It's Mr. Thunner's land and his refinery. Refinin's always gonna be dangerous. You got to be a man, that's all. Anybody who can't measure up to that, well, we might as well get a bunch of girls in there to run things."

"I think we need a union, not you goddamn yellow dogs," a short, rotund fellow yelled, jerking suddenly to his feet. "What you guys think? Anybody else think we ought to walk out, see if they can make Thunder Pure without us?"

The hall howled, divided against itself. Some men were shaking their fists and yelling. Others sat back, fingering their chins. "You guys are talkin' through your hats," Goerdeler shouted. "Somebody said they tried to get a union in here

before. They're right. I was one of the boys that tried, back
in 'fifteen. It didn't work then and it won't never work. A
union ain't going to do anything for you an honest man can't
do himself. You'd be damn fools to walk out in the winter,
anyways."

Goerdeler was banging on the card table, making it dance
across the stage. The girl steno had stopped transcribing, was
sitting with her legs crossed, looking amused. Vansittart sat
with arms folded, staring grimly out over the storm. Now a
physical current was pulling men toward the back of the hall.
Half rising to look, Halvorsen saw that the short, round fellow was the center of a group. He was explaining something,
gesticulating excitedly, but no one could hear him. Then
someone stepped out on the previously deserted balcony,
above them.

To his astonishment, it was Daniel Thunner. The owner
leaned over the gilded handrail, looking down at the crowd.
He still had his hat on and a long overcoat. It was dirty and
stained with soot. Heads lifted. Men pointed. Thunner didn't
speak, just waited as the noise rose and peaked and fell away.
He took off his hat, and the hall quieted.

"I understand there's some dissatisfaction here." His voice
sounded hoarse, cracked, as if he'd been sucking smoke. "So
I thought I'd come down and make things clear.

"I'm sorry about the fire, and the men we lost. Tom Callahan taught me to pitch, at the company picnics when I was
a kid. I knew Shaughnessey and Rapisczek. I think of us as
a family—the Thunder family. You all know there ain't a
man who works harder than I do to keep us all eating regular.
Just like any man does for his family, any man who's a
man."

Thunner half turned from them, coughing into his fist.
Then he raised his voice. "But I hear there's some swelled
heads here who want to tell me how to run things. Well, I
got news for them.

"That's this: I give the orders at Thunder Oil," he roared.
"My grandfather struck the first well in the Seneca Sand. My
father built Number One. There's plenty of loyal men here.

I'll see them at work tomorrow. And we'll put Thunder back together, and we'll keep it together.

"But any lousy bastard who wants to make trouble—go on! We'll take you on. And we'll beat you, just like we always have!"

Uproar and confusion. Shouts of support vied with raised fists and hoots. Above it all Thunner settled his hat back on his head, turned, and mounted the balcony with long, unhurried strides. He ducked under a velvet rope, pushed through a curtain, and disappeared from sight.

Behind him the hall was filled with shouting men. Some were fighting. Others were climbing up onto the stage, or thronging in confused eddies. "Meeting's closed. This meeting's closed!" Vansittart yelled. Halvorsen didn't see that it was, not by a long shot. But the chandelier lights snapped off, then the lights on the stage. He stood and started elbowing his way out.

The lobby was packed sardine-close with angry, excited workers. The managers had left by some back way. Then the doors banged open, spilling them out into the sparkling, ice-cold night air that smelled of snow and woodsmoke. The older employees trudged silently off into the night, faces troubled. But the younger ones stayed, arguing under the lit marquee, John Wayne in *The Dawn Rider*, Movietone News, Popeye cartoon, till it too flashed off and the night snapped closed on them like an old woman's purse.

"Say the meetin's closed. We never got a chance to talk!"

"To hell with those birds. Tell 'em where to get off."

"They got a fat nerve. We oughta convene our own meeting."

Halvorsen looked down the block. It was late, after ten. They couldn't stay out here—it was freezing. Then he saw the flashing sign down the street.

"Let's go down there."

"What, in the bowling alley?"

It didn't take long; the men were so cold they didn't want to stand around, and so angry they didn't care much where they went. They tramped after him and pushed through the grimy door, climbed stamping their boots up the narrow, worn steps.

"We're gonna have a meeting," Halvorsen said to the grandpa at the counter. "Don't look like you're too busy, anyway. We'll pass the hat, pay ya for the time. Okay?"

"Sure, sure, thatsa jake," he said, hands in the air like it was a stickup. "You want-a have meeting, go ahead. I stoppa the bowling, okay?"

He was surprised, when they sat and squatted around the foul line on the scuffed waxed wood, some perched uncomfortable-looking on the ball rack, how many had stuck. Some he knew, some he didn't, faces he'd seen but didn't recall names. For some reason they were all looking at him, maybe because he was the one who'd led them here. He said, "Okay, what exactly are we doin' here? Are we talkin' about goin' out, or what?"

"We ain't got enough guys here to strike Number One."

"Okay, then we'll just walk out. Till they fix things."

"What we want 'em to fix?"

"The safety gear first. We want a worker safety committee with teeth."

"An' we want our wages back up where they were, back before Thunder started cuttin' 'em."

"Forget it, Mac. You been drinkin' too much giggle juice. There's lots of jokers out there be happy to pick up our tools, we don't want 'em."

The old Italian, from the counter: "You fellas wanta start a strike at Thunder, that's-a right? That's what-a you do here?" Nobody answered him.

They finally decided to elect a committee to represent them. By show of hands they elected Lew Pearson—the field men all seemed to know Lew, maybe because he was always driving around from lease to lease; Stanley Melnichak, an assistant foreman from the pipe shop; "Shorty" Quarequio, another plant man, the stubby excitable fellow who'd spoken up at the Lind; and Halvorsen. He was surprised, but figured it was the exhibition bouts, guys recognizing his name from that, as much as him speaking up at the meeting. They agreed to stay out tomorrow, just to show they could do it, then go back in the day after. The committee would draw up a letter outlining their complaints about safety and pay. They'd meet in a week and vote on it, then present it to the company. At last Halvorsen said, "Okay, that it? Anything else?"

"Bar's still open, over at the Star Lunch," said Popovich. "We ain't goin' in tomorrow, might as well make a night of it."

Halvorsen hesitated. Guertin had made it clear he had to cut out the hooch, keep up his training regimen; and he had; he'd been pretty abstemious the last few weeks. But the whiskey old Washko had forced on him seemed to have given him the taste for the stuff again.

"Well? You comin'?"

"Maybe for just a Straub's," he said. And looking forward to the drink, feeling good but not especially excited, as if nothing much in his life had changed, he went on down the narrow, grimy stairs and out again, into the windy night.

Eight

When Thunner came down for breakfast a week later, Leola was waiting for him at the table. He sighed inwardly, but bent to kiss her cheek. "How are you feeling this morning, darling?"

"Not well. I hardly slept at all."

He shook out his napkin, eyebrows raised in an attentive mask as she droned on. When she paused he said, "I'm sorry you're not feeling well. Is Ainslee up yet?"

"Here I am, Daddy."

He held out his hands, and got an armload of amber-haired little girl. He held her squealing above his head, as his wife looked on disapprovingly, then set her in her chair. He thought she was beautiful, with sharp dark eyes and button nose and a direct, straight gaze that made him feel as if he had something to hide. He'd taken her to the works and been impressed with her attention, her probing questions as they strolled among the towers and tanks, the hulking railcars full of Thunder products. The workers had grinned at them, tipping their caps at him and at the little girl trotting along in her pinafore, holding her daddy's hand.

But still she wasn't a boy, and Leola was spending more time in bed, her vague complaints multiplying. She'd seen Doc Brainerd, gone to consultations in Buffalo and Boston, but there didn't seem to be anything the medical men could put their fingers on. One had recommended a hysterectomy. He'd made it plain she was not to see that quack again. Seeing now her expression of suffering and self-sacrifice, he suppressed disgust and disappointment. Once he might have looked elsewhere, but a few years ago a man-to-man with Reverend Crandall had made him realize that however much a healthy man enjoyed certain things, he had a duty of self-restraint as well.

"What are you thinking about?" Leola asked him.

"Oh, business. What are you two doing today?"

"This is my Tuesday Club day. It's dreadfully cold, but I need to get out of the house and see someone. And I might stop by Thalier's for the new frocks."

"You got a lot of dresses in New York."

"That was last summer, Dan! You wouldn't have me wearing something dowdy and old-fashioned. Would you?"

He heard the Chrysler starting up outside. He drank off his coffee and rose, pulling on his gloves, ruffling his daughter's hair. "I'll be at work late. We've got a lot of cleanup, after the fire. You and Miss Verre, you'll have fun today playing, right, sweet cheeks?"

Outside, the freezing wind slashed at his face. He stood at the top of the steps, buttoning his coat, looking out over the valley. His eyes saw a fast-moving blanket of cloud, the shining hills that cupped the town like white walls. He gazed out over the sea of roofs that slanted down from those hills toward the long basilica sheds of factories and machine shops. But his brain noted only the pall of steam and smoke that streamed up to stain the sky, the wavering red-orange banners of flame that writhed again within the veil. From here you couldn't see the damage to Number One. But he knew it was there, cutting his output just when the market was showing signs of life again, and his already bad mood, begun by his wife's petulant face and the thoughts it triggered, deepened.

The Chrysler slid down the driveway. Herrot hopped out and held the door, hand flicking up in salute. Thunner got in, face grim. "Back to Number One, Harry."

"Yes, sir."

As the car slid away down the hill he glanced back at the house. A small, sharp-eyed face stared out from the side window, down at him. He lifted his glove, but his daughter didn't wave back. Only watched, intent and unsmiling, until he disappeared from sight.

The guard at the Gower Avenue gate touched his cap as the Chrysler shouldered in. As the car swung right and braked, Thunner sat staring through glass, as if unwilling to meet what he saw face to face. He gritted his teeth, kicked the door open, and jumped down.

His boots ground on black ash, sand, cinders, and dirty-white Foamite residue. It stank of burned oil and scorched iron. He stopped motionless, looking around at a wilderness of toppled piping, blasted-apart scrap metal, half-burned and splintered beams.

And suddenly, just as he'd feared, he was back there once more. Back with the stink of cordite and burning, of death and fire and torn-open earth churned into a muddy porridge that sucked you down to your knees, sometimes to your thighs as the bullets sang past. The goddamned snipers, the goddamned Boche machine gunners. They left them behind as a rear guard as they pulled back, and they waited till you were past and opened up on you from behind . . . but even that wasn't as bad as being *buried*. Icy-cold sweat broke out all over his body. His hands trembled, clenched in his coat pockets.

He stood there sucking in deep, calming breaths, till the fit or illusion faded, then forced himself on across the blasted ground toward a group of men who were heaving twisted plate from a collapsed tank up onto a flatbed truck. He and the straw boss discussed how to take down a sagging framework. Then a younger man came striding across the desolation.

Jim Etterlin hadn't been with the company long. He was a process engineer, the first Thunder Oil had ever employed. The other board members had scoffed when Thunner had proposed him. They said if the old hands didn't know it, it wasn't worth knowing about oil. He'd chuckled and said they probably weren't far wrong; then gone ahead and hired him. A slim young man in glasses, he looked exhausted this morning, just like Thunner felt.

"We were lucky," Etterlin said, nodding at the wreckage.

"Yeah?"

"It could have been a lot worse. If the bubble tower had gone—or if we'd had a trainload of product on that spur . . ." He didn't finish his sentence.

"The last time we had a fire, in 'ought-five, the whole plant burned. My dad had it rebuilt and running again in eight months."

"Process was simpler then. Speaking of rebuilding, I looked at some possibilities." Thunner nodded, and Etterlin spread catalogs and diagrams over the hood of the Chrysler. In a moment he was deep in the maze of lines and piping and valves.

Despite the complexity of the diagrams, refining petroleum was a simple process. Raw crude arrived by pipeline. Pumped in a continuous stream through the stills, the light volatile fractions such as gasoline came off as vapor. The heavier ones separated out in liquid form. Both flowed hot into the bubble tower, a vertical stack of stripping and rectifying plates, four feet in diameter and a hundred and twenty feet high. Kerosene came off at one level, gas-oil from another, distillate from a third. It was more complicated than that, since you recirculated certain fractions, but basically that was it; you fractionated in the tower, then ran each of the raw "cuts" through further treatment, depending on what you wanted as an end product—lube stock, motor fuel, all the way down to the tarry asphalt that went out of the works solid, cooled to a glassy obsidian.

Etterlin slid his finger along the colored lines. "These should be Hortonspheres. That'll drop our evaporation losses. Since we have to replace the condenser assembly anyway, we should install DeLaval agitators, more interstage tankage, and a modern filtration and wax-press line. We need to talk about polymerization, too."

"Tiona's selling out, auctioning their plant off—"

"Their stills are older than ours. Why would we want to buy the equipment they just went broke with?"

"Well, how much is this all going to cost?"

The engineer squinted toward the blackened, twisted gap. "I'm not done pricing it out."

"A guess."

"Depends on what and how much you want to be able to stream, and how much capacity you want for the aviation-quality lubricants. Half a million? Could go as high as six hundred thou."

"That's a hell of a bill." Thunner showed his teeth in what wasn't a grin.

"Well, you'll have the insurance. That'll defray your investment. You'll end up with a bigger gasoline fraction if we go with the polymerization. Take the ethane and propane out of that flare-off and turn it into motor fuel. Plus a modern plant'll take you fewer men to run."

Thunner stared at the diagram. The trouble was—and this was something he had no intention of telling Etterlin, or the board, or anyone else—there wouldn't be any insurance payment. Plant insurance was one of the things he'd had to cancel in '32, when nationwide crude runs to stills were down to two million barrels a day and nobody was buying lube oil and damn little gasoline either. He'd run naked for three years, and been lucky—up to now.

So all this fire damage and wrecked equipment was a dead loss, and anything he replaced this twisted wreckage with was going to have to come out of the workers' hides. It was that or close the plant.

He cursed himself and the gods of finance for the thousandth time. Everyone had said the market would keep on going up forever. Or at the very least, move sideways. Who could have believed that all that equity could just *vanish*—

"Something wrong, Dan?" Etterlin said, and he jerked his attention back to the present: the engineer's questioning squint, the dragon-tongue slither of ash in the wind, the earsplitting clangor as more scrap iron went onto the truck. He shook his head, clapped the engineer on the back.

"No, no. But we'll have to discuss it. I want to buy as little in the way of fabrications as we can. A lot of the framing, supports, that kind of stuff, we should be able to make in the pipe fitters' shop, rivet it together ourselves."

"I can design it that way, if you like. Take slightly longer to get back in operation—"

"I'd rather keep the paychecks in town than send them to Pittsburgh."

"That makes sense. Then there's the safety equipment. This is our chance to get it all updated. Put integral antiflame blankets into the new tanks. New fire-fighting equipment—"

"Our current gear still yields a return on investment, Jim. Let's look at that again when prosperity comes back."

Two overcoated figures emerged from the brick building that housed the refinery offices and headed for them, heads bent under the lash of the wind. Earl Vansittart, the manager, and Bob Wheeler, chief of Thunder's plant police. Thunner asked them, "What's the latest on our hotheads? The men who walked out last week?"

Vansittart: "We had maybe eighty guys out one day. They're all back now. They bitch and moan, but what the hell."

"Bob, what's your feeling? Anything there?"

The head guard was in the gray uniform, gray cap with gold lightning-bolt of the Thunder plant police. He wore a revolver belted over his greatcoat. He said slowly, "There's a lot of jawin'."

"Anything more?"

"Hard to tell. One thing, it ain't just the guys in the refinery. It's the ones out in the field, too. They get to thinking they're independent contractors or something."

"Well, get them straightened out," said Thunner, wondering again where he could locate additional financing. "Check with the foremen. Anybody doesn't want to play with the team, we can do without 'em. Run the list by me first, before you pink-slip 'em."

Wheeler nodded; Vansittart pulled out a notebook. Thunner stood watching the cleanup for a few more minutes, then got back into the car. He stopped once more, by the lab, and listened as one of the research chemists briefed him on a new method of propane separation. Then, finally, he headed for the office.

The Thunder head office had been on Main Street since the company had been Thunder Sinnemahoning; a squat, sooty, three-story stonepile with cast-iron cornices and Ionic columns on either side of its little windows and the date 1878 on its cornerstone. Thunner hated it. In a few months he'd be able to move to the new building. For a moment he wanted to go and see it again, but he marched himself firmly into the old office's entrance instead.

Several men looked up as he came in. He nodded to several he recognized—salesmen, promoters, oil producers—and favored one with a grave "How're you, Whelan. Be with you in a minute" as he hung his hat and coat and went past them to the inner office.

The Sands belonged to Leola, but this belonged to him. A tea-urn steamed on a sideboard. Two aged leather wing chairs faced the massive walnut desk that had belonged to Colonel Charles. His father's collection of bronzes stood on the mantelpiece, and above them his Western art. The one modern piece was a Bellows boxing print, *Saturday Night at Sharkey's*. He regarded it for a moment, admiring the virile raw energy of the colors, like gas flames in the dark, the pale stains of the audience surrounding the beef-colored, violet-shadowed forms of the combatants. Have to call Guertin, find out how his Swedish challenger was coming along. The thought buoyed him a little.

He took the day's mail off the sideboard. Weyandt had been in early, and had already opened it, winnowed through it, and attached relevant references to the most important missives. He sat down; sighed; allowed himself one more glance at the print. Then rubbed his face, hard, and set himself to work.

Nine

Halvorsen sat slumped in an ancient sag-seated armchair, the paper spread out on his lap. There were some nutty things in it today. Like the Utah cult that was waiting for the resurrection of a woman who'd been dead for ten months. They were keeping her corpse fresh in a saltwater bath till the "rebirth." Then again, other things weren't so funny. The Lindbergh case; Hauptmann's lawyers had grilled the baby's little Scottish nurse till she broke down crying on the stand. Twenty people had been killed in San Francisco when someone put poison in baking soda. A guy in Milwaukee who had apparently been mailing bombs to banks and police stations had blown himself up accidentally in his garage, along with a pal and a nine-year-old kid. A mob in Tennessee lynched a Negro for slapping a white woman. The Japs were making a new nation out of North China. And a sharp zero spell was on its way down from Canada.

Clearing his throat—he felt listless, hot, and a little faint—he lowered the paper, glancing around the front room of Mrs. Fiona Ludtke's Gentlemen's Boarding House.

The parlor was uncomfortably furnished with the old lumpy chairs and a round oak table with claw feet that held carved balls and a big console radio shaped like a cathedral window and a Gramophone he'd never heard played. On the walls hung mounted penmanship copies and a chromo of the Old Homestead. A Holderlin Machine Tool Company calendar hung by the door, all but the last days of November crossed off. Fake-bronze reading lamps with brittle beaded-paper shades stood about on an age-browned carpet worn so shiny smooth by generations of boots you couldn't tell what its pattern had once been. The room smelled like sauerkraut and tobacco, and around it this Sunday morning, smoking and occasionally leaning to use the spittoons sat the bachelor men, young, middle-aged, and old, who called this bare house home. They sat with mouths open, and heads cocked; or bent forward, hands dangling at their knees, staring at the radio, from the cloth-covered grille of which a mellifluous, manly voice swelled and faded. A rich, deep, ingratiating voice, with a touch of Irish brogue that lingered over words. *The Golden Hour of the Little Flower* was on, and Father Coughlin was laying his lash on both political parties. *"Your actual boss, Mr. Laboring Man, is not so much to blame. . . . If you must strike, strike in an intelligent manner, not by laying down your tools, but by raising your voices against a system that keeps you today and will keep you tomorrow in breadless bondage . . ."*

An old man grunted in agreement, glancing at Halvorsen. Who avoided his eyes, staring at the paper, trying to push away the nervousness that made his feet tap the worn carpet.

"President Roosevelt has both compromised with the money changers and conciliated with monopolistic industry. . . . He who promised to drive the money changers from the temple has built up the greatest debt in history, which he permitted the bankers the right, without restriction, to spend, and for which he contracted that you and your children shall repay with seventy billion hours of labor. . . ."

"You listenin' to this, young fella? He's tellin' us the straight of the thing. We got to share the wealth, take it back from the Jews an' bankers as stole it from us. That Hitler fella now, he—"

"Say, it's all a bunch of hooey," Halvorsen interrupted him. "Why don't you turn that stuff off?"

"Hooey? Why, you goddamn pup. Still wet behind the ears."

Halvorsen rattled the paper, sorry he'd said anything as the old man mumbled on. He was feeling pretty down in the dumps. But he had to snap out of it; he was fighting tonight, out in Chapman, and this was no exhibition; it would be his first real bout. Trouble was, it felt like he was coming down with something. He hoped it wasn't the Spanish influenza again. They'd all had it in '19, that was what his mom had died of, and his dad not long after, out on the farm. He'd been pretty damn sick himself, only it seemed the bug didn't kill the kids, or the old people, only young, strong men and women in the prime of life. He hadn't been out to the farm for a long time. He ought to go back, fix the roof before everything went to hell. His sister didn't care; she'd gotten married and moved to Gary and he hardly ever heard from her except at Christmas.

Coughlin was in full oratorical flight now, ranting about a guaranteed annual wage and English machinations and the need for a third party to hold the Democrats to their promises. Halvorsen tried to lose himself in the comics. Popeye, the self-proclaimed king of Spinachova, was in love with a knockout Brutian spy named Zexa Peal. Andy and Min Gump were arguing over Uncle Bim's trouble with Mrs. De Stross. Joe Palooka was putting on weight for the Schmellinsaltz fight. As soon as he won, he was going to retire from the championship and marry Ann. . . .

"Aw, shit," he muttered, closing his eyes and letting his head sag back.

The real reason he felt so lousy was, it looked like it was over, him and Jennie.

The day after the big mass meeting, he'd woken late and just lay there in his room, groaning. Rolled over at last and found he was still in his work clothes. His boots had made big mud-smears on his sheets. Shoot, Miz Ludtke would kill him.

Then he'd remembered something else, and jerked upright and pulled the white-enameled alarm clock toward him. Then closed his eyes, cursing himself and the boys who'd kept buying him drinks the night before. He'd forgotten to set it, and it was ten-thirty, and *he'd missed Johnny's funeral*.

Too late to go, too late to do anything. He'd called the Washkos' house, but of course no one answered. They were at St. Denis's, or out at the cemetery. He debated going up there, but figured it would be worse, coming in hangdog smack in the middle of things, than not showing up at all. So he'd just hung around the boardinghouse, and after dinner when he wanted to try again someone else was on the phone. So finally he got his coat and boots on and went down to the candy store on the corner of Marshall and Labstain and called again from there, hoping he didn't get her dad.

"Hello, the Washkos'."

"Jennie? It's me."

A tone he'd never heard in her voice. "Oh . . . Bill. Where are you?"

"At the candy store, using the phone."

"What happened, Bill? Didn't you remember we were burying Johnny today?"

"I remembered. I just didn't get up in time."

"We waited for you. But you never showed up. Then I looked for you at church."

"Look, I'm sorry. I meant to go. I just forgot to set the darn—"

"I don't think you understand how much it meant to me, to have you there. My mother, my aunts all asked where you were."

"I'm sorry. Look, I can come over now, I can apologize to them—"

"It would be better if you didn't. I ain't slept or washed or anything, the house been so full of people. Everyone says we're just too different, you and I. They say I ought to find myself a good Catholic Slovak boy and not a cake eater."

"A what?"

"A cake eater, that's what they call you. They think you should find yourself an American girl. Somebody more up-to-date and classy than I am. And maybe they're right. We just don't seem to think the same things are important. And Pa—"

"What about your pa?"

"He says he heard about what you said, at the meeting last night. Being disrespectful, and all. He says I can't see you anymore, Bill. He says a fella who'll talk wild like that, you'll never keep a job. He don't want you coming around anymore. And I think maybe he's right. Because, you see, when I do get married, it's going to be forever. I do like you, Bill. But I don't want to make any mistakes, or lead you on. That would just make us both unhappy."

He'd argued with her, feeling sick inside and guilty too, because he was in the wrong, but she was inflexible, and finally he'd just said all right, figuring maybe he could talk to her later, talk her around; and hung up.

But he hadn't seen her since. He'd called the house a couple of times, but Mr. Washko just hung up without saying anything as soon as he heard his voice, and whoever else answered—Mrs. Washko or the kids—always said Jennie wasn't there. It made him mad. But he couldn't think of anything he could do about it. Other than go over there and crawl, and he wasn't going to do that. So all in all he was feeling pretty blue, and his life was about as messed up as it could get, and he just didn't want to think about it anymore. So he was almost glad when Dick Shotner came into the parlor and said, "Hey, Bill, d-did I hear Miz Ludtke say you were fightin' today?"

Shotner was younger than he was, eighteen or nineteen. He worked in a battery factory out in the east end, but he didn't do dirty work; he was some kind of clerk or book-keeper. He was too thin, and his neck was too long; his triangular, sallow face narrowed to a too-pointed chin, like the pictures of TB patients you saw in *Life*. His eyes were too big, and his ears protruded like handles, and his movements were jerky and huddled. He looked like a dog who expected to be kicked. He wore a rusty black suit, like a preacher, and hightop shoes scuffed to raw leather at the toes, and he was always trying to get Halvorsen to go down to the YMCA with him. Halvorsen didn't actually dislike Shotner. It was more like not feeding a stray. As if, if you were friendly, you'd never be able to shake him off.

"Yeah, tonight. Didn't know you followed that stuff."

"I don't, but since it's you—how you g-gettin' out there? Ridin' your cycle?"

"Naw, I quit since I skidded into that tree and bent up the front wheel. Been thinkin' of sellin' it. Interested?"

"Ha, ha, I don't think so. So, how you g-gettin' there?"

"Got a guy coming by to pick me up."

"Can I bum a ride?"

Halvorsen said reluctantly that he didn't think there'd be a problem, but it wasn't his car. Just be out front when he came. Shotner nodded and said, "You d-done with the comics, there?"

A hand was shaking him. He jerked awake, looking around the parlor. "Somebody just honked," Shotner said. "That your pal?"

He got up and peered between Mrs. Ludtke's yellowing lace curtains. A green coupe idled on the street, the round visage of Fatso DeSantis like a furtive moon behind the wheel. He told Shotner yeah, that was him. He grabbed his bag and pulled on his coat and galoshes in the mudroom and stamped down the steps, careful because it was icy.

"Hey, W.T. Let's go, get in."

"Len, this here's Dick Shotner. Wants to know if he can ride over with us. Dick, this is Len DeSantis, friend a mine from when we was kids."

"Sure, get in, plenty of room in back. We stoppin' for Jennie?"

"She ain't coming."

"What's the matter? Girl trouble?"

"We're on the outs, that's all."

"Don't know why," DeSantis crooned. "There's no sun up in the sky; Stormy weather—"

"Can it, Fatso. I ain't in the mood."

"Take it easy, W.T. Sorry to hear that, I thought she was real sweet."

He didn't respond. DeSantis put the car in gear and the wheels spun, then caught and they headed down Front Street. They slowed for the trucks and construction where they were putting up the new Thunder Building, then headed west along the river, out of town.

He took deep breaths, looking out, trying to shake this thing. The Allegheny was already frozen. You couldn't tell it was a river, except that there weren't any trees. It could have been a road: just a smooth wide expanse of white with here and there the humps of rocks beneath it. There were islands out there too. No one owned them; they were just little projections of earth and rock, and black sere bushes, leafless and to all appearances lifeless. When he was a kid he used to daydream about living on them alone, like Huck Finn. He cranked his window down and spat into the snow rushing past. DeSantis rummaged under his seat. It was a mess down there, which always surprised him. DeSantis was always freshly shaven and powdered and well dressed, but as far as his heap went he didn't seem to care what it looked like.

He came up with a quart of Old Quaker. "Slug a happy water?"

"No thanks."

"Want a snort, Dick?" DeSantis yelled, holding it up. "If you can drink it straight and stout, and it doesn't knock you out, you're a better man than I am, Guzzle Gin." Shotner said he didn't. "You a fight fan, Dick?"

"No."

"What you going for, then?"

"Just to see B-Bill here fight. I ain't never been to one, and I thought, well, I'd just see what it was l-like."

"Oh yeah. Well, I hope you got some scratch, they're

gonna charge us to get in and whatever we want to drink."

Shotner said he had a little kale, and they went along the river, not too fast, DeSantis driving in the crowned center of the road unless somebody was coming the other way. The chains whined and jingled. "Damn this snow," he said. "And look at that sky, it's gonna be ass-deep to a wild Injun come tonight." Neither of his passengers said anything.

Chapman was past Bagley Corners, just before you crossed the county line. There'd been sawmills there before oil was discovered, and a couple were still running; but mostly it was paper mills now. The smell hit them when they were still well east of town, invisible but solid, a smell to be respected, held in by the valley and boiled down into a concentrated reek of sulfur and dead skunks. "Man, that stinks." DeSantis wheezed. "How you gonna fight in that?"

"Hold my breath, I guess."

"For ten rounds? Where the hell we going, anyway?"

"Pull over, I'll ask." He cranked the window down again as DeSantis let the coupe roll to a stop. An old man in a battered gray fedora stood by the road, grizzled cheek-sunken face buried in his overcoat collar. "Hey, pop. Hey! Where's the Sons of the Piedmont?"

"Take a right, up by where used to be the Peoples' Grocery. You gonna see it up on the side of the hill."

"Hey, we're from outta town. We don't know where the goddamn grocery used to be."

"To hell with you. Take a right after the mill."

"Thanks, old timer."

The hall was built out of huge blackened hemlock logs so that it seemed to be growing sideways out of the hillside. A clearing in the scrub woods was parked solid with slush-crusted flivvers and worn-out trucks with rust-eaten running boards. Halvorsen got out and danced on the rutted snow and frozen mud, loosening up. Throwing punches at the air. Shit, he'd rather shoot a well than do this.

"Look at that," DeSantis said. "Want me to take that down, keep it for you?"

It was a fight card, tacked to the door of the club. He felt
the butterflies take off and whirl around in his stomach.

HEMLOCK BOXING ASSOCIATION
EXCITING FISTIC SHOW TONIGHT!
THREE BOUTS
STARTS AT EIGHT-THIRTY
MAIN GO AT TEN O'CLOCK
BRIMMING WITH ACTION!

ROBERT "THE WELSHMAN" ARTHUR (121), ST. MARY'S, VS. ED
"NICKEL PLATE" JESSON, (117), COUDERSPORT

———

W.T. "KID NITRO" HALVORSEN (157), PETROLEUM CITY, VS. "K.O."
LOUIS GIGLIOTTA (160), CHAPMAN

———

SEMI-FINAL HEAVYWEIGHT CHAMPIONSHIP BOUT!
JACK MCKEE, (175), RAYMONDSVILLE, VS. FIGHTING SAM SHANG
(179), CLEVELAND, OHIO

SEATS RESERVED FOR LADIES
AT SONS OF THE PIEDMONT HALL
NOVEMBER 21, 1935

He said "Sure," figuring to give it to Jennie, then remembered: She'd given him the air. But DeSantis was already
stuffing it inside his coat. So he just spat into the snow again
and pushed through after him, into the dim and the laughter
and the yeasty stink of cigars and needled beer and crowded,
sweating men.

Guertin and Picciacchia were waiting for him in the back, a
cramped mildew-and-urine-smelling closet disguised as a
dressing room with a stained curtain and a rack with a towel

hanging on it so paper thin you could see through it and a wash table with a crack-crazy crockery jug-and-basin with yellow flowers molded into the porcelain. A radiator hissed malevolently in the corner. He looked at the pitcher thirstily, but didn't dare reach for it. Guertin kept him short of water before a fight. While he was changing DeSantis asked the priest if he should put money on Halvorsen. Guertin shrugged. DeSantis hesitated. "Whatta you think, Billy? You feel like a winner tonight?"

"I feel okay, Len."

" 'Okay'?"

"Yeah, 'okay.' Not great, but okay."

"It's a tough fight?"

"Gigliotta's good," said Guertin, going after his own eyes with the heels of his hands as if trying to mash them back into his skull. "Best middleweight they got in the Gerroy stable. But the Kid here's come along pretty smart on his practice bouts."

DeSantis looked as if he wanted to ask something else, but finally didn't. He said, "Well, good luck," and patted Halvorsen's thigh. Then he went back out through the curtain.

"Hop up on the box there," said Picciacchia, and Halvorsen sat and held up his hands for tape. "Gigliotta's a good match for ya. I seen him box lotsa times. You oughta be able to take him, but watch his right. Be glad you ain't lacing it on with McKee tonight. He's a real mauler, ya know he knocked down Harry Greb once . . . you the doc? He's all yours, go ahead."

While the doctor was examining his throat and frowning, someone came in through the curtain and stood looking down at him. Halvorsen blinked when he turned his head and saw who it was. "Evening, Mr. Thunner."

"How you feeling tonight, Halvorsen?"

"Okay, sir."

"I've put a good deal of cash down on you. I'm counting on you to come through for me with Mr. Gerroy's fighter."

"Do my best, sir."

"I understand you've been talking union with some of those hotheads stayed out the other week. That right?" When he hesitated, then nodded, Thunner said, "Well, you're young yet. Take my advice, leave that kind of stuff alone. Just leads to trouble, doesn't do anyone any good. Okay, now, remember, you want it bad enough, you can show this dago what the canvas looks like close up. The Father here says you got the goods. Go in there and make me proud." Thunner slapped his back like a man encouraging a horse, and left.

Time passed. After he was examined and weighed, he sat restless for a while, robe over his shoulders; then slid down and paced back and forth—not far, the room was too small. Guertin sat with his shoes propped up on a stack of empty beer crates, collar undone, head back. He looked tired and old. Halvorsen wondered if the headaches ever went away, if they were there even when the old man slept. The crowd roared now and then on the far side of the wall, making the tin lampshade rattle and buzz.

At last Picciacchia came back. He said, "That tape tight enough? They're ready for us." He hoisted himself to his feet, thinking, The cat's in the cream crock now, and followed the crooked little man and the big priest out.

Into darkness, a haze of cigar smoke, a press of noise, a gauntlet of hostile faces. He sucked air, fighting the urge to vomit. He ducked through the ropes and came up bouncing on his toes, the robe swirling out like a cape. The grimy patched canvas was spotted with rust, or was it blood . . . men perched on chairs, on pool tables, barstools . . . an old-ster's cheeks folding around toothless gums like a worn base-ball glove . . . a grease-caked wooden ceiling scant inches above his head. He raised his clasped gloves, almost touching it as a voice yelled, "For the second fight of the evening. In the black trunks. From Petroleum City, at a hundred fifty-seven pounds, W. T. Halvorsen, the Nitro Kid."

Silence, and two quickly stilled cheers from a gloomy corner. Halvorsen squinted: Fatso and Shotner.

"And in the red trunks, from right here in Chapman, at a hundred and sixty pounds . . . Fighting Louie Gigliotta!"

The crowd welcomed the hometown fighter with a pro-longed roar and a hammering of bottles. Gigliotta was hairy and bowlegged, with a deep thick torso under his undershirt and well-muscled arms and a craggy, jutting brow like Alley-Oop. Halvorsen let Picciacchia's malformed strong little hands shove him down onto the stool as he studied his op-ponent. Short arms, just about the same height he was or a little shorter. Maybe a chance for a right cross he'd been practicing. But not too early. Guertin stood above him, chew-ing a cigar. "Stay focused," he rumbled. "Keep your mitts up. And watch those ropes, they're kind of loose." Halvorsen glanced at the heavy sagging manila cable. No bouncing back off that.

The bell clanged, and he got up and moved out into the light. The ref, compact and ugly in a starched white shirt, grabbed their gloves, slammed them together. "No butting, no gouging, no hitting below the belt. Break when I say to. Come out fightin', and may the best man win."

Halvorsen opened with a couple of jabs, then followed a left-jab body feint with a left hook to his opponent's head. Gig-liotta took it and came back with a right like a beer wagon. He danced back and circled, into the left, which seemed a little weak, a little hesitant. The Italian kept his head turtled and his guard well up. He'd be hard to sucker out. He wasn't like the guys he'd been fighting in the fields. Then again, he knew a lot more now than he had when he took on tool dressers and laborers over a dare or a misplaced word. Guer-tin had drilled him for endless hours, till he staggered, but now he didn't even have to think to inside slip a straight left or weave to the outside on a left-jab lead.

In again, a quick flurry of punch and counterpunch, and back out, circling, up on his toes. His head felt naked without the head protector. Gigliotta closed in. The guy liked his right, Picciacchia said. Okay. He dropped his left, letting the other fighter glimpse his chin, and drew a shot to the head. He shoulder-rolled and blammed a right back, just missing the other man's chin.

He tested the guy a couple more times, weaving out of the way when he counterattacked; drew him again, scored on a right cross; then the bell clanged. He jogged back to his corner and squatted, chest heaving already, chewing on the wet rag Guertin handed him out of the bucket. He stared across the ring as Picciacchia touched up a cut on his cheek. Gigliotta didn't look back. He was talking to his manager, face set and expressionless.

The bell, and up again. He didn't feel weak now. He felt full of power and light as air, light as the smoke that eddied around Gigliotta's glove as it came around slow as a switch engine trundling down the rails. He stepped back from it, then went on in and hammered him one, two, three to the body, faked a break and came back in and shoulder-rolled a straight right to his head and hooked hard, hard to the trunk again, steam-hammering them up into the other man's ribs.

"Kill him! Kill the little shit!"

"Get on in there, Louie!"

The cries barely penetrated his consciousness. He closed again and fought it out toe to toe for five or six combinations, head down, hitting as pile-driver-fast as he could. Gigliotta seemed logy and slow. Then he backed out and circled, catching his breath. Gigliotta seemed content to stand still, following him around.

Halvorsen figured he had him measured now. He feinted, then bent his knees and submarined in, following a left jab to the belly with a left hook and then a straight right hard and true to the Italian's head that sprayed sweat out in a cloud that he glimpsed for a flashing moment frozen in the brilliant light, lit against brilliant darkness. Like stars flung across the void. He hesitated, gaping at the beauty of it.

The left came through his defense too hard to parry. It knocked his head back, and Gigliotta came in after it, and he grunted to blow after blow, doubling him over. The ropes creaked and rocked against his back. He clinched, gripping the sweaty hairy shoulders tight, smelling the other man rank and stinking and wondering if he smelled as bad. Then the ref was yelling in his ear. "Break it up. Break it up, girls. Get outta there and box."

He broke and danced back, trying to fling a lock of hair out of his eyes. It kept falling back down. Gigliotta followed him, hammering at his face. He ducked and wove and escaped at last. The crowd-sound was a roar in his ears, like a great fire. He couldn't make out what exactly they were yelling, but it didn't sound like they were rooting for him. He was moving in again when the bell clanged and they broke and he jogged back to his corner. Sucking wind now, the burst of energy already leaking away. He coughed. All the damn smoke, and the shitty paper-mill smell . . . he kept coughing, unable to stop.

Picciacchia, in his ear: "Spit your mouthpiece. Hear me? You doin' awright?"

"Yeah."

"Five and four."

"Nine."

"Listen ta me. You doing good, Nitro, you doing good on points, but save somethin', kid. You got eight rounds to go. Make him chase you now, okay?"

"Yeh."

"Don't try to knock him out. You're winnin' this one. He's a palooka. A goon. Just stay away from that right."

"Yeh." He licked his cracked, dry lips. "Water—"

"Not till next bell. Open your mouth." The mouthpiece thrust in, he bit down on the soft rubber, and got up and went in again, into the light.

By the fifth he was exhausted. His feet dragged, and his hands were leaden. It was agony keeping them at eye level. But Gigliotta wasn't showing it. He had to be twenty-nine, thirty, but he didn't seem to tire. Blood and sweat sprayed off his face each time Halvorsen landed a glove. He just shook his head and kept shuffling inexorably forward. Still, he thought he had the edge. He was landing more punches, mostly lefts. He didn't get the feeling he was hurting this mug, but that wasn't how you scored a fight. Anyway he kept hammering away, wheezing and coughing. And watching that right. Every once in a while Gigliotta would gather everything up and throw the office at him, but it wasn't hard to dodge. Just had to keep moving. And not trip, like he'd tripped fighting Grau out at the lease. No holes to step in here, though.

The bell, at last. He dragged himself back to the corner through a storm of yelling, catcalls, boos.

"Spit it out. . . . Forget them skunks. You doing swell, W.T. Ain't he, Father?"

"You're doing good, Kid. How you feel?"

"Awful tired."

"Well, you're halfway done. Keep up just like you been doing. He's gettin' tired too, don't forget that."

He didn't have breath to answer, just kept heaving in air and smoke. He felt dizzy, lightheaded. "Gimme . . . wet my whistle," he gasped.

Picciacchia said, "You had some last round. No more goddamn water, you gonna cramp up. Suck that sonofabitch rag, that's all you get. An' just keep thinkin' a the money."

The bell rang. Guertin's heavy paw shoved him forward, and he stumbled out, eyeing the swollen, bloody, black-hair-matted face that swam in the brilliance in front of him.

He landed some punches, but it was like hitting a goddamn brick wall. He was taking more of them now. Too tired to slip or duck. Bludgeoning at his ribs, his chest. Christ, the guy could hit, even with his left. Where'd he get the idea his left was weak? Every time he took a shot in the gut, it made him feel hollow and sick.

The seventh round. He went out nauseated and woozy, feeling his legs going noodly. No question, something was wrong. He shouldn't be this tired. But Gigliotta lumbered out of his corner like it was round one. If he could get a clear head shot maybe he could put him down. Goddamn it, he was younger, he was in shape, he ought to be able to wrap telephone wire around this guy.

He bored in grimly again, and two jarring blows to the chest made him grunt. His own landed with a weak slapping noise. He wasn't hurting anybody. What the shit was going on? Had to keep his guard up ... he blinked, flinging sweat and hair back out of his eyes. The crowd howled like gas roaring out of a wild well.

Grimly, he fought on.

"Where the hell are we?"

"Huh?"

His goddamn lips, made of wood ... so numb he could hardly mouth words. "Where are we," he muttered again. He was lying down. Where was the count? He didn't hear a count. He tried to hoist himself off the canvas. His arms pushed, but nothing happened. His head felt like it was stuffed with straw.

"Come on, help me get him up." Guertin's rough voice, close to his ear. Past it he heard men talking, the chink-*ding* of a cash register, the gay ringing of bottles, guffaws.

It came back in a rush. The last rounds, being battered around the ring as point by point the Italian evened up for every punch Halvorsen had scored in the first half. Hanging on, head bowed, as the iron fists slammed into his gut, his ribs, his head. Clinching and playing the corner. Trying to remember the ringcraft Guertin and Picciacchia had hammered into him, not to win, but just to stay up and moving. Apparently it was over, but he couldn't recall from blackness if he'd won, or lost, or drawn. He shook his head, tried to throw off the hands that were helping him up, guiding him out of the ring. Somebody shoved his head down and he stepped automatically between the ropes. A warm wetness hit his face. It was a moment before he realized someone had spat on him. Then he was back in the dressing room. He collapsed onto the table, reaching inside for strength that wasn't there. "He didn't knock me down. I hit the goddamned canvas with my head."

"Oh, he knocked you down a couple times," said Guertin. "Though you kept getting up. Then as soon as the last bell rings you just sort of sag down, like they let all the air out of you. What the devil was wrong out there, Halvorsen? I thought you were gonna take this guy clean. How about it, Mick?"

"Oh yeah, I thought sure he was gonna clean his clock." Picciacchia was touching his face as he talked. He felt a sting and reared back; the trainer said, "Be a man, damn it. I gotta fix that or you'll carry it the rest of your life."

The monsignor's voice again, inflexible, accusing. "You're a better fighter than that. What in Hades happened out there?"

"I felt punk all this morning. I must be gettin' the grippe or something. How'd the decision go?"

"You lost on points."

As he was chewing on that bitterness DeSantis came in, Shotner trailing him. They hovered as the trainer rubbed him down with a damp towel, then liniment, then water again. "Hope you didn't lose too much on me, Len," Halvorsen muttered. His mouth felt all loose and puffy.

"Twenty goddamned dollars, that's all. Oh—hi, Father. Sorry."

"Somebody had to lose," said Shotner. "I thought he d-done pretty well. Lasted the whole ten rounds, didn't he?"

"Yeah, never mind them guys," said DeSantis. "They don't know what they're talking about."

"What guys?" said Picciacchia, rubbing Halvorsen with quick, hard, short strokes, like he was cleaning underwear on a washboard.

"The bastard—sorry, Father—the fellas out there."

"What were they saying, Len?"

"Oh . . . some of them was running their mouth. Sayin' you gave up after round five. You know how these lowlifes talk."

Halvorsen closed his eyes.

While he was putting on his clothes the guy from the bar came back with a grimy envelope. When Halvorsen thumbed it open he discovered forty well-used one-dollar bills curled inside. He gave Picciacchia five, then offered Guertin the rest.

"No, that's yours. You earned it."

"Take it for the collection plate, Father."

"I'll take ten for the poor. Well, I've got an evening Mass to celebrate, I'll leave you now." The priest hesitated, then added gruffly, "You didn't do too bad tonight. Mr. Thunner isn't going to be happy, but—at least you stuck."

"I'll take him home," said DeSantis, patting Halvorsen like a child who'd fallen down and hurt himself. "Hey, want a beer or something? You must be awful dry after all that fightin'. Not here—we'll go back to town, go to a joint there."

Halvorsen blinked. He'd forgotten it during the bout itself, blotted it out like everything else in the world that lay outside the ropes. But now it all rushed back, and suddenly he felt impotent and abandoned again. "No more booze, Len. Gets me in too much trouble."

"Buy you supper, then. Least I can do."

"Maybe. Lemme get my coat on."

They rode back in silence. Halvorsen bit off a chew and held it in his cheek, slumped in the back seat. His throat felt sore whenever he swallowed. By the time they got back to P.C. the streets were dark and the snow was whirling down steady and serious out of black clouds so low they scraped the tops of the hills. "Jesus, now it's coming," DeSantis said, peering out through the narrow space cleared by the wipers. "Crank faster, Dick, it's hard to see. There, there's the Slipper."

They parked near a storefront separated from the other buildings. Halvorsen stood on the street after the others went in, looking down it. Down a long vacant space of turbulent darkness, ceilinged by the new streetlights that hung like caged little suns from the heavy wooden poles. Here and there deep in the storm headlights moved down on Main Street. There weren't many people out. Those who were waddled slowly and clumsily as deep-sea divers, booted and overcoated, barely glancing at him as they passed. The freezing wind pressed his face like a heavy door. He shivered, pushed his cap back, and went inside.

The Scarlet Slipper was a one-room joint with a sanded-

---

oak floor, a stand-up piano, and a glass dome light above the dance floor. They got a table by the single window and a fella came over in an apron. "What we got for eats?" DeSantis asked him.

"Spaghetti and french fries. All we can do on a hot plate. And three-two, two for a quarter. Iroquois, Schlitz, and Manru."

"Schlitz for me," said DeSantis, and looked at Halvorsen, who didn't feel like drinking, but finally shrugged and said he could stand a Manru; let Fatso play the host. "Make that two. And a couple plates of spaghetti. Dick?"

"I don't drink."

"We got pop, you want it."

"Sure, a pop. Orange Nehi?"

"Comin' right up."

A pianist, a drummer, and a clarinetist started playing "Ain't Misbehavin' " to the empty dance floor. There weren't that many people around, for a Saturday night. Two girls in knit cloches and rolled hose sat across from them, smoking, still wearing their coats and galoshes. Halvorsen kept looking at them, wishing Jennie was here.

DeSantis ate all his spaghetti and half of Halvorsen's, and ordered more beer. Halvorsen kept replaying the fight in his head, looking out the window at the snow falling endlessly through the dark.

"Len. Was they really sayin' I took a dive, back there in Chapman?"

"Don't pay no mind. Buncha loudmouths."

"I don't like people sayin' that."

"They're just flipping their lips. You were ahead on points right up to round six or seven. Every time he knocked you down, you came back up."

"I thought you f-fought really well," Shotner said earnestly. "It ain't your fault you're feeling punk. You'll wreck that bum next time, I bet."

The owner came by to clear. "So, I know you boys? Been in here before?"

"Lots of times," said DeSantis. "This here is Kid Nitro,

you know, the fighter? And this is Dick Shotner, helps run the battery company."

"Kid Nitro, huh? Wondered what happened to your face. You boys play? Got a craps game going in back. Only honest game in town."

"Want to play some craps, Bill?"

"I don't care. You?"

"Nah, gotta work tomorrow. You gonna be all right from here?"

Halvorsen said yeah, they could walk back to the boardinghouse. DeSantis paid for the beer and food, wouldn't let him kick in, slapped him on the back, and left.

"Ever play craps?" he said to Shotner. The kid shook his head, eyes wide.

The back room was narrow as a line shack, badly lit by a single dangling Mazda. Mustached men in suit coats glanced up from around a table as they squeezed through the veneer door behind the john. Two others leaned against the bare board wall, arms folded, watching everything. Halvorsen saw cash on the felt, green on green. Well, he'd shoot the twenty-five. Then go home and get some sleep, try to shake this cold. His throat felt rawer by the minute.

The banker wore a black fedora. He reeled off the rules in a cracked whiskey voice. Fifty cents to the house.

Halvorsen held the dice to the light, looking for marks, and balanced them between his fingertips. Then rattled them and shot. They bounced off the side and came up four. "See, now I gotta make the four," he said to Shotner. "You put your bet in here, you're betting you come, and the other guys here, they cover it. Get it?"

"Think so, yeah."

The others didn't talk. They kept their eyes on the dice, or on their money. A bottle of Three Rivers stood on a side table. Occasionally someone touched it to his glass, but nobody swayed or slurred. The smoke haze burned his eyes. He finished his beer, bit off a chew, and kept the long-necked bottle to spit into.

He didn't bet much at first. Just a dollar here, a dollar

there. He asked Shotner if he wanted a turn but the clerk said no, he'd just watch. The dice were cold. Player after player crapped out. His turn. Halvorsen warmed the dice and shot. They hopped off the side and came up nine.

"Make the nine," he said. A couple men bet he'd come, but an old fella with a walrus mustache put money on the "won't come" spot. Halvorsen shot a two, then a four, thought for a minute he was going to make it; then sevened out. He grunted. At this rate he wouldn't be in long.

The dice kept going around, and he kept losing. He was down to four bucks, and he felt like finishing up, getting cleaned out and going home.

Then he won a little back.

Around eleven, he all of a sudden turned hotter than a two-dollar pistol. Shot fast and reckless, not caring, and it was like that was the secret, the key. Shotner stood gaping, Nehi forgotten in his hand. Halvorsen kept shoving the growing pile of cash back onto the table.

Around one someone knocked on the back door. The players stretched, reaching for drinks as the banker opened it and leaned out. When he came back Halvorsen said, "Who was it?"

"Just a cop. Wanted a loan. Ready to play?"

When the game broke at three A.M., he was up three hundred dollars. The owner shooed the players out into a black, snow-choked alley walled by blind brick. They scattered silently as they reached the street. Halvorsen stopped under a streetlight, looking up at the snow blowing past the bulb. He felt dizzy. His throat hurt so bad he couldn't swallow. Brew him up some mullein tea, that was what he needed. What his ma always did when one of the kids took sick.

Shotner muttered over his turned-up collar, "Gee, you won a lot."

Halvorsen shrugged, then bent into the freezing wind. They fought their way down long empty streets, boots squeaking as they plunged into the snow, then finally uphill. Stamping snow off on the boardinghouse porch, he looked down. The town was nearly invisible in the blowing dark, save for the one light that made even the distant hills flicker like the walls of a cave. The fiery column that roared, like a foretaste of Hell, above the stacks and flare-offs of Refinery Number One.

Ten

When Halvorsen stilled the alarm a week later, on the first day of December, the boardinghouse was dark and silent. He threw back the covers and lay for a moment shivering in waffle-knit longies. Behind the snore from the next room he heard the tick of the clock and behind that, just above his head, the secret whisper of the settling snow.

He'd laid his clothes out the night before. Cotton socks and over them a pair of gray wool edged in red. He found his wool twill work pants in the dark, recognizing the rough cloth by feel. He thrust his feet into his boots and pulled his hunting coat on over a plaid shirt and sweater.

Sleep had left him, replaced by anticipation. He groped under his bed and felt the heavy, smooth weight of the guns. He jacked each open to make sure it was empty, and slipped a few rounds of ammo into his pocket.

In the hall he tapped at another door. On the spur of the moment, he'd asked Shotner the night before if he wanted to go hunting. And the kid had gaped at him, as if he'd offered some inestimable treasure, before saying, "Yeah. Sure, you b-bet!"

The parlor was dark, the radio silent. He pushed the button to click on the light and went down the stairs to the furnace room. He stoked up with five shovelfuls of icy-cold anthracite, heavy and shiny as black glass, opened the damper, and went back up to the kitchen. He sawed curling pieces of cold meat, slathered them with mayonnaise, folded them into bread and tinfoil. The sandwiches went into a doughboy pack, along with matches, compass, blanket, and rope.

Shotner came downstairs. "Take somethin' to eat; we're gonna be out there awhile," Halvorsen told him.

"I got a couple ham sandwiches, an' some candy—"

"Ought to do her. We better get going. Lew's gonna be waitin'. Here, you can carry this. It's a Krag. Used to be my dad's. Wait a minute, let me check on the furnace."

When he swung the door open tiny blue flames danced over the bed of new coal. He half shut the damper, checked the boiler gauges, and went back upstairs.

When the door clicked behind them the icy wind made his eyes tear. It was cold and snowing hard. The street was pitch dark, but he felt the fat flakes patting his face.

It was blowing even harder on Main, but at least he could see. The snow fell in whirls around the vibrating white-hot filaments of the streetlights. Above them was nothing, no moon, no stars. Despite the ungodly hour the street was a parade of vehicles, chains jingling, lights searching through the snow. He rubbed his hands together, shivering.

"Hey, W.T.!"

He turned, to the old Ford truck shuddering by the curb and Lew Pearson leaning out, yelling, "Get in. Throw your packs 'n' guns in back."

Three men made a tight fit in the cramped cab. Halvorsen said, "This here's Dick Shotner, Lew. Rooms with me at Miz Ludtke's. Okay if he comes along?"

"Sure. Glad to have you."

"Where we headed?"

"I got a place in mind, y'all ready to do some walking."

Leaning back as they joined the procession, Halvorsen envisioned what was happening in this dark dawn. All over Pennsylvania the towns were emptying, boys and men streaming up into the forest in their old cars and on foot and some still mounted. Carrying the weapons, the food, the pints of cherry brandy or rye, the ropes and knives. The cold, empty land was alive with men moving silently into coverts, seeking out ledges and vantage points. So that when vision came—

The Ford jolted, locked its wheels, and half-spun before steadying again. "What's the plan?" he asked Lew.

"I figure Bobwhite Run. Fella said he had good luck out there last year."

The road grew rougher, finally becoming an icy, near-vertical slash along the edge of a drop. They saw fewer and fewer other hunters, and then, after a time, none. At last Pearson pulled off. As the engine and lights died together, utter darkness rushed in on them. Halvorsen blinked at the red and yellow afterimages, groping for his gear as the door slammed open.

The freezing air numbed the membranes of his nose. The hill was a black mass. He saw nothing else, not the road or the truck or the sky.

Shotner: "Either of you guys bring a flashlight? I can't see a thing."

"We don't need no flashlight, Dick. Just follow me."

The snow squeaked as they moved off. Before long Halvorsen felt the crackle of cold-brittled brush under his boots. It was quiet now, with no wind and the only sounds their panting in the thin cold air. He stumbled and something hard stabbed him from behind. Only several yards on did he think it might be Shotner's gun muzzle. He was glad he hadn't given the kid any cartridges yet.

They climbed and climbed, until still feeling weak from the tail end of being sick, his legs shook and the air flowed like fire around his tongue.

"Let's go quiet now," Pearson whispered.

They turned and went downhill for a few rods and then along the level. At last Pearson whispered hoarsely, "Hold up."

Halvorsen froze. He heard a rattle, a crackle, then a series of soft thuds. "What you doing there?" he heard Shotner murmur.

"Dried apples. There." The last thud was followed by the rustling of paper.

He lay full length against hard frozen ground, icy rock, cradling the Winchester. From his left came Shotner's labored breathing and an occasional sniffle. Beyond, from Pearson, came no sound, no movement.

Halvorsen checked the waxed paper he used to keep snow out of the barrel. Snowflakes brushed his ears, quiet, white, like frozen silence. The season opened at sunrise. But he couldn't even make out his front sight yet.

He tried to relax, letting his body sag into the holes and hollows. He shivered.

Gradually his mind wandered. He moved his hips gently, imagining pressing himself down into a woman. But the ground was hard as stone, and even through trousers and heavy underwear it chilled his genitals.

In the lightening gray he saw the trees, dimly, for the first time. Lew had placed the stand beautifully. The long clear-cut down which they'd come was visible to his left, slanting up the hill for three hundred yards. To his right it continued down to an angular black-iron oil-jack. It wasn't pumping now; the rod-line was motionless. And straight ahead, where his rifle lay on the breast-high embankment, was more forest, the birches stark against the fresh snow.

"Bill." Pearson was holding up his watch.

Halvorsen rolled over. Shotner was watching him. He put his finger to his lips, then gestured him over.

When the kid reached him he got three of the long bottle-shaped Krag rounds out of his pocket. He showed Shotner how to charge the magazine, how to use the single-shot cutoff and the safety. "Don't shoot unless you're damn sure it's a deer," he whispered. Shotner nodded.

He rolled back over and stared out again, toward the dark dots that were the apples, toward the edge of a thicket. He pushed cartridges into the Winchester and worked the lever, making as little noise as he could. As he checked the hammer with his thumb something caught his eye, a flicker of motion, and he looked up. Held his breath, searching through the morning gray. A leaf, maybe, dead but still clinging to a branch. Or maybe he'd imagined it.

The light was coming fast now. The world was colorless, monochrome, white snow, black trunks, gray sky. He glanced at the others. They were still, frost-smoke drifting from their open mouths, hovering around them, then moving away slowly, like a spirit or ghost reluctant to part with the body it had inhabited so long.

Several minutes later the barrel of Pearson's carbine swung slowly. Halvorsen followed it out into the woods.

The motionless deer were the color of the birches. Their thin legs were like saplings. The snow swirled between and he lost them for a moment and when he saw them again one had moved a few yards nearer the apples. The others hung back, screened by the dead brush.

He glanced down at his sights. When he looked up the deer had moved again. He hadn't seen it jump or run. They moved in bursts, and stayed stock-still in between.

This one was wary. Its flanks rippled with uneasy muscle, ears pointed and alert, nostrils flared. But the wind was in their faces, and the animal couldn't smell them.

The deer bent and nuzzled the ground. His gun wavered, almost in line. He squirmed again, not caring when a point of rock grated in his belly. If only he could see a little better . . . his left arm slid forward on the stock, lifting the brass bead until it gleamed on the deer's back.

The deer began munching loudly on the sweet, cold fruit. Then his vision focused on its head. He breathed out, dropping the butt from his shoulder.

Then he glanced to his left, and saw Shotner squinting

along the barrel of the old Krag, saw his gloved finger curling into the trigger. He hissed, "Dick. *Dick!* Don't shoot! It's a doe!"

Pearson glared their way. He made a shut-up gesture behind the rock.

When the other deer trotted out from the thicket the southerner frowned. "Damn does'll eat 'em all," he muttered. "I want a buck, damn it." He reared up and heaved a chunk of rock. It came down yards short and the deer scattered, bounding away stiff-legged across the snow.

Nothing happened for the next hour. Lying prone on the ground, Halvorsen's legs and arms passed through pain into a deathlike numbness. The snow, whirling down fine as sawdust off a crosscut blade, gradually buried them beneath a translucent white glaze. At last Pearson pulled back his carbine and scrambled to his feet. "Well, hail. I can't lie here no longer. Let's take a look around."

"Weather like this, they'll be lyin' low."

"Yeah, down in the valleys, out of the wind." Pearson rubbed his face with a glove. "They ain't gonna come out, I guess we gotta go in after 'em."

Late that afternoon he sat perched on an ancient stump, as big across as he could stretch both arms, looking out over a valley that thirty or forty years before must have been filled with massive hemlocks. Before the loggers came, and ripped them down for tanbark and building wood. If he thought back and closed his eyes he could just remember the last of the logging, not far from the farm. Just barely remember lying awake in the dark and listening to them shooting those big logs down the creek. The boom of dynamite as the splash dam went, then the thunder of the great logs shooting down the gorge on a tide of water brown as bean soup and powerful enough to roll boulders. So that now years later the stripped earth had eroded from the rocks and ledges and the ribs of the Alleghenies bulged naked over second-growth pitch pine and maple. Sheltered from the wind on this back slope of hill, the dark short-needled evergreen boughs had

absorbed the snow, holding it suspended in a mass that reflected all light, absorbed all sound.

He gazed out, mesmerized by memory. He'd hiked and
trapped these hills since he was a child, and worked and
hunted them before he became a man. Their savage beauty
awakened a peace in his soul, as if saying, Only in conflict
can mountains rise; only in strife can a man or a nation grow.

After the long day's hunt, hours of walking, hours more
in stands Pearson said were surefire, they'd seen eight deer.
All does. He wondered now whether there were buck in these
woods at all. So he sat on the stump and gradually slipped
into wishing Jennie was beside him. Thinking what he'd say
to her, and how good her hair would smell if he buried his
face in it.

Some time later a branch snapped on the far side of the
rock.

He was surprised to find himself still in the woods. Shadows were blue ink on the snow. He was about to call out to
the others when he became aware of breathing not far from
him, followed by a muffled snorting like a horse.

He leaned forward, and peeped cautiously around the boul-
der.

The buck stood twenty yards off, half hidden by trees. He
blinked and looked again. It was the first buck he'd seen all
day and he watched it for some seconds with delight before
he remembered it was to be killed. He poked the .30-30
around the stone, laying the bead over the buck's heart. Its
mule-gray winter coat was glossy and smooth over a swelling
chest and chunky, powerful hindquarters.

It lowered its head, swinging its antlers forward from behind the boughs. Then it tensed, lifting its tail, gathering
itself to spring.

Of its own volition the hammer eased back, pressed back
to cock by his gloved thumb.

Beyond the trees, up the slope, Shotner waded out into
view, toting the Krag butt-aft over his shoulder like a shovel.
The deer saw him too. It seemed undecided to run or stay
where it was, crouched amid the pines.

"Hey, Bill!"

The shout decided it. It flattened its ears and leaped, legs extended in a bound that sent it four feet into the air. Simultaneously a crash rang back from the mountain, bouncing and booming back like thunder as it racketed away across the valley, fading in the slow, repeating tide of echo on echo till it too was lost and gone.

"Jesus!" Pearson, sliding down the slope. "Did you see that? Was that you that shot?"

Halvorsen stood, jacking the lever. The ejected shell landed smoking in the snow. He looked downhill, where the buck had disappeared. He figured he'd missed, and to tell the truth, he wasn't even sorry.

"What was it, W.T.?"

"Buck, all right. Couldn't count points, but he was a big un."

"Too bad. How about a sip a smoke?"

"Don't mind if I do."

Pearson handed over a pint of Cobbs Creek, then waded over to the clump of pine into which the deer had vanished. "Hey, you hit him. Splash of blood here. Sometimes they take a while to go down."

They found the whitetail two hundred yards down the hill, lying at the edge of a lease road. The tracks showed that it had collapsed at the uphill side, struggled to crawl across the dangerous open space, and almost made it. Its eyes were still open. Pearson poked at them with his rifle, then whistled. "Nice shot. Just under the backbone. Look here, where the ball come out."

Halvorsen said nothing. He was looking at the glossy dark spheres of its eyes. The living liquid gleam of them went away as he watched, gradually filming over till they were opaque and dead as two black marbles rubbed with coarse steel wool. It must have died just as they came up. He felt a strange thing, not regret exactly, but some sadness akin to it. He stared down at the animal, frowning, trying to work it out into something that made sense.

"Good rack, too. Eight-pointer. Nice shootin'."

"Dumb luck, he was flyin' through the air like some kind of airplane. Let's dress him out before he freezes." He caught Shotner gazing rapt at him, admiration shining in his eyes. Looking quickly away, he squatted and pulled out his knife.

His Case moved with the casual speed of long familiarity. He'd skinned a lot of animals as a kid, trapping with old Amos McKittrack down on the Blue River. He sliced the hairy glands from the back legs. He tied off the loose sack of balls and shrunken penis, sliced them off and threw them aside. He rolled it over, carrying the neck cuts around to the collarbone, then whetted the blade on his pants and worked it carefully up through the hide from beneath. The blood-smell welled up as the skin parted, showing yellow fat, red muscle. He reached inside. "Dick, see this? Got to close this hole. Put your hand in here."

Shotner knelt, pulling off his glove, and after a moment plunged his hand in beside Halvorsen's. His narrow throat worked. Pearson glanced across. "He okay?"

"I'm all right. What am I f-feeling for?"

"That little thing, right there. Got it? Now roll it over this way a little."

He yanked and everything came out at once, a soft glistening eggfruit-colored mass of entrails and organs. Shotner looked up into the clean powdery snow suspended in the pines. He muttered, "I never d-done this before."

Pearson held the bottle out. "Maybe this'll help."

"Oh. No, thanks."

"Dick's in the WCTU," Halvorsen explained. "I mean, the YMCA. Clean livin', all that kind of stuff."

"Ah, take a drink. Put hair on your chest."

Shotner looked doubtfully at the bottle. Then, suddenly, he wiped his hands off in the snow and reached for it. When he was done coughing, and the others were done laughing, Halvorsen finished it in one long draft. He wiped his mouth with the back of a bloody hand, and leaned forward again.

*   *   *

By the time it was full dark he was exhausted. Slogging through deep snow all day, plus pitching the tent and then dragging wood. Good thing he'd found a couple of bird's nests; nothing was as good as last year's nests for starting a fire. He leaned against a tentpole and knifed off a chew of Mail Pouch, relishing the heat of the fire on his face and hands. Over it, sizzling and spitting, slanted three huge cuts of venison impaled on green maple branches. His stomach rumbled eagerly. He glanced at the others. Pearson was hunched forward, staring fixedly at the food. He blinked as the smoke eddied toward him, but made no effort to move. Shotner sprawled on his unrolled blanket, to all appearances dead.

"Meat's ready. Wake up, Dick, time to eat."

The deer steaks were charred on the outside, fire-bitter, but inside rich and juicy with a wild gaminess. Blood-gravy ran down their chins. When they could stomach no more Shotner opened his pack and shared Oh Henrys, Klein Bars, and cold red penny licorice. Pearson reached back into his, and came out with another pint. "I was savin' this for tomorrow," he said. "But I guess we can go ahead now." They sat around the fire, passing the ginger brandy from hand to hand. They talked for a while about work, about the letter the grievance committee had written and sent off to the company. Then Pearson told a story about an old coon dog he said his father had had once, and Halvorsen countered with a couple of the Seneca tales he'd had from Amos McKittrack. Shotner lay there listening, not saying much. Gradually the talk and the stories petered out, and they just lay around the fire looking into the red glowing heat-wavering heart of it that always made Halvorsen think, with a little shiver, of Hell. He shook it off and said to Shotner, "Well, what you think, Dick? Like huntin' with us?"

"Sure. A lot. Thanks for taking me, Bill. I mean, letting me go with you."

He shrugged, embarrassed again. Shotner was just about his age, but he seemed a lot younger. He got up and dragged one end of a fallen tree over the waning fire. The thick bole would smolder all night long, and give them red coals buried under gray ash to fry breakfast over. The snow glittered redly, still unmelted, on its upper surface. Pearson yawned, snapping his jaw shut with a click. "I'm about ready to turn in."

"Me too. Dick, toss your bedroll in the tent. You can sleep with me."

The pup tent was cramped and chill inside. It smelled of leaves and old canvas. He unrolled his mummy bag in the dark. They'd have to lie close together; the guns took up a lot of room. It filled with rankness, tobacco and brandy, sweat and blood as they pulled off their clothes and boots.

"I mean it," muttered Shotner. "Thanks for bringin' me, Bill. I ain't had too many friends."

"Forget it." Halvorsen wriggled his toes deep into the bag. It wouldn't take long to get to sleep tonight.

"I wanted to tell you something," the voice came again, after a while.

He jerked awake. "What, dammit?"

"Oh, I didn't know you were asleep. I'm sorry—"

"Forget it. What?"

"You remember, you and Lew were talkin' about Dan Thunner? How he stood up, there at your meeting, and how you wrote the letter to him?"

"What about it?"

"He's my dad."

Halvorsen blinked. Then rolled over, to face Shotner in the red-flickering dark.

"What did you say?"

"I said, he's my d-dad. My mom was his mistress, before he went away to the war. When she got in the family way he gave her money to go away, but he never married her. When he came back from France he married somebody else."

Halvorsen didn't know what to say. It might be true, but it struck him as the kind of thing a man had ought to keep to himself. "I'm sorry to hear that. About your mom, and that. But why are you tellin' me, Dick?"

"I had to tell somebody. I never did before. And you been

my friend, and all." He heard a gasp and a choked sob.

Finally he reached out and patted the thin shoulder. "Look. Thunner's hard, but I think he's square. Does he know about you?"

"I went to see him. That's why I came here, to Hemlock County. I went down to his office. I wouldn't tell his secretary why. I waited in the office. I wouldn't leave. Finally he let me in. He listened to me. Then he said, 'I don't have a son, Mr. Shotner. And if I did, he wouldn't be a weakling like you.' "

"Damn."

"He talked like I wasn't there," Shotner whispered. "Like I didn't exist. You know what I'd like to do? I'd like to kill him. I'd like to shoot him down just like you shot down that deer."

The fire snapped outside, a pine-knot exploding in the flames, and through the chink in the door-flap he saw a column of sparks shoot upward. Shotner didn't say anything else, and after a while he closed his eyes again.

Eleven

Four days later the steam pipes creaked and clanked in the hot, close air of the coach. The few passengers sat scattered, heads sagged against the horsehair seats or nodding as the wheels clattered and the coach swayed. Suitcases and grips rocked beside them, jolting in their overhead racks.

The woman sat with closed eyes, but she was not asleep. She wore a plain slightly shabby green tweed coat, buttoned tight despite the heat. Her dark, glossy hair was concealed beneath a plain black hat. One gloved hand was draped over a cardboard suitcase.

She'd sat awake there all night, staring out through the windows at the hills. Remembering another train trip, years before. That time, on a flatbed railcar.

Doris Gurley Golden had changed since that night, but not because she'd forgotten it. She stared out as the crossing bells clanged and the train slowed, swaying and clacking over the points as country stations pulled smoothly closer. They looked so peaceful, those sleeping houses, those night-lit streets. But here and there along the right-of-way fires glowed like scattered stars come to earth. People called them Hoovervilles, the makeshift cities evicted families hammered together out of flattened kerosene cans and cardboard. And when the cold white morning came the ragged boys ran along the tracks in the snow, pulling toy wagons, and climbed up on the tender at the stop and threw down coal to their sisters.

When the conductor called, in his long singsong, "Petroleum City . . . Petroleum City," she opened her eyes. They were startlingly dark, filled with shadow. She raised her hands and massaged the back of her neck, where the harsh plush of the seat irritated it, then pulled down one glove to check her wristwatch. The conductor felt his way toward her down the aisle. He checked the ticket on the back of her seat, nodded and went on. She heard the door between the cars open, and for a moment the clatter of the couplers and the jolting jangle of the chains and the rumble of the wheels were loud, immediate, ominous as thunder; then they slid closed, and the steam heat clanked, and she blinked at fields of snow sliding by outside.

Snow, and the bare rails shining like sharpened blades, and beyond them the riveted black iron arches of a bridge as the train, still slowing, snaked and clanked across a frozen river. Brick factory buildings swayed past. Power lines, dipping and then rising as the train rumbled on. Silvery tanks, capped with pointed crowns of dirty snow. Skeletal parallelograms she recognized after a moment as pumping-jacks nodding in steady self-absorption in deserted pastures. Beyond them the hills rose suddenly, steeply, white barriers from whose flanks distant trees looked on, black and stripped like disinherited multitudes.

And like some whale or monster from the deep the fear rushed upward, the terror she'd held at bay all through the trip out. Her breath came faster, and her fingers clamped on a small heavy purse as if on the iron bracing of a flatcar.

When the station came into view she forced herself to rise, gathering her things for departure. The purse, the gloves, the grip. The air brakes hissed, and she braced herself against the seat.

The train eased to a halt. They stood waiting in the cramped hot smoky-smelling vestibule until the conductor came back. He opened the outer doors, went down the iron steps, and stood extending his hand to the women and old folks and kids. She caught her breath as snow and smoke and steam blew up into her face, along with a strong oily smell like the garage bay of a gas station. For a moment she felt faint, as if she were going to fall. Then it passed, as it always did, if she was brave and kept going. Recovering, she directed her steps across the platform, struggling with the grip, and passed through the doors into the station.

The town stretched off beyond it on the other side, a big-town main street, with cars plowing through soot- and cinder-stained snow and banks of it heaped up as high as her head. The sidewalks were shoveled clear in front of the stores, though, and she picked her way between piles and across streets until she reached the Hemlock. She paid a dollar fifty at the desk and got her key, asked when the dining room would open, and went up.

She felt safe in the little room, once the door-chain was on. She went to the washstand and cleaned the night's soot from her face and hands. She opened the suitcase, took out several skirts and blouses, and hung them in the tight little closet that smelled of dust and hair oil and mothballs. She bounced on the narrow, squeaking bed, then crossed to the window and bent to peer out.

From here she could look the whole length of the town, from the shingled roof of the train station to an enormous new building still surrounded by a construction fence. She eyed the legend atop it. She turned away, glancing at her wristwatch, and made two circuits of the room. Then pulled her coat on again, and went downstairs, the snaps of her galoshes jingling.

The nickel tolled as it dropped, and she waited, tapping her pencil in the phone booth. It rang twice, then a man with a foreign accent answered.

The excitable voice rattled in her ear. She listened expressionlessly, making notes in a black book taken from her purse. She interrupted him from time to time, making sure she had proper spellings, first names.

Finally she thanked him and rang off. She went to the desk and asked if there was such a thing as a city directory. There was, and she consulted it for quite some time. Then went into the adjoining room for dinner.

That evening she was sitting in the lobby after supper when three tired-looking men came in out of the snow. She watched the shy way they glanced around as they stripped off their muddy overboots. Their denim trousers and heavy wool coats, the caps they took off self-consciously as they crossed the carpet toward her.

They introduced themselves as Melnichak, Pearson, and Halvorsen. They said there was one other man on the committee, but Shorty was on night shift. Then fell silent, regarding her with barely veiled suspicion.

She said she was sorry she couldn't invite them up to her room. The lobby, on the other hand, was too public. Where could they could adjourn for a private discussion? They suggested Cassidy's, next door.

Cassidy's was long and narrow and beery-smelling, with scuffed linoleum floors, dangling clear bulbs with emerald glass shades, old-fashioned wooden tables, a long counter bar, and heavy-looking twin-spouted iron pots hanging from the stamped-tin ceilings. They followed her to a corner table and, after a moment of hesitation, ordered a pitcher of Straub's. Her eyes lingered on the iron pots. "What are those?"

Halvorsen twisted in his seat. "Them? Those are yellow-dog lanterns. Used to, back before the electricity, they'd drill by 'em. Put crude oil in them, put rag wicks in those spouts, and hang 'em in the derrick. Give you enough light to work at night."

"Interesting. I haven't seen the oil industry at close hand before."

Halvorsen coughed—the cold was proving hard to shake— and took a slug of his beer, examining her. She wore her hair in a close Louise Brooks helmet, and it gleamed like fresh-poured asphalt under a strange, almost mannish little hat. Her hips had a pleasing chunkiness as they fitted into her chair. Her heavy eyelids blinked slowly as she sipped at her beer.

"Where exactly you from?" he asked her.

"The CIO."

"No, from where, New York or—"

"That's right, Lower East Side. Born and raised on Rivington, but I live in the Village now."

Pearson said, "Gee, seems to me they might of sent us somebody who's done some oil work."

She pulled cigarettes from her purse, stuck one in the corner of her mouth, and snapped a match across the book. It was damp and didn't light. "Wrong. You don't need another oil worker. *You're* oil workers. You need a labor organizer. I've organized in textiles, coal, electrical machinery, ladies' garments, shoes, metal, rubber. The problems you face and the tactics you employ are exactly the same."

"The CIO," said Melnichak. "You're split off from the AF of L now, right?"

She studied him. Stocky, tousled black hair, high Slavic cheekbones, and obvious intelligence in his dark eyes. "It may end in that. But as of this moment, we're still officially within the American Federation of Labor."

"But you're the radical wing?"

"That's a misconception. Mr. Lewis simply disagrees with Mr. Green and Matthew Woll over craft unionism versus industrial, or trade, unionism." She looked off toward the bar as she spoke; she'd had to explain this many times before. "The AF of L had its place and time. But since the World War they've assimilated the bourgeois world-view. When the crisis came, and millions were dumped into unemployment and want, they made a conscious choice to corner the market on their own little craft skills, and abandon the common workingman. So the progressive elements have to make their own way."

"What's the difference between craft and industrial union-ism?" Halvorsen asked her.

"What do you men do?"

"I'm a driller; Lew's a transport man; Stan here works in the pipe shop, in the refinery."

"In the AFL each of you would belong to a different union, according to the type of work he did. In the CIO you'd be in the same big union, because you're all in oil. We organize vertically, the same way modern industry does." She tried another match; it didn't light either. Almost apologetically, Halvorsen offered his Zippo. She squinted into the flame, then leaned back, exhaling smoke. "All right; spill the dope, boys. You're the grievance committee? Let's hear your grievances."

Pearson gave her the lowdown, filling her in on the fire, the deaths, the walkout, and how things had gone since then.

"You presented the resolution?"

"We tried."

"To who?"

"The refinery manager first; then at the Thunder office. We couldn't get anybody to take it. So we finally just put it in the mail with Dan Thunner's name on it."

"That's clever. And what happened?"

"Nothing, yet."

"That was how long ago?"

"A week."

"Have the men gone back to work? Or are they still out?" No one answered, so she pressed on. "Are you three working now?"

They looked uneasy. Finally Melnichak said, "Yeah. We are."

"Don't look so sheepish. If you weren't, that was the first thing I was going to advise you to do at this point. Do you have a list of the men who walked out? I suppose you know to keep that locked up."

Halvorsen said slowly, "I sort of thought you were going to tell us to go out on strike."

She swiveled to face him. "That may come. But there are

a few things we have to get straight between us, first."

She blew smoke into the dark air, thoughts momentarily elsewhere. She'd noticed him studying her, the one who'd lit her cigarette. Halvorsen. Blond hair, a hard young face, strong hands lying on the tabletop. She let her eyes dwell on them for a moment. She could see callus on the fingertips, the marks and scars of old cuts and burns. They would feel rough no matter how gentle the touch. He caught her glance and dropped his, fiddling with his glass.

But then she reminded herself sternly: *You cannot concern yourself with individuals.* Only one thing really mattered, and aside from how they affected its advent no one man or woman's life made a difference. Certainly not the things her old self had wanted once, before that night at Beech Woods. Before she had been touched by the hands of many men; and later the back-alley butcher's dirty hands; and then had come weeks of fever and last of all a slow, bitter afterknowledge that certain things were forever denied her.

No, she had no time for that sort of selfishness anymore.

"All right, let's talk about what I can and can't do for you. If four hundred men are willing to walk out on their own, it would seem there's enough unhappiness with this company to at least explore the possibility of setting up a union. Has there ever been one here?"

Halvorsen remembered the old-timers talking. "They tried, years ago," he told her. "But the producers brought in new hands to work the leases. Hunkies, wops, other foreigners. They finally had to go back to work."

"We're going to learn to stop thinking in those terms. 'Hunkies.' 'Wops.' 'Foreigners.' Okay? All workers are equal. As to losing, that might happen again. Can you risk that?"

"Some of us," said Melnichak. "Other guys'd say we're lucky to still have jobs, even if they cut the pay—"

"And it will keep going down," she told them. "Just so long as there's no pressure on the other side keeping it up. You think the owners ever pay higher wages than they absolutely have to? When that money could be in their pocket, instead of yours?"

She pushed the beer glass aside and began giving them chapter and verse. Explaining how at a certain point every industry began to sweat its employees, through either wage cuts, speed-ups, or mass layoffs. This was how the capitalist system worked. The Depression had only sharpened that process. No individual had the bargaining power to stand up to management. Only by banding together could they make their power felt. Not only would this benefit them and their families, it was patriotic. The plutocrats had to be forced to share buying power if the country was ever going to recover. "That's what Section Seven-A of the National Industrial Recovery Act meant," she told them. "We had the right to organize free of employer coercion. The right to bargain collectively without intimidation. It's not un-American to fight for what you can get. The owners certainly operate that way."

"But the Court killed the NRA," Melnichak said, and she saw the suspicion in their faces again. "You're talking about capitalism, and all. What are you? A communist? We ain't going to get far with that around this town."

"No, but if you called me a socialist I wouldn't disagree. I happen to think we workers could manage things a hell of a lot better than the bosses. We sure couldn't do much worse. But you're right, the New Deal's shot its wad. So if you think you can sit on your can and wait for FDR to bring you the promised land in a basket, your kids'll still be sitting there when they're carrying you off in a pine box.

"Now, there's been a lot of activity recently in oil. I looked it up before I got on the train. The OWIU has had quite a few successes out West. That's the Oil Workers International, out of Fort Worth, what used to be the Oil Field, Gas Well and Refinery Workers. That's who I recommend you affiliate with."

"I heard of the OWIU. Can we get one of their organizers?"

"I keep telling you, I *am* their organizer. They've got their hands full in Oklahoma and Kansas and Texas. Since the Court decision, they're trying to hold what they got, and it's going to be a fight. They'll grant you a charter, but if you want a union, you've got to build it yourselves."

She'd seen a lot of men shake their heads at this point. Give it up before they'd even tried. And there was no point forcing them. You couldn't organize from the outside. "And it will be a long, uphill climb," she said softly. "You're going to lose friends, and maybe members of your family. It'll mean risk, and hard work. They'll hook your pals into being informers. Tar you as radicals and troublemakers. If you lose, there's still a blacklist, and don't think those sons of bitches won't use it. See, I've been out on the line. I know no matter how high they talk, there ain't a dirty trick in the book these birds won't pull.

"I guess that's my question, boys. Are you game?"

Halvorsen was the first to nod. His face had hardened. He was remembering the smell of roasted meat in the Washkos' little house. And how the foreman, Goerdeler, had said conditions in the refinery weren't the workers' business, and how it would cost too much to scrap the old hoses and fire-fighting gear and put in new safety equipment. So that it was pretty plain right from that how it stood, that to the company a dollar was more important than a man's life. That was what he'd stood up to protest, back at the opera house. It was time for a change. If that made him a troublemaker, well then, a troublemaker was what he'd be.

"We'll never know unless we try," said Melnichak. And Pearson nodded too.

"Good," she said, lighting another cigarette and sitting forward. "Okay, now. How many men work at this refinery?"

Pearson furrowed his brow. "Around eight hundred, I think. It don't look like that many when you go in. But they're there, in and out, night and day."

"How many shifts? And when's shift change?"

Melnichak told her work hours varied, according to what part of the plant you were in. The "units," like the dewaxer or the Dubbs cracker, had to run around the clock. Refining was a continuous process; they ran on twelve-hour shifts with a swing shift each week. The maintenance and repair crews, pipe fitters and electricians and carpenters, who were still called barrelmakers at Thunder, worked the same hours and shifts. The packaging plant, where the cans of Lightning Triple-Filtered were filled and packed twenty-four to a case by a big Continental Can machine, ran ten-hour day shifts and closed at night.

"Do any women work there?" Golden asked him.

"Women?"

"In the can plant."

"No, no women. The only girls are the typists and clerks in the head shed."

Halvorsen said, "Now, all those are in the refinery. Remember, in oil, you got the plant, and then you got the field. We got drillers, tool dressers, roustabouts out there."

"How's the solidarity? Could they split us, field versus plant?"

Halvorsen considered that one. "I don't know," he said at last. "Maybe."

"Is there any time when all the men are together, at the plant?"

They thought it over, then said the peak time would be at the morning shift change. Eight o'clock, the offgoing unit shifts would be there, the oncoming ones, and the canning employees and the transport people who ran the spurs and loaded the packaged oil onto the boxcars would all be reporting in.

"So, we going out or not?" Melnichak said at last. "We don't want to wait too long. We want this thing over by Christmas."

"Hold your water, boys. First I got to call one of our printers. I guess Erie would be the nearest one, from here. I'd use a local printer, but there's always somebody can't keep his mouth shut. I'll tell them to work fast, and throw it on the next train."

She leaned forward and lowered her voice. "Then, here's what we're going to do."

Twelve

A couple of days later, standing outside the gloomy-looking building, she realized suddenly that she was too bone-tired for an action that really hadn't even started yet. Maybe she was burning out. Too many deaths, and threats, and beatings. Too many confrontations.

Then she straightened her back. Her feelings didn't matter. Neither the fatigue, nor the fear. She couldn't give up. Too many ghosts marched with her.

The men in the waiting room examined her silently as she stamped snow from her boots, unbuckled them, hung her coat on a stand. She checked her watch, then said to a thin-lipped, disapproving-looking receptionist, "Miss Golden, to see Mr. Thunner. I'm expected."

"Just a moment . . . go right in."

The terror woke, making her heart pound and her feet drag as if through some cold, thick fluid. She took a deep breath and forced herself through into the inner office.

It was just as she expected, expensive and masculine: dark varnished bead-boarding, soft-looking leather chairs, desk as big as a battleship. The receptionist closed the door softly behind her. She noted a bronze statue of plunging broncs, and a boxing picture on the wall. The only unexpected touch was the samovar. As she crossed the carpet the men rose together. She held out her hand, manlike, to the tall one at the desk. After a moment he took it.

"Good morning, Miss Golden. I am Daniel Thunner. These gentlemen are Rudolf Weyandt, my personal secretary, and Ellis Hildebrandt, our corporate attorney. Will you have a seat? Tea?"

"Thank you." She opened her purse, held up a pack of Camels. "Do you mind?"

"Not if you don't," said Thunner. He selected a cigar from a desk humidor, clipped the end, and flicked flame from a match. She didn't look like his idea of a union organizer. Plain and dark and dressed plain and dark, too. Somewhere between frumpy and sultry, like, he thought, so many women of her race. But utterly cool and matter-of-fact.

Weyandt came around the desk and lit her cigarette for her. She leaned back and for a moment the office seemed cheery, the four of them like businessmen contemplating a deal.

"If you'll forgive me," said Thunner, breaking the illusion, "I don't have a lot of time today. Can we get right to whatever it is you wanted?"

"Of course. Thank you for seeing me. I'm here this morning as a representative of the Oil Workers International Union—"

"Are you an oil worker?" Weyandt interrupted.

"I'm a professional business agent, Mr. Weyandt. My home union is the International Ladies' Garment Workers, of New York. At present, I'm working under the auspices of the CIO."

"So actually you're working for John L. Lewis," said Hildebrandt, tenting his fingers.

"Mr. Lewis is the head of the CIO. Mr. Harvey Fremming is the president of the OWIU, which is a member of the Committee for Industrial Organization."

Weyandt said, "The CIO is a fiction. Lewis heads the UMW, a radical organization that promoted industrial turmoil during wartime and even now fans the flames of violence in our coalfields."

She said evenly, "Not true. Lewis never struck during the war. It was over for a year before he terminated the Washington Agreement. Is he a radical? He supported President Hoover during the last election. And what you term 'turmoil' would not exist if not for the stubborn blindness of business interests. Gentlemen, I'm here to deliver a message. If I may proceed?" Thunner nodded. "As I was saying, I represent a major union with agreements with Sinclair, Cities Service, Louisiana Oil and Refining, Ashland Oil in Kentucky, Tucker Oil, Witt Franklin . . . I could go on."

"Anyone in the Pennsylvania fields?" Thunner asked her.

"Not as yet, but our organizing efforts here have just begun. You need not fear you will be the only one to deal with us."

"No, I don't think we'll worry about that." The owner half smiled at the others.

"I'm here this morning, first, to show you that I'm human. Labor organizers and business leaders have more in common than you might expect. Second, I would like the opportunity to show you why it's to your advantage to do as many other companies have, and recognize organized labor as a partner, rather than as an adversary." She went on, giving him the standard speech: How an effective union equalized labor costs across an industry, how once the workers were organized and a fair contract signed he could forget about wildcat strikes like the one he'd had the month before. Thunner leaned back, puffing on his cigar and looking skeptical. Weyandt was smoking too. Only the attorney abstained. The smoke from their cigarettes and cigars drifted upward and mingled, forming a thin haze.

She finished, "I have spoken with some of your workers. It is their intention to apply for a local charter. Once officially organized, they will ask you to recognize them as an agency for the adjustment of labor grievances. We can save a great deal of trouble and ill feeling, Mr. Thunner, if you would recognize the union now as their bargaining agent. Are there any questions I can answer for you?"

She stopped there and stubbed out her cigarette.

"Well," said Thunner at last. "You certainly have the brass, Miss uh, Golden. To stroll in here and threaten me, to say you represent my men, when obviously you haven't the slightest idea what goes on in our town, or in our plant."

She waited, knowing what was coming. She'd heard it so often before.

"In the first place, my boys are satisfied. To me, that's the message behind what happened last month. A few hotheads walked out; most of our men stayed on the job. Those who walked out came back once they'd thought it over. We're rebuilding from the fire. In a couple of months we'll be back up to full production. We're all up against hard times, but I believe if we face them together, we can lick this Depression. We have a great esprit de corps here at Thunder.

"On the other hand, *I* run this company, not them. If you've talked to the men at all before you thrust yourself into our affairs—"

"I assure you, Mr. Thunner—"

"I say, if you've talked to them at all, you know that we've come through business crises before, in 'ninety-three and 'o-eight; and floods, and fires, and we and the other Pennsylvania producers fought Rockefeller to a standstill twice. I'm not saying Thunder is a one-man show. But in my view, you are nothing more than an outside irritant, and we have no need of you."

Weyandt, the secretary, said, "The best thing you can do for the company, the town, and the workers themselves, miss, is to get back on the train this afternoon and go back to wherever you came from."

"I'm not prepared to do that."

The attorney: "What exactly *are* you prepared to do, Miss Golden?"

"Assist your employees in achieving recognition."

"To gain what? What is it they expect to get through agitation that they can't obtain through honest work?"

She took a breath. "I can't speak for them, Mr. Weyandt. Let me make that clear right now. I'll advise them on union procedures, legal issues, and so forth, but you will actually be dealing with a committee of your employees. So I can't say what their demands will be. I will say that they have several serious grievances. They want improvements in safety; they want the National Recovery Act wage and the forty-hour week. They want their right to representation, to be part of standing committees—"

"Let's take those one at a time," Thunner interrupted. He glanced at his watch, to give her the message that the interview was drawing to an end; she in her turn lit another cigarette, to show it had only begun.

"First, we are making improvements in the plant, including some modernization of the safety equipment. But fiscal constraints limit the amount of perfectly operable capital equipment I can afford to replace.

"Second, there is no National Recovery Act anymore; therefore, there is no NRA code wage and no forty-hour norm in this industry. It is true we are obliged to retrench with a temporary lowering of wages. But the men understand it's unavoidable if we are to remain competitive in an extremely weak market.

"As to a 'right to representation'—Ellis, what were you saying about that?"

"That it's nonexistent," said Hildebrandt. "The Supreme Court has been consistent over the years; there is no 'right' to join a union. Whatever this Wagner-act hue and cry involves, I believe the Court will strike it down as well. There is absolutely no obligation upon any employer in the country to recognize, negotiate with, or even meet with so-called representatives of the workers."

"Then I must thank you for receiving me," she said.

"It was an enlightening experience. But it will not happen again, Miss Golden. I don't make it a habit to waste my time with outsiders and Bolsheviks."

"You are making a mistake, Mr. Thunner."

Thunner said coldly, "I will not be intimidated, by you or any other so-called labor representative. Nor will I permit intimidation of my workers."

"You mistake me, Mr. Thunner," she said evenly. "That was the hand of peace I just extended. The question is: How far are you prepared to go when the hand of peace is withdrawn?"

He didn't bother to answer that. Instead he shoved himself abruptly to his feet. She rose too, stubbing out her cigarette. The men did not bow as she left.

They were waiting in a green Oakland coupe a block from the office, in front of the five-and-dime. When she got in, the blond kid, Halvorsen, looked at her expectantly. For a moment she didn't understand. Then she said, "Oh. Nice car. Whose is it?"

"Just bought it this morning."

"You must be doing all right," she told him.

"Made a killing in a crap game. Well, how'd it go?"

"He won't negotiate and he won't meet with representatives. He's maintaining the wage cut and he won't give on hours. In other words, exactly what we expected."

"We have some news too," said Shorty Quarequio grimly. "Guys coming back in from the hunting—we all sort of take time off for the season up here—they tell me they broke the old work groups up and moved everybody around. Like, I'm on day shift now."

They looked glum, so she gave them a smile. "Cheer up, boys! Actually, this is the best thing that could happen."

"It is?"

"Sure. If he gave in at this point the union would be very weak. If the men don't have to fight for it, they don't value it. Did our shipment come in from Erie?"

"Lew picked it up down at the station."

"Where is it now?"

"In his truck, down at the main gate."

"Okay, let's go start this thing," she told them.

*   *   *

She stood at what they told her was called the Gower Avenue gate, digging her hands into her coat pockets. She looked to the left and the right, noting things like the width of the sidewalk, the width of the street, the distance to the river, flat and white on the far side of the tracks. Much of the coming battle would take place on this territory, and she scanned it with narrowed critical eyes against the white glare of morning light on snow. Then raised them, to the brick-pillared gatehouse, the iron gates, swung wide now, the gray-uniformed guard snug and warm inside his post. And beyond that, a plumber's nightmare of piping, tankage, steam-plumes, smoke, and fire.

"What's on the hill side?" she asked Halvorsen.

"Well, you know, I ain't never worked in Number One."

"Tell me what you know."

"Well, there's the office, inside the gate there. Then the lab, and the power station, there with the chimney that says 'Thunder' on it. Past that's the units, where they break the crude down into gas and lube oil. That's where the guys got killed in the fire. To the right, you can see the product tanks through the fence. That low building's your packaging plant. Past that, up where the hill starts to rise, there's your crude tankage. Another power station, a pumping station, an' a fire station past there."

"I see. Past that?"

"Well, nothing. I mean, there's Seward Avenue, and then just houses, and so on up the hill."

A truck pulled up with a screech, and half a dozen rough-looking men she didn't know jumped out. She tensed, then saw that Pearson was with them. They started tossing down bales of print. She pulled a handbill and ran her eyes down the cheap, cold, speckled paper.

REQUEST FOR UNION REPRESENTATION

I _____ , officially state that, under the protection of applicable State and Federal law protecting my right to collective bargaining, I

desire to be represented by Local No. 178 of the
Oil Workers International Union for the purposes
of bargaining and grievance with my employer,
The Thunder Oil Company of Petroleum City,
Pennsylvania, that it is my intent to join such
Union as a voting member; and that
henceforward I will treat with the company and
its representatives only through my duly elected
Representative, President of said Local 178 and
such official negotiators as he may from time to
time appoint.

Signed, _____ , Dated, _____ , 1935.

"Looks all right," she said. "How about to you boys?"

Halvorsen said slowly, "I got one problem with this."

"Just don't tell me anything's misspelled."

"No. But when we hired on, we had to sign a pledge not
to join a union."

"Sure, a yellow-dog contract. That worries you? You
mean, like you're breaking your word?"

"Yeah."

"What happened if you didn't sign it?"

"They didn't hire you."

"Exactly. If anyone brings that up, explain that the 'promise' was signed under duress. A promise exacted under duress isn't binding. That's what the lawyers say, and as far as
what's right or wrong, I say let those who got money in their
pockets worry about that.

"Any other questions? Swell, everybody grab a couple of
handfuls and stuff 'em under your coat. That dick on the
gate ain't going to search anybody. There you go, boys. Get
your work group together when the foreman ain't around.
Make it fast. Talk it up, pass 'em out, let 'em discuss it for
a couple of minutes, then ask for their John Henry. What is
this—the eighth? Make sure everybody puts down the right
date, that can get a ballot thrown out right there. If they want
to think about it, tell 'em they already had a month to think

about it. This is their chance to show the company they're serious."

The men loaded up on the far side of the truck, using it to shield them from the view of the gate shack. Then they broke up, and began drifting in one by one. Halvorsen took a bale to his car, to run around to the leases.

When they were gone she stood looking through the fence after them. Then told herself: No point hanging around. So she turned, and headed back toward her hotel.

It was a long walk. The tracks lay on her left, and past that the open river, and on the far bank what looked like a small and struggling village. Fischer Town, the men called it. They talked of joints over there, of "the line." Apparently it was where the town authorities relegated the prostitutes and the colored. The railroad bridge stretched across the frozen Allegheny a mile ahead of her, two black ruler-lines connected by a brocade of trusswork. The snow-laden breeze came from behind her, pushing her along. Once this thing started she wouldn't be doing any more strolling around alone. Past the refinery were long blocks of industrial buildings. Machine shops. The Holderlin Company. A stocking mill, a glass plant, a window-shade factory, more machine shops, most specializing in oil-field equipment, or so it seemed from the signage.

She trudged on, until at last there was the Erie station and past it the main street. She stopped at an eatery and warmed up with a cup of coffee. She ought to report in, call New York. But she delayed, feeling sleepy, and had a doughnut and then a piece of pie. Knowing all the time she ought to get to work. She had to rent a storefront, one with parking nearby, preferably with a good open space around it and a back way out. She needed a lunchroom to set up the soup kitchen, and a shoe-repair shop that would run a tab. She had to pay calls on the mayor and the police chief, the local clergy, and the editor of the town rag. Class enemies, but any fair play the strikers got would help.

For just a moment, sitting there, she felt that familiar fist knot itself in her stomach. It didn't depend on solidarity, no matter what she told them. She'd seen unions stay out through bombing, injunction, hunger, and lose in the end. It didn't depend on clever tactics. Get too Machiavellian and the rank and file turned against you. It didn't depend on any single thing she'd ever been able to put her finger on. But if it all went right, she could walk away leaving something bright and new behind her, leave hope in men's hearts and joy on the faces of women and full bellies for the children.

But if they failed, she'd leave only wreckage. Not just the present misery, but the desolation that meant the death of hope.

She didn't believe in God, or any of that pie-in-the-sky nonsense. But if she had, she would have prayed. For the strength to keep on, and for the wisdom to make the right decisions.

Because to a large extent, it would depend on her.

"Number, please."

"5475, please . . ."

"Thunder Oil Company."

"Hello, is Dan there?"

For some reason the switchboard girl didn't ask her who she was; just put her through. "Mr. Thunner?" she said brightly, pressing the earpiece to her head in the booth in the hotel lobby. "Is that you?"

"Yeah. Who's this?"

"This is Miss Golden. We met in your office yesterday?"

The voice turned brusque. "I recall it. What do you want now?"

"Well, you said you wouldn't see me again, so I figured this time I'd phone. I guess you know by now what we're doing."

"My foremen confiscated your little cards, if that's what you mean."

"Did they confiscate twelve hundred of them? That's how many we put inside the gate. And out on your leases. We're tabulating them now. We have a lot of signatures, Mr. Thunner. Did you know how angry your men are?" He didn't answer and she added, "I wanted to give you a last chance. We're still counting, but there is really a very nice turnout. We also got our charter, and we'll meet tonight for elections. You now have a union to deal with! Will you follow Sinclair and other large oil companies, and recognize it?"

"No."

"Will you let me present my credentials?"

"I told you, no deal."

"Then I have to warn you, I suspect the men will vote tonight to go out. The only thing that might prevent that is immediate union recognition, followed by negotiation. Now, I have been in this business a few years, Mr. Thunner. I will give you two pieces of advice."

"You're giving me advice? Why?"

"To save us both a lot of unpleasantness. First, don't try to interfere with our meeting tonight. We will have men posted to protect it. Second, this is a chance for you to cut your losses. Do you play poker, Mr. Thunner? If you fold now, the men will be satisfied with much less than they will after you and they keep upping the stakes."

Thunner cursed her. For a moment she debated replying; years with hard men and harder women had left her no compunction in doing so. But she finally decided it would be best if she simply lowered the hook gently, until the humming line told her he had been cut off.

The meeting that night, held in the auditorium of St. Bartholomew's Catholic School, went pretty much as she expected. She sat primly on the platform as the committee explained their rebuff by Thunner. She gave a pep talk, welcoming them to the CIO and explaining in simple terms how the local would work; then turned it over to a grizzled oldster who'd been in the tin-plate strike in McKeesport, for the nominations and the vote. Just as she expected, the first motion after the elections were complete was a motion to walk out. It carried by acclamation. The few "no" votes were booed down.

She took over then, pointing out that they had to go about

this in an organized manner. Before she stepped down they had a picket schedule, and men assigned by name to get barrels and wood to burn in them and tents to warm up in on the line. Quarequio had suggested a vacant barbershop a relative of his owned between South Street and Ivory as their headquarters. And they had a strike fund, not much of one, but it was properly set up and an accountant appointed.

Standing in the street outside when the meeting ended, listening to them boast and joke as they streamed past her, loud eager-sounding men talking about how quickly they would win, she shuddered, whipped by a dark foreboding.

They'd taken on the monster, and nothing in this town, or this county, or in the lives of the people who had challenged it, would ever be the same.

Thirteen

The dark-colored Terraplane, so coated and rimed with frozen slush and mud that its true inherent hue was impossible to determine, slowed as it cruised by the refinery gates. Quiet green eyes peered out through the dirty windows. Studied the faces under pulled-down working caps. Read the placards they carried. Noted the cordwood and old tires stacked beside the flaming barrels, and beyond them, the smokeless, deserted, motionless acres of stills and tank farms.

Then the car sped up, and plowed on, throwing salt and slush from beneath its wheels.

"Deatherage," the lean, tense-looking man said to the desk manager at the Grant House. He held a snowy white handkerchief to his face for a moment, as if dabbing on cologne, though no scent was evident; then refolded it and put it carefully away.

"Very good, Mr. Deatherage. Yes sir, we have one of our deluxe rooms reserved for you. With running water and private bath, that will be three-fifty a day. There will be a radio in your room, and we have free service to meet all trains. How long can we expect your company?"

"I may be here for some time."

"Very good, sir. Will you require a telephone in the room?"

"Please. Can you recommend a garage?"

"Freas Brothers, left on Mechanic Street, right on East Mahoning. Triple-A recommended, fireproof inside storage for fifty cars, complete repairs, and Thunder gas." The clerk chuckled. "Though that might be in short supply."

"What do you mean?" Deatherage looked toward a sign that read WILLIAM PENN TAP ROOM.

"Thunder shut down day before yesterday. Labor trouble."

"That so? How do folks feel about that?"

"Well, to tell you the truth, the company had it coming. Not that it's so swell to have it happen, but—"

"I'm sure there's right on both sides."

"You're probably hitting the mark there, sir. Yes, definitely, hitting the mark. Well, about your car, would you like it delivered?"

"Please. Have them wash it and wax it, change the oil, fuel it, and have it back here at eleven. A local paper?"

"Here you are, sir, the *Deputy-Republican*, compliments of the Grant House."

A five-dollar bill appeared on the counter. "Why, thank you, sir!" said the clerk. He slid a key across the desk and struck a handbell. "If there's anything else I can do for you, sir, please let me have the opportunity to be of service. Sal, show Mr. Deatherage to room 364, please."

In a clean, spacious room overlooking the main street, Deatherage gave the bellhop another five. He asked for ice, a carton of Old Golds, and a quart of decent scotch. Door closed, he lit a cigarette, sank into an easy chair, and gave himself up to ten minutes of thought.

At the end of that period, he resumed his activity. First he inspected the door lock; then went over the room carefully, walls and ceiling, paying special attention to any small holes or cracks, moving the washstand and bureau to check behind them. When he was satisfied, he removed his suit and shirt, placing everything from his pockets in order on his bureau. Change, keys, handkerchief, and a heavy, gleaming silver dollar. He bathed his face, then took a clean, starched shirt from his valise and hung it on the bathroom door. He set a varnished case on the bureau. He took a set of gold cuff links from an upper drawer, then slid open the lower to reveal a selection of rings, lapel pins, and tie-clasps, engraved and stamped with a multitude of fraternal and professional symbols and devices. He hunted through them, evaluating and then rejecting several, until he found what he sought: a small, silver-colored button embossed with a five-pointed star.

A tap on the door. He opened it a crack, leaving the chain on, then let the bellboy in. He gave him another dollar. Poured himself three fingers of scotch, and drank it off.

He sat listening to the radio, holding a refilled glass, and smoked another cigarette from the fresh carton. Then he opened the newspaper.

He studied this for some time, the news, the editorials, even the employment columns. Then he set a clock, turned off the light, and lay down.

At eleven-thirty, freshly shaven and crisply dressed, he was shown into an inner conference room in the Thunder offices. He recognized Thunner from a photograph in that day's paper. "Mr. Thunner," he said, shaking his hand firmly. "I'm Pearl Deatherage."

"This is Mr. Weyandt . . . Mr. Hildebrandt."

He shook hands with each, then took the chair to which Weyandt showed him. They all sat at the same end of a heavy long table that looked as if it had occupied this room since 1890. Thunner said he had a couple of other fellows coming over. Deatherage said he would be happy to meet them. Thunner offered tea; he declined.

"Interesting first name you have," Thunner began.

"Yes, it is."

The oilman caught the gleam on his lapel, and leaned closer. His eyes moved from the pin to the damaged mouth of the man who wore it. After a moment he said, softly, "What division?"

"Seventy-ninth A. E .F. And you, sir?"

"Saw the elephant with the Twenty-eighth."

"A good division. Do you find life looks different after having been under fire?"

"Indeed." Thunner studied him a moment longer, then picked up a correspondence file. "Well, to business. I was somewhat skeptical when I received your initial inquiry. Yours was one of several, as it happened. We received letters of solicitation from—Rudy?"

"Sherman Service, W. J. Burns, Pinkerton, and Railway Audit and Inspection."

"All in the same line of activity. But your call seemed more . . . sagacious. And events have transpired pretty much as you predicted."

"I've spent a lot of time in the field, dealing with things of this sort."

Hildebrandt said, "May I inquire as to your qualifications?"

"My qualifications are that I succeed in my chosen endeavors. I wouldn't be a partner in the agency if I didn't give value for value. However, I will lay two testimonials before you. Needless to say, I can't leave them." He removed an envelope from his briefcase and flattened the letters within to be read.

"Impressive," said Thunner, raising his eyes at last. Deatherage refolded the letters, and replaced them.

"Tell us what you had in mind," Weyandt prompted.

Deatherage cleared his throat. He sat back and hooked his thumbs in his vest.

"American Efficiency Engineering Associates was established in nineteen twenty, to specialize in the area of labor relations and management consulting. We are not a detective agency, and we are not anti-union per se. We are pro-management and pro-employee. Our business is the improvement of labor-management relations. Now, it has come to our attention that a situation has developed in your plant." He paused. "I would like to ask that further conversation will be kept confidential among us."

"Mr. Hildebrandt?" said Thunner.

"I think it may possibly be found more convenient if I withdraw," said the attorney. He rose, and shook hands again with Deatherage. The agent waited until the door was closed, then resumed.

"As I was saying, it has come to our attention that you may be in need of our unique industrial services . . . and now that we are alone, let me be frank as to their nature. As those letters from prominent industrialists attest, we are the recognized experts in union prevention and union breaking, strike prevention and strike smashing."

A short silence, before Thunner cleared his throat. "Well, uh, Pearl, I appreciate this consultation. Appreciate your coming up to talk with us. But I don't believe we are really going to need outside help with this. We have our little troubles from time to time, back here in the hills. Usually it doesn't amount to much. See, these are my troops, in a sense. As an old army man, you'll understand what I mean. They gripe from time to time. Once in a while they have to blow off steam. But they're good boys, basically, and there's not the distance between labor and management out here that there might be in Pittsburgh or Detroit. I appreciate your coming down to see us, and if it seems necessary we should hire a detective, I will be certain to bear American in mind."

Deatherage listened respectfully, nodding now and then as Thunner made a point. When Thunner paused he said, "Sir, I would like to present you with this copy of a report we recently received from one of our sources."

Thunner leaned forward to take the document. He flipped up the stiff paper cover and read the crackly onionskin beneath. It was a faint but perfectly legible carbon copy of the minutes of the organizing meeting of Local 178, Petroleum City, recording the discussion and the vote to strike. Appended to it was a list of union officers, committees, and committee members. Each name was followed by an address and a telephone number, either that of the member or of a neighbor who could contact him in case of need. He stared down at it, and his lips slowly compressed.

"How did you obtain this?"

"You don't have a personnel information system operating in your plant?"

"I haven't felt it necessary to spy on my men."

"Would you go into battle without reconnaissance, or intelligence reports?" asked Deatherage softly.

"But how did you get this? These appear to be the official minutes of their meeting."

"That is exactly what they are. But as to how we obtained them—with all due respect, Mr. Thunner, we must protect our sources. You will understand that."

"I find it hard to credit. That you already have someone in your employ inside their—association. Yet it's obviously genuine. I know many of these men." He looked back down at the list, brows knitting into a frown. "This is very, very impressive work."

"Thank you, sir. Now, let me also present you with this special report on the infiltration of radical elements into the CIO—which is the organization that is now attempting to unionize your company." Thunner received this and leafed through it, then laid it aside. He looked at Weyandt, who returned a slight elevation of the eyebrows but said nothing aloud.

Deatherage crossed his legs. "May I smoke?"

"Please do."

"Please go on, Mr. Deatherage," Weyandt said. "This is very interesting."

"Thank you. Gentlemen, your current troubles stem primarily from two men: Franklin D. Roosevelt, and John L. Lewis. Roosevelt's counting on labor for his reelection next year. The Labor Relations Act and now the Wagner Act basically lifted all lawful boundaries to organizing. Consequently, Mr. Lewis has thrown himself into the project of organizing industrial unions."

Thunner listened intently. "I knew some of the boys were disgruntled over the wage cuts and so forth. And we had a bad accident recently. But you set it forth as rather more deliberate."

"It is much more deliberate, sir, and much more ominous. It takes Americans quite a while to wake up to anything so foreign as these radical ideas certain undesirable types are pushing, and what it might mean to you and me and all the rest of us who are just foolish enough to love this country with all our hearts. Our free enterprise system has its faults. But when outside agitators come in to sell your men on crazy notions that they can run your business better than you can— and when our own government encourages them—"

"What precisely is your point, Mr. Deatherage?"

"I don't believe this strike is your men's fault, Mr. Thunner. In a certain sense they are misguided. How else could they think a total stranger could look out for their welfare as well as one of their neighbors? Make no mistake: Those who are dangling promises in front of them are skilled hypnotists: professional radicals, labor racketeers. And perhaps even worse. You see this as a local disturbance. Would that it were so. I personally believe this organizing drive is a fully conscious and carefully prepared penetration of an industry vital to our prosperity in peace and defense in war, driven forward by a ruthless and cunning foreign power which is a sworn enemy of the United States."

Weyandt frowned. "Are you saying the Soviet Communists are behind this?"

"You have said it, not I," murmured Deatherage.

A discreet knock. "Come in," called Thunner. "Earl Vansittart, my plant manager. Bob Wheeler, my guard chief. This is Mr. Pearl Deatherage. He's got some interesting ideas about what we're facing here. Go on, uh, Pearl."

"As I was saying, it's unfortunate they've chosen your company as their point of attack. Perhaps we will return to that subject later. But now let us examine its impact on you." Deatherage lit another Old Gold. "I think you've already realized that an operating union in your plants and fields means financial loss. But that really is the least of its effects. This new Wagner Bill . . . Are you aware that under its provisions, if you recognize a union in your plant, you might as well resign yourself to operating under closed shop conditions? That even your loyal employees will be forced to join the union, pay dues, and conform to union discipline? That you will basically lose all control over rates and hours; that the shop rules in the trade agreement mean you will be unable to change or update your production practices without their say-so? That you will be unable to transfer a man from one part of your works to another without their approval?"

"Why, you can't run a refinery like that," said Vansittart.

"Earl's right. We couldn't operate under those conditions," said Thunner.

"You'll have to if you don't defeat this. And are you aware that even if you capitulate, your production can still be interrupted by a union seeking gains in other plants, or other industries? Let us say the Erie Railroad strikes again. Your employees are very likely to go out in support. Do you really want to try to execute a business plan under those conditions?"

"But that's a national issue," said Thunner. "It's certainly a threat, and it might be worth a political contribution from an association several of our major refiners set up not long ago. But let's get back to our current difficulty here. We've faced strikes before, Mr. Deatherage. I can't say I remember much about the one in 'ninety-seven, but I recall the one in nineteen fifteen very clearly. My father defeated it, without any outside advice. And I'm not entirely sure what advantage I would gain from your presence now."

"A fair objection. Let me ask a question, then. Have you prepared a spoiling attack? Or do you simply plan to react to your opponent?" He smiled at Thunner.

"A spoiling attack?"

"To interrupt their plans—"

"I'm familiar with the phrase. Please be more specific."

"With pleasure. For example, I would like to address a meeting of individuals who might be interested in cooperating with us to save the town. Persons such as the mayor, leading clerics, newspaper editors, other molders of public opinion. I would also advise you to take certain steps to make it perfectly clear in the minds of those of your men who remain at work, what the ultimate outcome of this work stoppage will be, and who will benefit at that time. There are other concrete steps you need to take now. I could enumerate them, but I should much prefer to be able to advise you in detail. I would strongly suggest that you retain me to be, let us say, your chief of staff in the coming battle. I can't fight it for you, Mr. Thunner. But I can help you select the terrain, train your men, counsel you on tactics, and plan how and where we will defeat the impending offensive."

Thunner pursed his lips. "What would American's terms be, Mr. Deatherage?"

"I would say, surprisingly modest. We believe it is our patriotic duty to counter this massive effort to undermine our liberties. I myself require a personal retainer of only fifty dollars a day. There will be expenses, but they will be far lower than the price a Red victory would force you to pay."

"Bob, you haven't said a thing," Thunner said to the man in the gray uniform. "What's your attitude to taking on a little outside expertise?"

Wheeler cleared his throat. "I'm not sure we need it, sir. So far things are quiet out at the gate. If there's trouble, we've got guns."

Deatherage laughed aloud. "This isn't the nineteenth century, gentlemen! This isn't Homestead Steel!"

"What do you mean?"

"I understand you've met Miss Doris Gurley Golden."

"I have."

"What did you think of her?"

"Seemed like a cocky little girl."

"That 'little girl' put six mines into receivership down in West Virginia. She won a dock strike in Portland and took down a hotel in Brooklyn the owners swore they'd close before they organized. Who'd she say sent her here?"

"I don't recall her home union. She mentioned the CIO—"

"Sure, that's Lewis. But did she tell you some of the organizers he's using carry Party cards?" Deatherage lifted a hand, palm out, to Wheeler. "Don't take offense, Chief. But it isn't guns you need. Or not *just* guns. Don't make the mistake of underestimating your enemy. You need to know how these people work. There are ways to defeat them. Some simple and inexpensive. Others, less so. But consider what's at stake."

Thunner sat silent. Deatherage reached into his briefcase again, and slid the paper toward them across the table. "Consider what's at stake," he repeated quietly. "I guarantee my results. Those testimonial letters should convince you that they are worth their modest price. And after all, this is about more than money, gentlemen. This is about defending the American way of life. Isn't the precaution worth taking? To make sure we keep everything our fathers fought to bring the world—and that we hope to pass on to our sons?"

Thunner raised his gaze from the contract, to meet Deatherage's chill, sardonic orbs. Gazed into them, his own eyes narrowed. "You said you *guarantee* your results? That if I employ your services, we'll break this strike, and smash this union talk forever?"

"I most certainly do."

Deatherage smiled slowly, dabbing at his lips with a snowy handkerchief as Thunner uncapped his pen.

Fourteen

Halvorsen gasped when the wind grabbed the car door and flung it open. The day was dazzling, the snow-silvered land so blinding bright that the cloudless sky itself seemed darkened above the hills. Across the tracks the men were singing "Oh, the moon shines bright on Pretty Red Wing. As she lay sleeping, a brave came creeping." He bent, helping Golden pull out boxes of heavy cold doughnuts and thick-sliced sandwiches of fat-dangling ham wrapped in translucent waxy Cut-Rite and tied with string. Then slogged through the snow toward the gate, the men changing the words to the union version as they got closer.

Gate Two was closed, the iron-barred gates chained shut, the pillars slimmed by the snow clinging to their sooty brick. The pedestrian entrance was open, though, and a path had been trodden through it into Number One. Beyond it, though, flare-offs and smokestacks rose still uncrowned by their usual billows of smoke. No doubt the reason the day was so unwontedly bright, the snow so startlingly immaculate . . . he peered through the bars, but saw only one tiny distant figure, trudging across the empty expanse of cleared site where the accident had been.

There once was a union maid
Who never was afraid,
Of goons and ginks and company finks
And the deputy sheriffs who made the raids.

"Can you bring out the coffee?" she said, and he nodded and headed back to the car.

This union maid was wise
To the tricks of company spies.
She never got fooled by a company stool;
She'd always organize the guys . . .
Oh, you can't scare me, I'm stickin' to the union,
I'm stickin' to the union,
I'm stickin' to the union,
Oh, you can't scare me, I'm stickin' to the union,
I'm stickin' to the union,
Till the day I die.

He lugged the sack of ground Eight O'Clock to the tar-paper shack the picketers had thrown up across the street from the gate. He set the sections of iron rod-line across the oil-drum fire, dumped four spilling-over palmfuls into the big blue graniteware pot, and set it to boil. Then stood watching the line.

It moved as slowly as tired men trudge through snow. The first day a lot of the boys had showed up in their Sunday best, but Golden had sent them home to change. They were workers, she said, and they should look like it. Now they wore their heavy rough coats, worn boots, workaday overalls, and some of the zing had gone out of them. They walked with faces sunk in scarves or turtled into pulled-up collars. Their signs lay propped against the fence. Only when the cops drove by did they pick them up.

They'd been on the line for almost two weeks now. It still

felt strange, not to go out to the rig every day. He'd driven
out once, to see what was going on out there. An old man
had come out of the engine house, a caretaker. Halvorsen
had pitched him to join up, but the oldster just shook his
head and shrugged. But in a way, the strike was work, too.
He'd figured, maybe picket, listen to some speeches, some
shouting, then it would be over. He'd never figured on this.

And as they'd marched, and the temperature had dropped
to cruel lows, Thunder had counterattacked. The picketers
had watched truckloads of furniture, beds, and food rumble
through the gates. Placards had appeared in town offering
bonuses to men who came in, and the *Deputy-Republican*
had extolled the company's generosity and forbearance.
Foremen called their men on the phone, offering them escorts
and rides in. They mentioned job security and promotions,
and there were rumors of hundred-dollar Christmas bonuses
for men who stayed "loyal."

Some had listened. Sometimes a face had disappeared
from the picket line, and the next day would be one of those
who swung down fast off the trolley and walked rapidly toward the gate, shoulders hunched as if they expected the
impact of rocks instead of the catcalls and curses of their
abandoned comrades. One day he saw old Mr. Washko climb
down, which was funny because he knew Washko didn't
work in the refinery—he was a field man. Their eyes had
met for a second, he in the picket line waiting and Washko
headed for him. They'd stared at each other for a moment;
then the old man had turned his face away, giving him a
profile as fierce and cruel as a hawk's, and forced his way
through them to the gate.

Hands thrust deep into the pockets of her coat, Golden stood
watching them too.

She didn't like stepping into spontaneous strikes. It was
an opening, but a treacherous one. Going in without any of
the usual preparation, the risks of failure were greater. And
if you failed, you crippled any chance of organizing for
years.

But you couldn't say no, either. The opportunity had to be grasped. And then another dilemma faced you, even if the boss caved and sat down. You had to satisfy the workers, or they'd call you a sellout and curse the union and it would die. So you had to walk a tightrope. You needed a visible victory to pacify the rank and file. But the smart thing after that was to settle as soon as you could, then start the real job: developing the workers' consciousness, building a union and a treasury, before you went out again for real gains.

Looking at the trudging line, she forced herself to see them not as freezing and probably hungry men, but as a term in an economic equation. Her job was to provide relief, sustain morale, and maintain discipline. She had to figure out how to make Thunner agree to talk. Then she'd have to help negotiate the settlement.

She reached out suddenly and snagged a man's coat as he slogged by. "You there. This is a picket line, not a hangout for bums." His hand came up to his chin. Fingered it, as guilt dawned. "Tha-a-a-t's right. Go home and shave. Then come back." She released him and swung back to Halvorsen. "Let their appearance go to hell, their spirit follows it right on down."

He grunted and peered into the barrel, blinking into the heart of the flames. "Oak. Where'd we get oak? They was burning green pine here last night."

"One of the local farmers. He brought in some milk for the kids, too; we gave it out this morning down at headquarters." She peered in. "You can tell what kind of wood it is just by looking at it?"

"And the smell, and the color of the ashes. Sure."

"More than I can." She hugged herself. "Gives a good heat."

He glanced at her. She was slapping her arms, rubbing her gloved hands together. She nearly always wore gloves, he'd noticed that, even indoors. She wasn't a bad-looking woman. Reddened, plump cheeks, a curl of black hair twisting out from under the man's cap. Deep-breasted, wide-shouldered, wide-hipped. But there was something separate about her.

Like she never trusted you, or anyone, not all the way. Or, no, it wasn't that exactly; more like she didn't want to know anyone too well. It sort of made a man wonder what would happen if.

Not that he had any plans. He didn't need any more woman trouble than he already had. But just out of devilment he grinned and said, "Well, the harder the wood, the better the heat." She cut him a sidelong glance and turned away, giving him the air as definitely, he thought, as he'd ever gotten it.

The shift ended. She'd timed the pickets to turn over half an hour before the shifts in the plant, to have fresh, spunky boys out front when the men inside tramped out. She watched Shorty Quarequio pass out the meal tickets. A round on the line got you a free sandwich and bowl of soup at the Alpine Diner. The men going off eased themselves down onto the tire piles and old ties dragged up from the river-edge. Some lifted their feet skyward like weary infantrymen. Those going on stood in a tight group, fists bulging their pockets, glancing alternately at the gate, the tracks, and the coffee.

Which should be just about ready . . . Halvorsen wrapped a rag around his palm and pulled the pot off the fire. He poured it empty into the mugs and field cups thrust out toward him, then stuffed it full of snow again and put it back on the grate.

Golden looked around, at the locked gate, the fence stretching off, the silent tanks and stills, the empty tracks and switchyards, the frozen motionless river. Hard to believe so peaceful a scene might be the battlefield on which men's futures would be decided, maybe even Man's future—but it might be. One of these days.

She shook herself and took a slug off the chipped teacup Halvorsen held out. The boiled coffee tasted flat and harsh, and the grounds grated under her tongue. But many a day on the line in West Virginia she'd been damn glad of a cup of coffee and a hunk of bread. While the mineowners lived like kings, in their big houses on the high hillsides. Not that they were responsible for the squalor and want, the broken bodies and broken lives below them. Oh, no.

She caught Halvorsen eyeing her again and blinked, coming back to the bright hard day, the cold-pinched faces around her, still hoping, but racked already by doubt. She looked around, then clambered onto the stack of ties, onto the fender, then up, with an assist from his strong arm, up onto the roof of the used car he was so proud of. She straightened and took a deep breath, smoothing her coat.

"Morning, men!" she yelled, making it deep and all the way from her diaphragm.

"Morning, Miz Golden."

"Anybody out there? All I hear is the wind—"

"Morning, Miz Golden!"

"All right! Here we all are together again, this thirteenth day out. Thirteen's an unlucky number. Unlucky for those sons of bitches who think making a few bucks out of the boss's scrap pail is more important than standing with us."

A feeble cheer, all too thin in the open air. She hurried on, and a few minutes later got to cases.

"Now, they tell me the company's runnin' scared. Like Shorty told me his foreman called him up, offered him a bonus to come in. He'd have an escort, they'd give him a ride. Ain't that thoughtful? Limousine service for the working stiff. Fellas, I don't see how you can even think a strikin' against a company that takes such good care of its folks as this here Thunder Oil does. Who says there ain't no Santa Claus?"

Chuckles, shuffling feet. There, they liked that.

"Hear they're offering bonuses. A hundred bucks. And talking job security and promotions if you go back. Well, sure are. Didn't they offer Judas a nice raise and a good job? But where's that scratch coming from? Out of the bosses' pockets? Bet your bottom dollar it ain't. It comes out of the same place as everything else: your work, your hands, the product of your labor. The worker creates everything you

see. The only reason you don't *own* it all is that you don't
know your strength."

Halvorsen stood at the edge of the crowd, watching her.
She made strange exclamation points, dashes, curlicues in
the air with her hands as she spoke. She talked different in
front of a crowd; simple words, short sentences even the
foreigners in her audience could follow. She didn't seem to
be shouting, but somehow she made every word fly past the
fence and on into the plant and come echoing out again.

"Now, I know it ain't easy for you. I know the landlord's
after you for the rent, and the time payment's due on the
Ford. The kids are counting the presents under that tree and
the butcher's told your wife he ain't going to put no more
on the tick. The good news is that we got five hundred dollars more in the kitty today. Strike fund contribution by our
brothers in Tulane and Houston, the Oil Workers' International Union. They sent this with it." She read a short telegram wishing them luck and promising solidarity. Then held
it aloft, like a banner fluttering in the cold wind. "That'll buy
us bread and beans, and shoe repairs, and ointment for your
feet. We ain't in this alone. But another thing I want you to
remember after we win this thing is the folks here in town
who pitched in too. The merchants who put you on the book,
and carry your families. Especially Red and White Groceries,
who extended us a line of a hundred dollars' credit.

"Now a little refresher.

"What is a strike? A strike is when we stop the owner's
income from his property, and make him unable to operate
it on his own terms. What is a *successful* strike? When the
workers win recognition of their right to bargain as a group.
We ain't asking for the moon, boys. All we want is recognition. After that we want a safety committee, an eight-hour
day, seniority, and true collective bargaining. But all that lies
down the line. What this strike is about, right now, is getting
them to figure out what they can see right in front of their
eyes: that we're going to stick, and we're going to stick together.

"Now who the hell is going to stand with me, right to the end?"

When the cheering and stamping was over, he reached up to swing her down. She stood by his jalopy, talking to several of the men. He was thinking about another cup of coffee when he caught a face that was familiar, yet out of place.

It was Dick Shotner. The kid hovered awkwardly at the edge of the crowd. He caught Halvorsen's eye and smiled and pushed toward him, long gangly arms writhing around as if they were radio-controlled by Ming the Merciless.

"What you doin' here?" Halvorsen asked him.

"I heard she talked out here every morning. Thought I'd come out and hear it. Gee, she's something, isn't she?"

"She's a piece a work, all right."

"I'm kind of in a funny position myself. I'm on a salary. I guess that makes me management, right? But I feel like she was talking to me. What she was saying about how the owners earn their bread by the sweat of our brow, and all that. And that song they sang, there at the end. I never heard that before."

"She taught us a lot of old Wobbly songs," Halvorsen told him. "But bein' a bookkeeper, that sounds like work to me. You wouldn't get me in there, adding all those numbers up. Probably get half of 'em wrong. What, you thinking of starting a local down at the battery plant?"

"A union, down there? I don't know. My b-boss wouldn't like that," said Shotner, and he looked so envious and at the same time so afraid and so weak that Halvorsen had to look away. Maybe he was old Dan Thunner's kid, but he could see why the old bastard might not be too enthusiastic about owning up to it.

"Here they come!" someone shouted, and like a pile of suddenly magnetized iron-filings the crowd realigned itself. At the same time a police sedan drove up, rocking onto the snow-heaped walk in front of the gate.

Inside the plant a whistle began to blow, sending a low, gradually swelling note out across the river valley. The men listened to it drone on and on, filling the gap between sky and earth with a vibrating music that seemed to stop all thought and all movement. Then it ended, and a shining commacloud of steam drifted thinning into the bright sky. Silence reigned again; but long seconds later the shriek moaned eerily back from the south and east and north, echoing and reechoing fainter and fainter as it wandered lost amid the endless hills.

A squad of gray-coated Thunder Oil police came out of the guard building. They unlocked the gate and pulled it open. The strikers outside heard everything in the cold, still, hollow air: the pant of their breath, the protest of the hinges, the rattle of the chain. When it was open the graycoats took up a position before it. Their gazes didn't meet those of the workers. They stared straight ahead, or lifted their eyes to the hills.

The trolley clanged its bell and squealed to a stop. Forty yards separated the tracks on Gower Avenue from the refinery fence. The strikers reoriented again, this time into a rough funnel, one end open, near the rails; the far end nearly closed, to the width of one or perhaps two men, at the gate.

Two city cops got out of the patrol car and stood in front of it, not exactly between the oil bulls and the men on the pavement, but not too far away, either.

The first worker appeared at the trolley steps. He looked uncertainly at the silent gauntlet ahead. Then his face closed, and he jumped down into the snow. Holding his arms close to his sides, he walked toward the gate.

"Javie, hey, Jav! Where you think you're goin'?"

"C'mon over here, have a sandwich."

"Don't be a sap, you sap."

"Goddamn it, Javinovitch, we're doing this for you."

"Be a man, not a goddamn scab!"

At first cajoling, the voices turned hostile toward the middle of the trek. Halvorsen saw their target's face pale toward snow-color as the gauntlet closed in, men leaning forward to point accusing fingers, to shout into his face. The city cops stood straighter. One put his hand on his billy. But then the oil bulls pushed their way forward, and the lone man lifted his head as he reached them and flashed back one glance mingled of shame, rage, fear, and relief. "We'll be waitin' when ya come out!" rose a voice as he disappeared into the plant.

A car approached along Gower, slowed, then nosed in. The windows were cranked closed. The men within slumped low in their seats. The tires crunched the snow as the picketers moved reluctantly out from in front of the moving bumper. Halvorsen saw one lower his lunch bucket and brace himself. A dragging shriek of metal against metal cut the air, raising the hair on the back of his neck. The automobile didn't stop. It just kept on rolling in through the gate, its lacquer showing a long, raw silver scratch.

Past it, inside the fence, Halvorsen suddenly noticed a man looking down from the fire-escape landing on the second floor of the office. He had on a gray coat and gray hat.

"Who's that?"

Golden, beside him. He shaded his eyes and looked again. "Don't know him," he told her.

"Shorty? You work in the refinery. You know that fella up there?"

Quarequio didn't know him either. They stood looking up.

As if he could hear them, the man took a pair of opera glasses out of his coat and focused it on them. They stared at each other across a hundred yards of snow and fence and milling bodies, as the rest of the streetcar's passengers emerged and followed, one by one, their individual path through the furnace, each enduring in his turn first the cajolings, then the insults, and finally the threats of his fellows.

She turned abruptly and walked away. Halvorsen hesitated, then followed. She went back to his car and reached inside, to the worn leatherette case she never let far from her sight. Shielding what she was doing with her body, she was jotting something down. "I think I know *what* that sonofabitch is," she muttered. "But I need to know *who*. Here." She turned, and he watched a small pink pointed tongue run along the flap of an envelope. "Take this in to him."

He gaped at it, then at her. "Take it *in*?"

"You heard me." She squinted toward the crowd. "Go on now, they'll let you through. Act like you just got off the trolley. Just don't wait for an answer."

He got the idea then. But just then the streetcar clanged its bell, meaning it was about to start off again, and before he could think too much about it, he ran a couple of steps and threaded through the crowd and came out in front of the gate just as the bulls were turning away, heading back inside.

"Just a minute," he said, trying to sound out of breath. "They almost wouldn't let me off that damn toonerville."

"Better move faster next time, Jack. That's an ugly bunch of bos, out there." The bull pulled the gate closed behind him and wrapped the chain around the metal bars. The lock snapped.

He followed the others in, slogging after them, but instead of heading on into the refinery, turned and climbed the stairs of the refinery office.

He'd been in this building before, to get requisitions signed for drilling equipment and parts and so forth, but the steam-heated wainscoted hallways felt different now. Ominous, like enemy territory. The close, hot air made him sweat. At the top he pushed his way through swinging doors and came out at a counter. Here the occupied desks, the clatter of typewriters, seemed almost normal. Not many of the clerks and secretarial staff had gone out with the other workers. A woman in a dark blue polka-dot dress with a lace collar looked him up and down. "What do you want?"

"Deliverin' a message."

"To Mr. Vansittart? I'll take it in."

Vansittart was the refinery manager. "No, not Mr. Vansittart. Him. Mr.—" He pointed past her, to where the gray-coated fellow's motionless back was visible. He was still standing out on the fire escape.

But instead of giving him the name, as he'd hoped, she swung part of the counter up like a drawbridge. He grunted and went down between the desks, the clerks and bookkeepers glancing up at him, leaning back now from empty blotters so that he could see that their pretense of busy-ness was only that, a pretense, and then out into the narrow iron of the platform, out in the bitter air.

The stranger was still standing there, holding the field glasses in one hand and taking a drag off a cigarette with the other. He was taller than Halvorsen, with a straight slightly hooked nose and deep grooves around a sagging mouth. Outside the fence the guys on the line were singing "I Dreamed I Saw Joe Hill Last Night." From up here it sounded distant and plaintive. Halvorsen tugged his cap down over his face. "Message for you, sir."

"For me? From whom?"

"You got to sign for it."

The fella looked at the envelope, then the pad and pencil Halvorsen proffered. He took a swipe at a signature and handed the pad back. Halvorsen looked at the name. Then, before he could turn to escape, "P. Deatherage" tore the envelope open with a quick motion and ran his eyes down the contents.

He raised his eyes slowly from the strike flyer. "This somebody's idea of a joke?"

Halvorsen shrugged. He turned to slide past him, but not before his shoulder was seized. He flung it off with an instinctive, loathing quickness, the way one rids oneself of a large insect unexpectedly glimpsed on one's arm. Deatherage reacted too, and without thinking about it his guard came up. They were squared off on the little ice-covered iron platform, thirty feet above the pavement.

Deatherage's emerald eyes were icy cold. Then they dropped, to the pad crumpled into Halvorsen's fist; and tiny crinkles appeared around them, like used tinfoil. "I see," he said, and studied Halvorsen's face again. "Yes, that's my name. And what's yours, friend?"

"I'm W. T. Halvorsen."

"I've heard that name before. Where? Thunder employee?"

"Driller. Out on strike." He reached for the door, but

Deatherage stepped in front of it. Face to face on the narrow
fire escape, he couldn't get around him.

"Stick around a minute, Halvorsen. Want a fag?"

"Don't use 'em. Let me by."

"Wait a minute . . . the committee. Pearson, Melnichak,
Quarequio, and Halvorsen. The boys who started all this
fuss."

He didn't answer. Deatherage gave it a moment, then said,
"You know, we could use a friend on the committee. You
could make a little cash, and the others'd never know. Plus,
whichever way things turn out, you'd have a job. Interested?"

"In bein' a stool? Gnatz to you. You gonna let me by? Or
am I gonna have to knock you down?"

Deatherage raised his hands then, palms out. "Keep your
lid on. Hands off is my motto." He stepped aside and nodded
toward the door. "You're free to go."

He had his hand on the handle when Deatherage said,
"What do you think she's after, W.T.?"

"Who? Miz Golden? The same things we are."

"That's where you're wrong, friend."

"This ain't her strike. It started before she got here. She's
an organizer. That's all."

"Sure, she's the little glass angel up on top of the tree,"
Deatherage said. "And you're all so smart you can talk Italian with one hand. Let me tell you something. You can even
pass it on to her if you want. You know who I am now. That
should tell you Thunner's serious about holding out. You
boys are gonna get left holding the bag on this thing. The
shutdown's not going to last. We've got production going
out on the tanker train tonight. We're pumping again; we'll
be lighting the stills off again pretty soon. It'd be good to
have you there with us."

"You're talking to the wrong man, mister. I'm staying out
till the company recognizes us."

"Well, we can live with that, too. Just plan on making
your living some other way than oil. You can take that back
to your friends on the line." He smiled then, and stood aside.

"Don't believe everything she tells you. And feel free to come in and chat anytime you want to get warmed up."

When he handed her the pad a shadow came over her face as she studied it. "Who is he?" Halvorsen asked her.

"A sonofabitching strikebreaker. And the best. I wonder how Thunner got hold of him."

"You know this guy?"

"I don't *know* him—I don't think we ever were present at the same action. At least that I know of. But every organizer's heard of him. Tell me what happened." He told her what Deatherage had said, about going back into production, about a tanker train going out that night. She nodded silently, like her thoughts were somewhere else. Then asked him again about the tanker train, if he'd said exactly when it was going to leave the plant.

He stayed with her the rest of the afternoon, accompanying her back to the headquarters for a meeting with the wives, then to the *Deputy-Republican* office for an interview with one of the reporters. He knocked off at his normal quitting time and drove to Gasport, to the gym, as the snow started coming down.

Since the strike started he'd been working out there every day, sometimes seeing Guertin, most times not. Picciacchia still worked with him, giving him pointers, and he sparred with whoever was around. Since he'd lost to Gigliotta, nobody had mentioned any more fights. There weren't as many men hanging around at Doherty's these days. The great bay seemed empty and cavernous as he jogged out and began his workout. He felt funny sometimes, on strike against Thunder Oil, yet being here at Thunner's expense. But as far as he could see, one was company, the other was personal. He hadn't mentioned it to anyone in the union, and he didn't see why he should. As long as nobody threw him out he'd stay. He put in a hard two hours, then showered down and got dressed again. He didn't want to go back to Mrs. Ludtke's, but he couldn't think of anyplace else to go that didn't cost money. Buying the Oakland had just about cleaned him out. He hadn't known then they were going out on strike, hadn't known that the nice fat foreman's pay envelope would suddenly stop.

It was dark outside and snowing hard when he came out. He was driving down Main Street when he suddenly saw her on the sidewalk, galoshed and babushka'd, bent against the wind. He pulled over and stretched to push open the door on her side.

"Jennie," he yelled. "Jennie!"

She looked at the ground but didn't come over to the car. She had bright-blue knit mittens on, like a kid, what a kid would wear. "Bill. How are you? About ready for Christmas?"

"It might be a little late this year. What are you doin' out in this weather?"

"Just going home from work."

"Well, how about a ride?"

"I don't think I ought to. We ain't going together anymore. . . ."

"Jeez, come on. It's only to get you home."

She got in reluctantly, and settled into the seat beside him. She shook out her kerchief, then her hair. She looked around. "This your new car? I heard you got one."

"It ain't new, but it runs. Don't know how much longer I can keep it, with the strike and all. But she's got a good heater, don't she?"

"Yeah, that's nice and warm."

She didn't say anything else and he concentrated on driving on the slick road. "How's your folks doing?" he asked her at the corner of West Washington.

"Ma's not doing so good. She took Johnny's dying real hard. Pa just comes home and drinks." She hesitated, looking out, then added, "It ain't much fun these days, Bill."

He said casually, not looking at her, "You going out at all? Got yourself a new beau?"

She shrugged, and he could see just by the way her shoulders moved how tired she was. He thought about asking her to the movies—Shirley Temple was on in *The Littlest*

Rebel—but finally he didn't. Just dropped her in front of her house and watched as she trudged up the walk, paused on the porch to wipe off her boots, lifted a timid mitten to him, and disappeared inside.

That night somebody left an iron bar on the tracks outside Number One, and the tanker train derailed. Nobody was hurt, but the salvage crews from the Erie were there all the next day hoisting it back onto the rails. Halvorsen stood with a silent group of the boys, watching, listening to their curses when their hands froze to a piece of bare metal and the skin came off. Seemed like no matter what you did, it was the working stiff who finally paid in sweat and blood. Never the one who really mattered. He stood there ruminating. So how did you reach the men at the top? How far could they go; how far *should* they go?

It would take some thinking on. It surely would.

Fifteen

The house frowned down from near the crest of the mountain north of town, a somber and brooding pile of dark stone, but dressed tonight for welcoming. Electric light sparkled through the heavy plate windows. Holly and pine garlands twined up the tripled columns of the porch. Thunner and Leola stood by the door, welcoming guests and pointing the way to the traditional nog.

It was the night before Christmas Eve, and the occasion was the annual holiday party at The Sands. For as long as anyone now living could remember, the family had opened their home during this season to friends of the family, senior management, those worth knowing in Hemlock County. It was a link with the glorious past, and sometimes through the chatter of conversation and murk of good cigars Daniel Thunner heard his father's confident baritone, his grandmother's silvery laugh, his grandfather's guffaw. When he was a boy he'd thought it feudal and old-fashioned. But with the passage of time he'd understood; and adopted the custom, after Colonel Charles had passed on, as his own. Later,

Mother might come down. Lutetia Kane Thunner was self-conscious about her age. She would no longer eat in public. But she would hold court in her high-backed chair for a few minutes, looking regal, before the nurses took her back to her room on the electric elevator.

He stood by the door, observing himself in a pier glass. He looked well in black tie; beside him, Leola, vertical for once, in a violet silk crepe evening frock sprinkled with rhinestone dewdrops. Her bare shoulders glowed in the candlelight.

"Reverend Sloan. How nice to have you." "Hello, Rudy, help yourself to eggnog." One by one and couple by couple he welcomed them as they emerged from their automobiles and mounted the steps. Conrad Kleiner, Keith Colley, George White, independent producers whose crude fueled and underpinned Thunder Oil. Vansittart and Hildebrandt and Etterlin, from the company. Ward Van Etten, who owned Seneca Glass, and who was building a new airport outside town in memory of his son, a noted local flyer who had died in a plane crash. Mr. Henry K. Holderlin, owner and president of Holderlin Machine Tool Company. The local Methodist pastor. The directors of the Board of Commerce, of the YMCA, the principal of the local high school. Industrialists, doctors, attorneys. Some brought marriageable daughters and sons as well as their wives, and the house was always thronged by the time the buffet opened.

Tonight, though, nearly every man, as he took his hand, muttered something encouraging about "holding out" and "beating those Bolshies." Thunner was forced to maintain a smile and say something sanguine in return, but every repetition of the shibboleths increased his rage and anxiety. Without fire roaring beneath the great stills he wasn't turning a dollar. But the outflow of cash barely slackened. He couldn't interrupt pension payments, heat and power, salaries for the men still on the rolls. He'd already tapped his personal credit out in order to replace the equipment lost in the fire. Now Weyandt was secretly negotiating with a New York bank for a mortgage on the family's lease lands.

He shook off the feeling of doom, grinning at Kerfoot Inskeep, the chairman of the county Republican Party, and his obese simpering wife. "Merry Christmas, Daniel, Leola," Inskeep boomed, taking Dan's hand in two sweaty paws and squeezing it like a letter-press. "Hold out, man. They shall not pass! Don't give an inch!"

Thunner gritted his teeth. "Delighted to have you here, Kerfoot. Marguerite, you're looking *especially* lovely to-night."

Twelve below zero, and down in the valley the river lay black and still under the lash of the wind. Only the faintest glimmer showed from the window of the tar-paper shack. A kerosene lamp, trimmed low.

Engine off, the sedan rolled to a halt up on the road. Then the doors swung open. Four men piled out, carrying clubs and lengths of wire rope. One lifted a large can out of the trunk. They cased the empty riverbank, the gates across the road, the lightless hills. Then trudged and stumbled through the thigh-deep snow, down toward the shack.

As the others stood guard, the one with the can upended it and ran the splashing stream along its back wall. A flicker; then golden flame ran rapidly up the boards.

The night guard erupted howling, swinging a pick. The dark figures scattered, but the hurtling point caught one in the side. He uttered a short scream and sank down onto the snow. The others closed on the figure that stood alone. For a few seconds a glittering arc wiped a space clear around it. Then it slowed, and the wolf-circle closed.

The sodden sound of blows and kicks rose toward the icy stars.

Finally Thunner was able to break away. He left Leola talking to Mrs. Van Etten, and circulated.

Great fires roared in the living room, the bar, the garden room, the dining hall, its panelings and carvings imported entire from a Tudor house in Kent; in every one of the eight fireplaces in the immense house. Bare shoulders glowed, bare necks and backs must be kept warm beneath jewels and thin silken sheaths. Thunner thrust his head into the kitchen, checking with Mrs. Himes on the progress of the roasted turkey, mincemeat, pumpkin pie, frothy pudding.

In the garden room, the president of Raymondsville Bank and Trust was sharing Havanas with Hildebrandt and the new Episcopal minister, young Reverend Sloan, and discussing Social Security. "I would be the last person in the world to stand in the path of any program which would bring happiness and an increased standard of living to any American," said the banker. "All my life I have attempted to help my fellow citizens attain security in their old age, by building up their savings during their earning years. But this scheme, it's nothing but a perpetual motion machine. I'm astonished so many people have fallen for it."

The attorney: "I read something recently that said by nineteen forty-nine it will add a billion and a half to the cost of U.S. products. Making us totally uncompetitive with foreign manufacturers."

"Surely there's something to be said for providing for people in their old age," ventured the minister, a pale young man with a tentative mustache.

"Granted, but is that government's responsibility?" said the banker. "Now, don't misunderstand me. I'm as liberal as the next fellow, but where this fellow Roosevelt's gone wrong is, you just can't fool the multiplication table. People were so shocked by the market crash that they are vulnerable to these ABC schemes, these economic nostrums. Someone profits by them. Very handsomely, I'm bound. But once prosperity returns, these false prophets like Coughlin and Long—yes, and your beloved FDR—will fade away. Dan'l, I'm sure you agree."

"There's a great deal to what you say." He smiled, then half bowed and withdrew, winking at the younger man, who gave him a dawning smile.

In the living room, in the hallway, his guests stood about with highball glasses and cigarettes. He turned to slide through, catching fragments and remarks as he pressed hands and lifted his glass in salute.

"It's so sad. Poor Mrs. Lindbergh. And now they're going to England, just to be able to have a normal life."

"It's perfectly obvious what's happening in our colleges. They're just cutting educational standards in order to get more students into the classrooms."

"I see where Ickes says we're making twenty-one cents a barrel. Not in Pennsylvania we're not. With crude at two-thirty I make barely enough to keep my rod-lines greased."

"Of course, they blame the missionaries for the agitation. But how many missionaries can there be in North China? Doctor, how many would you guess?"

"The bill's prima facie unconstitutional, and the court will rule as such. The federal government simply doesn't have that kind of regulatory authority over the mine operators."

"It's a new vitamin C nose drop. The Rockefeller Institute says it prevents infantile paralysis in monkeys."

"I don't care how many that fellow prints. I still can't look at it and think of it as a negotiable currency."

"No, it's actually seal fur, from Australia. I found it at Bonwit's."

"Bombing women and children. Someone's got to put a stop to it. That's no way to wage war, even if they are savages."

"It's a new drug. Incredibly effective. My sister tried it and lost twenty pounds. But it's rather dangerous, prescription only. . . ."

A masking smile on his lips, glass raised like a knight's shield, he made his way through the crowd.

Jennie Washko lay in the dark, in the low-ceilinged upstairs bed she shared with her sister. Viola's breathing sounded harsh and ragged. She got bronchitis every winter and was sick and had earaches for weeks, so bad she would cry. The upstairs was unheated and there were no lights up here. Her mother was afraid of fire, and would not allow them to bring so much as a candle upstairs. Jennie's whole body ached.

Ten and a half hours on the carding machines made her faint and dizzy. She made eleven dollars a week. She gave all her pay to her mother. So did her father, and her sisters. So had Johnny. He'd only made one paycheck before he died, but he'd been so proud, handing it over. A man at last, bringing money home. Then he'd died, and Billy hadn't even bothered to show up for the funeral.

She'd tried to forget him, after their argument. But seeing him the other day, riding with him, it had been hard to. She'd trembled the whole time in his car, afraid her father would see her. She wasn't allowed to be in an automobile with a boy, and her pa had a heavy hand when one of the kids disobeyed him or talked back. Her ma didn't like Bill at all. He wasn't Catholic. That made him the next thing to the Devil, as far as she was concerned.

She listened to her sister's struggle for breath. Please, Mary, don't let her get pneumonia again. Hail Mary, full of grace. Blessed art thou amongst women. And blessed is the fruit of thy womb, Jesus. Holy Mary, Mother of God, pray for us sinners, now and at the hour of our death, amen. She wanted to be good. She wanted to be pure. But sometimes her whole body ached just to be held. Sometimes she could not help doing what she knew she should not.

She closed her eyes as her fingers moved under her nightdress, her mind filling with a terrifying jumble of images, memories, imaginings; whispering to the Virgin in the narrow cold darkness as her sister coughed beside her; praying to know what she should do; praying desperately for forgiveness, even as she committed the mortal sin.

Deatherage stood by the bar, holding a glass of whiskey. Thunner observed that the bottle by his arm had emptied noticeably since he'd come by last. He said to the servant, "One more martini, please, Ty." To Deatherage he said, "I meant to ask you where you had served. You said France, didn't you?"

"I believe I did."

"Whereabouts? The Seventy-ninth was in the Argonne, wasn't it?"

Deatherage nodded offhand, glancing away. He didn't seem eager to discuss his war service. Thunner understood; he had unwelcome memories himself; so he moved the conversation on. "Well, I hope you're enjoying yourself tonight."

"Quite a shindig. You hold this every year?"

"A way of showing our appreciation, Pearl. To our friends and associates. And please, call me Dan."

"I'm surprised you invited me."

"Whyever not? For the duration, you're one of our senior managers." Thunner noted the ashtray, the crumpled pack the servant scooped away even as he noticed it. Deatherage looked ill at ease. Something he'd seen before in certain guests visiting the Sands for the first time. They usually dealt with it one of two ways: either by withdrawing or by talking business.

"I keep looking for Miss Golden," Deatherage said.

They both chuckled. "I don't think she'd respond to an invitation."

"She might surprise us."

"She might, at that. But I didn't invite her."

"Probably just as well." Deatherage reached for the bottle again. "She's figured out who I am. Whatever else she is, the bitch isn't stupid."

"Did you find anything more about the derailing?" He'd hoped not to talk about this tonight, but forgot as anger reoccupied him.

"No. But we posted guards. Since then transport's been going in and out. Are you going to restart one of your lines?"

"I still don't have an adequate labor supply. And I'm running up against another factor." He explained in a low voice his difficulty meeting fixed expenses. He finished, "We've got to break this thing before the new year. I can't afford to stay shut down much longer."

"I'm working on it," said Deatherage. "I think, when morning comes, our friends are going to realize we're through feeding them slow pitches."

"What does that mean?"

"It's better if you don't know."

"Jim Etterlin came to me yesterday. Said I ought to at least consider recognition. They'd take care of employee grievances, act as a safety valve—"

Deatherage opened his eyes wide. "Steady on, man. Do you want to lose everything?"

"I doubt we'll 'lose everything.' These are still my men."

"They *were* your men. Now they belong to her. This isn't just a question of the Thunder Company any longer, Dan."

Thunner said, keeping his voice low, but only with an effort, "You're not listening to me, Mr. Deatherage. I explained to you, there are limits to my resources."

"You've got it backward, Dan. You're running out of ready cash? Fixed costs eating you up? That means you've got to start production again."

Thunner said sardonically, "How penetrating. I've been through that line of reasoning myself. The question is, where do I find enough hands? I've run ads in every oil-country paper since the day they went out. I even called in my pensioners. Two showed up."

"What about this association of refiners you organized?"

Thunner's face went still.

Leola, from the doorway: "Dan, are you coming in? The monsignor's about to say the benediction."

"Excuse me. We'll discuss this further tomorrow. Are you coming in to dinner?"

"Think I'll pass, thanks," said Deatherage. He watched Thunner expressionlessly as he left, then drained the last ounce of amber liquor into his glass. He tossed it off with a quick backward jerk of his head. Patted his lips with one of the bar napkins.

Then, with a quick motion like a man presenting a knife, Deatherage extended his hand out before him. Watched it for long seconds. It was perfectly steady. Perfectly controlled. A slow smile took his twisted lips.

"Another quart here, boy," he said to the barman, flicking the empty bottle with a thumbnail and lighting another Old Gold.

*   *   *

Golden hesitated, looking up at the lightless windows of a massive 1890s brick pile two blocks from her hotel. They'd called her at the Hemlock half an hour before—just enough time for her to phone Shorty. She wasn't going to any meetings alone. Even if the voice on the phone said it was with the police chief and the assistant mayor.

For the fact of the matter was, once a confrontation began you never knew what *they* were capable of doing; you could never be confident that law meant law and order meant order or that any of the other words commonly supposed to mean certain things in America would still mean those things when the men who owned mines and mills and factories decided it would be more convenient for them another way. Words were not always what they seemed, and beneath the streets you saw lay other thoroughfares, and under the faces they turned to the public were others, faces that were never more naked than when they were masked. Now, hesitating, she felt the terror well up, even with Quarequio beside her. She breathed deep and slow, reminding herself there was only one way through the fear. "Are you sure this is where they wanted us to go?" she asked the Italian.

"This is City Hall," said Quarequio. He looked wary too. "They said downstairs. Here's a light left on. Must be it, huh?"

She forced her unwilling legs down a short flight of antique brick steps, to a lower-level door that when they tried to open it turned out to be locked. She knocked. While they waited she studied an emergency warning from the chief of police posted on the wall. It advised housewives against admitting peddlers to their homes. People had experienced costly property losses and bitter experiences. Strangers might be "spotters or locators" for professional criminals. It was safer to patronize local businesses, who employed your neighbors and paid city taxes. The police should be called at once if any itinerant applied for work or handouts.

The door swung open suddenly to an expectant face. "Miss Golden? Thanks for coming. Can I take your coat?"

She'd expected a cop, but when she went in, of the eight men sitting at a table only one was in the dark blue uniform of the Petroleum City police force. She stopped to stare around, masking her apprehension with truculence. "What the hell kind of kangaroo court is this?"

One of the men rose. "Please come in. Miss Golden. There's no danger here. We just wanted to . . . discuss the situation unofficially. For the good of the town. And that includes the people you represent, the workers at Thunder."

"I don't represent them. Their union does that."

He looked confused. "Aren't you with the union?"

"I'm only an adviser, gentlemen." She tilted her head toward Shorty. "Mr. Anthony Quarequio here is the president of Local One-seventy-eight. He's the man Thunder's got to deal with."

The cop said, "Anyway, we want to talk. You want to do us the favor of listening?"

After a moment she and Shorty took the chairs opposite them. She set her purse gently by her chair, hoping it didn't come to a search. The blued .32 would be good for a few nights in the local hoosegow. Well, she'd been in the can before. Never a pleasant experience, but part of the job, and now and then she'd had conversations with hookers that had come in handy in negotiations. She extracted a pack of Camels and lit one, waving the match out, sucking in the harsh smoke with sudden hunger. "Okay, boys, what's on your minds?"

A fat fellow in a red tie and pince-nez stood up and began to read a statement. He was sweating, though it wasn't warm in the basement. In fact, it was so chilly she and most of the men still had their overcoats on. The statement sounded like a Kiwanis speech. It was about cooperation and responsibility and marching toward prosperity together. She sat through three minutes of it, then rapped the table. He stopped, startled.

"Enough horseshit. You're cutting into my beauty sleep for this? Let's get to the point."

After a moment the cop said, flatly, "There's been an incident out at Thunder."

"What kind of incident?"

"Arson and battery. Four fellas were driving down Gower. Minding their own damn business. They saw that your shack was on fire. The driver stopped to see if he could help. A man comes out of the dark and swings a pick at them. The others had to jump in and rescue him."

"I see," she said coldly. "How badly did the goons beat him up?"

"He's at the hospital."

"Dead?"

"Unconscious."

"Sounds fishy to me, boys. I suppose he set the fire himself?"

She loaded it with sarcasm, and they sat for a moment not meeting her eyes. At last a younger man cleared his throat. "Miss Golden. This strike is hurting us all. If you could break the stalemate, accept Thunder's back-to-work offer—"

Shorty said, "There's been no back-to-work offer."

"The one that was in the paper."

"That offer was not made to us." She still didn't know their names, but she was beginning to get the picture.

"Of course it was. Thunder's willing to set up a safety program, offering a twelve-and-a-half-cent raise across the board—"

"We want recognition as sole bargaining agent. Everything else is ancillary."

They blinked at the word *ancillary*. Then a slim, polished man leaned forward. She was admiring his carefully combed-back dark hair when she saw that he was wearing a tuxedo under his overcoat. As if he'd just come from a party. The others quieted as he said, "May I put in a word?"

"Sure thing, Mr. Gerroy."

"Miss Golden, let me introduce myself. I am Elisha Denton Gerroy, the publisher of the *Deputy-Republican*, and I am deeply concerned about the welfare of the people of Hemlock County.

"Do you recall, as a child, when you threw a pebble into a pool of water? The ripples started small. Then they spread outward to fill the whole pond.

"That is what is happening to this county right now. The majority of our people are not doing well. This is the fault of economic circumstance beyond our control. But so far we have managed to stave off the worst. We have managed to keep everyone fed and most of the population employed. But this strike has lasted over two weeks now. The circles are getting larger. Thunder's the largest employer here. Probably eighty percent of our people depend on it, either directly or selling it parts and services or producing the crude oil that goes down the pipelines to Number One. Wait a moment; hear me out.

"No one is happy about this situation. But what worries me is, so far there hasn't been so much as a meeting between company and union representatives. It is not our purpose to propose terms. But without rancor or emotion, let me ask the question that is troubling us all: When will this matter be settled?"

"Ask Daniel Thunner."

"It's true, Mr. Thunner's not an easy chap to deal with when he has his back up. But the mayor's right. Thunder has tabled an offer. It may not be exactly what you want. But the situation is only going to degenerate. Tonight's incident is only a foretaste of the way things may go. Isn't it possible, Miss Golden, Mr.—Quarequio—that your members could go back to work, and continue negotiations with the refinery back in operation, and everyone making a wage again?"

She sucked on the cigarette, giving the impression of thinking it over. Then blew a stream of smoke in his direction. "Not on your fucking life," she told him.

Their faces, God help her. It was enough to make a cat laugh. "Goddamn it," growled the cop. "I told you talking to this commie bitch was a waste of time."

Just then a back door swung open, and a well-built, balding man in his thirties with a William Powell mustache looked in.

She breathed out. It was their attorney, Harvey Mulholland. He was actually on retainer for the local trade union council, representing the AFL tool and die makers at the Holderlin works, but he was a labor man and had agreed to make himself available during the strike. He nodded to the mayor and chief and pulled a folding chair off a pile and snapped it open beside her. "Topic under discussion?" he said briskly.

"Labor violence," said the cop, and "Management violence," she said at the exact same time. No one smiled.

"Actually, Harv, we were just about done with Doris here. It was more in the nature of a warning."

"What kind of warning?" asked the lawyer, taking command in a way she and Shorty hadn't managed. She didn't quite see how it was done, only that he was a man, and a big one at that. Like a pack of dogs, they were.

"About keeping this whole thing in the bounds of fair play. There's been a good deal of hooliganism so far. I wanted to nip it in the bud before somebody got hurt. Now it's too late. We've got two men in hospital. Now, tomorrow's Christmas Eve. We're not sitting here to say this side's right, or that side's wrong. But you got to understand, a lot of the businesses in this town depend on the payroll over at Thunder."

She said, "Then put some pressure on Thunder. How about getting Vansittart and that little rat Weyandt down here for a grilling in the basement?"

The city attorney said, "Can I say something here, Ted?"

"Go ahead." The younger man sat back, looking frustrated.

"Thunder's a responsible business. They don't derail freight trains. They don't set fires and start fights. There wasn't any trouble in this county before you showed up. This is a warning, miss. You've got an organized minority down there trying to terrorize the others into following the dictation of a few radicals. Now, there are means of ridding the community of people like you—"

"I know them," she said. Her voice utterly cold, like her heart.

"Legal means. Trespass, breach of the peace, littering, violation of the public safety ordinances."

"Where were you born, Miss Golden?" asked the cop.

"Passaic, New Jersey. The year Elizabeth Gurley Flynn came to town. Hence my middle name." She smiled slowly. "You mean, the undesirable alien racket. Won't work, Chief. I'm as American as you."

"We're leaving." Mulholland stood up. "If you have grounds, arrest her. Otherwise we have no further business here."

"Warn these people, Harvey. No more violence. Or else."

She barely resisted the impulse to show them a hand gesture that she'd learned on a strike out West. Instead she simply kept her mouth closed, picked up her purse, and left.

The light streamed blazing out across the snow from the tall windows. Outside, men in fedoras sat smoking in automobiles, looking grimly out as the wind covered the street with a wavering icy veil.

The men and women inside were playing a party game Leola had brought back from New York. Thunner found it boring, but the kids were having a ball. The older people drank, or stood about talking. He excused himself after his turn, and took a cigar out onto the porch.

The black chill struck instantly through his evening clothes. It was a cold he'd felt before, lying on the fields of France, waiting for the god of war to decide whether he would freeze or smother or bleed to death. It must have dropped ten degrees since dusk. He shuddered, turning his back to the wind, sucking flame up into the cigar from his patent Austrian lighter. Then realized he wasn't alone on the long gallery. Someone else was standing in the shadows, not far away.

"Mr. Thunner," the shadow said. It detached itself from the triple pillars and came toward him as he stared wide-eyed, wondering how this person had gotten through his guards. And what he wanted. "Don't call anyone. I just want to talk."

The hesitant voice was young. It seemed familiar, yet he couldn't place it. He rapped out, "What do you want? Who are you?"

"I told you—I just want to talk," said the shadow querulously. It was as tall as he was. "I think I m-might have something that you n-need."

Sixteen

A week later the New Year arrived in a flurry of gunfire. Halvorsen took his .30-30 out into the backyard at a quarter to midnight. When the whistles began to sound, car horns and factory whistles and the far-off despairing shriek of a locomotive, he lifted it and pumped round after round into the freezing sky. Half the male population of the county had the same idea. The night-shrouded hills echoed with the rattle of gunfire. Between the cracks from down the street he heard distant pops from over toward Gasport and farther off, from Rich Falls. The sound reached a crescendo, then gradually trailed off. Till the gray sky was still again. A little later he went back in, and the old man who believed Charles E. Coughlin, Francis Townsend, and Gerald L. K. Smith had the answers to all America's problems passed around a bottle of Guckenheimer and they drank to 1936. A little while later everyone went to bed.

The next morning he woke to a tremendous hammering on his door. He sat bolt upright on his cot. "What the hell is it?" he yelled.

"Bill?"

"Yeah, goddamn it, what?"

Shotner yelled back, "Lew Pearson's on the phone. Says Thunder's bringing in a bunch of boys to break the strike. Get down there right away."

He pulled his pants on and ran downstairs.

Pearson said he'd got the word from one of the pickets' wives who lived just outside the Seward Avenue gate. He was headed down there, and for him to pass the word on to Shorty before he came. "And make it snappy," he finished, and hung up.

Outside it was snowing again. He had an anxious minute or two as the Oakland wouldn't turn over. He cursed it and thumped the wheel. Finally it started.

Ten minutes later he locked the wheels and skidded to a snow-throwing halt on Seward.

A line of motor buses stood backed up at the rear gate to Number One. He racked the parking brake and cut the engine. He jumped down and ran through the fluffy falling snow down toward them. Lucy Amoretti, the chairwoman of the women's auxiliary, yelled at him as he went by, "Stop them bastards, Bill!"

The committee hadn't put many picketers here. It was the back way, going in from uphill. That was probably why the company had decided to route their buses this way. Old lease houses crowded siding to siding opposite the fence. They were called "cloth and paper" because there wasn't any studding; the outside was rough-finished hemlock, the inside walls just painted cheesecloth that moved when the wind blew. Their occupants stood watching. Within the fence rose the metal-hooped wooden cylinders of crude-oil storage tanks. The Cherry Hill pipeline came in not far from the gate, on a narrow right-of-way down from the hillside between the shabby houses, then over the street suspended on elevated iron trestlework like a miniature bridge.

As he pelted up to the idling buses, faces watched him from their windows. The sides held the names of city lines from Warren, Titusville, Bradford, Oil City, the other producing centers in the northwest and center of the state. The men inside were dressed for work. They looked down with mingled hostility and curiosity as he ran past, panting as the drifts dragged at his boots; headed for the first vehicle in line, which was now blowing its horn furiously but not yet moving.

Then he saw why. There were bodies in front of it.

His worst horror faded as he reached the gate. They were bodies, but they weren't dead. Stan Melnichak and two other picketers had lain down in the snow in front of the wheels. The Thunder guards were hurriedly unlocking the swing gates from inside, cursing and yelling at the picketers. The bus horn was blaring. The picketers were yelling at the driver and the guards. All in all, it was a noisy start to the morning. He debated lying down with them, then figured they had that job nailed. Instead he reached up and rapped on the side of the bus. He must have looked like he belonged to the company because the driver leaned on the horn again, then swung the door open for him to climb up.

"Knock it off. Jesus, a guy can't hear himself think."

"Who the hell are you?"

"W. T. Halvorsen, foreman for Thunder Oil. Who are these men?"

The driver said they were all from Freedom Oil. The other vehicles were from Quaker State, Wolf's Head, Pennzoil, Wolverine-Empire, United, and Crystal Oil. Halvorsen gave it a second, letting them all wait for what he was going to tell them to do. Then he asked the front row of guys, "What, you're scabs?"

"We ain't no lousy *scabs*. We're volunteers."

Through the windshield he saw Lew Pearson's truck plow to a halt, saw Pearson and Golden jump down and begin running toward them. He said, "You're not tellin' me you're oil workers?"

"We sure as shit are, buddy. Time 'n' a half and a free ticket."

"And you're comin' in here to break our strike? Is this what you're tellin' me?"

A burly Irisher with a swollen nose caught on. Rising up, he roared, "An' you're one of these stinkin' Reds. Get the hell off our bus." To the driver he snarled, "Honk one more time, then roll over 'em."

"I'm not driving over no women," the driver muttered. He leaned on the horn again, though.

The burly mick bulled past Halvorsen, carrying a baseball bat, and jumped down into the snow. Others were emerging from the other buses. Halvorsen scrambled down after him.

The Hibernian got to Melnichak and started to kick him, then lifted the bat. Halvorsen was a step behind him. As the club started down he grabbed the guy's shoulder, spun him around, and planted his right as hard as he could in the center of his face. A broad, flat face, simple and expressionless as a coal shovel, save for a moment of astonishment as Halvorsen's fist crashed into it.

The others hesitated as their leader toppled, then came on, circling him like a pack of dogs around a bear. He kept glancing over his shoulder at the buses, waiting for the mob, but to his surprise they just stared down at the face-off, as if it didn't matter to them, as if they were just waiting, curious, to see what would happen.

He shifted his attention back to his opponents, realizing suddenly that these were some truly ugly customers. All were scarred, all carried either a knife or some other weapon, heavy cane, ball bat, or a blackjack in a curled palm. They had empty, cruel eyes. He didn't know any of them. They weren't from around the county.

The one with the blackjack stepped forward, feinted, and whipped it in aimed at his skull. Halvorsen bobbed, then popped him with a dead-on left-right combination. The other waggled his head, as if flinging water off, but stopped coming. Fists up, dancing and shuffling in the snow to face first one, then the other, he yelled happily, "Now we're cookin'! Come on, who's next?"

The bulls charged out of the gate in a gray mass, having finally gotten it open. They made for the picketers on the ground. Two cops each grabbed arms and legs and dragged them out from under the wheels. The bus's gearbox grated, and it moved forward with a shuddering groan. Halvorsen stood, hands dangling, watching it pass, watching the plug-uglies stroll in with them. Then the next, then the whole parade. Christ, he thought. There's enough guys there to start the whole plant up. Thunner had taken them by surprise, outmaneuvered them. He snatched off his cap and threw it down, cursing.

Golden came over, brushing her coat off. "Does that help?"

"Some."

"I'm glad." She stared after the buses. "Can those really be workers from the other refineries?"

" 'Volunteers.' Selling us out for time and a half and a free ride. The sonsabitches." He retrieved his hat, ashamed of his display of temper when she was so cool about it. "What's up? We goin' in after 'em?"

"That wouldn't be wise." She pushed a curl of black hair off her face, frowning like, he thought, a disappointed and puzzled child. "The other owners shouldn't do this. It's not in their best interests."

"What do you mean?"

"I mean, it's dog eat dog, and when one's down the others should be at his throat. When Thunder stops supplying product, its competitors share its market out among themselves. That's one of the prime reasons he has to settle. But if they've discovered the virtues of combination . . . I'll have to think about this."

Halvorsen remembered the thugs then, and told her about them. She told him those were hired goons, finks, and they wouldn't be the last he'd see.

Melnichak and Pearson were sitting up. Stan's lip was bleeding, and he held a hand to his side where someone had kicked him. Halvorsen helped him pack his cheek with clean snow, then gave him a hand up. "That was pretty brave, Stanley."

"Stan."

"Yeah . . . that was smart, too, lyin' down in front of the bus. Don't know if I'd of thought of that."

More cars pulled up, a belated flying squadron of strikers and relief picketers the telephone chain had pulled in. Golden put them on at the gate. "If any more show up, we'll do your lie-down thing again," she told Melnichak. "But legally, Thunner's got access to the plant. He can send men and material in and out. So we've got to figure something better. And pretty damn snappy, too."

Looking down from the office, Thunner and Vansittart watched the workers get off the buses. They stood gazing up at the unfamiliar buildings, the towering, cold equipment. Then the plant foremen waded in, separating them by trade, then leading each group off into the alleys and recesses of the refinery. A remnant stayed leaning against the vehicles, making no move to work. Thunner stared down at them. He had nothing but contempt for such men, yet Deatherage had persuaded him they might have their uses.

He said to the manager, "Now, this is the way to start a new year."

"I'm surprised as hell they sent this many."

"So am I, actually, Earl. Though we're paying for them, double time to their companies . . . But by God, the Refiners' Association kept their word."

"And when they have labor trouble, we do the same for them?" Thunner nodded. "How long have we got 'em for?"

"I asked that they be made available for a week. But I doubt we'll need that long. Two days of production, three, and our men will start slinking back in. Seeing a closed plant is one thing. Watching another fellow doing your job, that's another." He examined the diagram on the wall, showing every valve and line and cutoff in the refinery. "What's your plan?"

"I'm setting up to start Number Two. Three shifts. We'll run a thousand barrels a day."

"Downstream?"

"Wait till the charge stock builds up, then fire up waxing

and Dobbs and so forth one at a time. Question: What about the bottoms? They're the lowest value-added fraction."

"That's what the river's for. Dump anything we can't move out fast for cash. Where's Etterlin, and Otis?"

"I'm here, sir," said the plant engineer, coming in from the next room, where he'd obviously been listening.

The three men discussed how best to tune the plant for limited production. Then Vansittart left. Etterlin lingered. He said, "Mr. Thunner, could we have a word?"

"Sure, Jim. Shoot." Thunner felt more cheerful than he had in weeks as he contemplated a restart. A thousand barrels a day was only a quarter of full production, but even a modest income stream would ease his financial squeeze. "The polymerizer installation going okay?"

"Yessir, but it wasn't that. It's about this strike. I don't think we're treating the men fairly."

Thunner stopped rubbing his hands. "You've played me this violin before, Jim."

"Sir, I went to an API meeting over in Titusville just before Christmas. American Petroleum Institute. I talked to a couple of the other engineers. It sounds to me as if we're about the lowest in terms of pay scale of any works in the area." The young man added hastily, "I didn't mean, as applies to me. I'm perfectly satisfied with my present salary, sir. I was speaking in terms of the men's wages. It seems to me that we could meet at least part of their demands—"

"How many hands have they thrown off?" Thunner interrupted. "These high-wage refineries you're talking about? I had to reduce hours, I cut pay, but I haven't pink-slipped a single employee. Can they say that?"

"Well, sir, that's a point I hadn't considered."

"I have. A lot of these men, their fathers, their grandfathers, worked all their lives for this company. I'd a hell of a lot rather have them call me cheap than have to throw them out without a job in the middle of the fix this country's in. I have an obligation to them, Jim. Consider this, too. It's not ten cents this way or that way I'm worried about."

Thunner waved out the window, at the mass of tanks and

piping and acres of silent machinery. "This isn't a refining plant, to me. It isn't even capital. What is capital, after all? The crystallized product of genius, and sweat, and desire, passed on from generation to generation for the good of mankind.

"This is my legacy, Jim. My grandfather founded Thunder, and my family has run it ever since. Someday I'll pass it to my son. Now, those men outside the gates are a trifle confused right now. Because of this East Side Jew, or whatever she is, peddling her foreign ideas. But they'll come around. And when they do, I'll take care of them, just as my family has since we came to these hills.

"But in return for everything we've given, we demand one thing in return. I will never let outsiders dictate what I do with my property. Before that happens, I'll burn it to the ground again, just like it burned in 'ought-six."

He studied the younger man's furrowed brow. "I know. You're young, and it looks simple, doesn't it?"

"It looks—imbalanced. Sir."

"Then you're going to have to trust me on this, Jim. I've seen what happens when the forces of destruction are unleashed. Once this is over, I promise you, I'll look at our scale again. Maybe ask you to recommend what we should be paying. And what's more, we'll need men like you for our employees' association. But right now I need you to stand with me." He put his arm around the younger man's shoulder. "Can I count on you? To put your doubts to one side for now?"

"Yes, sir," said Etterlin, straightening. "I admit, I don't understand some of the things I'm seeing—but I *do* trust you. You can count on me."

"Good." Thunner gave his shoulder another squeeze, then slapped his back. "Okay! It's nineteen thirty-six, boy! Let's get this plant runnin' again!"

Halvorsen was standing with Stan Melnichak, thumbing a fresh chew into his cheek, when he saw her picking her way down the bank toward the shack. The cops had forbidden

them to rebuild it, after it had been burned. They said it was
a public eyesore. They said the river edge, rocky and useless
though it was, scoured by ice in winter and covered by the
flood-melt from the hills in spring, was city property; building there was forbidden. Golden had waited until they left,
then waved the truckful of scrap materials in. Pitching in
together, the strikers had thrown it up in two hours. When
the police returned, they looked sourly at it, but did nothing.
"Score one for us," she'd said.

"What would you have done if they tore it down?"

"Built it again."

"And again?"

"Use an old Wobbly tactic." She'd hugged herself, her
cheeks the only color in a world occupied by winter. "They
want to arrest us? Let them. Let 'em jail us *all*. Say we get two
hundred men arrested, they got to feed us, keep us warm. . . .
They know they can't afford to, that's all." She'd shrugged.
"The question is, what they'll do when we push them beyond
that."

Now she picked her way across the snow-covered rocks
down to him, past a couple of tents that someone had put up
to keep warm in during the off-picket hours, and he straightened. "Bill. Stan," she called. "How many scabs you figure
were in them buses?"

He thought about it. "Eighty?"

Melnichak offered ninety. She said, "About what I estimated." She dipped fire out of the can with a long pine-sliver
and held it to her cigarette. Puffed, looking toward the
refinery. "They ain't goons, at least not most of them.
They're working stiffs, like us. All they need is to be persuaded to make common cause with their striking brothers."

Halvorsen turned his head to spit. "Sounds reasonable,"
he said. "But how you gonna make them see it that way?"

"They're starting up the stills," someone cried, and they
turned.

Black smoke streamed upward above the plant. With the
sky so clear, the smoke looked strangely dirty. Halvorsen
wondered suddenly what it was doing to everybody in the

town, breathing all that stuff their whole lives long. It was a strange thought, unsettling, and he put it aside for later.

"The trouble is, I can talk to them, but I'm not one of 'em." She fixed her eyes on him. "Who do we need to talk to them? I think one of their own."

Halvorsen almost swallowed his plug. "Now hold your horses, here. I ain't no speech-maker."

"They tell me you made one when this whole thing started. In a bowling alley, was that it?"

"That wasn't no speech. I just said some things had to be said."

"And that's all I'm asking you to do now."

He sucked the juice from the wad of Mail Pouch, but already his mouth was going dry.

The truck from Raymondsville slowed as the gates swung open, then growled ahead. Golden stood watching it. It had been a hectic few hours. Typing, mimeographing, then persuading Maria DeLucci, who owned the diner in the neighboring town, to do it. A ten-dollar bill had helped. But inside each of the ham sandwich, apple, and fried pie box lunches was a hastily printed flyer.

She raised her eyes to the curtain of smoke and steam that seethed above the refinery now. She could hear it, too, a hum and roar like the engine room of an ocean liner. And smell it: a heavy, cloying, chemical odor of oil and steam and hot metal, brought to them on a faint cold wind. It had begun about nine, and grown with each passing hour. The men on line watched it silently, hands dangling by their sides. She didn't like the look in their eyes. The hungry way they looked at the open gates with the sign that read PLANT OPEN. NOW HIRING. START THE NEW YEAR RIGHT. WELCOME BACK LOYAL THUNDER EMPLOYEES.

Melnichak, beside her: "The boys were up on the hill with a toy telescope some kid brought in. They've got Number Two fired up."

"What can they produce with that?"

"Well, it's complicated to explain—"

"Give me the women's version," she said, sighing.

"They'll concentrate on gasoline and lube oil. The other stuff, they'll probably save up the fractions left after the gas and oil comes off, and fire up units downstream' a that as they get enough for a run."

She asked him what percentage of normal production that would amount to, and he said about a quarter. She lit another Camel, rubbing her throat. The harsh tobacco was making her throat sore. She was smoking too much. Maybe she should switch to Kools. "Are we ready? It's almost time."

He said they were almost ready.

The band struck up at noon, lugubrious, but unmistakably music, booming drums and tinkly glockenspiels. Faces peered out from the windows of the office. A bit later a milling commotion began. He saw the outstretched gray-coated arms. Then the cops were shoved aside, and workers emerged, coming down out of the gate and across the road and down the snow-covered riverbank toward the stack of boxes and ties strongbacked into a makeshift ring.

Shorty Quarequio, bustling up with a steaming pot of coffee and a fistful of mugs. "How's it going in there, brother? Surprised they let you out of your cage."

"They tried to stop us," said a red-faced worker. "But we told 'em we were volunteers, not slaves. Come down to see what you had to say. And to see this boxing exhibition." The others gathered in a group, shoulders hunched against the chill wind, hands mining their pockets. Around the edges, the strikers filtered unobtrusively in among them.

Doris rose, and they quieted.

She started easy, thanking them for coming out to hear the other fellow's point of view. "Now we know you boys ain't anti-union. A worker to be anti-union, that would be like a Rockefeller or a Mellon being anti–Wall Street." A chuckle drifted up. Halvorsen licked his lips; it wouldn't be long now. "And what's more, I figure the bosses ain't told you everything. I bet if you'd known, there's more than one of you wouldn't have climbed on that bus.

"But anyway, thanks for joining us—"

"Where the hells's the exhibition?" shouted a voice from the back. A rough voice. He got up on tiptoe and saw who owned it. The plug-ugly from that morning, the Celt who'd started in on Stan Melnichak with a baseball bat. And looking here and there in the crowd, he saw more of them, scarred, cold, ugly Neanderthal faces, bindlestiffs and crooks, the thug-muscle someone had bought to stiffen the scabs' backs.

"Glad you asked that," said Golden. She lifted her arm and pointed at the kibitzer.

Quicker than he could react, the goon found himself circled by four husky riggers. Arms pinned to his sides, he was dragged like a performing bear toward the ring. Halvorsen followed, cracking his knuckles and breathing deeply. The other troublemakers in the audience started to move after him, then stopped. They too were ringed by strong men, slapping sawed-off lengths of iron rod-line against work-hardened palms.

Halvorsen ducked under the rope as the others unstrapped the goon. He stood at bay, snarling like a hyena in a nature newsreel. Get them alone and they weren't so brave. Quarequio asked him his name, and he snapped, "Kelly."

"In this corner, Mr. Kelly, from—"

"Erie," Kelly snarled, head down. The throng laughed.

"And in this corner, 'Kid Nitro' Halvorsen, a driller from right here in Petroleum City." Halvorsen finished stripping off his jacket—the air was icy without it, but he knew in a couple minutes he'd be warm enough—and turned to face them in his shirtsleeves, pasting a big grin across his kisser. This time he was the hometown favorite, and he milked it, turning around and around with his hands locked in salute.

A harsh clang, a piece of angle iron wobbled on a rope, and he moved out into the center of the ring, guard up, eyes squinted against cold, flat winter light vitreous and hard as a porcelain commode. Kelly hesitated, looking around; then, cornered, lumbered out to face him.

Halvorsen limbered up a little, staying on the move, and

tried a couple of teasing jabs. Kelly responded slowly, backing away. He had big arms, but he looked like a wrestler, not a boxer. Stay out of range of bear hugs. And eye gouges.

He closed suddenly, left flicking in fast as a diamondback's tongue. Kelly's head rolled before he shrugged his guard up and swung. Halvorsen danced back, then slammed into the rough wooden barrier at his back and ducked away as Kelly took another wild swipe. Not far enough, though, because the man followed him into the corner and pinned him there, denting in his ribs like a frenzied boilermaker. He took three solid blows before he could twist free. He danced away sucking air, more cautious now.

Visibly emboldened, Kelly circled after him, big hands out now like an advancing crab. "Come on, you Red bastard," he crooned. "Gonna break your back, squarehead. Then I'm gonna knock a piece off your Jew cooze, there."

"Get in here and take your medicine, ya fat mick." Halvorsen popped one off his nose, or tried to; but Kelly jerked his head forward and down as the punch came in, and his knuckles snapped on the guy's skull. The pain was incredible. He backpedaled, shaking his hand out. Damn, should have waited for the gloves.

The Irishman suddenly planted his feet and rushed. Halvorsen feinted and dodged, hooking a right into his neck as he went by. Kelly slammed into the timbers and staggered back, hands going to his throat. His face went red, then white. Cries of encouragement mixed with outraged yells. Halvorsen held up his hands, shrugging.

When Kelly turned around again he stepped in and hammered him hard in the body, left right left right, ignoring the pain in his hand, just jackhammering. The other man was bleeding from a slash on his face. Halvorsen hit him again and again, as hard as he could, till the Irishman's fists curled open slowly and fell to his sides, till finally he slumped down against the timbers, eyes staring open. "Enough," he muttered through the blood that dripped down into the snow. "Gimme a break, mac. I give."

Shouts and cheers broke out as Halvorsen staggered to the

platform. Hands reached down and he let them haul him up. He jerked the keen wind deep into his lungs. Face to face with the crowd, now. Past them he saw the guards watching from the gate. Somebody handed him up an uncapped beer bottle. He tilted it, then held it out to salute them. A scatter of clapping eddied up.

"That's it, boys," Golden yelled. "You just seen how a real man treats the scum the bosses sick on us. Anybody else want to step up and take him on?"

Nobody did, and he for one was damn grateful. For a moment he hoped she'd forget about him and keep talking. But instead she pushed him forward. "Okay, they're yours," she muttered. "Go on. Give it to 'em."

He took another deep breath, dashing beer-foam off his mouth with the back of his hand, blinking in the icy light. What the hell was he going to say? His guts hurt where Kelly had hammered him, trapped in the corner. Shit, he hoped he didn't have to wear a truss after this.

"Uh, I ain't much of a speech maker," he said, to scattered laughter. He ran his hand over his hair, staring at the up-turned faces.

"Ain't much of a speech maker . . . but I got to tell you fellas something. About what we're tryin' to do here."

He took another deep breath. "See, about two months ago we had an accident in this plant." He told them how the guys had complained about the safety gear, about the fire-fighting equipment. "Then one day some fellas were up on the iron. Maintenance crew, up on the bubble tower. Tom Callahan, Donnie Rapisczek, Mark Shaughnessey, fella named Pecora, don't recall his first name, and a fifteen-year-old kid named Johnny Washko. I knew Johnny. A nice kid. *Hell* of a nice kid. Only workin' because his old man, he was a roustabout, he couldn't make enough slavin' at Thunder to keep a roof over his family's head.

"Anyway, there was a fire. And the guys couldn't get off the iron fast enough. Why? Because the rivets were rusted off their escape ladder. And they all roasted to death. All of 'em. I went to Johnny's wake. It smelled like somebody burned the ham; I tell you, it turned my damn stomach. I couldn't stand being in there, and his family—I didn't know what to say to his maw."

He took another swig of beer. The faces stayed his, hooked now, listening. Soon as he was done with this, though, he needed a chew.

"Anyway, that's why we went out, boys. It wasn't about jack, but I want to talk about that, too." He told them straight up what the pay scales were at Thunder, and saw their faces go still as each man compared that to what he was making. "Now, the goddamn supervisors is tellin' us it don't matter, they pay so low. They say we're lucky to have jobs at all these days. And maybe there is somethin' to that. But we're done takin' what they give us, like it was charity. There comes a time when a man's got to take things into his own hands. When people are dyin' because the company's too cheap to fix the equipment, in my book, that's when we walk out. And try to build a union that'll stick up for the workingman, because there goddamned sure ain't nobody else who is.

"Now: Where do you fellas fit in?"

He smacked his fist into his hand and it hurt so much he lost the thread of his argument. He looked past the crowd, to where the cops were forming up, getting ready to charge out. Better finish up. And get some ice on his mitt. Should have packed it with some of this snow soon as he got out of the ring.

"Anyway, we're all workers here. I ain't got nothing against you fellas. But without you, see, Thunner can't run his plant. If you was the ones walkin' out, I sure as hell wouldn't be crossing no picket lines to take the bread and baloney out of your kids' mouths.

"There ain't really nothing else to say. The union's all we got left, here. We ain't goin' back through those gates without it. If we don't get it we're all gonna have to leave town, I guess. Take our families and go. And I don't want to do that. I don't want to live nowhere else. Like to get married here, settle down and raise some kids. That's my dream, anyway.

"So if you go back in there—and maybe you got to, I don't know—but if you do, all I ask is one thing: Don't help them beat us, boys. Put in your time, draw your pay, but don't help them beat us. Because once they got us crushed down, you're gonna be next."

A distant screech, a plume of white; the plant whistle signaling the end of the noon break. He didn't have anything more to say, so he just stood there, shaking the tension out of his shoulders.

"Let's go, boys. Back to work." That was the head bull, "Whiny" Wheeler. Slapping his truncheon into his glove. The other cops behind him, hands on their revolver butts. A moment of uncertainty, abeyance.

Then one man moved and then others, and the meeting broke and the men from outside straggled back up the bank, across the tracks, back through the gate. Golden blew out, and the others gathered around Halvorsen, slapping his back.

He blinked, then realized, looking down, that not all of them had left.

The kid was red-haired, freckle-faced. He swung himself up on the platform and stuck out his hand. "Nice speech, Red," he said. "Nice fight, too."

"Thanks, kid. But I ain't no Red. Union, sure; but I ain't no Bolshevik."

"I'm Frank Latimer. And I'm with you guys; I say the bosses can shove it up where the sun don't shine."

"Hi, Frank. You better get back in there. Whiny's headed for you."

Melnichak laughed as he shook his hand. "Red," he repeated. "I like that." Halvorsen gave him a disgusted glance.

The men from Bradford and Titusville and Oil City went back in, but they didn't work. They stood watching gauges and controls, hands in their pockets . . . and did nothing. The foremen first reminded them what they had to do, then cajoled them, at last raged and threatened. They stood idle. The straw bosses rushed madly about, trying to keep the stills running, but there weren't enough hands. Gauges kept climbing. Finally they had to shut down. The plumes of smoke thinned, easing from black toward gray and then becoming faint wisps of upcurling white as the fires flickered yellow, and red, and then guttered out in furnaces and stills and crude-heaters.

Not long after that the buses started their motors again. Golden had the boys ready at the gates when they came through. Hastily trudged signs on the snowy hillside read THANKS BROTHERS and SOLIDARITY and SPREAD THE WORD. She watched the buses swing onto Route Six and vanish.

Only a disappearing wisp of flame floated over the flare-offs which that morning had roared anew. Only a ghost-wing of smoke drifted from the stack above the power station. Around her the pickets talked in boasting voices. There was much slapping of backs and shaking of hands. She gave Halvorsen a brief hug, feeling the taut, hard muscle under his red-barred coat.

When Quarequio and Pearson and Melnichak came over, she gave them each a quick embrace as well. But the stocky Italian barely returned it. He said, "Yeah, dancing and singing. We licked 'em. This time. But what if they get some real hungry boys in here? Folks who ain't got a job waiting back home? Like from someplace their damn farms're blowing away."

Melnichak said, "Spill it, Shorty. What's on your mind?"

"I'm thinking we better figure out some way to close this goddamn place down for good."

Pearson asked him what he meant, and Quarequio said, "I mean, what if some morning they wake up and maybe the power plant burned down. Or the dynamo, somebody put sand in the bearings. Or busted up the pipeline, so they can't get no crude."

Halvorsen took a slow look around, making sure there wasn't anybody else listening. He said in a low tone, "You're talking sabotage. I don't know, Shorty."

"You don't know. Well, this here's the goddamn committee, boys, right here, and I'm telling you we better start thinking about it pretty soon because there's some lads in that picket line mad enough to bust. They burnt down our goddamn shack, damn near killed the night guy. I tell ya, it's time to stop playin' patty-cake here."

While they were arguing about it, she walked away from them. Wanting to be part of it, but knowing it was best for them all if she wasn't. Pressed to the wall, the workers had to progress to the next stage in the development of the struggle. It was the inexorable force of history, moving them all on with as little regard for their volition or hers as an ocean tide. She hugged herself in the wintry air, thrilled for a moment by their victory, and the foretaste of the ultimate and final victory to come.

Then she saw the gleam of field glasses, the somber figure watching her from the second story of the office. She dropped her arms, conscious of a sudden apprehension replacing the triumph.

Maybe they'd won this battle. But the war had only begun.

Seventeen

The basement of the Petroleum City police station, a few days later, and blue-uniformed city cops and Thunder plant cops in gray standing contemplatively around several heavy wooden crates stenciled AGRICULTURAL HARDWARE.

"Invoice," said Chief Foster, waving the flimsy paper. Deatherage pointed to Wheeler, who came over and took it out of Foster's hand.

"We don't want any trouble, now," said the police chief. "That's why we agreed to help out on this."

"There won't be any trouble, Jerry. That's what this is all for, to make sure there won't be any. This all must be secret, by the way. I don't want to show we anticipate anything. That would only aggravate the situation. I'm sure you don't want to do that."

"Of course not," said Foster, stroking his mustache. His eye lingered on a small blue pin on Deatherage's overcoat lapel. He leaned closer. "What force were you with?"

"Sorry?"

"That's an FOP pin, ain't it?"

"Honorary member. Awarded by the national committee. Well, let's take a look," said Deatherage. The company cops looked at Wheeler, who nodded. They started prying off the covers.

Inside the boxes were long red tubes, short-barreled break-open guns, and boxes of shells marked CAUTION. GAS. A guard picked up a mask and tried it on. They looked at his goggled eyes, the queer unhuman muzzle. Deatherage selected one of the guns. He broke it open across his arm and tried a shell in it.

Wheeler. "Something wrong?"

"No, no. Just checking that they sent us the proper caliber." He replaced the gun, rooted around in the crate a bit more, then beckoned to the police chief. He handed him a small black object. "Looks like a pen, doesn't it? It's yours. Here's a box of cartridges."

Foster turned it in his fingers. "How good is this stuff? Ever seen it used?"

"Indeed I have. I think anyone who comes in range of it will not invite another dose. Please be careful. You don't want to fire that in a closed space."

As the chief examined it, the Thunder guards finished laying everything out on the floor. Deatherage walked along the line, splitting each pile of equipment down the middle. When they were all divided, the gas shells and guns and tear-gas clubs and nauseating-gas jumper-repeaters, he made a peremptory motion. Wood screeched as the guard nearest him pried up the lid on the last crate.

Four Thompson submachine guns nestled in their wooden compartments. Deatherage handed two to his men, along with drum magazines and boxes of .45 cartridges.

When the division was complete, the guards replaced the half reserved for Thunder into the cases. They positioned the lids and hammered them back on.

As they carried the crates up the steps and into the back of a well service truck, Deatherage took out a cigarette and a box of hotel matches. But munitions were still exposed, and he held it unlit as he asked Foster where a good place might be to demonstrate the gas bombs and gas guns, and get everybody trained and used to working together in case things turned sour. The chief suggested the Hemlock County Gun Club, east of town. Deatherage asked if it could be reserved and privacy assured. They agreed on the day after tomorrow.

By then all the crates were gone, Thunder's share to the truck, the city's disappearing back into the steel-doored basement armory. Deatherage winked at the chief, extracted a flask from his overcoat, and they shared a nip.

Foster said, "So what's Dan planning? I hear he couldn't get the workers from the other refineries to lift a hand."

"They did at first. But that Red bitch got to them, poisoned them against working at all. I'm telling you, she's gonna have to be dealt with." He lit the cigarette, then held the match steady to light Foster's. "Something like that, I've always seen it as a local responsibility. Aren't there any wide-awake, patriotic Americans in this town?"

"There's a few. But—"

"But what?"

The chief didn't answer. Instead he said again, "So what's Dan planning now?"

"We've arranged for some outside missionaries. Men who are available for temporary work and are reliable hands."

Foster lowered the flask. "Strong-arm boys? I don't want any trouble, Mr. Deatherage."

Deatherage carefully kept contempt from his face. The sheep kept bleating that: "No trouble, no trouble." What good was a cop who recoiled from a scrap? "That is my goal too. But to settle this matter, we have to get these slackers back to work. It's gone beyond a disagreement about safety and wages. The company has offered to compromise, yet still they refuse to return. It's simple pigheadedness now. Or worse. You must see that. This can't be doing Main Street any good."

"No, holiday sales are way down."

"Everyone's losing money. Isn't there something the city

council, the mayor, can do to fix this thing up?"

"We've tried. You're right, they don't want to listen. Oh, and I heard a rumor about trouble over at Holderlin. That's going to shut the town right down, if they go out too."

"See how it spreads? Chief, we need to talk about making my men deputies. If those Reds down at Number One start any rough stuff, I'd hate to have them walking around without legal protection."

Foster said he'd ask the city attorney. Shortly afterward, Deatherage touched his hat brim. They shook hands, and he climbed the stairs up to the street level.

The truck was gone, and the alley behind the great sooty brick pile of City Hall was filled with the motionless mist of early morning. This high in the hills, the clouds seemed to descend at night, filling the valleys and hollows with vapory tendrils of cloud-stuff. Deatherage stood by his car, musing over his preparations. The munitions had been the last item. That fool Vansittart had objected. Said he didn't like the idea of gassing his employees. He'd pointed out patiently that the idea was to have protective measures in place; if things got ugly it was far better to depend on gas than bullets. But this says machine guns, Vansittart had said. Why am I ordering machine guns?

To guard against the worst, Deatherage had told him. Better to have the wherewithal to put down violence and not have to use it, than to be caught short when agitators whipped a mob into riot. As they had in a number of cases in which he had been involved. Anyway, the Thompsons were registered to the city police; they were only on loan to the plant protection force. He'd advised the plant manager to see to several other matters along the same lines. Another fire-fighting line and a steam line should be run to the main gate. Trucks should be furnished, ready to rush reinforcements from point to point. And he'd recommended to the mayor that city employees remove the motley collection of used railroad ties and tires and so forth from the riverbank in the vicinity of the gate. So far, he hadn't seen any action taken on that one; but those he'd recommended to Thunder, all had been completed.

When the noon train came to a stop, the broad man in a black sack suit and scuffed brown brogans swung down off it carrying a cheap cardboard suitcase. Others came off with him, congregating in front of the station.

The man in the black suit was named Kevin Shannon. He was from Philadelphia, where he did jobs for the company Deatherage represented, and other companies in the same line of business. He'd worked for an importing organization during Prohibition, but with the return of legal alcohol had to find some other means of earning a living. He'd gotten the word about this job and gone down to the area around the Reading Depot, and found other men he knew and gotten them together and put them on the train.

They were standing in the cold air, smoking and passing around a bottle, when Deatherage's dark green Terraplane drove up. He cranked down the window. "Mr. Shannon?"

"Here, sir." Shannon stepped out, flicking his cigarette aside and coming to a lazy attitude of attention.

Deatherage asked him if everyone was accounted for, and told them to head across the street, to Cassidy's.

"One beer apiece, that's all he's going to give you. I don't want you going in drunk. You'll need your wits about you. All right, here's a gentleman from the company, to say a couple words."

"Hello, boys. I'm Otto Goerdeler, senior foreman down at Thunder. I understand you're hard workers. Glad to have you with us." The men stared back expressionlessly, slumped in the worn chairs spaced out on scuffed linoleum. There was no one else in the bar. One of the newcomers lounged against the door, arms folded, in case anyone should drift in.

When Goerdeler fumbled to a stop, Deatherage stood and outlined the situation in brusque sentences. The plant in question was an oil refinery. Entrances were being blocked by strikers; they were ignoring injunctions. "The police chief started soft, but he's going to see reason. On the other hand, the union sonsabitches are starting to play rough. They already beat up one of our boys, caught him outside the gate and beat him up. Isn't that right, Kelly?"

The shovel-faced man nodded from over by the bar. "Four of 'em," he said through swollen lips. "Held my arms, and beat me up."

"So that's the situation, the kind of scum you're gonna be head to head with. We could take you in at night, or sneak you in in a freight car, but we're not going to do that. You have the legal right to go in, and we're going to insist on those rights. You're here to teach these people respect for the law. Anybody packing?"

Several men nodded almost imperceptibly. "Don't show 'em unless one of them pulls one first. We don't need any martyrs, okay? And there just might be some boys from the press there looking on. Fists and sticks and coshes. Understand what I'm saying? Now, there any questions?"

Shannon raised his hand. "Sounds like it might not go so easy at the gate."

"That's why there's a bonus. A fin for each man who gets past the pickets."

"Ten."

"No good, Kevin. It's set up with the client already. You're each getting one-ten an hour for every hour you spend in the plant. Plus chow and a bed and incidentals. That was the agreement and it's no good asking for more." Deatherage checked his watch. "Okay, the trucks are waiting outside. Go to it, and good luck."

None of them noticed the barkeep, who turned from washing glasses as they crowded out, crossed the floor to the phone booth, and groped in his change apron for a buffalo nickel.

Halvorsen stood against the fence, hands in his coat pockets, the sign leaning against the chain link. Nobody had come by all morning, no cars, nothing but the nearly empty trolley rocking and squealing past every hour. That and the steadily

falling snow. His breath eddied around his face, then drifted
away in the crisp air. Christ, if only this cold would back
off. Made sense, the winter they went on strike had to be the
coldest anybody could remember. He glanced at the others.
Since the incident with the scabs, Melnichak had doubled the
pickets, and Golden had given them some tips as to what to
do if anyone tried to get in again.

One good thing about it, they'd stopped the trickle of men
back to work. A few had even come back out again. Old Mr.
Washko, Jennie's dad, was one of those who'd returned to
the fold. He and Halvorsen still hadn't passed a word, but
he'd told Shorty he just didn't feel right, looking out and
seeing them standing out here. Made him feel like a heel and
a backstabber. So he'd grabbed his lunchpail and sashayed
out past the bulls. Right now he was huddled over the trash-
can fire down by the shack, rubbing his gloves together.

But there were still scabs in there. They watched them
walk in at seven thirty every morning. There wasn't any
more joking. When they yelled an insult or warning now,
they meant it. And if a man encountered another in a bar
after hours, and one had spent the day on the picket line and
the other inside the gate, well, there might be words exchanged. And then punches, till their friends had to pull them
apart, and the two sides would separate again, silent and
watchful until they were out of sight of each other.

In a way, he figured they were winning. Thunder hadn't
produced a quart of oil in a month. That had to hurt, even
if they'd built inventory before the boys actually went out.
But the strike treasury was busted, the money from the
OWIU gone now, and most of the guys' savings were gone
too, those that had had any to begin with. The ones with
families came in every morning looking haggard. You could
see they weren't getting enough to eat: they were saving it
for the kids. It was too goddamn bad.

We just got to stick, Halvorsen thought. There ain't nothing else for it. Just got to stick, till Thunner gives out.

He was thinking that when the trucks swung around the
corner and headed down along the frozen river toward him.

*			*			*

The man in the gray overcoat lit an Old Gold and flicked the smoking match away, leaning against his car inside the Gower Avenue gate. The picketers at the east end of the plant had given way sullenly before his nudging bumper. He'd stared them down through the windscreen, until their eyes dropped and they sidled aside. Scruffy, pallid wraiths. Why the hell didn't they get wise?

But it was a good thing they didn't. Without their stupidity, their cowlike loyalty to the other fools, there'd be no call for his services.

At the moment, he was content. Forty men at a dollar ten an hour. Shannon and the other nobles got a little more but not enough to make a difference. Vansittart didn't realize yet that they'd be drawing pay for twenty-four hours a day. But if they were inside the gates, that was damn well how they'd be billed. Thunner would squawk, but once he saw they were all that stood between his precious plant and destruction, he'd pay up. Would pay for much more, now that he'd chosen to ride the whirlwind . . . his eyes narrowed as the total assembled itself in his head. Over a thousand a day for Shannon's boys. Fifteen percent of that was the agency's, and half of *that* was his.

A very nice seventy-five a day, on top of daily billing and expenses. With proper nurturing, it would grow fast now.

He didn't mind advising executives, ordering munitions, training the guard force. It all went on his daily rate. But the real money was in violence, the longer and more widespread, the better. It was a rule of the business. The rougher things got, the more readily the money flowed.

Stick to the union, boys, he thought. We work together, you and I, and we can make this go on a long time.

A faint smile curved his lips. Then vanished, as he felt the telltale trickle at the edge of his damaged mouth. Dabbing his chin dry with the freshly laundered handkerchief he was never without, he looked out coldly on the field of coming strife.

*			*			*

Halvorsen was still thinking this, that no matter how rough it got they had to stick, when he saw the trucks bearing down on him. At the same moment an auto horn began honking in town, in staccato bursts. The danger signal.

He pulled himself off the fence, and sprinted for the far side of the avenue. The vehicles grew steadily, looming out of the falling snow as they plowed toward him.

His yell brought men spilling out of the line shack and the tents. They stared blankly at the oncoming trucks, then began running across the field toward the gate. They carried axe handles, two-by-fours, and lengths of rod-line. They came silently, running intent across the snow.

He reached the pile of ties and with another man grabbed one and lugged it toward the road. Saturated with ice, it seemed heavy as the earth. After a few yards they had to drop one end and both grab the other to drag it along. Finally they got it to the center of the street. Dropped it there, then levered it over until the spikes that had been hammered into it faced up. Behind them other teams dropped a second and then a third across the roadway, making a solid barrier of heavy oak baulks and sharpened iron teeth.

The trucks' horns sounded suddenly, together and all at once, like a herd of charging, trumpeting animals. The wheels locked, and snow leaped up, compressed pellets of it spraying up as the brakes slammed on.

He left the road and ran back for the gate, where a grim-faced phalanx of maybe twenty workers holding clubs and weapons now confronted the vehicles as they plowed, rocking, to a halt.

The canvas flaps at their backs jerked aside, and men jumped down to the snowy road. One slipped and went sprawling, but the others stepped over him to deploy. They spread out, then stopped, standing with legs apart, surveying the gate and the grim line marshaled before it. Most wore dark overcoats and hats. Some carried clubs of their own. Others slipped on brass knuckles, or slapped blackjacks lovingly into leather gloves.

"Damn, they're big," said a man behind Halvorsen. Another muttered, "Sluggers, they call 'em. I seen boys like this in Oil City, the tankmakers' strike."

The leader, a broad man in a black suit and high-topped brogans, stepped slowly forward. He rocked as he came, like a seaman. The others waited, immobile save for the steady slap of cudgels and blackjacks.

"Hey, you. We're new hires. You fellas know what's best for ye, you'll step out of our way."

"You ain't crossin' our line," Halvorsen yelled. He wasn't the official leader, but the men had all looked his way.

"Better clear out. Law's on our side, boys."

From behind Halvorsen, a youthful high voice yelled, "Hey, we don't give a good goddamn if you're Jesus Christ on a band box. He *said* you ain't crossin' our line."

The suited man turned his slow attention to Halvorsen. "We're crossin' it, all right. Oney question is whether you're goin' to be standing up after we do."

The high voice from behind him again, and this time he glanced back to see that it was the redheaded kid, Latimer. "Why, they ain't nothing but a bunch of goddamn finks. You want a taste a this, come on and show your cards," he yelled, swinging his sign like a baseball bat. "Right, boys?"

The black suit came striding in, and the others fell in behind him. Their boots crunched in the snow.

She saw the two faraway lines of men come together, and for a moment it was like an Eisenstein movie; soundless but full of drama; black shapes locked in struggle against the stark, incandescence of the snow. Men crouched, then reeling away. Raised clubs, fists, bludgeons. Then a flurry of motion, and tiny figures collapsing.

She was watching from Pearson's car, up on the hill, as they sped downward toward Number One and the river. Then they passed in front of a line of houses, and she couldn't see it anymore.

"Faster," she said, filled all at once with a terrible fear.

*   *   *

Halvorsen was still tender in his fist, so he held on to the sign. The black-suited man had locked eyes with him, and kept coming; so he stood his ground and waited. The other held a short strapped object in one hand. A sap, a cosh, a leather club, no doubt weighted with lead.

As they met, the other guy reached for his sign, and Halvorsen kicked the butt of it up from the snow, aiming for his gut. The thug parried it, grabbing it with his left, and slammed the cosh down on the length of wood so hard the shock tingled his hands. Then reached under it for him. Halvorsen evaded his grab and kicked him in the shin as hard as he could.

"I'm gonna take you apart piece by piece, scumbag." The man grinned. "And it's gonna be fun."

He came in again, evading Halvorsen's clubbed sign to slam the cosh down on his arm so hard a lightning-flash of pain burst behind his eyes. Or was it in his eyes . . . no, the flash had come from over by the gate, where several cars had drawn up. He jerked his attention back just in time to catch the blackjack whipping in again. He tried to slip the blow, protecting his head, but memory and consciousness alike ended there.

Thunner stood watching from the second-floor office. He hadn't wanted this. But he'd tried the gentle approach. The malcontents hadn't responded. They'd intimidated the other workers so thoroughly they wouldn't lift a hand. Descended to derailings, arson, beatings. Now the men who'd stayed loyal were slipping away. It had become a test of wills.

He glared down, fists clenched, wishing he could go down there himself. By God, he'd love to get his hands on one of them. He couldn't understand how a man could turn his back on his work, his employer, his country, his family. But the men out there were in some mysterious thrall. The drab little woman he'd thrown out of his office had some hold over them.

Well, he was through coddling them. He'd blow Thunder up with dynamite before he'd turn it over to people like that.

Because they could never build. Only destroy.

Iron in his heart, he watched the lines crash together. Saw men close, and struggle; saw some go down, and others stagger back, tottering about holding their heads in their hands, until other figures caught up and clubbed them down into the trampled snow. And his fingers dug into his palms and he shuddered as it became another snowy landscape; far away in space and time; yet ever immanent, present, in his memory and his nights. Where men in greatcoats and coal-scuttle helmets bayoneted and were shot by other men in khaki over a landscape foul with death and burning, the skies roofed with the greasy gray snow that fell through the smoke of burning French villages.

He remembered one November night after he lost three men to the snipers the Boche left behind in every factory chimney and ruined churchtower. The company had lagged back in the advance, afraid to stick their heads out of cover. And it was terrifying; he'd felt naked and vulnerable himself every moment there was enough daylight to sight a rifle. He'd gathered them in an abandoned Hun dugout and explained to them how they had to accept the danger, in the name of a greater good. How their sacrifice meant this horror would never touch their own land, their own families.

He watched for a long time, teeth bared, hands twitching at his sides. Then turned away abruptly, sick with the fullness of what he himself had willed.

Halvorsen blinked, conscious only of tremendous light and tremendous pain. The light came from a pale square of pinkish blue. The pain filled his skull, so jagged and huge it left no room for thought.

Then something cold came down across his forehead, and the square was eclipsed by a woman's breast.

He rolled his head, to see that he was in a small, nondescript room. A white iron bedstead. A chair, with Doris Golden in it, leaning forward again to adjust the cloth.

When her eyes caught his she raised her eyebrows and sat

back. "So, you're awake. We had the doctor up. He said to keep an eye on you when you came to. Can you talk?"

He grunted, "Uh-huh. Where am I?"

"The Hemlock Hotel. My room."

". . . my place."

"You needed looking after," she said brusquely. "Several of our boys were injured. We set up an infirmary down at the restaurant, but there weren't enough beds. So I volunteered mine."

He cleared his throat with an effort, eyeing the peach-colored wrapper she was wearing. "Where are you gonna . . . ?"

"Don't bother about that. I can sleep on the floor. It won't be the first time, I assure you."

He stirred and tried to sit up, but she shoved him down. "You better let me up," he said.

"You're staying right there till the doctor comes back."

"I got to use the bathroom."

"Then you'll just have to let me help, won't you?"

It was embarrassing, but only, apparently, for him. When she eased him back down and pulled up the coverlet, he closed his eyes. He heard her heels tap across the room, a door creak. Before she went away down the hallway he said, "I feel kind of thirsty. Could I have a drink?"

When she returned he sipped at the glass, then sank back. Damn, his head . . . he suddenly remembered the fight, and struggled to sit up again. "What happened? Did the finks get past us? We stopped them, didn't we?"

"They got through. They had to drag some of them in, though."

"Well, that's good, anyway."

"Yeah, you boys put up a good fight," she added, but he saw that she was worried.

"What is it? What's wrong?"

She unfolded the evening *Deputy-Republican* and he saw the photograph on the front page. Himself, clubbing back at the fellow who'd attacked him. The angle at which it had been taken didn't show the other man's blackjack. It looked as if he were unarmed and Halvorsen was striking him down. STRIKERS ATTACK LOYAL WORKERS was the headline. Below that it read TEN INJURED IN PITCHED BATTLE AT THUNDER NUMBER ONE. MAYOR WARNS OF WIDER VIOLENCE.

"The bourgeois press in action," she said. "Can you read that? Does it look like you're seeing double? Good, there's probably no concussion then." She folded the paper and tossed it aside with a look of distaste. "They *know* what happened. The son-of-a-bitch reporter took down my statement. Is it in there? Look in vain."

He looked up at her profile, her dark hair cupping it, her determined, fiery eyes. She wasn't a beautiful woman. Not the kind you'd pick out first at a dance. But her anger made her beautiful. And without thinking about it, because if he had he probably wouldn't have done it, he reached out and took her hand.

To his surprise, it was trembling. She looked down at it. "There's no place for this," she said after a moment.

"Don't you feel it? I do."

"What do you feel?"

"Admiration," he said. "Friendship. I'm not real good at talking about it." He closed his eyes, then opened them again to hers. "Don't you?"

"All I feel is mad, Bill. There's no room for anything else." She went on, lashing out against the bosses, the criminal scum they employed, the corruption that oozed everywhere through the veins of a sick and dying system; it was quite a speech. It almost made him forget that her hand was still in his, that her fingers were searching across his palm. Lingering on the scars. Exploring the pads of tough skin where the bull-rope had burned. When she fell silent at last, he hesitated; wondering if what he was doing was betrayal, of the cause, of his comrades; then decided he didn't care. And she must not have thought so either, for when he reached up she resisted for only a moment. Only enough to make it her own act, when those fiery lips lowered themselves to meet his own.

Eighteen

Dick Shotner was walking along the crooked broken brick sidewalks of Seward Avenue when he saw the shadows moving up on the hillside. It was six o'clock in the evening, the middle of January, and the city had never put lights in this part of town. It was where the few colored people in Hemlock County lived, here and across the river. He stopped. It would be wisest to walk on. Then he wondered, with a surge of excitment, if it might be something his dad and his new friends would want to know about.

He left the walk quietly and slid up between two shotgun houses, hardly any snow at all between them, the paintless cracked siding boards so close on either side he could have touched them both without extending his arms. His heart began to pound. A cow mooed, sidling aside, and he smelled its ordure and oil smoke and human waste. The shadows were full dark now, and he was one with them. Uphill, through another, even more ramshackle and crowded street of shacks and tin-roofed sheds, the ground between them unpaved but the snow swept neatly away to reveal frozen black mud.

There they were again, running lightly along the top of a boxed-in structure that ran above the roofs, upward toward the high woods above the sleeping town.

He halted, wondering what he was getting himself into. He looked through a window not three feet away, seemingly into the face of an old woman who sat staring at something out of his range of vision. Dance music seeped through the rotting wood. He stood in darkness. To her he did not exist. His lips curved bitterly. It was how people had looked at him all through school. The boy with the weird writhing gestures, the halting, tongue-tied speech. Kids who hardly knew what a bastard was knew he was one. Yes, he was used to whispers, averted looks. So that when the man who had never been there all your life looked your way at last, acknowledged you existed, even in the dark, even as a secret—

A hammering came from above, then the crash and splinter of wood breaking.

He bent and ran awkwardly, past the last henhouse and chicken run, and scrambled up through briars and snowdrifts into the treeline. Here and there vast gradual depressions, as if of shell fire, still marked where the great hemlocks had been torn from the soil decades before. He stepped into them, staggering as he fought through the icy black claws of brambles.

He crept out from the woods, farther up the hill, toward a pool of flickering yellow that gradually came into sight.

In the light of an old-fashioned railroad lantern, four men were swinging pickaxes. With each blow the crack and echo of hollow wood splitting came to his ears. He huddled, hugging himself, eyes wide in the dark.

When the last plank was pried away, the lantern rose. It showed them all what lay within the long coffin-box that snaked down the hillside, braced and undergirded with heavy timbers, stuffed and insulated with rags and straw.

The men conferred over it. Then they bent, and his fox-cocked ears caught the creak and squeal of long-untouched bolts being unfastened. Simultaneously he made out a familiar voice.

He got to his feet, understanding now, and stumbled down the hillside toward them.

Halvorsen whirled, and he saw the others jerk around at the same time; Melnichak leveled a revolver. They stared at the coated figure that waded through the deep snow toward them.

"Hey, Bill, is that you? It's m-me. Dick."

The tension broke in curses. "What the hell is he doing here?" "Pipe down. Goddamn it."

Furious, Halvorsen hissed, "Is there anybody following you? Goddammit, Shotner, you got no business mixed up in this."

"Ain't it enough that I hate my lousy dad?"

"What'd he say?" asked one of the others.

"Nothing," said Halvorsen, and led his boardinghouse mate a little way off. "Look, you told me about Dan Thunner and your mom and all that, and I sympathize. You got a rotten deal. But it ain't going to do you any good getting beat up by his bulls, if they come out of those woods. Or get thrown in prison for destroyin' property. So why don't you just get going on down back to Miz Ludtke's and let us do what we gotta do."

"I know what you're doing. Sabotaging the c-crude line."

"Yeah, that's what we're doing." Halvorsen peered back down the hill, fearful lest somebody had seen the kid climbing up along the pipeline that carried heated fresh petroleum from the Cherry Hill field down to the refinery.

"W-well, I w-want to help."

"This is our fight. You want to pick a scrap, start something over at the battery plant. Start a union, like you said."

"I never said that. I got nothing against the boss over there. He's an all right guy. Kind of hardheaded, is all. Him and me, we get along. Last week he said—"

Halvorsen debated simply planting one on the point of his chin and dragging him off into the woods. Now he was saying, "I know you fellas are acting up. Tipping over the cars,

when people try to drive into N-N-Number One. I read about
it in the paper. Hey, I think it's great. Oh . . . heck."

Simultaneously with his exclamation, Halvorsen realized
that a dark slow flood had crept through the snow toward
them; was even now sliding and trickling around his boots,
Shotner's galoshes. The sweet, heavy odor of Pennsylvania
crude eddied up, filling his nostrils. The heavy fumes made
his head spin. That would be the natural gasoline, the lightest
fraction of the crude when it came out of the ground. Years
ago they'd thrown it away, burned it off. It was too volatile,
too dangerous.

He shoved the kid suddenly, then again, making him stagger. "Get down the hill. Get out of this stuff. Run. Run!"

Behind them a flame glowed. It danced in the forest darkness, struggling with the wind. Then it grew brighter.

Shadows lurched toward them, running and jumping over
uneven ground. The fire grew swiftly behind them, yellow-
white flame licking hungrily out over the surface of a black
stream. Building and spreading. Until by the time they
reached the street and separated it was a massive column of
golden fire, towering above the town, lighting from within a
flickering immense column of smoke far darker than the winter night.

Left alone on the pavement under a streetlight, Dick Shotner realized he had a choice to make.

The clock ticked slowly in the office on Main Street the next
morning. Deatherage sat at the long table where Thunner had
first received him. He was reading letters and reports, occasionally making a notation, or squinting his eyes at the fireplace as he thought.

At precisely nine Vansittart and Hildebrandt came in. The
plant manager hung his hat, looking tired. "Good morning,
gentlemen. Any progress?" said Deatherage, turning the papers over, facedown.

"Line's back in operation. But they spilled two hundred
barrels before the pumper station noticed the pressure dropping."

"Is that a lot?"

"Not really. And we don't actually own the oil till it comes through the fence, you see, so the loss is not ours. It's Connie Kleiner's, or rather, his father's."

"What do the police say?"

The lawyer snorted. "We don't have Mr. Sherlock Holmes on duty, apparently. It's obvious who opened the valves, but as for an arrest . . ."

Rudy Weyandt came in from the outer office as the senior men seated themselves. The executive secretary took a chair at the foot of the table, and listened attentively as Vansittart told them about hearing the news on the radio that morning, a ten-cent advance in East Texas crude to $1.15 a barrel. "The first price increase since nineteen thirty-three," he said. "Now, tell me that's bad news."

"It is if you don't have an operating refinery."

"What about this wrecked pipeline?" murmured Deatherage, returning the papers to his briefcase.

"It's back in operation. Didn't I say that?"

"But what's to prevent them doing it again? Tonight, if they wish?"

"Nothing, far as I can see. The only solution is to post guards along it. Kleiner won't. He says he'd rather just stop pumping, avoid the chance of loss and damage. Foster refuses to help. Says he needs his boys in town."

Vansittart: "We can't operate without a steady supply of crude."

"Wheeler has barely enough men now to hold the perimeter." Deatherage took out a small book and leafed through it. "I can phone up more personnel. If you approve."

Vansittart looked torn. "We've got to keep the crude flowing, or we can't operate," he said at last. "I see no other solution. I believe Mr. Thunner will have to agree."

"How many miles of exposed pipeline up there?"

Vansittart told him. Deatherage made a calculation and recommended fifteen additional men. The manager protested that that was too many. Deatherage pointed out that they had to have three shifts, plus a spare man or two for sickness or unexpected absence.

Thunner arrived at nine-thirty. "Earl, Rudy, Ellis; Pearl. Sorry to keep you waiting," he said, crossing to the sideboard and drawing a cup of tea. "The Ministerial Association asked me to come down and explain the situation. The Presbyterians are on our side. They asked the others to come out against the strike. The Methodists and Catholics voted it down. But Reverend Sloan and Father Guertin offered to speak to the strikers, if I thought it might do any good. . . . What have you got for me? Where's Otis?"

Vansittart explained that he and the senior foreman were alternating duty at the plant, sleeping in the office, in case an emergency arose. Etterlin spent most of his time there anyway, since he was single. Each man briefed in turn on the area under his charge. Thunner listened with a frown, looking at one of the Remington bronzes as if he expected the bronc to begin bucking. When they reached the events of the night he said harshly, "I read it in this morning's news. I want the man who did it. What's Jerry say?"

"He says he can't tell from the evidence. Most likely the strikers, but—"

"That's perfectly obvious. No one else would deliberately dump and destroy crude. Mr. Deatherage. Your source on the committee, the one who's feeding you the minutes and so forth. Can you find out names for me?"

After a moment Deatherage said quietly, "I quite possibly could."

"Do so, then."

"But there might not be enough to prosecute in a court of law." Deatherage waited, then, when Thunner did not respond, took out his notebook. "I'll put my man on it," he said.

They discussed the need for protecting the pipeline. Thunner's lips tightened, but he approved additional armed guards. He asked Vansittart how the plant restart was proceeding. The manager said it wasn't.

"It isn't? Why not?"

"The outside men won't work."

"The ones we're paying a dollar-ten an hour to?"

"These are not scabs, Mr. Thunner," Deatherage explained. "These are strikebreakers. Those men you had in from surrounding refineries, those were scabs. The men we've been advertising for in the papers, new hires from TioPenn and elsewhere, they would be scabs. But these are not. I believe I explained to you prior to their hire, that they were not trained oilmen. I am afraid they are not now inclined to add that skill to their list of special qualifications."

"They won't even sweep out their quarters," said Vansittart. "It's getting to be a sty over there in the infirmary. I've spoken to Shannon about it. About the drinking and card playing, too. He does not seem to be a man singularly penetrable to reason; if I may say so."

"Mr. Shannon gets a job done," said Deatherage. "He's talented, in his rough way. But I will speak to him about those matters."

"Anything else?" asked Thunner, putting his hands flat on the table, preparing to rise.

"I have a proposal, sir," said Weyandt.

"State it."

"The plant has been idle over a month now. But so have the strikers. I think it's time to move in for the knockout."

"How?" said Hildebrandt. "They've shown no signs of buckling. It seems to me that whatever we've thrown at them has just made them harder."

Deatherage said, "Which is exactly what they want you to believe. In reality their condition is desperate. Would you like to know how much they have in their treasury?" He tapped his briefcase. "I'll tell you: thirty-five dollars."

"What can they be living on?" said Hildebrandt.

Weyandt said, "Hope alone, and desperation, and the charity of the few merchants who will still extend them credit. I've spoken to some of our local merchants, sir. Grocers and so forth. Trying to feel out just how strapped they're getting, on the other side. The average worker's savings are minuscule at best, and now they are exhausted. They've sold, or hocked, everything they can carry. Their kids are hungry. They're afraid. I think that with one last push, that line will break."

"What do you suggest?"

"The velvet glove of forgiveness and, beneath it, the iron hand of fear."

Thunner said quietly, "Not quite so flowery, Rudy. Just give it to me straight. I'm as eager to get this over as they are."

"Very well, sir. Let's make them a final offer. We can't do it directly, but perhaps we can use these clergymen you mentioned as mediators. Give them the safety committee. Bring your wages up a bit more. But hold firm on the big one: no recognition. The public will support you. You can't recognize an organization that gives way to violence. The police will back you too. Foster understands that any further sabotage must be ruthlessly suppressed."

"I don't believe raising wages is economically possible in this market," said Deatherage, who had followed the conversation closely.

"Perhaps not for long. But surely we can afford it for a time. Once the union is out of the ring, we can reduce them again. In six months. A year."

Thunner nodded slowly. The secretary continued, "That's the velvet glove. The iron is: You've got to make it plain that this is the last chance for your former employees, not only here, but throughout the oil region. Any man not coming back as of the thirty-first, say, is not only fired, but blacklisted."

"The blacklist has been outlawed," said Hildebrandt.

"All of us here understand that," said Weyandt. "But is it our fault if the men should not believe we still, as employers, occasionally discuss matters pertaining to employment policy? The foremen are contacting their men occasionally at home, right? They can pass that along confidentially."

They discussed it for a time and decided to back up a feeler via Reverend Sloan and Monsignor Guertin with an advertisement in the local papers. As the clock struck eleven,

Thunner got up, slapping the table. "Rudy, I feel good about this. The churches on one side, the whip on the other. If we hammer hard, this time they'll crack. If only there was some way to get that message across to the leadership."

He and Deatherage exchanged a wordless look. Then they left, one by one, each man with his own thoughts locked in his heart.

Mr. Cassidy turned them away when they tried to come in for their weekly meeting. Said, wiping his hands on his apron, that he was sorry. He was on their side. He'd proven that, hadn't he? They were welcome as individuals. But he couldn't host the union meeting anymore. Mr. White owned his building. They'd understand, he was sure.

"You think I'm ever coming back through these doors, you're wrong," Pearson told him. Cassidy started to protest, then fell silent. He went back behind the bar.

Halvorsen suggested the back room of the Scarlet Slipper, where he'd won his bundle. So that now they sat around one of the tables, the only folks there this early in the day, eating spaghetti off the hot plate and drinking Manru from the icebox. The five of them: Lew, Stan, Shorty, Halvorsen, and Doris. He watched her wind pasta around her fork with a strange mingling of desire and questioning. There was some barrier between them still. One kiss had passed between them, almost chaste, but unforgettable. One kiss, and no more.

"You must be feelin' better, Red. You're sure goin' to town on Timmy's spaghetti."

Halvorsen grunted that he felt all right.

When D'Orso went back into the kitchen Melnichak said, sitting forward, "Okay, here's the deal. Four ministers came to see me this morning. Did you see the paper? The same offer as in there. Thunder's giving us two weeks. Come back by the thirty-first, the last day of January, or we're fired."

"Not just that. I heard they're drawing the blacklist up."

"They can't do that no more."

"You tell Dan Thunner and the other bastards who own

this state what they can't do. It ain't gonna be on paper. We just ain't gonna get a job after this."

They sat silent. Then Quarenquio burst out, "I tell ya, we've got to use our beans. Come up with something. We wreck a tank car, hell, it ain't Thunder's railroad. We bust up the pipeline, it ain't Thunder's oil. It makes us look like Bolsheviks and that's what people are startin' to call us. He can set all the deadlines he wants, I ain't going back, but we got to hurt Mr. Daniel Christly Thunner. There ain't no other way to make the sonofabitching company crack."

Melnichak said quietly, "What you mean? Blow up his house or something?"

"A little dynamite might get things moving."

After a moment Golden said quietly, "It could also land us all in the electric chair."

"Maybe you got a better suggestion."

She shrugged. "I've seen lots of strikes. They ain't any of them easy. You just got to stick."

"We can't stick forever," said Pearson. "Oh, I can, and Billy here. Hail, we can live in the woods and shoot deer, and eat dandelions and blackberries in the spring. But the boys who's got families—they're just about at the end of their row."

Quarequio: "I heard a good one yesterday. One of the fellas on the line, he says, why, if I found fifty cents in my pocket, I'd know I had somebody else's pants on."

"Har de har."

"What about Holderlin? Anybody know if they're coming out?"

Golden said, "I met with the shop steward and several of the men yesterday, to ask for money and help. They're discussing a strike vote themselves. The trouble is, they're AF of L. I got the laying-on-of-hands routine, but no contribution."

"Bastards."

"But we still got to stick."

The southerner upended his bottle. "Thunner's hurtin' too. They ain't shipped a can or a case since we walked out. I got a guy on the inside, he's a scab, but we talk. He tells me them finks in there ain't turning a hand. Boozing it up, playing craps all night long. They even been bringing girls in from Miss Minnie's. That adds up to heavy sugar. We keep poor-mouthing ourselves but old Dan ain't got all the money in the world neither. All we got to do is give him that last shove."

"Let me tell you about something the workers did in Akron," Golden said then.

She told them about the baseball game one day when the teams from two factories refused to play because the umpire was a company man they hated. The ump refused to leave, so both teams simply sat down on their bases, in the outfield, wherever they were. They wouldn't play ball. They just sat, until in confusion and rage the ump was replaced. And how the next week a dispute had broken out between some workers and a supervisor in one of the plants, and they were on the edge of giving in when one of the men said, "Aw, to hell with him, let's just sit down." And how their simple refusal to touch their machines had brought the whole factory to a halt.

Shorty looked puzzled. "Swell, but we ain't in the plant no more. How can we sit down when we ain't in the plant?"

But Melnichak was nodding. "Use your noggin, sluggo. Don't you hear what she's saying? We go in and occupy it."

"What's Chief Foster gonna say about that?"

"What can he do? He can't arrest us all. Remember when we rebuilt the shack? We called their bluff and they backed down."

"We'll have to fight. Them finks, and the oil bulls—"

"We fought them before. This time we do it our way."

Heads together, they began to plan.

Deatherage was sitting in his room at the Grant House, listening to the radio news on KDKA. Federal government expenditures had just gone over the four-billion-dollar mark, with almost half of it deficit spending. The Japanese delegates had walked out of the five-power naval conference, ending all armaments limitations. Three little girls in Ebensburg were being questioned over the shotgun slaying of their father. When the phone rang he set down his glass, took a last drag on his cigarette, and stubbed it out. Cupping the mouthpiece, he said guardedly, "Hello."

"Mr. Deatherage? This is L-390. When the moon comes over the mountain."

"Unknown yesterday are the stars of tomorrow. Give your report."

The voice on the other end spoke for some time. The agency man listened, then reached into his coat, which was hanging on the valet, and got his notebook. Scribbled a line, holding the earpiece close to his ear.

"That's it. That's the decision."

"What time is it planned for?"

When the other rang off he looked for a moment at what he had written. It read, *Mass attack on No. One main gate six a.m. Refinery to be occupied. No guns.*

Deatherage poured himself another whiskey and drank half of it off. He looked out the window at the dark sky, eyes narrowed against the smoke from a fresh Old Gold.

At last he decided, and picked up the phone again.

"Sir? Pearl Deatherage here.

"I believe the time has come to smash this union business forever."

Nineteen

The next day it snowed about as hard as anyone in the county could recall, and to their horror and astonishment the snow was black. Some murmured about prophecies and the Bible, and disquiet persisted even after the radio said it was soil, from a great dust storm on the Plains. The streetlights burned all day as it fell, filthy and oppressive and even smelling somehow of the hopelessness and misery people knew from the newsreels lay to the West. By evening, with it still coming down hard from an immobile sky, the streets were empty. The committee called the picketers in from the refinery as dark fell. Nothing was moving, and they needed to ready themselves.

Halvorsen came awake startled in the cold dark, jerked upright by the ringing grind of his windup Westclox. He dressed without turning on the light and went padding downstairs through the icy boardinghouse shadows, carrying his boots in his hand.

By the time he got the furnace stoked and his heap shoveled off and cranked up and down to the diner, the others were already there. They sat in the booths, looking at the still-dark windows, warming their hands with mugs of the watery coffee and gnawing at slices of hard bread. The wives sat with their men, looking anxious. Some carried babies, or had small children clinging to their skirts. The children looked on with apprehensive eyes, some with thumbs tucking into their mouths, others exploring their streaming noses with their fingers.

Golden got up for a short talk. First she thanked those who were not members of Local 178 for being there. She appreciated the support of the active membership of the Holderlin works and other industrial organizations of the city. She reminded them that this was to be a peaceful occupation. They would defend themselves if attacked, but they would start it orderly and peaceable. She told the secretary to make sure he got those words down. Then she turned the meeting over to Melnichak.

Stan shrugged and looked around. "You all look pretty grim here, boys."

"We're hopin' for d' breaks, Stan."

"Okay then. You guys all got your stewards' orders. Remember what Doris said. We don't hit back till we're hit. But if you're hit, give the finks and goons something to remind them they don't want to mix with us again."

"Just a minute," said Golden, standing again. She held up a box, rattled it, then handed it to Halvorsen. "Pass these around, Red. Something to keep your spirits up."

Halvorsen picked one out and passed the box on. It was a simple disk of stamped metal, colored red, white, and blue. The shields read OWIU LOCAL NO. 178. And below that, IN UNION THERE IS STRENGTH.

Silently the men pinned them on coats and hats. Quarequio murmured, "Bill, you want to say anything?"

"Yeah, go it, Red."

He stood slowly, worked his chew, and spit brown juice into a pop bottle. "You guys sure are wantin' a lot of speeches out of me these days. Might change my mind about workin' fer a living, turn me into some kind of politician."

"Kiss my patootie if you do," someone yelled in a drunken voice. He was instantly silenced with hisses of "There's ladies here, you loudmouth."

He looked out on them, tired-looking and ragged and packed close together and smelling not all that great. They were hungry, and probably scared, too, of what was going to happen that morning. Propped against the booths were homemade saps and clubs, sucker-rod wrenches and bit hooks and lengths of rod-line and lead pipe. Italians. Hunkies. Germans. Irish. Scandahoovians, like him. Just workers. Just men, sick at last of having nothing, and ready to fight for their share.

All of a sudden, he felt proud.

"Boys, they may bust us, but they'll never forget this day. And neither will any of us. We're fightin' for the union— little 'u'—like our granddads fought for the Union with a capital U. Only this time, the slaves we're freein', it's every one of us.

"See, I figure we're not fighting for another nickel, or even for the safety committee. I know that's how this thing got started. But somehow along the way, it's got bigger than that.

"I know what I'm gonna be fightin' for this morning. It's the right to stand up and be counted. The right to take care of our wives and our kids. And just for the chance for all a us to hold up our heads. This here, this right here, is the liberty they make the speeches about on the Fourth of July. I don't know, but seems to me you got to fight for your freedom every few years. Or you lose it. And that's what we're gonna be out there marching for today."

He took another breath, wondering what the hell was wrong with him, why his eyes burned and his throat felt funny. "Anyway, I just wanted to say—I been in a few scraps, but there ain't been a one I been prouder of than this one. And there ain't nobody I'm prouder of than us. Damn it—let's go out there and show Dan Thunner what kind of stuff we're made of."

They didn't cheer. It wasn't the time to cheer. But he saw

the light in their eyes as he sat down. And it was the best feeling he'd ever had in his life.

Not too long after that, they went outside and began to load up. Halvorsen took three loads of them over, and the other men with cars took people who hadn't any, too.

The committee and several men with military experience had sat up late over a map of the plant. They had decided to attack the east gate this time. The Lincoln Avenue entrance was the farthest from the office and the infirmary, where the goons and bulls were stationed. The main powerhouse, the fire and pumping houses, were just inside the gate. Beyond them were the railroad spur and then mostly open ground, dotted to the north with crude tankage and to the south of O'Connor Street with the refined-product storage tanks.

He dropped his passengers two streets away and out of sight from the gate, in the playground of the Fifth Ward school. The old stone building was a lightless backdrop as they stood shivering in the morning dark, huddled against a cruel wind and the still-falling snow. He went back to the Alpine to make sure no one had shown up late. Then drove back, parked the Oakland on a side street that sloped down toward the river, and set the brake.

He got his tire iron out of the trunk, and walked up to the schoolyard to join them.

A woman stood in the darkness; he didn't recognize Doris until she said, "That was a good speech, Red."

"Thanks."

"Take care of yourself." She glanced around, as if to assure herself that no one was looking; then gave him a quick kiss on the cheek. "Take care."

When they moved out between the houses in front of the gate, Number One looked deserted. Head bent, he peered into the storm, but saw no one. The powerhouse smokestack rose into the gray sky till it was blotted out by the snow. A black line of freight cars stood motionless on the spur, every rivet and stringer and coupling traced in white shadow.

The line of men advanced, boots crunching and squeaking in the grimy snow. The quiet was weird, palpable. He swung the iron, relishing its weight. He kept blinking flakes from his eyes, trying to see who was holding the gate. Funny, he didn't see anyone there at all.

"Double time!" yelled somebody, and the column began to run.

They got to the fence yelling and screaming, and the ladders and ropes came up out of the crowd and dropped across the fence with a clash of steel. The ladders swayed as the younger men rushed up them, the older workers reaching up to steady them against the chain-link. Halvorsen pulled himself up hand over hand. He teetered for a moment at the top, then jumped down. He landed so hard the breath came out of him, but got up unhurt.

When he was sure nothing was broken, he ran for the gate.

Quarequio was there before him. Two blows of his sledge-hammer and the padlock flew apart. Dozens of reaching hands and shoving boots immediately drove the grilles inward. They opened like sluice gates on a great dam, and the flood of men poured in, already dividing as they entered the yard, each with a destination: a building, a valve, a tank.

Then the falling snow parted, like a curtain, and he saw the forms ducking beneath the freight cars, stepping around them, climbing over the couplings. Pausing for a moment on the ballast stone before stepping down in a ragged line toward them.

Every one carried a rifle.

A warning yell from behind him, and he whirled to see another party, all in gray greatcoats, trotting out from behind the powerhouse. The bulls were hauling a long hose. It dragged in the snow between the men who tugged on it.

Stand fast, or retreat? He whirled again and saw behind them, filing out from one of the houses outside the gate, yet another stream of uniformed men. The city constabulary. Trucks nosed in from side streets. The bobbing dark head of a horse, then another: mounted policemen debouching from a backyard, blocking the way back toward the school, barring their escape.

Just as he realized they were surrounded, Shorty yelled "Charge!" The mass of men quivered, then surged into motion, half headed farther into the plant, the others doubling back toward the gate.

He spun and went with the ones headed in, toward the railcars and the dimly seen line of riflemen before it. He saw Pearson ahead of him, running all-out toward the freight spur. A strange, confused surge of feelings clenched his throat. Fear, and rage at whoever had sold them out, and, from somewhere, a godlike, leaping joy. He swung the tire iron, hoping to get in at least one good lick before the sons of bitches shot him.

A ripple of flashes came from the spur. Unaccompanied by sound, strangely, but he did not mind the absence of hearing. He ducked, still running, expecting at every moment the blow of a bullet. Instead he saw that the shooters were aiming upward, and raised his eyes.

A swarm of black objects arrowed downward toward them. When they struck the ground some bounced up again, leaping like dolphins before burrowing under the snow. One struck a worker not ten yards from him; the wounded man fell to his knees, covering his face with his hands.

A fine mist streamed up, driven into their faces by the wind. It seemed to come from under the snow. His eyes began to burn, then his throat. He pulled up his coat, attempting to breathe through the cloth. But stumbling toward them, he couldn't help sucking it deeper into his lungs.

Suddenly he realized he was alone. That the line of shooters was advancing, that they were reloading their guns. He could see their faces now, set with hate. Fixed on him.

Gasping, weeping, he turned tail at last, and stumbled back into the stinging mist.

Driven back by the gas, half the crowd surged back toward the gates. Men fell there, gored against brick walls and iron fences by the blind tossing of the crowd, before a section of it collapsed outward, dragging down posts and fencing under the pressure of bodies. A short, rotund figure bent to grope beneath the snow, as if trying to free his boot from something; then straightened suddenly, breaking into a strange jerking dance before falling prone.

Then the crowd contracted, and forced itself outward through the gap into the street, where the horses waited, prancing nervously, blowing and snorting in the cold, snow-laden air.

The police line held firm for a moment, then began to bend inward.

Someone crouched, and pried up a brick from the road. It arched through the air, and fell into the midst of the blue line.

A hail of rocks, pipes, debris, and brickbats followed it, lofting, then raining down. A horse reared, screaming in terror and pain.

A cop leveled a revolver. For a moment, human voices faded away; there was something almost like silence, broken only by the the clatter of hooves and the distant yelling of the men still engaged inside the plant. Then Foster lunged across the line of uniforms and snatched the gun away.

Screaming hoarsely, the strikers charged. The blue line held for a moment more, then broke. The police scattered, retreating, chased by the strikers; and the horses reared, whinnying into a darkened sky.

Halvorsen emerged from the gas-shroud near the powerhouse with maybe a dozen men still with him. They were coughing and wheezing. Long strings of mucus dragged down from their faces. Their eyes stared red and weeping through blinking lids.

He was thinking he probably didn't look that great himself, when a cloud of whiteness burst out not far from them. A hoarse sibilance came from its heart, and, a moment later, screams.

The cloud was live steam, from hoses dragged by the plant guards. From other hoses water sprayed out. When the icy water hit men it dealt a shock almost like death. They reeled out of the spray unable to breathe, sinking to their knees, then getting up to run a few paces before falling at last to lie motionless on the snow.

The steam was choking, and blinding. It drove them back, unable to battle the men who stood behind it. Colorless, invisible when it emerged from the charged steam-nozzles, it flashed into white scorching vapor, burning and choking anyone within its range.

Only four of them made it into the powerhouse. Scabs stared as they came running in, then turned tail, abandoning the boiler room. He was still staring around at the maze of asbestos-padded pipes and steam drains when the steam-line gave an expiring hiss. Someone had found his way to the proper valve.

Outside the plant he heard someone yelling, a heavy, commanding voice. "Drop it, men. Ready your tear-gas bombs."

He hoisted himself to a window and smashed out a pane of frosted glass with the tire iron. He was surprised to find it still in his hand. It seemed as if he had run for miles, and had been battling for hours. But, peering through, he saw that it was only a hundred feet to the gate. Parties of men still swayed in struggle here and there inside the fence. The strikers were outnumbered, though, falling back in disorder.

They had to escape.

But before that, he wanted to make Thunder pay.

He went from valve to valve, spinning those that were open closed and those that were closed, open. Then he saw the clear tube half-full of water. He found the feed line and twisted the wheel closed. Then he ran from the door.

He was halfway back to the gate when a group of cops spotted him.

This time the attack was at close range. From the line of gray arched a thrown volley of cylinders, fat batons, tumbling over and over as they fell. One of the men who had come out of the powerhouse with Halvorsen bent to seize one. He was raising the smoking bomb to throw it back when it exploded, cartwheeling again into the air. The man grasped a shattered hand, staring at the bloody mass in disbelief until a police truncheon clubbed him to the ground.

Halvorsen ran on. The bluish mist of gas was thicker now, lower to the ground, and different. His eyes did not burn so much, but . . . a moment later he doubled, retching uncontrollably into the trampled snow. Another man ran by hatless, blood streaming from a long gash on his temple.

He was still doubled over, gagging, when a staccato sound echoed off the tanks and sheds. A worker spun and fell. Halvorsen dropped into the snow, hugging the solid earth beneath it as he heard lead going over his head with a buzzing hiss. Not a rifle bullet; it didn't crack the way a rifle bullet did.

Rolling over, searching desperately for shelter, he looked up for whoever was shooting at him. There: a dark-suited figure on an overpass. The winking light ceased the moment he glimpsed it. The figure dropped back out of sight.

As soon as the firing stopped, men leaped up and began to run for the gate. He found himself carried with them. Through the confusion of running strikers, through the drifting gas mist and the screaming. On the way out he stumbled over a heap in a snowdrift, realizing only after he picked himself up that it was a human body. He was running again before he realized what he was doing. Sobbing, he made himself stop. Forced his terrified body to turn and retrace its steps, bending in terror beneath his fear of more bullets.

Tugging at the outthrust hand, he felt something strange for a moment, almost like an electric thrill coming up from the limp flesh he grasped. He dropped it, startled; then made himself grasp it again.

Yelling to those streaming past to help him, he began dragging the wounded man to safety. He dragged the heavy body quite a few yards through the scuffed-up, dirty snow before he realized Shorty Quarequio was dead.

Twenty

When the interment was over, in the high old cemetery that overlooked the valley, he followed the others down the steep and icy slope. He and Pearson walked together. Golden was a little way off, with some of the women. The Italians were a black-clad shoal stumbling downhill together, enfolding the weeping family. Halvorsen crumpled the paper in his hand, thrusting it into his overcoat the way they'd thrust Shorty into the earth. He felt strange in the suit. He didn't own one; he'd had to borrow it from the old man at the boardinghouse. In the pockets he found old Huey Long pamphlets.

He hadn't wanted to speak, but Doris said somebody from the committee had to testify about the cause Quarequio had died for. This time he'd written down what he wanted to say. It was harder work than he'd thought, writing a speech. Damn near as hard as standing up in front of a bunch of people to give it.

And when he was done and sat down, there hadn't been any clapping. It was a funeral, after all. But he'd given it all he had. Told how Shorty had always been up front when it came to looking out for the workers. How he'd been one of the men who spoke up first, that night at the Lind, and later at the bowling alley when they pledged themselves to a union. How he'd never looked for anything for himself. Only for all workingmen.

And how he'd paid for that, falling over a live wire down at Thunder.

The cops had found it when they were clearing away the wounded, after the battle ended. Someone had connected a cable to the generator in the powerhouse, and led it out across the yard just inside the gate. Only the heavy snowfall had saved a lot more people being electrocuted. The company denied any knowledge of it. The state police said they were investigating what the *Deputy-Republican* called a "regrettable accident."

He spat into the snow.

He raised his eyes to see Jennie, trudging along with her head down not far away. He thought about it for a couple of steps, then said to Pearson, "I see somebody I know," and went off toward her.

"I didn't know you knew Shorty."

"His sisters work at the stocking factory. I came with them."

"Oh." He couldn't think of anything else to say, so he just dropped his eyes. They went along for a few steps, then the Italians stopped and began to argue about something. High-pitched keens split the air.

"That was just right, Red. Oh—excuse me."

Golden turned her dark eyes from him to Jennie. He was momentarily nonplussed at seeing them together. Beside Doris Golden, Jennie looked much younger than she was. She looked childlike, innocent . . . unmarked yet by whatever had dug its claws into the other woman's face, chilled her eyes, crimped her lips like a fork on a piecrust.

"Doris, this is Jennie Washko. Her brother was one of the fellows who died in the refinery accident. Jennie, this is Doris Golden."

"I'm sorry, kid. This must bring back painful memories."

"I just wonder how many more are going to get hurt before this is settled," Jennie said. She examined the woman carefully. She'd seen her before, but never up this close. She looked tired and old. She had to be in her thirties.

"That's up to the bosses, not to us. Anyway, W.T., I wanted to say that was just right. A funeral's not the place to whip the men up. We'll do that at the meeting tonight." He nodded and she said good-bye, with a last glance at Jennie, and went on down the hill, back erect, arms swinging.

Jennie said, "I never met a Jewish person before."

"Pretty much same as anybody else, seems to me."

"You seem to be good friends with her."

"Well, we're both on the strike committee," said Halvorsen, feeling uneasy, though he didn't think he had any reason he should feel guilty as far as Jennie was concerned. "There's my machine. Can I give you a ride home?"

"I guess so. As long as you let me off at the head of the street."

He didn't drive her back directly, though. Instead he turned east and took the north road along Todds Creek toward Beaver Fork. She didn't ask where he was going. Just sat with her purse in her lap, looking out as the woods and then the snow-covered fields went by. Her hair covered her face. Finally he said, "You heard about how he died."

"Mr. Quarequio? Yes. The electric wire. But nobody knows who put it there."

"Inside the fence like that? The goddamned company put it there, who the hell else? Sorry—I didn't mean to swear."

"It's all right. I'm getting sort of used to it, working at the factory."

"The cops say they're lookin' into it. It's an 'accident.' Two, three days, you watch, they're gonna say one of us strikers done it." He hammered the wheel. "The mayor, the town . . . I never knew this was how it really worked. You know how they tell you in school, about voting and all that. But it don't work that way. The goddamned owners run everything. And there's not a damn word they say that isn't a lie."

He caught a troubled flash of eyes. "You sound like a radical, Bill. I even heard her call you 'Red' just now."

"I didn't start out that way, but hell if I ain't getting to be one." He blew out, forced himself to relax. "Sorry, my nerves are shot. Want to stop someplace, get a cup a coffee or something?"

She said sure. Not another word passed between them all the way to Beaver Fork.

LUBE OIL PRICES CLIMB ON SPOT MARKET, said the *Wall Street Journal*.

Thunner pondered the article, which was spread out on his desk in his office. Pondered the ramifications, the meanings.

He was pale with anger.

Apparently the on-loan workers who'd come to Thunder from the other refineries had taken word of the strike in Hemlock County home with them. The CIO and OWIU had seen it as an opportunity, and thrown additional organizers into the oil fields of western Pennsylvania, southern New York, and eastern Ohio. Now, one by one, the other refiners were going out too. The *Journal* estimated that sixteen thousand men were out, with more walking out every day. He'd already fielded calls that morning from Schoenfield and Ruffenach. There was unrest at Wolverine-Empire and at Crystal. Both men were livid and, for some reason, at him. Ruffenach had called him a Typhoid Mary, and said his firm's participation in the Refiners' Association was ended as of that call.

A tap at the door. "Mr. Thunner?"

"Come in," he snapped.

Weyandt admitted Deatherage, with two young men in dark suits and identical ties; waited for his acquiescence; closed the door silently behind them at his peremptory wave. The strangers gazed curiously around the office. Thunner rose grimly to shake hands as Deatherage introduced them as Mr. Brecher and Mr. Alinsky. "They're joining our agency as consultants. I suggested to the home office that this might be a good place to break them in. To blood them, as it were."

"I see. We need to talk, Pearl."

Deatherage slipped a letter in front of him. "Before we do, I prepared this for your signature."

"What is it? Another bill?"

"It's your letter of condolence for Anthony Quarequio's death."

"You must be mad. I'm not signing any apologies."

"You're signing this," said Deatherage. He tapped it. "I know you don't like it, but one of my duties is to manage your public relations."

"They're the ones who broke down the gate. I've checked. Etterlin and Wheeler swear none of my men put that cable out there!"

"I know that, and I know who most likely did. She needs martyrs; why not manufacture one? But it happened on your property. Right now, you're cast as the villain." He tapped the paper again. "Alinsky here wrote this for you. He's a Harvard man, going to be the next Sinclair Lewis. Hell of a piece. Damn near made me cry."

He didn't bother to read it. Just uncapped his pen and slashed his signature across it so violently the nib protested. Then tossed the newspaper across the desk. "All right, that's done. Have you read this?"

Deatherage, coolly: "I have."

"The other refineries. Producers too. Sixteen thousand out and more downing tools every day. Biggest industrial dispute since the 'eighties. The spot market's going crazy."

"It's excellent news, isn't it?"

Thunner stopped in midspeech. "What the hell are you talking about?"

"For you, I mean." He looked around the office. "May we sit down? And turn this into a civilized discussion?"

Thunner glared, then motioned brusquely to the settee. The younger men hovered uncertainly by the fireplace. Deatherage lit an Old Gold, blew out the match, and studied it. "Very well. As I was saying: This is excellent news. Why? Two reasons. First, the other brands aren't grabbing your market share anymore."

Thunner waited. Looking at him, Deatherage thought, unaccountably, of the famous photograph of J. P. Morgan, the one showing him in a chair the polished arm of which resembled, by some trick of light, an unsheathed knife gripped in the financier's hand. "Second, in our situation, the more desperate things become, the closer we approach a resolution."

"All it looks like to me is, we're digging ourselves into a hole so deep we'll never get out of it."

Instead of answering him, Deatherage turned to the new men. "Let me make this point right now, boys. Mr. Thunner here's the fellow we work for. Not the stockholders. Not the rest of management. Remember that. Find out where control resides. Your job is to make sure he keeps that control."

"Goddamn it! Answer my question!"

The agent stood coolly. "Perhaps we should continue this some other time. Your intemperate language—"

Thunner mastered himself, but not by much. He said, "I will attempt to moderate it. But damn it, I wish you'd talk a little plainer."

"Gladly." Deatherage sat again, then hitched himself forward. "The workers attacked your plant because their resources are at an end. That's what violence means: that they've given up hope of winning fair and square.

"Do you remember, when this started, how the mayor and the city council tried to stay neutral? You were annoyed at the time. I told you it would change. And it has, hasn't it? Now they're on your side. Oh—I hear we got the injunction, the one against camping on public land."

"Ellis got it, but Foster won't enforce it."

"He won't enforce a judge's order to vacate?"

"He's temporizing. Says it'll lead to violence."

"You need to do something about him, next election. But if you want those scum out from in front of your gate, I can take care of that for you. Do you?"

"If it can be handled reasonably."

"I keep telling you, every outrage, no matter how it originates or how it ends, redounds to our advantage. Sooner or later, and I think sooner now rather than later, the state government will have to take action.

"But: to the market. If I were you, I'd start selling advance deliveries. Ride that bull market, Dan. Because inside of a month, maybe less, you'll be shipping Thunderbolt Triple-Filtered as fast as the Erie Railroad's locomotives can pull it out of here."

Thunner stared at him, and at the two young men. Instead of answering he snatched his hat off the table, flung the door open, and stormed out.

He stood alone in the falling snow on Main Street, chest heaving with helpless anger and bewildered fear. The walls around seemed to lean inward, as if to crush him. He hadn't brought his overcoat. Ought to go back, get it—the snow was already building epaulets on his shoulders—but he couldn't stand being indoors when he felt like this. It was like being buried alive.

Like being buried alive.

He turned, shuddering, and began walking with his head bent. The single picket posted before the building stood so ragged-shivering, pinched-cheeked, and abstracted that Thunner walked past him without the man's recognizing him. Other pedestrians slogged toward him. One was an acquaintance; he noted that the man's nod, when it came, seemed forced, and he kept on, whereas once they would have stopped to share a political opinion or the latest Roosevelt joke. He glanced back and was startled to see Weyandt behind him, carrying his overcoat over one arm. His secretary dropped his eyes. Thunner almost called to him, then saw he hadn't meant to be seen. And understood why.

Anger shook him. He did not look back again.

He didn't know where he was going until he reached it. He stopped on the torn-up pavement, looking up to where it towered into the lightless sky, rivaling the snow-shrouded hills.

The Thunder Building. The construction workers had gradually left, one by one, and, heedful of the need to conserve his resources, he had not insisted they return. The great building stood as empty as the streets around it. He crossed the muddy space before it and picked his way in. A guard started up from a chair, trotted forward; he dismissed him with a wave and went on into the lobby.

He stood there for a long time, looking up first at the sparkling steel ceiling, then down, at the great mosaic. Complete now, pristine and shining. The great buildings and rushing trains, the speedy automobiles and soaring monoplanes frozen in midflight. He couldn't believe how beautiful it was. Even if it were buried, in some unimaginable war of the far future, it would be rediscovered someday, and marveled at, like the excavated wonders of Herculaneum.

But even it left him feeling nothing inside. Last fall, he'd taken his rivals around and grinned as they gazed open-mouthed. Now his triumph had turned to ashes. He'd snapped back at Deatherage, but he felt guilty about the dead man. About the dozens of wounded, police as well as strikers. He kicked a timber savagely, sending it skidding out across the floor. Damn them all! All he was trying to do was run a business. Now his secretary had to follow him, fearful he'd be assaulted, or worse.

Fists clenched, he stood speechless amid the monument and ruin of his mighty dream.

The Beaver Hot Luncheonette was stainless steel and glass, a startling piece of modern times plunked down on a slanted street of tired company houses, a timber-era beer joint, a storefront candy store. The inside was steamy and food-smelling, and the faces that turned as he held the door for her were blessedly unfamiliar. They got seats together at the counter, in front of a sign that read EAT HERE—WHY GO SOMEPLACE ELSE TO GET CHEATED? The waitress had a hair-net and a pencil over her ear and razor-drawn eyelashes like Jean Harlow's. Jennie studied the menu. "Seems like I'm gaining weight, on my feet all day at the carder. Maybe I better not have anything."

"We got a cottage cheese plate, kid."

"Then I'll have that."

He was hungry but he realized suddenly he didn't have a goddamn dime. He said in an undertone, "Jennie, I forgot. I'm flat busted."

"Let me get it this time, Bill."

"I don't want to take your money."

She clicked down two quarters and told the waitress, "Whatever he wants."

He ordered pie and coffee. When she left Jennie said over the clash of silverware and the talk and Ida Cox crooning a torch song on the radio in back, "I'm worried about you, Bill."

"I'm all right."

"I know we're not . . . friends that way, anymore. But I still worry." She shuddered. "When I heard about somebody getting electrocuted, I thought sure it was you."

He put his hand over hers, wondering at how tangled up his feelings and thoughts had gotten. Once, everything had seemed so simple. Marry Jennie. Save his money. Study to be an engineer. Now it was like opening a drawer, the kind where string and old pocketknives and dead flashlight batteries, rubber bands and kitchen matches were all jumbled up together. Her hand lay still for a moment, then turned up shyly to grip his.

She murmured, "Sometimes I miss you."

"Geez, sometimes I do too, Jennie."

"You ever thought a getting together again?"

"I don't know. Your family . . ."

She said she knew. Neither of them said anything until the waitress came back with their plates.

When Thunner got back to the office, Deatherage was explaining to the young men how to use supervisors to influence the outcome of union actions. They looked up as he came in. In an icy, resolute voice Thunner said, "Mr. Death-

erage, you and your associates will leave my county on tonight's train. All of you. The guards, the skull-crackers, the
'consultants.' Just get out."

Deatherage pushed back his chair. "Excuse us a moment,
please," he said to the young men. They scrambled up, eyes
wide, and left the room. Alinsky closed the door behind him,
darting back one curious glance.

"Now, Dan, what's this? Let's get it out on the table."

"I told you, I want you out. All of you, the thugs and
grifters and spies, whoever laid that cable and whoever shot
at my men."

"They aren't your men anymore, Dan."

"My workers aren't my enemy," said Thunner. "I never
thought that, from the beginning. But somehow you've persuaded me they are. If I could sit down with them, we could
come to some agreement. But all these other people keep
pushing in between us."

Deatherage thought: It had to come. It always did. And
when it came, you had to let them talk. When the angry man
across from him paused for breath, he said, "You know, Dan,
I agree. You are perfectly correct. If you and your boys out
there could sit down together, you'd come to an agreement.
Unfortunately, that has now become impossible. We're both
in the grip of larger forces."

Deatherage tented his fingers. "This latest outrage . . . it's
not an isolated incident. I've tried to keep you informed
about what they've been doing. The beatings along the picket
line. The threats. Do you know, they telephone the wives of
the loyal men? Telling them they're sorry about what happened to their husband at work today? Can you imagine their
state of mind, what they say to their husbands when they
come home?"

Thunner grunted something.

"Not to mention slashing their tires outside their houses at
night. Making outcasts out of their kids at school. Listen to
me. They realize that this is war."

Thunner sat down. He put his hands on his knees. "No,"
he said, in a level, tired voice. "I've thought about it, Pearl.

War? You and I have seen it. I don't want it here. But it's coming. Sabotage. Hired thugs. We're pulling each other down to it, step by step. And if we don't stop, that's what we'll have out here. Civil war."

"You mean we're getting down to brass tacks at last," Deatherage told him. "What are you proposing? Surrender in the field?"

"I can afford to compromise."

"Can you? Set your emotions aside. Think it through logically with me. You recognize this union, this 'Local One-seventy-eight.' Then what happens?"

"They come back to work."

"No, what happens is, they carve your guts out at the table. Maybe not so bad this first time. They're hurting too. But a year later the contract comes up for renewal. Their bellies are full. Now they want revenge. They let your blood again. And again. Weakening you. Year after year. Gradually they take control of the plant, work rules, new hires, everything you thought was your prerogative.

"Till at some point you say, 'I can't run my business anymore. It's no longer mine; it belongs to the union.' Then you go to a lockout, only guess what? They're stronger, and you're weaker. Meanwhile your production costs rise. You can't lay men off, you can't trim wages or cut back hours as you once could. That's all fixed cost now. All you can do is pay. Till you slide under. They can't see that coming. You can't expect them to. All they see is their own paychecks, week by week. Until it's too late, and Thunder's history.

"Or don't you think it will happen that way? They'll come back to work, swinging their lunch pails and singing the company song, and everything will be like it was? Do you really think that? Go ahead. Look out two years. Tell me I'm wrong."

Thunner scowled, not answering. Finally he grunted, "I'm not sure I run the company *now*."

"Oh? Who does?"

"It seems to me you're taking over that position."

Deatherage smiled, then touched his lips quickly with the

back of his hand. "Okay. Maybe I deserved that! But there's a big difference. When this is over, I'll be just an unpleasant memory. While a union will have a bit in your mouth from here on in.

"No, you've got to go for the throat, Dan. There's only going to be one winner here. And that is my talent. To win at all costs, by whatever method is necessary. That is what you hired me for, isn't it?"

Thunner sat motionless, feeling the familiar horror as the walls closed in. Sweat broke cold beneath his suit coat, the starched shirt. He gripped the armrests of his chair to keep himself in it. From leaping across the table at the cold voice that spoke on and on, telling him things he knew were true but that he did not want to hear.

"Dan, I heard the pride in your voice when you told me how your dad and your granddad built this company from nothing. Fought Standard Oil and won. Rebuilt after the fire. Beat back strikes before. They fought to give you this company. If you want to keep it, you've got to fight, too. And the best chance you'll ever have to win is right now." He put an urgent hand on Thunner's knee. "I'm talking to you as one old soldier to another now. Don't break up the squad. We beat the Krauts because we stuck. It's the same battle. The same enemy—you know the Kaiser was behind the socialists, the Reds, the pacifists in the war."

"I don't want more men to die."

"No sane man would! But what difference do a few Gentile lives make to Golden? All they're thinking about is power. The power they'll win when they take over the country from the men who made it great."

Thunner sat motioness, and Deatherage saw that this was the moment. "Listen to me, goddamn it. The past is past. It'll never be the way it was again. But we are going to beat these people! We're going to burn out this union infection so thoroughly that your son isn't going to have to deal with the next one.

"I understand your misgivings. They do you credit. This is a dirty business sometimes. You can step back from what

I do. Even condemn it. That's fine with me. I don't have to live here the rest of my life. But you can't do without me, Dan. You're in the deep woods now, and I'm the only one who knows the way home." He waited, then leaned back. "But of course the decision is yours. We came at your invitation; if you want us out of Hemlock County, we'll go. Do we? Or do we stay, and fight shoulder to shoulder till this is over for good?"

Thunner stared into the fire, hands locked together so firmly his knuckles grew white. He stayed that way for nearly a minute as gradually his expression grew harder; as all remaining doubt and softness vanished, put away with an immense effort of will; as his features became at last older somehow, bleak and thin-lipped. Finally he said, "You'll stay. Till it's over; then I want you to leave. Immediately. All of you. And never return."

Deatherage rose; stood for a moment at wordless attention; then left the room with swift strides.

Thunner remained, still staring into the fire. And for some reason, rubbing at his eyes angrily, felt them sting with tears.

Twenty-one

Coming up out of the grimy echoing tunnel of the Seventh Avenue IRT, ears still ringing from the grind and shriek of steel wheels, she turned up her collar as the bitter wind gnawed at her neck. Channeled by the great buildings, the snow whirled down from a sky as closed and lightless as Hemlock County's, but held at bay by the vertical bayonets of the skyscrapers.

Manhattan on a Monday, January 27, 1936, three-twenty P.M. Summoned by telegram for a meeting with the executive committee. Holding her coat closed, she pushed her way with hurrying scores across Thirty-fourth toward the second-rate hotel. The meeting was scheduled for four o'clock. She was early. She wouldn't be surprised if it was still going at eight. Around her, men and women bent into the wind, faces shuttered, each closed and intent on his or her own errand in the great metropolis.

She'd boarded the train from Petroleum City before dawn, and stepped off at Hoboken for the ferry. The South Ferry Local brought her here, across the street from the McAlpin.

She glanced at her watch one more time, then went into the
Nedick's on the corner for a hot dog and an orange drink
and four more pages of the S. S. Ván Dine mystery she'd
found abandoned on the train.

Half an hour later she was admitted into a bare third-floor
office that smelled of steam heat and old cigars. A typewriter
clattered behind a partition. A poster on the wall read, IF I
WENT TO WORK IN A FACTORY, THE FIRST THING I'D DO IS
JOIN A UNION. It was signed with FDR's unmistakable flourish. In the next room faces she knew turned from a long
table.

"Doris. Come in."

"Hello, Sidney."

Short, squat Sidney Hillman, leader of the Amalgamated
Clothing Workers of America, and a founding member of
the new CIO. She went around the table, shaking hands with
the reserved-looking Charles Howard, of the Typographical
Union; fiery red-haired Mike Quill, head of the New York
Transport Workers; Al Hartwell, of the Labor's Nonpartisan
League, tall, dark and handsome in a conservative suit. Max
Zaritsky of the Hatters Union, chunky and truculent, always
ready for an argument; David Dubinsky, president of the International Ladies' Garment Workers, casual in an open-
necked shirt under a tan lounge jacket, but perhaps the
shrewdest of them all. She noticed one man's absence: Harvey Fremming, president of the oil, gas, and refinery workers, to whom she was on loan. She was the only woman in
the room.

A stir in the front office, and a huge shaggy-browed man
in a tent-sized black suit occupied the doorway, brushing
snow from his overcoat with one enormous paw as he removed a black hat with the other. A moment later he was
bent over her hand, muttering, "Doris, ah, my Doris." She
snatched it back as the others laughed, but could not avoid
being enfolded in a bearlike hug. She smelled cigars and hair
oil. When he let her go at last she took her seat, smiling
faintly as John L. Lewis grounded himself at the head of the
table with the cautious gravity of a liner entering a drydock.

"Let's open with a report from the front lines," said Hillman. "Harvey telegraphed he couldn't be here. Sister Golden?"

"I'm here from Pennsylvania, where the unrest in the oil country is spreading." The other labor leaders listened closely as she outlined the situation in Petroleum City. She didn't need to tell them details. These men had been through dozens of strikes and lockouts. They knew what she meant when she said "Management continues to resist. The town is divided, and the police are hostile." They knew when she said "Road transport in and out is uninterrupted" that she'd tried to enlist the local teamsters, and found them on the other side of the steadily widening A.F.L-C.I.O. split. When she ended with Quarequio's death, silence vibrated. Lewis lit a cigar, puffing out a slow, heavy writhe of smoke. Hillman said, "Can you hold out?"

"For a few more days, yes. But our funds are exhausted. A thousand from the general fund—"

"I wish we had it to give. Do you need another organizer?"

She shook out a match, hungry for the nicotine she sucked in. "No. The workers are developing their own leaders."

Lewis cleared his throat. He sat drumming his fingers, then said abruptly, "Will they settle for status quo ante bellum, plus recognition?"

"I can't predict that, John. The owner's stubborn."

"Of course he's stubborn. They'll all be wearing asbestos suits in hell before they give us a thing we don't spill blood for. But the essential thing now is to settle, make Thunder the bellwether and exemplar for the other refiners."

"I understand that. But now that they've gone out, struggled for it, the workers want tangible gains—"

"Of course they do; but you must explain the tactics of temporary compromise." He scowled at her. "We must conserve our resources. Do you understand me?"

"There are safety, other issues in the way—"

"*Settle*, Doris. End it. We must secure our flanks before we advance."

Lewis launched into an impassioned speech, half tub-thumping oratory, half a canny explanation of where the AFL had never dared tread but where American labor had to go, or surrender to darker forces. "I have just about decided we have got to unionize steel. We have the railroads, by and large. We have coal now. If we can unionize steel, coal, oil, and automobiles—those are the basic industries of the twentieth century.

"The nineteen thirty-six UMW convention will open in Washington this week. At that meeting we will respond to Brother Green's ultimatum that we dissolve the CIO and return to the house of our fathers. Our response will be a resounding roar of 'Never!' Then we will be free to carry the battle to the commanding heights.

"I spoke last week to the rubber workers and auto-parts makers in Akron and Cleveland. They are spoiling for a fight. So is steel. The mighty will smite us hip and thigh, but right merrily shall we return their blows.

"The time is ripe. But we must do this right. Trained organizers, and at least a million and a half in the organizing fund. We can't go the craft route. Green will want to, but we can't make the worker join craft unions. Unless we show the way, the laboring man and woman will do the very thing we do not want—join either the company unions or the communist unions. Neither have his true interest at heart. The sheep must be gathered into one fold, and that fold must be ours."

He hammered the table, and once again, as she did every time she saw the leader of half America's workers, she could not decide if he was deadly serious or the best actor she had ever known. "We must organize the unorganized! The nation needs a labor movement that represents the millions whose exploited condition makes them a drain and a boil upon the body of every American citizen, whether he works with his hands or with his brain. Free in their industrial life, partners in production, with a decent standard of living, they will form the finest bulwark against alien doctrines of government.

"This is the opportunity to forge a mighty engine to be-friend the cause of humanity! But if we let it slip away, not only will high wassail prevail at the banquet tables of the privileged, but we will end by falling prey to either fascism or communism."

Lewis ranted on, looking more like an enraged sheepdog than ever. She tapped ash from her cigarette, returning to earth from the transports of his oratory. Sham, or visionary? Saint Francis, or power-hungry Mussolini? She really didn't know.

The night was black as she came up out of the local at DesBrosses. The empty streets stretched off into the freezing emptiness of lower Manhattan.

She gripped the heavy purse, then, glancing around, slipped out the .32 Savage and slid it into the pocket of her coat.

Gathering her courage, she began walking. From here on she did not know the names of the streets. In the underground one trained oneself not to know certain things. She looked down each alley she passed, turning her head to check for anyone following her. But no one else seemed to have busi-ness on these deserted, empty byways, silent save for the sigh of the wind and the squeak and jingle of her galoshes and the distant hooting of a nightbound ship somewhere off on the wintry Hudson.

The door was a black square in a windowless wall. It opened the moment she knocked. But it gave way not into light and warmth, but into an inky gloom nearly as impen-etrable as the starless night.

She followed a hunched old man who said nothing at all through a winding maze of narrow corridors. The chill air stank of old leather and damp. His flashlight bobbed over a splintery wooden floor that creaked with each step. He tapped on a door. Held it as she slipped within. Then his slow footsteps and hollow cough crept and shuffled away, back into the shadowy echoing recesses of what seemed to be a huge storehouse, abandoned and deserted when the Crash closed its doors forever.

The door clicked shut behind her, leaving her in utter darkness and a close choking smell that closed her throat. She stared into it, seeing only a random seethe and mill of colors as her pulse accelerated. Her fingers tightened on the gun in her pocket.

"Who's there?" she whispered.

The light clicked on above her, an old-fashioned hand-blown bulb dangling from a cord.

"Elena," said the goateed little man at the table. He did not rise, but pointed to a curve-backed swivel chair set across from him. She adjusted it, blinking in the sudden electric brilliance. The room had once been someone's office. Pale patches glowed on the plaster where calendars or pictures had hung. A litter of yellowed invoices or receipts lay in a corner, where rectangles of pristine varnish showed file cabinets had once stood. One wall she took for a map, until she looked more closely. It wasn't a map. It was a spidery reticulation of mildew burrowing along the cracks in the ancient plaster. Now she understood the choking smell. Aside from these things, the table, the chairs, the harsh light that drew shadows beneath her interlocutor's features, the room was empty.

She had met this man three times before. Sergio was not his real name. She didn't know his real name. She did not know how to contact him. She did not ask him questions, but she had to answer his.

All this was common, inside the underground Party.

"Sit down, please. Something to warm you?" He pushed forward an unlabeled bottle.

"I wouldn't mind a small one."

"To the revolution."

"To the working classes."

It was rum, straight, and she drew a long breath after it and set the glass down. The bearded man tapped a wide cigarette of the kind she had heard called *papirovki* from a tin case and lit it. With a practiced awkwardness; for the thumb and two fingers of his right hand were missing. Then he leaned forward and his match-flame touched the end of her cigarette.

"Your report?" he said.

This time her description of the situation in Hemlock County was different. She touched on many of the same events and personalities she had once before that day. But the prism through which events were seen was not the same. Sergio listened without comment, skull tilted to one side. Occasionally his eyes widened, as if to convey attentiveness. His slicked-back hair, the pointed goatee, made her think of a Chekhov character.

"My most recent direction from the executive committee of the CIO is to settle the matter as soon as possible. A major offensive is being planned to organize the steel and automobile industries. Lewis and Hillman want the oil action ended before that begins. My instructions are to settle for recognition and whatever minor improvements in the workers' conditions I can secure. But, above all else, to settle soon."

"Interesting," he said. He sat for a moment, studying the end of his cigarette. Then he began speaking, in a soft, accented monotone.

He told her that the unrest in the oil regions coincided with developments in the coal regions of Pennsylvania and West Virginia. Radical unions there were contemplating a major work stoppage. But the Party had conceived a more advanced tactic: to bring them both into an offensive alignment; to operate two sets of labor actions in synchronization.

"Coal and oil?"

"On which, structure of capitalist industry rests. If supplies of both are interrupted, the entire mechanism must grind to halt. No?"

"You're describing something like the General Strike. It didn't come off in England."

Sergio said softly, "They were not properly coordinated. Was no revolutionary vanguard to exercise discipline. This will be something new. A general energy strike. In middle of a winter like this, it will destroy any chance of American recovery from the Depression. If this country remains paralyzed, Europe will plunge even deeper into same economic twilight."

"That is our goal?"

"No. Only intermediate step." He poured himself another shot of rum and tossed it off.

He tilted the bottle toward her glass, but she covered it with her hand.

She said, "A fuel strike in the middle of winter like this—it won't be the rich who will suffer. They will purchase warmth whatever the price. It will be the masses of workers, the poor, and the unemployed."

"Have you heard saying, 'the worse, the better'?"

"Meaning, the worse for the capitalist system, the better for us."

"Exactly."

She felt the cold of the room penetrating her legs, her heart. "So we deprive the proletarians of one of the necessities of life. With the ultimate goal being—?"

Sergio said dryly, still looking into the glass, "The open Party has grown tremendously since nineteen twenty-nine. Contradictions of American society are exposed to all who have eyes to see. This is coldest winter in many years. Eleven million men without work, without hope. Roosevelt is last gasp of the old system, a dabbler in revolution who understands neither revolution nor history. The artificial stimulant of New Deal is wearing off. Time is ripe for revolutionary transformation. Spain is moving rapidly toward the dictatorship of the proletariat. France will follow. America is like cocked gun. If we can wreck coal, and oil, it will detonate Soviet Revolution here as well."

She sat in the close-choking room, staring at the spidery web of mold. "We're to wreck the country, for the sake of the Party?"

Sergio's eyes flickered. "What is 'the country' but an artificial concept foisted on us by the ruling classes? What is revolution but a wrecking of twisted structure of capitalism, to build a finer edifice on its ruins? The Communist Party of the United States has always had two missions: to speed the revolution here, and to safeguard the Home of the Revolution overseas. We are not concerned with bourgeois notions of morality. The end of world revolution sanctifies all means. For example. We have the capability to sabotage every aluminum aircraft propeller made in the United States. We have already made certain that if American torpedoes are ever used in a future conflict, not one of them will explode. Your activity will also cripple the supply of essential aircraft lubricants."

She said, "But what if we should find ourselves on the same side as America?"

"On same side as the arch-capitalist power? Not likely." Sergio looked around the room, then shot a cuff to consult his watch. "Very well, enough democratic centralist discussion. Your instructions. You will continue your activities as directed, and intensify your efforts to bring about the decisive confrontation."

"You do not wish the strike settled."

"No. The turbulence in the oil fields has only begun."

"I have no higher loyalty than to the Party. But the workers are suffering. My advice would be to settle the strike, let them recover, meanwhile building up the apparatus from within—"

"I will not include that remark in my report on this meeting," said the man across from her. "For your own protection. Listen closely now! We speak of historical necessity, and world crisis. The party line in this matter has been decided at the highest level. Let me warn you against identifying too closely with those you lead. The moment you see them as human beings, the moment you become interested in alleviating their present lot, that is the moment you cross the boundary into trade-union consciousness and right-deviationist error. You must make yourself hard, for the Party is vigilant, and knows all that we do and say. Do you understand?"

She said through a dry mouth, "I believe I do. But I must

also be objective. Our strike funds are exhausted. The CIO has refused further support."

He took a small notebook from his pocket as he spoke, centering it on the table. A stubby chewed pencil joined it. "We can furnish some resources. Provided that you understand your orders. Do you understand them, Comrade?"

She said quietly, "I understand now. And I will carry them out, to the best of my ability."

The money came in new-looking fifty-dollar bills. He counted the cash out, made her count it too, and made her sign for it. She understood. The Party was careful with its funds. Sergio rose a moment later, ending the meeting with a curt nod. He led her through the mazelike rooms, down long, badly lit corridors until she was quite lost. Then opened a door, and ushered her outside again.

Where she paused, alone in the empty street, surrounded by the freezing city night. Feeling the doubt still burdening her heart. Not of the tactic, but of those who so coldly dismissed the human suffering it brought inevitably in its train. She couldn't help wondering how Sergio and those whose orders he carried out could be so certain of themselves. How they could place themselves on a mountain, directing the faceless masses beneath as coldly and passionlessly as if they were a lower species, born only to toil and die for the greater good.

For just a moment she wondered: Wasn't that how the capitalists saw them?

She put her fingers gently to her cheek. It came, then, knowledge from the body clearer and more certain than brain-memory or dialectic. Closing her eyes, she lay again on rough swaying iron. In the cold dark her fingers closed on themselves, unconsciously digging into the flesh of flogged, bloody men.

It was the only way this unjust world could be smashed, and remade anew. She had to become hard as steel: to rise above the cost, above broken lives and pain, trusting that the glory of the coming dawn would wash away all human tears. Those whose orders she received had accomplished that, had turned themselves into iron, into stone, into the implacable and remorseless agents of History. She had to do the same, until that new world was born.

Understanding now, she tapped with firm and resolute steps toward the light.

Twenty-two

Eli Gant died on the first of February, 1936, standing up in the back of a truck. He never saw the bullet coming. Never saw who fired it. Never knew that this jolting, freezing ride was the last one of his life.

Eli was from down South, from Smackover, Arkansas. The funny thing was, he'd been a union man, once. Just pushing a broom around by the stills because that was all a colored boy could do in the Henry H. Cross Company, but still and all in the union, until Lion Oil smashed Local 97 over the Labor Day weekend of 1934. The labor board reprimanded the company and ordered them to bargain, but the board and the union and Eli Gant too had been swept away when the NRA fell like a bursting dike.

Since then he'd worked one summer building roads on a WPA gang. Put in a vegetable crop on two acres of his aunt's, string beans and black-eyed peas, okra and beets, and peddled it from door to door. But nobody had the money to buy his vegetables until they were so wilted he let them go for a penny or two. You couldn't feed three younguns on that. Then he tried fishing, but one night somebody busted in the bottom of his john-boat and stole all his poles.

So that when he saw the ad for stillmen in the El Dorado paper, he went down to the post office and invested two cents. He wasn't no stillman, but he'd watched the white boys while he was pushing that broom. Give him a chance and he'd figure out what he didn't know. And damn if he didn't get a ticket all the way to Pennsylvania back in the mail. So he'd kissed Naomi good-bye and told the kids to mind their ma, and went north on the Missouri Pacific. He'd never been North before, and sat looking out the coach window as state after state went by, seeing the shacks and Hoovervilles crouched along the railroad right-of-way. And a slow bitterness took him, thinking how shitty things were.

And now he was here, and the white-cloaked hills were like prison walls and the mist-wreathed river was nothing like the wide sandy-green Ouachita. But what the advertisement and the printed letter that came with the ticket didn't say was that he was going to be a scab. He didn't know that till he got into the truck. There was room in the cab, but the ginks driving it got a look he knew on their faces and said there wasn't no room there, he better climb in back. And to keep his head down as they went through the line.

He didn't like it. But he didn't have a dollar in his pocket to go home with. When times were rough, you just had to stick.

But the cold had struck him numb; he'd never felt cold like this before, and sitting down in the back of the stake truck meant squatting in two feet of snow and he just wasn't going to do it. So he rode standing up, his arms over the front of the stakebed.

He saw the river, and the hills, and the drab hill-huddled city; and after a while, the dead chimneys of a refinery loomed slowly ahead. He saw the woods and the bare flood-littered riverbeach and bent, huddled figures at the gate and the tar-paper shack with the smoke yarning up from the trash fires.

The sight twisted his heart because it was exactly what

they'd done in '34, down in Arkansas. He'd spent months on that line. Watching the scabs go in, a few more every day. And now he was one of them, and men were looking toward the truck as it came closer, and getting up, and raising their fists. Shaking them at him.

That was his last thought before lead crashed through his skull and spattered the bed of the truck with blood and brains and teeth and bone fragments. His body reeled back, arms flailing. But long before it stopped jerking and writhing in the bloody snow, Eli Gant was dead.

He was sitting in the Alpine warming his mitts around a mug of weak joe when the cops came in. One clamped a heavy paw on his shoulder. "Red Halvorsen."

He pushed it off. "That's what they call me."

"You a hunter, Halvorsen?"

"Who ain't?"

"Got a rifle? What kind?"

"Want to take a look? It's in my car. Right outside."

"You better come with us."

Lucy Amoretti came out of the back, wiping her hands on a threadbare red-checked dish towel. "What you bothering him for, Eddie?"

"Been a shootin'. Down at the gate." The policeman pulled Halvorsen's hands behind him. Handcuffs clicked, and icy metal bit into his wrists.

"That's goddamned tight," he said, as one of them held the door.

Their faces were hard as WPA concrete. "Shut the hell up and get in the wagon," said the cop behind him.

They took him to the station, then down to the basement. When the iron door clanged shut behind them he felt his skin tighten, felt the sweat start despite the cold, still air. It smelled of limestone and shit and oil. The cops set him down and let him wait.

"Think I could have a chew?" he asked after a couple of minutes. "From my pocket, here?" But they didn't even look at him.

*   *   *

After they were done with him they pushed him into a cell and threw a blanket in after him. It was cold, the walls rough-mortared brick. It stank of feces and something else, a dank sharp smell, and mice skittered away from where he collapsed.

He pulled the blanket over him before he passed out.

He must have lain there all night. He couldn't tell when the sun came because there were no windows. All he knew was that he was awakened by a pounding and then a clink of metal. When the door shivered open, he blinked, sitting up. He didn't mean to, but a groan came out anyway.

It was Doris Golden and a young-but-balding guy in a suit. Doris said, "Are you all right?"

"A little bruised up. See you're back from New York."

"That's right, I'm back. Bill, this is Harv Mulholland. He's an attorney. There's been some discussion of getting you out of here."

He got up slowly. "I'd sure like to. But they say I shot some colored fella."

Golden stared at his bare chest, then at his face. Her fingers touched his cheek gently. "They beat you."

"Figured to loosen my tongue up, I guess."

Mulholland said tightly, "Who did it? We'll bring suit. We'll wreck this damn department—"

"Forget it. Just get me out of here," Halvorsen said.

The attorney had a couple of questions for him. Such as what kind of rifle did he hunt with. Whether he owned any other guns. "Can we spring him on bail?" Golden asked when he was done.

"Maybe. Let me get in touch with Judge Wiesel. See what I can do, okay?"

A knock on the door, and it creaked open. "Time's up."

"We'll be back, Red." To the cop she said, "Lay another hand on him, and we'll see you in court. Not the department. You, personally." The officer glowered, but didn't say a word.

He came back a few minutes later, after the others were

out of the building, Halvorsen figured. He stood just inside
the door, thumbs hooked in his Sam Browne belt. "You son
of a bitch," he said. "You think your Bolshie-vik friends are
gonna get you out of this?"

"I got my hopes. Ain't that I don't like it here, but—"

"You just button your goddamned lip," said the cop. He
had a thick face, not brutal, just heavy. "We was talking
about you people last night down at the Legion hall. There's
still some real Americans left, Halvorsen. An' they're gettin'
fed up. You hear me? We had about a bellyful of this."

He turned over wearily on the iron bunk. "You want to
whale on me some more, go to it," he told the cop. "Till
then, whyn't you just let me the hell alone."

Late that afternoon he stood outside the station, hands in his
pockets, shivering with cold and relief. Around four o'clock
Mulholland had come back with a piece of paper from the
judge. The cops had reluctantly let him go. He didn't know
for how long, but he was glad as hell to be out.

"Need a ride?" said the lawyer.

"Got one?"

"Sure, where to?"

When he got out of Mulholland's Buick at the Alpine, his
whole body felt like it was made out of Jell-O. Pearson and
Melnichak looked up as if to Lazarus as he strolled into the
diner. "Jesus Christ, it's Red," said Lucy. "What are you
doing here? We just been hearing about you on the radio.
Sounded like they was ready to strap you down in Old
Sparky."

"Well, that lawyer fella got me sprung for now." He eased
himself down, and Lucy bustled around and pretty soon he
was digging into chocolate pie and a big glass of milk. He
was suddenly hungry as hell; they hadn't given him a thing
the whole time the jail.

Melnichak slid a Buffalo paper in front of him. "Maybe
you ain't seen this yet," he said. "We're famous now. Went
out all over the country, I bet."

NEGRO SHOT IN OIL-FIELD STRIKE

A recently hired colored man from Arkansas was murdered from ambush today in Petroleum City, Pennsylvania, near a hobo camp outside the strike-bound Thunder Oil Company.

The shooting of Eli Gant, 34, escalates tensions in a labor dispute already rife with accusations that neither the company nor the union is willing to compromise or negotiate.

Thunder Oil executives say the murder was a conspiracy hatched in the pickets' shack and offer a $1,000 reward for information leading to identity of the shooter.

Halvorsen whistled. "A thousand smackers. No wonder them cops wanted to beat it out of me."

Melnichak said slowly, "A lot of folks would be friends to a porcupine for that. Especially fellas without jobs, with families . . ."

Pearson: "You mean the guys on the line? You don't need to worry about them."

"I ain't worried. I didn't shoot the poor bastard."

"Hell, I believe you, Red. But what I'm thinking is, the way this goddamn town's getting, they won't need a lot of evidence to pin it on you."

"Here's another piece a pie, W.T. Eat all you want, it's on the house."

"Thanks, Lucy. Who you figure *did* do it?" Halvorsen asked them.

"Wasn't one of us. The guys on the line hate scabs like poison, but if we was to shoot anybody, it wouldn't be some poor sonofabitchin' scab. It'd be one of Deatherage's sluggers. Or Deatherage himself, better yet."

"Whoever laid that power cable killed Shorty, I bet is the same one who killed this nigger scab."

Halvorsen said, "Lew, I know you don't mean nothing by it, but it ain't necessary to call him that. He was a goddamn worker, same as us, like Doris says. He just got off the train. He might not even of known we was on strike."

They sat wordless for a minute, then he got up. "Guess I'll head down and see how the line's doing."

"It ain't," said Melnichak. "We're losin' heads again. They ain't gone back to work, but they ain't out there, either. A lot of 'em I bet are just sittin' at home tryin' to make up their minds how much farther we got to carry this thing."

"Till the goddamn end," Halvorsen told them. "We got to carry it till the end. And I got the feeling it ain't going to be too much longer."

Thunner sat back in his leather chair, listening to the voice coming over the phone. Across from him Weyandt sat alert, ready to hand him files or references should he demand it. The steno hovered outside the open door.

George Howard Earle was the first Democrat to govern the state since before the turn of the century. He was a Philadelphia blue blood, a financier, a close friend of FDR. He and Dan had met once, at a dog show in Harrisburg. Thunner loathed him. He listened to the aristocratic Harvard accent now with mounting disgust and anger. But he couldn't hang up on the governor.

"And we're reading the wire services and the national news. What in the devil is going on up there, Dan?"

"Well, we've got a fairly serious labor dispute on our hands."

"I would say so. You've had several deaths, isn't that so? What are you doing to these people?"

"Those are not my doing, George. Those are accidents—"

"Getting shot in the head is an accident?"

"That was one of my men, not one of theirs."

"I'm hearing from Harv Mulholland that you're not negotiating, Dan. That's not a sign of good faith."

"I'm not negotiating because this strike is being run by outsiders. There's a Red agitator here, woman named Golden, who's got the men all stirred up."

"Who shot this colored fellow, Dan?"

"That murder was hatched in the pickets' shack. I've put up a thousand dollars for information."

"Your mister mayor told me that."

"His people picked up a suspect, but then your friend Dick Wiesel let him go. Some specious nonsense about the slug they dug out of the boy being a forty-four—the suspect's rifle not being right."

"Judge Wiesel's one of yours, Dan. Not one of mine."

"He doesn't take orders from me. Obviously. But I've got my men working on this. We'll find the murderer."

"I don't want to talk about that. That is a secondary issue. Now, listen. Are you listening, Dan?"

"I'm here."

"This strike is hurting the economy of this commonwealth just at the moment it looks like we're making some progress against this depression. I want it settled, and I'm not telling you what to do. It's a personal opinion. Riding with Black Jack Pershing in nineteen sixteen, I saw how things can get out of hand when there's no give to the situation. Like it was with the big landowners down there in Mexico. Eventually you get a Pancho Villa. We don't want that. *You* don't want that. Give up a few cents, Dan. Show some *noblesse*. I don't want to have to call out the Guard."

Thunner's knuckles whitened on the phone. "I've *made* offers. They want full recognition—"

"Why, that's little enough. Why not recognize them?"

"We don't bargain with criminals up here, Governor." The title tasted nasty in his throat. He signaled Weyandt, pointed to the sideboard. As the secretary set a whiskey in front of him, Earle was saying, "Dan, there's more interest in what's going on up there than you may realize. Harry Hopkins called me this morning. Yes, from Washington. Harry said someone he knew was interested; we might see her sooner than we think."

"Who?"

"You think about it. My advice is to settle, Dan. Settle *now*. Good-bye."

When he heard the disconnect, Thunner slammed down

the handset. Weyandt stood as he leaped to his feet, as he crossed to the sideboard and poured himself a stiff drink and swallowed it straight. Then remembered he already had one on his desk, and kicked a trash can across the office. "Get Deatherage in here," he said. "Get Wheeler, get Foster, get Vansittart. We have got to finish this thing."

"We're dealing?" asked Weyandt, expression carefully ironed blank.

Thunner tossed off the drink on the desk too. He stared down at the street. "Deal, hell. They ignored my deadline. Refused my offers. Defied me. No, we're going to smash this scum once and for all."

Twenty-three

It was one of the narrow, slanted streets that clung to the hillside above town, where the tiny cheap frame houses crowded together so close a man could barely slide between them sideways. Looking at them, Halvorsen wondered how they'd been able to swing a hammer to nail the siding on. The rotting steps sagged under his boots as he climbed onto the porch of Number 15, steeled himself, and knocked, staring at a withered petunia frozen forever in its lard-can planter.

Morning rounds. When a man didn't show up for picket duty you couldn't just let it go. Strike discipline, Golden called it. So every morning the committee divided up the names and headed out. Sometimes a woman peered out, cheeks flushed with shame and hate, and spat, "Go away, and don't come back here. He went back to work." Then there wasn't anything to do but tip your hat and leave.

A curtain twitched at the window, but the door stayed closed. He rapped again, louder, shaking the whole wall.

The woman had a blanket wrapped around her, with taut

terrible lips and steel spectacles held together over the nose with sticking-plaster. She stared out from the narrow slit of open doorway. "W. T. Halvorsen, from the union," he said, taking off his cap though it was bitter cold and turning his lapel to show her the button. "We missed Nikolaj this morning, down on the line. Come to see if he's gonna make it in. He here?"

"He's here," she said. Her voice was low and cracked. He didn't like the look in her eyes.

"I talk to him, ma'am?"

For answer she eased the door inward. He stamped his boots off, stepped across the threshold.

The ceiling electrolier was dark, and the air inside the little house, a shack, really, was as icy cold as the air outside. No wonder; the walls moved with the wind; they were cloth, papered over with glued-on comic pages, Tim Tyler and Dixie Dugan, Dick Tracy and the Gumps. The only piece of furniture on the bare pine floorboards was a broken chair. Past a flowered calico curtain that screened the back of the house, he heard a child coughing, agonized and horrible. He stood for a moment, head bent under the low ceiling, but the woman didn't say anything. She went to the broken chair and sank down into it, pulling the blanket tight around her shoulders.

"Nick?" he said, not too loud. No one responded, and after a moment more he pulled the curtain aside and thrust his head behind it. A stink of feculence met his nostrils, and he squinted into dimness. "Nick? You back here?"

A figure started up from a rag-cloaked bed, swayed, and moved toward him in the dark. Halvorsen became aware of a child's stertorous breathing, too loud in the icy air. "What the hell you want?"

"It's Bill Halvorsen. Wondered if you was sick, or what." Halvorsen stared past him at the bed, fumbling at his jacket; held out a meal ticket. "We ain't got much down at the kitchen, but maybe it'll—"

"They run out of bread yesterday," said the woman, from her huddle in the chair.

"I know times is hard—"

"Mabel's bad off," said the man, voice not harsh, not angry, just wondering and stunned. "M'daughter. She ain't never had good lungs. We been taking our furniture an' stuff down to Wink's, to buy coal, but now we ain't got nothing left but that chair and he says it ain't no good. He won't give us anything for it."

Halvorsen stared past him at the child's face. White and sucked-out, it lay upturned to the plank ceiling. The blue eyelids fluttered as the terrible cough went on. He'd been about to say what he always said, that they just had to stick. But the words died in his throat. His eye caught on the stove. The door stood open, showing nothing but a little heap of gray ash. The wind moaned in the chimney pipe.

"I been stayin' in bed with her. Tryin' to keep her warm," the man muttered. "Wife's close to bein' out of her head."

Halvorsen fumbled in his pocket. He'd been saving it for a new battery, but now he held out the last dollar he had. "Here. Buy yourself some coal an' some medicine."

"We don't take no charity, mister."

"This ain't no goddamn charity. It's strike funds," he lied. Then flinched, startled as the woman's hand came around him from behind. It grasped the bill, then slowly withdrew.

He said something else, what, he couldn't recall, and pulled himself out onto the porch again. Looking across the fog-shrouded valley to the gray dead hills across from them.

Then a rage shook him, so great he clutched the rotting porch-post till his fingers cramped.

They were sitting around the table when he came in. He didn't bother taking off his coat or unwinding his scarf. Just crossed the floor toward them and slapped the money down in front of Melnichak. The small greenbacks that had replaced the big notes of his youth still looked like play money to him. But he knew those bills represented food, shelter, all that men worked for and needed, not just for themselves but for those who depended on them.

"What's this?"

"For the relief kitchen."

"You hit it playing craps, again?"

"I sold my thirty-thirty."

"You sold your rifle?" said Pearson. "You?"

He ignored that, dropping into the last empty chair. "I held back five for one of the guys on the line. He's got a sick kid, needs coal and a doctor. And that taps me out. I'm gonna have to move out of the rooming house, maybe down to the shack. This afternoon I'm going to go down to Tracy's and sell him my auto back. Probably won't get what I put into it, ain't many people buyin' Oaklands these days—"

"No. We need it," said Golden coldly. "You can't let it go, Red."

"What are we gonna use for gas?" he asked them. "And a new battery? Them tires ain't going to go many more miles, either. If we can't run it, what good is it?"

"I hadn't mentioned it, yet," she told them, "But I brought some funds back from New York. Not a great deal, but enough to keep gas in your auto, and pay our telegraph expenses, and the rent on the union office for a couple more weeks."

"We don't need any of that. The boys need food and coal and medicine more."

"No. That money's for strike overhead," she told him, and for some reason he did not fathom, her eyes were utterly depthless, dark and unrevealing as a hole through river ice. "Not for family maintenance. They're going to have to get along as best they can."

"Get along as best—I told you, they're dying up there in those shacks."

"Tell it to Dan Thunner."

Halvorsen stared at her, not understanding what was going on. He passed a hand through his hair. "Look, we got to talk about this. Shorty's dead. We're broke—or just about, and you're tellin' me we can't buy food with however little or much we got from the CIO. The boys have been out huntin' but there still ain't anything in the soup. Keepin' that office open and sendin' telegrams ain't going to change the way this is going to turn out. The families are dead down to it. I hate like hell to say it. I hate like *hell* to say it. But I'm thinking, maybe it's time to fold."

They stared back at him. Finally Golden rose. "Let's go for a little walk, all right?"

Outside, Main Street was deserted in a wilderness of blowing snow. Only a few stores were open. Most were shuttered, closed down for the depth of winter and the strike. Beside him Golden's boots crunched in the snow. She said, "Okay, what's this crap about giving up?"

"The families are starving, Doris." He told her about the dying child, the bare room. "It ain't the first time I seen things like that, but it's like all of a sudden it hit me right here. That little girl sounded like she was dying. I think she *was* dying."

"What you saw was the hidden face of capitalism," she told him. "What the hell kind of party game you think we been playing all this time?"

"Yeah, but kids—"

"Children die all the time. Does that sound heartless? The heartless one's the man who's locked us out. If he breaks us, your wages are going to rock bottom. There ain't no two ways about it. And more kids will die, only slower. Rickets and rotten water, bad food and no shoes—they're dying all over this country, tonight, tomorrow, every day, and they're gonna keep right on dying as long as we let the owners run things."

"God, Doris, I—"

"Hear me out, Red. I know it ain't easy. It ain't so peachy for me sometimes either. The only way to keep going is, to stop seeing the faces. You can't think about individuals. Not once. Not ever. The only way to save any of them is to win this strike. And the only way to save all the kids, all over, is to smash this lousy bloodsucking system to bits and build something better."

He stared at her, suddenly aware that her speech had changed since she'd come among them. Little by little, till now she sounded like she'd been born here, in this narrow

valley. Her hard, pinched features didn't look Jewish anymore, or foreign, or different. She looked like one of them.
"You're talking communism."

"No, not that. I ain't a communist no more than you are.
But some of the things Abe Lincoln said sound awful much
like it." She looked away then, and went on in a lower tone,
"We all go through this, Bill. You think I don't get blue once
in a while? But it ain't as hopeless as it looks. It ain't just
in this valley now. You know that. Refineries are going out
all over the state and up into New York. It's the biggest oil
strike ever. Do you want to see something?"

"What?"

Her hand came out of her coat holding the familiar buff-
colored envelope of a telegram. He stared at the little purple
sticker that read *An Answer Is Expected by the Sender of
This Message*. The pasted strips of words read NEW WALK-
OUTS REPORTED OIL CITY BRADFORD WARREN CONTACT LO-
CAL LEADERS AND COORDINATE YOUR GOAL TO END ENTIRE
STRIKE SOONEST WITH RECOGNITION OWIU THROUGHOUT
PENNA OILFIELDS SENT LETTER TODAY-JOHN LEWIS

"So Thunner won't get any more scabs from outside. And
here's something else he's bound to be thinking about. If he
settles with us now, he can place product without competition. He's smart enough to know that market gain would
persist."

"What are you sayin'? That you're ready to make a deal
with that son of a bitch?"

"Whoa, there! A minute ago you were ready to throw in
your cards, Red. Which is it?"

He couldn't answer, under her steady skeptical gaze. She
took his arm and they walked a few more steps. "You're
getting angry," she said. "But this is like a boxing match,
Bill. The one who keeps his head longest wins."

Like a boxing match. He puzzled over that phrase for a
second, wondering what it was that made him feel like he'd
almost been on to something. But in the end couldn't come
up with it. He told her, "That ain't all that gets you points,
in the ring."

"I know, maybe I shouldn't use boxing talk with you. But what I'm saying is, we can't give in now. We got to keep on. Or all our sacrifices up to now have no meaning. Shorty's death—the hunger—the lost wages—all the hours the boys have spent on picket." She took a breath, and said the words he knew she'd say, at the end of whatever explanation or analysis she had: "We just got to stick."

And he realized something else: that there wasn't any room in her heart for anything but what she was doing.

Then he remembered the hopeless, agonized coughing in a dark back room, as if a child were being torn apart with pincers. As the steely anger leaped up again he began, dimly, to understand why it was she kept herself on such a short rein; began to sense how much that icy control cost her, and what flame it might conceal.

"Anyway, I can't take this no more," he told her. "I got to do something."

"We're already doing what we got to do."

"How? Even if I sell my jalop it ain't going to keep everybody fed more than a day or two—"

"*Don't* sell it, I told you." Her voice softened. "We didn't ever thank you for the use of it. Did we? And now you want to sell it. For the cause. You're a good comrade, Bill. But we'll just have to tighten our belts another notch. I been thinking, though, what you said about the kids. Somethin' we did in the coal country. We got to get them out on the streets. Give them boxes and get them asking people for money."

"They ain't going to get much, around here."

"We'll win this, Bill. If we can only—"

"I know, if we can just stick. But damn it, I can't stick it much longer," he told her again, slamming one fist into his glove and looking angrily around at the hills. "I got to do something. If only somebody would tell me what."

She gave him a long, speculative glance.

Twenty-four

The moon rose high and white that night, flooding the snowplains with a quiet, icy light. It was a clear night, calm, snapping-cold, and the chill radiance silvered the smoke that curled upward from the clutter of tents and makeshift sheds that edged the riverbank.

The strikers called it Thunderville. The little camp had grown up gradually, first a tent or a lean-to here or there between the river and the railroad right-of-way, on the sloping rock-strewn land that flooded every spring. As two long winter months of strike and eviction had passed, more had accumulated, till now twenty dwellings, patched tents and flimsy shacks of boards and packing-crates and hammered-out tin cans, meandered along a scuffed-bare pathway of creek pebbles and slush. At its heart a common fire roared and smoked. Men and women sat on logs, watching the shimmering dreams that danced in its embers. Gnarled fingers strummed at a guitar.

"Long-haired preachers come out every night,
Try to tell you what's wrong and what's right.
But when asked about something to eat
They will answer in voices so sweet:

"You will eat, by and by,
In that glorious land above the sky.
Work and pray,
Live on hay,
You'll get pie in the sky when you die.
(That's a lie!)"

The singing and the music traveled on and out into the darkness, growing fainter as it crossed riverstone and ice, echoing under the cold stare of the stars. Till it reached the line of men who stood motionless along the road. Some wore long coats and hats. Others, khaki uniforms and trench coats.

Deatherage stood smoking a cigarette from a cupped palm. Around him the men murmured quietly, or stood silent, waiting.

A runner, breathing hard. "They're in position, down by the river."

"Right flank?"

"In position."

"I guess you can start things off, Captain," he said to one of the men in uniform. He tossed the butt down hissing into the snow, ground it out with his boot.

A truck engine ground to life, and the shadows started walking forward.

"When a scab dies he goes to hell,
Parlay voo
When a scab dies he goes to hell,
Parlay voo
When a scab dies he goes to hell
The rats and skunks all ring the bell,
Hinky dinky parlay voo.

"The boss is shaking at the knees,
Parlay voo
The boss is shaking at the knees,
Parlay voo
The boss is shaking at the knees,
He's shaking in his BVDs
Hinky dinky parlay voo."

Then a dog barked, and a woman screamed.

The truck lurched into the encampment, and suddenly its lights blazed on.

And all at once yelling, the roar of engines, the flat crack of shots let off skyward filled the valley. Tents collapsed as the wheels plowed through them, grinding over beds and campstools and boxes filled with meager, worn belongings. Pots and pans clattered on stone. The dog yelped again, high, then screamed. Sparks scattered beneath the churning tires, the snorting tilted roar of the high-tipped hood. Screaming and shouting rose from the camp, clearly audible to the tall man who stood watching still from the road above. And behind the lurching shadow the skirmish line swept forward, and sticks and rifle butts rose and fell, boots and fists slammed down into open mouths. Blazing sticks were snatched out of fires and thrown into tents where children cowered.

"Get them the hell out of here."

"Goddamn Bolsheviks. Get the hell out of our town."

"Clear out, you goddamn beggars. Anybody here in ten minutes we're gonna shoot where he stands."

Carrying their clothes, fleeing, the inhabitants cast back and forth; then, perceiving the only way of escape, headed out into the river. Over the solid snow-covered ice, toward the dark humps of islands and beyond them the lights of the far shore. Behind them a tent collapsed in fire, sending a column of sparks yearning toward the stars.

The committee members paced slowly over the field of battle the next morning. Heaps of ragged clothing and smashed furniture still smoked. Halvorsen bent to pick up a bent tin-type of a grim-looking aged couple that had been trampled into the snow. He held it for a moment, then laid it carefully back down.

"Fischer Town," Melnichak said, as if the words tasted foul. "That's where they drove 'em. Burned our goddamn camp an' our shack and drove 'em all off across the ice. Christ, just like the Cossacks, in the Old Country."

"Who was it?" Golden asked quietly. "Deatherage's goons?"

Pearson kicked snow over a smoldering pile of debris. "Not this time. I heard, somethin' called the Citizens' Committee. A lot of 'em was from the Legion. Wearing the uniforms, and the blue caps. Came in behind a truck. Damn lucky they didn't run over some kid."

"Our brave veterans."

"A lot of our guys are vets too. Makes 'em wish they had their machine guns back, I bet. Well, now they're over at River Street. Miss Minnie called and said the women and kids was in her parlor, the girls gave them blankets and are makin' 'em all breakfast. God bless her, I say."

Golden and the others started making plans, but Halvorsen didn't participate, didn't even really listen. He was shaking. He strolled a few feet away, looking at a torn, trampled doll, a smashed mirror, the flaking detritus of poverty; all these people had, once they lost their homes, or were kicked out of their company-rented drafty houses. All they had.

He came across a dead hound, frozen in a glassy spread of blood, its muzzle raised and eyes open, frosted, unseeing.

Raising his fists to the empty sky, he held them aloft. Then lowered them slowly at a cough behind him.

It was Latimer. The young man had followed him away from the others. He stood mute, looking around. At last he muttered, "Back where I come from, we don't let the owners get away with shit like this."

"I'm about there myself, Frank."

"You about ready to do something?"

"What you got in mind?"

Latimer looked toward the refinery. "I was thinking of dynamite."

"I know something bigger," Halvorsen said.

"Nitro?"

"Packs a hell of a bigger wallop."

"Where would you get it? Make it?"

"Could do that, but it's dangerous, cooking bootleg nitro."

"Then where?"

"Steal it."

He was thinking of Bryner's, of the factory and storage house far out at the bottom of a distant hollow. Where he'd picked up his loads, back when he was a well shooter. Then he shook himself. "No. What the hell'm I talkin' about? It's swell to think about, but we ain't no bomb-throwers. Blowin' things up, that ain't the way to settle nothing."

Latimer kicked up ash and watched it drift downwind. "When does it get bad enough?" he muttered.

"When there ain't any hope left."

"You still hopin', are you?"

Halvorsen didn't answer. They stood together for a little while longer, silently watching smoke rise, watching people hunting about for their belongings; then began to help.

Twenty-five

The redheaded youth slogged slowly on ahead of her, head bent against the wind, breaking the trail. Golden lurched after him, wading through the snow on numbed feet as they moved out onto the frozen river.

She'd worked in New England and the high Appalachians, but she'd never felt cold like this. Or maybe she'd just never been this hungry and this cold at the same time. Because of course she'd been slipping her meal tickets to people who needed them more.

All about them winter lay on the land like a curse, turning the clay ridges along the riverbank into iron and the stunted bushes into torn black embroidery. The bitter wind tore up curtains of snow and sent it whirling across the flat ice like tormented ghosts searching the barren earth for those they'd lost. Her belly felt as empty and cold as this hill-hollowed valley. Dizzy, weak, she paused to scrape at the snow with the side of her galosh. Revealing impenetrable ice beneath, hard and lightless as obsidian.

She pulled her scarf tighter and plodded on, following Latimer's bent back.

She didn't know how much longer the men could hold out. But their determination so far had impressed her. They'd begun without class consciousness. But their native independence had hardened under the blows of the oppressing class to a steely unyieldingness. A few would break, a few always did, but she knew now that most would stay out until the end. Just as she'd told Lewis, the struggle was developing its own leadership. And with skill, some of that leadership, refined in the crucible of class struggle, would graduate into the Party.

But it would take a delicate touch. There were still those who thought in terms of compromise. Politicians. Short-term thinkers. Like John L. Lewis himself, blustering and histrionic and overbearing, but at heart nothing but an accommodationist: END ENTIRE STRIKE SOONEST.

For nearly two months now she'd had to look like one of them. Act like one. Maneuver like one. While deep down she knew: You couldn't reach an accommodation with the bosses. They had to be destroyed.

It was an impossible mission. Sometimes she felt like two people.

But the Party had asked it of her.

She thought about this all the way across the river, till they reached the far side and a treacherous rocky slope where snow-hidden rocks tried to turn her ankles.

Fischer Town was a raw scatter of shacks and barns and dilapidated houses along the slope of a shallow hill. Ramshackle piers stretched out into the snowy flatness, board outhouses teetering at their ends. A sunken barge lay canted, half buried by ice. Neither of them knew the way, so Latimer stopped to inquire at one of the shacks. A dark face peered out, apathetic and incurious. A dusky hand pointed to a two-story Victorian with a broad sagging porch and turrets and a discarded Christmas tree tilted against the wind in a side yard.

There wasn't any red velvet, or chandeliers, or nude paintings in Miss Minnie's parlor. Agemeasled mirrors reflected a speckled linoleum floor and varnish-flaking pine benches along the walls. But it was warm and the toddlers playing on a throw-rug didn't seem to mind. Golden stripped off her gloves while she briskly interviewed the workers' wives about the raid. She'd already called Chief Foster and asked him what he was doing about it. Got an evasive answer, but at least the man had had the grace to sound abashed. She didn't expect action from that quarter, but you had to try. Just as you had to call the editor of the local rag and ask why he'd run nothing about a public outrage by local vigilantes.

A middle-aged woman in a flowered wrapper introduced herself as Minnie Delite. She had a smooth powdered face and wore her bleached hair up. Golden shook her hand firmly and thanked her for taking their people in. Delite said, "Well, when the fox is loose us chickens got to roost together." She winked. "You look hungry, honey. There's java and angel-food cake in the kitchen. Go on back and ask Christine to give you some. I think one of your men's already back there."

She found Halvorsen sitting in the kitchen, drinking coffee. A wedge of cake sat half eaten in front of him on a white-enameled table. He looked up a little guiltily, and stood. "Sit down," she told him. "Finish your cake. Been here long?"

"No. No, uh, just came over."

She sat down with him and they discussed where the children could go. They decided that the last nineteen dollars in the fund would go to train tickets, to take some of the kids to relatives in other towns. Latimer sat in for a time, long enough to wolf two large pieces of angel food, then went back out front to talk to the girls.

When they had made the decision—and it was not an easy one, to tell parents they had to send their children away, the union couldn't feed or protect them any longer—she sat motionless for a few minutes. Finally she sighed. "Well, I guess that's that. We're broke."

"I can still sell the car—"

"I don't want to make you do that. It won't change the outcome." She looked at her hands, at the fingers twisted together in her lap.

Halvorsen got up. He stretched, then bent to look out the back door. Past him she saw a line of icicles swaying on a bare clothesline, shadowy snow-humps that might be bushes, a gray-black scattering of fresh coal-ash on the snow. "Well . . . I guess I better be gettin' along."

"Already? Stay and warm up a little."

"I don't know. Thought I'd check on the pickets, make sure everybody showed up."

"You're not on duty."

He opened the door, stepped halfway through. "Not till tonight. No."

"Then wait a minute."

She cornered the madame in a sitting room off the parlor. Delite was spreading butter from an ice-sweating crock onto hunks of bread while dirt-smeared children looked on, their dilated eyes following each motion of the knife like kittens fascinated by a dragged string. She asked if there were somewhere she could lie down for a few minutes. Delite hooked a key dexterously from a rack on the wall. The metal disc attached to it was stamped with the number eight. Their eyes met briefly; then the madame turned away, setting the bread in front of the urchins. It was snatched off the plates instantly, pressed to voracious small mouths.

Halvorsen was still standing on the back stoop when she put her head out. She said nothing, just showed him the key. His eyes widened, a comical reflection of the childrens'. "Give me three minutes," she muttered, and went up the stairs.

A high-yellow girl in a saffron nightgown passed her in the hall, a cigarette dangling from her lip. Her dark eyes ran up and down her body. Doris thought she was about to speak, and smiled at her; but she didn't, just cut her eyes away haughtily or arrogantly or maybe just without any interest in her whatsoever, and went on down the hall to what must be her own room and slammed the door.

The room was nine by eight, narrow and high-ceilinged, with urns printed on the water-spotted wallpaper and a border high up with lilies and peonies. A Mazda bulb with a dusty leatherette shade. Boards nailed to the wall in the rough shape of a closet, with a dusty black georgette teddy hanging from a cardboard hanger. A bed with a doubled blanket the color of wet clay laid across the foot. The room smelled like face powder and whiskey, and the ceiling was the color of coffee.

She'd thought about this for a long time. This was not the place she would have chosen, but it was the only place it was possible. Certainly she could not have entertained him in her hotel room. The staff would eject her instantly and would no doubt have had her arrested as well.

She stared out the little window for a moment, looking across the river at the distant town. Then pulled down the blind as he tapped at the jamb.

Afterwards she got up and did something by the washstand. He lay with his arms behind his head, breathing deeply. When she was done she slid back under the covers, shivering. She hand-rolled a cig, parked it between her lips, and groped in her purse for matches. Pulled fire off one with a thumbnail, man-style, and lay back. He shifted on the pillow and she felt him staring at her. She dragged down that deep satisfying first lungful and said, "Before you get any ideas: I'm not in love with you. And I'm not going to be. Understand?"

"I don't have any ideas."

"Good. Because this is all there is. And this was the only time. We both have more important things to do."

"Then why'd you do it? Did you like it?"

"Sure. What do you think?" But really she hadn't; she usually felt very little, sometimes nothing at all. She debated telling him about what had happened in the coal fields, how something in her body or maybe in her head had died that night and never grown back again, desolate as a burned-off field. Finally she decided he didn't need to know that. She blew smoke toward the ceiling. "I did it to clear your mind. Sort of like blowing your nose. So we could talk, without the sex thing between us. Get some things straight. Do you remember what you asked me? About what you could do?"

He stared at the side of her face, the smooth curve of cheek and jaw and neck descending to plump, rounded shoulders; looked at her without understanding her; unable to comprehend how anyone could be so self-controlled. He didn't know whether to admire it or not.

The cheap bedstead protested as he half-rolled away from her, and she saw his jaw muscles bunch. "I been thinking about it."

"What did you decide?"

"Nothing, yet. Sometimes I think about things."

"What kind of things?"

"Oh, like how they killed Shorty, leavin' a live wire laying out; and them kicking Stan when he was down; and gassing us, and that poor sonofabitch colored scab they shot. And then I think, maybe we ought to do like them. If that's the only thing they understand."

"To 'do like them'—what exactly do you mean by that?"

He was silent, and she felt proud that he understood, as if by instinct, that a secret shared was a secret no longer. Reminding herself too that she had to be on her guard as well. "That's right," she murmured. "It's better if you don't tell me. Or anyone."

"Don't intend to. Ain't decided to do it yet."

"But you said, if that's the only thing they understand—"

"Uh-huh. There's no other way to get to Thunner. We tried to negotiate, and reason with him, and make a deal. He's not making any deals. Instead he gets goons in from outside. Gets the local flag-wavers to burn our camp out." The pale eyes, blue and distant as a far stand of spruce, studied the wall. "He's got to understand that only goes so far. Then folks start kickin' back."

"I can't disagree. But let me warn you about something." She lifted her head and searched the room, examining the ceiling and walls for the tiny peepholes places like this often had. Satisfied at last that no one could hear them; they might see, but they couldn't hear, she lowered her lips again to where fine blond chest-hair crept through the unbuttoned neck of his long underwear. "Remember the Molly Maguires? How the Pinkertons infiltrated them, sold them down the river? Don't let anyone into the circle you don't trust utterly. Not family. Not even me. I never heard this. You're never to talk to me about it again."

"I know that, goddamn it. And I ain't said I'm goin' to do it, yet."

"Whatever you decide, don't get caught, Bill. And don't get hurt." She squeezed his upper arm, buried her face in the pale skin of his neck. He smelled like sweat and oil and man, and for a moment that passed so quickly she could only snatch futilely after it, like a fish already flicking away the moment it touched her hand, she glimpsed like a long-ago memory what she might have felt if her life had not been different. But as rapidly as it occurred it was gone, and she was glad, for she did not regret missing it. She murmured, "And when this is over, there's a place for men like you."

"You're talking about—what? Something like the Communist Party?"

Despite herself she tensed, realizing she'd gone too far, said more than she had meant to. "I didn't mean that. Forget it. We shouldn't stay up here much longer—"

"Wait a minute. Don't get up yet."

He rolled over, levering his lithe muscular body above her on corded freckled arms, his leathery work-hardened hands pressing down, his rough chapped lips and unshaven prickle of beard-stubble passing across to her neck, her shoulders. His mouth smelled of coal-ash and chewing tobacco and cake. Rolling her thighs open again, she reached up to lock her arms around his neck, smiling faintly up into his close blue eyes. But instead of penetrating her, he lingered there, eyes squinted as if against the sun. She felt them examining her skin, the fine creases where age settled first, the first silver lines in her hair.

"What *do* you love?" he muttered.

She was startled; she didn't expect it. A worker didn't ask questions like that. "What do *you* love?" she asked him back, changing the emphasis, stalling for time.

"I love the woods, an' the way they look. A deer jumpin' through the snow." He blinked, returned as he said it to that endless moment on the back slope west of Songbird when he and the buck had regarded one another. It had seemed to last forever, so long he could go back into it in his mind as if he were still there. He said softly, "That's about the most beautiful thing I ever seen, I guess."

Beneath him she watched his eyes recede, sinking away into a place that she could not follow. Then he came back, and whispered, "I answered you. So now you answer me. What do you love?"

"The people. The masses, and what has to be their destiny. That's what I dedicated my life to."

"That why you're here with me?"

"No. That kind of love doesn't leave any room for any one person."

"Maybe that's what I ain't getting. How can you care about a bunch a people unless you care about 'em one by one?"

She didn't answer that—it was just playing with words—and after a moment he bent his head again, and his beard-stubble pressed itself to her naked belly, exposed beneath the hem of her hiked-up slip. "I ain't gonna love you, if you say not to."

"No. Don't."

"But I'm always gonna remember you," he whispered, and shifted his hips above her and she rose to receive his peremptory hardness with a gasp of something not far from pain.

Above her, entering her, joining himself with her, Halvorsen suddenly thought of a way through. He didn't tell her, or mention it. But it might be a way. Then he forgot about that, forgot about the strike, lost her and himself too as consciousness itself vanished into a white hard focused light.

On the far side of the river, Daniel Thunner tapped his fingers together, glancing now and again at the antique London-made clock that had kept time in the Thunder office since his grandfather's day. The woman had called at two sharp, asking if he would be available to take a call at three. Then he drummed loudly on the desktop. His inner door was locked, and Weyandt had strict orders not to open it.

At eight minutes after three the phone jangled. "Mr. Daniel Thunner? Long distance from Ormond Beach, Florida. Can you hold?"

"I can."

He cleared his throat, shifting in the leather chair, waiting for the voice from the past. *He* was incredibly aged, in his nineties. They said he spent his time building foundations and charities, playing golf, and sitting in the sun. Thunner had no idea what this call was about, what *he* wanted. He sat alone in his snug office, with the fire crackling, and felt apprehension tauten muscle and nerve like a deliberately drawn wire.

A whispery voice crept over the hissing crackling long-distance line. It said, "Good morning. Am I addressing Mr. Charles Thunner, sir?"

He cleared his throat. "That was my father, Mr. Rockefeller. He's passed on. I am Daniel Kane Thunner."

"Well, I declare. It is your grandfather I remember best, then. I recall how Beacham used to sign the hotel registers. 'Mr. Beacham Berwick Thunner, four dollars a barrel.' We had our—business differences. But ah, I admired his drive. At any rate, you are the principal up there now, am I correct?"

He said he was. John D. Rockefeller said, "I believe you know I had interests in the Pennsylvania fields. Earlier in my career."

"Yes, sir." The Rockefeller "interests" had tried to crush every independent producer in Pennsylvania and Ohio, and came within a gnat's whisker of succeeding. There had been war in the oil fields between Standard Oil and the Independent Producers' Association, war with guns and nitroglycerin bombs. "We still have a great deal of . . . respect for you here, Mr. Rockefeller. What can I do for you today, sir?"

"I've been reading about your troubles and thought I might offer some advice. Since I have been semiretired for some years, it may not be germane—"

"I'd be glad to hear whatever you had to say to me."

"The first one is economical operation, of course. That is really the whole secret of competition. Do you know, your operating equipment, pipes and lines and so forth, everything made of iron, loses a tenth of its mass every year to rust? Careful attention, just coating it with a layer of crude oil, will save you considerable funds every year in replacement costs."

The whispery voice went on and on, about rust, and book-keeping, and making sulfuric acid, and buying coal-dust waste. Thunner was wondering if the old man was still right in the head when Rockefeller muttered, "Now, I understand that right now you are experiencing a good deal of labor trouble. I have faced a good deal of that sort of hetchling in my time and I have read the wire reports coming out of there very carefully, and here is my recommendation to you, Mr. Thunner. I offer it to you in the interest of labor peace. Do you understand what I am saying?"

For a moment he didn't; then suddenly he did. "You mean the unrest might spread to Standard."

"Something like this is dangerous to us all. Now, I want you to listen. I faced a very similar situation to this at Ludlow back in nineteen thirteen. There have been a good many false reports put about concerning that, by the way, by those little people who write these narrow, prejudiced books; but we did win it in the end. So that if you are serious about bringing about labor peace, I would advise you to find or manufacture some excuse to bring in the military, the militia, or guard, or what have you up there in Pennsylvania. The first step to that is to make perfectly plain to public opinion that these strikers are dangerous men, Reds and anarchists, without honor, or respect for the law. I read there's already been several incidents up there, one apparently involving a helpless Negro."

"That's right, there's been—"

"That is your entrée, Charles. Demonize your enemy and you are three-quarters of the way toward vanquishing him. That benighted Miss Tarbell and her friends attempted to do that to me and in a large measure they succeeded. I am sure you know the local police. I am sure you know the merchants who supply these misguided men. You can find ways to effect the resolution of the matter in a suitable way. In a healthy economic climate, I might recommend exercising patience, until the men see their way clear to return to their covenant with you as their employer. But not at the present. In these times I would recommend immediate action."

"I appreciate that, sir."

"There is a lot of flammable tinder lying about, in present economic conditions. A wide-awake businessman will stamp any sparks out as soon as possible. Sometimes a fellow has to do things he doesn't enjoy doing. But you do not do it for yourself. You do it for the company. No man takes a deeper or more friendly interest in his fellowman than I do; but sentiment has no place in business."

"I understand, sir."

"I will promise you one thing that I have learned in a long life: They will forget. Put your doubts aside, and act boldly for the general prosperity. Act now, and when that prosperity returns no one will place a jot of blame against your account."

Thunner promised that he would consider that, and thanked the ancient voice for its advice. Rockefeller rang off, and a moment later, Thunner did too. Then he leaned back, and tented his fingers again.

The old fox had spoken.

But could he trust the fox's advice? Was it really in

Rockefeller's interest to have a strike against the independents settled? He could see it just the other way: that the big producers would be perfectly happy to have their capacity off the line. What were they all pushing him toward? He didn't want to go that way. A chill touched him, as if cold metal stroked with infinite lightness along the back of his neck. He had the sense he'd gotten now and again in France, a sense that some unseen eye was following him, some unseen finger bending slowly tighter on a trigger.

Ludlow. Rockefeller had mentioned Ludlow. Why did that ring a bell? He leaned forward and pressed his call buzzer. When Weyandt answered, he asked him to ring down to the Carnegie Library and find out what he could about an industrial dispute at Ludlow in the year 1913. No, he couldn't recall what state Ludlow was in.

Then he leaned back again. He sat tapping his fingers against his mouth, feeling again that familiar sensation of being closed in, crushed, imprisoned.

The buzzer. He pressed the contact. "Thunner."

"Rudy here, sir. Answer to your question: Ludlow, Colorado, nineteen fourteen. United Mine Workers struck the Colorado Fuel and Iron Company, one of the Rockefeller concerns. Strike lasted from fall of 'thirteen to spring of 'fourteen. Finally they called in the state militia. The troops fired into the tents. When the women and children crawled into the holes they'd dug inside the tents, the troops poured kerosene on them and set them on fire. Total thirty-three men, women, and children shot or burned to death. Commonly known as the Ludlow Massacre." Weyandt's voice hesitated. "Is that what you wanted to know, sir?"

He didn't answer. Sweat prickled on his forehead. He rose swiftly and poured a deep whiskey, staring sightlessly at the painting of two fighters, both bloodied, but striving blindly on in a shadowy terrible ring, as the avid faces stared from the encroaching darkness.

He felt clearly at that moment just as he had once or twice in France, in those dreadful dragging moments in the trenches, waiting to go over the top: that he stood at the locus of both decision and immense danger. Only now he was no lowly lieutenant. He was the point man in a momentous struggle, the stake and meaning of which he only dimly grasped. He was the fighter in the foreground of the painting, struggling manfully against some obscure but just for that reason even more menacing shape, half man, half beast or demon. He thought he knew some of the demon's legion of names. They were anarchy, obliteration, violence, and civil war. Struggling manfully . . . but at the same time he suspected he was nothing more than a puppet in the supple hands of some far more powerful force.

Which was he, general or pawn?

And if he was the puppet, who held and manipulated the strings?

God?

Fate?

History?

He had the weapons. He could gun down the strikers. But if he did that they would curse the name of Thunner forever. And there was another reason. He had fought and seen his men die to keep the war far from home. He could not bring himself to break faith with them. War was no convenient abstraction. He had seen it. He knew what it looked like, what it felt like, what it smelled like.

And yet he could not surrender. He *could not* surrender.

In the cozy warm firelight the tall man wiped sweat from his forehead, staring into the writhe and dance of blackness, emerging slowly and inexorably as a poisonous smoke toward him from the four corners of the gradually darkening room.

Twenty-six

Monsignor Jules Guertin was standing by one of the radiators, looking off across the empty echoing space of the gym, when Halvorsen came up to him.

He'd thought about this all day, since he'd left Golden off at the union headquarters. Thought about whether it was a good idea or not. And finally had to admit he really couldn't make up his mind. So that this was a chance to sound it out with somebody he respected.

No question he had to do something. He couldn't get those kids out of his head. Damn it, they shouldn't have to go to no whorehouse to get a piece of bread, a warm place to play. He felt like it was his fault. Crazy, sure, but hadn't he helped start the thing, that night at the Lind, and kept it going ever since? So that when he'd had the idea, there in bed with her, it had felt strange at first. Maybe stone-stupid, the kind of punch-drunk idea you'd expect a boxer to get. But then the longer he'd thought about it, the better he'd liked it.

So that now as he took Father Guertin by the arm and led

him toward the bleachers, he almost felt it might not be so crazy after all.

When he told him Guertin sat still, the grizzled massive head regarding him like some ancient Roman bust chiseled out of ruddy marble. Finally the priest blinked painfully and rasped, "But he's a heavyweight. You're what, fifteen, eighteen pounds lighter than him, Kid."

"But I'm fast, and I'm young. I can take him, Father. Or at least make a pretty good show of it."

"More likely he'd stretch you out on that canvas like a tailor. That, or knock you so high in the air you'd starve to death waiting to come down. What in the world are you thinking about, son? You can't go up against Jack McKee!"

"Father, you told me once that it wasn't the size of the fighter that counted, or even so much how fast he was. It was the fire in the belly, you said."

"That I did, but—"

"I got that fire, Father." He rubbed his knuckles with his right hand and kept arguing. He'd almost beaten Gigliotti, after all, even though he was sick. He'd trained hard all winter since then, marched for miles on the line, and eaten hardly anything. He was fined down till he was all muscle. The old priest kept shaking his head, even getting up to leave once. Halvorsen pulled him back down again. At last he said, "Look, Father, I figure you been following the strike in the paper and all. But what the paper ain't telling anybody is how hungry and sick the kids is getting. I don't see no other way to get them fed than this. That's the God's truth, and I ain't cursing when I say it. Are you gonna turn around and say you won't help them?"

Guertin scowled. "Sure, I'd like to help 'em. But how's you getting yourself beat into doll rags gonna do them any good?"

"If I win, that's where the purse goes. Right to the kids, strike relief. Hey, maybe a gate too. Set this up for us, Father. You got to. That's the only way they're gonna get food and medicine and warm clothes. Some of 'em, it's the only way they're gonna make it through the winter."

Guertin peered at him, the old eyes suddenly sharp and examining. Finally he said, as if to himself, "What exactly are you proposing here? Supposing I were to take this craziness to Mr. Thunner. What kind of purse did you have in mind?"

Licking his lips, he said, "All or nothing, Father. That's the bet I was figuring on. All or nothing."

They were in the back of the headquarters when he told them late that night. Golden, Melnichak, Pearson, and the red-headed kid, Latimer, who had been hanging around so much making himself useful that now they let him sit in on the meetings.

Halvorsen said, to their somber, withdrawn faces, "I got an idea this morning."

"Well, spit it out," grunted Melnichak.

He told them about it. Halfway through, Golden cut him off. "No, no, no. That's not the way we run a negotiation."

"It's something he'd go for. I'll damn betcha Guertin will come back with a deal."

Melnichak ran a hand over his dark curls, looking skeptical but interested. "Snow again, Red, 'cause I ain't sure I get your drift. You want to take on some killer heavyweight Thunner owns. And we ride the goddamn strike on it?"

"This is insane," said Golden. She gave him a hard hostile look, as if that morning had never happened.

"Look, right now this thing's over. Kaput. We ain't got change for a damn match between us. Know how much he had riding on me when I fought Gigliotti? Two large. Thunner's a sportsman. He likes fights, horse races, he's a betting man. If I win, we get cash for the fund. It don't hurt nothing, having Guertin check it out."

Pearson: "What if you lose?"

Halvorsen shrugged. "We go back to work. Which we're gonna have to do pretty soon anyway, since we're dead broke, last I heard."

Pursed lips, gravid silence around the table as they thought it over. "How about if it's a draw?" Latimer asked at last.

"Then we ain't no worse off than we are now," Halvorsen said.

Melnichak said slowly, "Well . . . we'd have to get the boys together, take a vote on it—"

Golden slammed to her feet. "I can't believe this. I cannot *believe* you're actually discussing this nonsense."

"Jeez, don't go all womanly on us, Doris. It ain't the end of the world."

"After all the work the men put in. After Shorty got killed—"

Melnichak said grimly, "We ain't doing no disrespect to Shorty, Doris. This wouldn't be no party for Red. He could get himself killed in that ring. I seen this McKee box. He's a goddamn murderer. But Red's right. We're out of money. Out of food. Out of credit. The families can't hold out on air and snow. If this is a chance to go on, I say, hell, let him go ahead and try, see if Thunner'll go for it."

"You're insane. Completely insane. And I won't be part of it."

They sat and watched her as she stalked out.

Twenty-seven

I thought you should see it right away," said Weyandt, leaning anxiously as Thunner, already livid at being disturbed at his breakfast table, ripped the telegram out of its envelope. Then after a brief perusal crumpled it and threw it to the floor, cursing.

Across the table his wife rose with frosty dignity. "If you're going to use coarse language, Daniel . . ."

"I'm sorry. Forgive me, darling." He mastered himself, smoothing back his hair with one hand. "They don't give you much warning, do they?"

"Probably deliberate."

"Why does she have to stick her nose in here? This is no concern of the damn—of the government."

"She turns up everywhere. You know that. She's his eyes and ears."

Thunner sighed again. His wife, meanwhile, had continued buttering her breakfast roll. He had to admire her sangfroid. Now, at last, she asked, "Who is it?"

"*His* wife, Leola. Eleanor."

"Eleanor Roosevelt? Coming here? How tiresome. We shan't have to receive her, shall we?"

"I wouldn't have her in our home. But it might be wise to set something up at the club. The more time she spends chatting, the less she'll have to cause trouble. Rudy, give Berke a call, ask him to set up a luncheon and reception. He'll know what to do. Better give Elisha a ring too, let the paper know."

His daughter came in and took her chair. She'd just had her hair bobbed, and he examined her shining amber helmet. On impulse he leaned forward and brushed a strand back from her face, getting a mysterious smile in return.

"Guess who's coming to town, darling?"

"Who, Mother?"

"The wife of the President of the United States."

Ainslee didn't answer, she was deep into her Cream of Wheat. Then she said, "Can we see her?"

"We shouldn't care to, darling. She's not interested in people like us."

"She doesn't like us?"

"She and her husband want to take away everything we have. Does that sound like someone you want to welcome to your town?"

"No-o," said the child slowly, considering. "But why are we letting her come here, then?"

Thunner tried to resume reading an article about a millinery strike in New York City, but failed. Weyandt lingered expectantly by the door. Outside came the snarl, then purr as the Chrysler's engine started. Slapping the paper down, he got up and left, not stopping to kiss his wife or daughter. His mind was already moving ahead, to the business of the day.

By eleven the B&O platform was already packed. Hemlock County had always been Republican, at least until the election of '34; but as the news spread, stores had put up CLOSED placards, the Catholic high school had let out, housewives had hurriedly tied kerchiefs over their heads or pinned on hats. Now the Knights of Columbus band stood gripping their instruments in the shifting watery light that wavered down between heavy but for the moment snowless clouds, and the mayor and most of the town council waited shivering on the platform, and at their feet an expectant crowd lined the cold-shining rails for two hundred yards on either side of the station house.

A distant wail drifted down the valley, and heads turned. A murmur of anticipation rose into the wintry air.

Deatherage stood not far from the platform, observing the hollow, pallid faces of the women, the weak-chinned, thread-bare male citizens, the Babel of foreign accents. Save for the council, there was a noticeable absence of the town's better sort. An ironic smile pinched Deatherage's mouth. The Forgotten Man incarnate, turned out to meet one of his patron saints.

The interesting thing was that there really weren't many cops. Across the platform he saw Chief Foster, bulky and flushed in a blue wool greatcoat from the shoulders of which he brushed dandruff with a fussy, old-maidish gesture. Aside from him, only three boys in blue stood along the platform, doing their best to look alert and efficient, but not succeeding very well.

He was still coldly angry from his meeting with Thunner half an hour before. The Thunder Oil president had made it very clear that there was to be no trouble while Mrs. Roosevelt was in town. "You will do nothing to interfere with, injure, or embarrass her," were his words, accompanied by a painful prod in the chest with the Thunnerian finger. "I want your word on that. Do you understand me? She's no nigger scab. I don't want this county in the news any more than it is."

Deatherage had given his word; of course. Thunner was the boss. But now here he stood, and suddenly he could not help envisioning it. Envisioning the headlines if the victim of an anonymous assassin should happen to be the wife of the President of the United States.

He had not come here with that intention. But once elucidated in his mind, it grew second by second, as if the seed had lain for years and only now sensed the moment of its imminence; unfolding bud to petal, petal to a dark malevolent blossom even as he stared in the direction of the approaching engine.

Deep in his pocket, his fingers closed gradually on the cold steel of a revolver.

Her hands deep in the muff, Jennie Washko stamped her feet on the icy macadam as the locomotive came into view. A tiny black speck, far down the valley, and behind and above it the towering steam-and-smoke cloud that pulsed up again and again into the lowering sky. Beside her Viola chattered on, excited as a squirrel. "My gosh, Vi, can't you be quiet just for a minute?" she said at last. "Listen, the band's going to play."

It opened with a blare of brass and a crash of drums, and swung into "Happy Days Are Here Again." The onlookers straightened, rising on tiptoe, some singing with the music as the whistle hooted again, again, and the driving thud and hum of the locomotive drew closer. Then it was on them, radiating heat that those who stood closest to the tracks could feel on their faces, and ashes and smoke swept toward them on the gelid wind, and clouds of steam and through it the rattleclatterjangle of the cars and at last the slow expiring hiss and groan and squeal as the train eased to a stop.

The woman standing in the close, overheated vestibule rubbed the palms of her gloves together nervously. She'd inspected the valley as she came in, noting the condition of the forest, of the rails and roadbed, estimating the percentage of homes with outdoor privies, the state of repair of the bridges. *He* would expect a complete report.

The door slid open with a sudden startling bang, and she looked out and down at a sea of gray hats and turned-up collars. The local band was making up with volume what could barely qualify as music. But they were welcoming her, and she waved and smiled, stepping carefully as she descended, and the conductor, looking serious and dignified as if he did this every day, handed her down to the platform where the local bigwigs stood jostling each other.

Jennie could hardly contain herself. There she was, just as tall and awkward-looking as she was in the photo sections, slowly coming down the steps from the Pullman not ten feet away. Viola jumped up and down, pumping her sister's arm in excitement. Mrs. Roosevelt wore a shapeless black suit open at the collar, with a rather dowdy traveling hat. The muzzle of her fox stole dangled over her right shoulder. Her brown shoes were sensible and her hose was shiny. She carried a well-worn suitcase in her left hand, and in her right a leather briefcase, a purse, and a shopping bag. Slips of paper peeped out of her jacket pockets. "Viola, stop *jumping*," Jennie scolded her sister. "You're going to tear my arm right out of the socket."

"Jen, I can't *see* her. I can't *see*!"

"Well, all right. Hold still and I'll lift you up."

Deatherage stood irresolute, bewildered by the impulse that had surged up from some unknown depth of his heart. That had begun as a random pebble, bouncing through his mind, but which had triggered a landslide that thundered down now sudden and overwhelming and uncontrollable.

He began drifting forward through the crowd, the gun heavy and snug against his thigh.

There she was, only a few feet above him, stepping down onto the platform as a young woman lifted a girl in front of her. There was nothing to stop him. All he had to do was get a little closer.

Clutching the gun even more tightly, he began pushing his way forward. Pulling a colored woman back as she started to mount the steps. Her indignant angry face turned, mouth open, but stayed soundless and open as she caught sight of his face. Beyond her he saw one of the cops, hands deep in his greatcoat, eyes not on the crowd but on the tall, spare woman who stood a few yards past him, fiddling with her purse beside Foster and the mayor.

Deatherage pushed past more spectators, wedging them aside. He felt a light sweat break on the very surface of his skin.

She set down her bag and stood smiling and blinking in the glare off the snow as a short man in a gray topcoat launched into a speech of welcome.

"I believe you have probably all heard Mrs. Roosevelt on the radio, speaking for Simmons Mattress Company and Selby Shoes. Although, as yet, the Petroleum City *Deputy-Republican* does not yet carry 'My Day.' On behalf of the citizens of Hemlock County, I bid you welcome to the Pennsylvania Crude Oil Metropolis of the World."

She gave them all her smile, and took a deep breath.

"I do not usually make speeches. But I was reminded, coming in here today, of the One Hundred and Twenty-First Psalm: 'I will lift up mine eyes unto the hills whence cometh my help.' I could not help noticing your beautiful snow-covered hills. And though it is a bit brisk today, you know that I am a New York State girl myself! So winter weather is nothing new to me.

"I do apologize for coming in unannounced. One of my lectures was canceled, and the opportunity was there, and I decided to take it. I do find, that when people learn I'm coming, there's a great deal of cleaning up and so forth. And I really didn't want to put you to all that trouble."

She had not intended to make an address, but the naked yearning in their faces led her on. And presently she found herself speaking of the want and privation she had witnessed in her travels across the land. "I have seen the dank, dark working conditions in mines and the sorrow on the faces of sharecroppers. I know you are on strike here, and not living on much—raw carrots, perhaps, or a little bread.

"The message I would have all of us take away is that either we are going to learn to share, or we will all end up with nothing.

"It has always seemed to me that there are two ways of looking at politics. If you believe that a nation is really better off which achieves for a comparative few, high culture, ease, opportunity, and that these few from their enlightenment should give what they consider best to those less favored, then you naturally belong to the Republican Party. But if you believe all people must struggle slowly to the light for themselves, then it seems to me that you are naturally a Democrat.

"We have accomplished a great deal in these three years of working together. But the New Deal cannot be considered complete. What I have learned in politics is that significant changes in national direction cannot simply be declared. They must be worked at long and patiently, and it is as much of a process of education as it is of argument.

"I do know that there is no native resentment of the well-off in the breast of the American worker. All he asks is to be allowed to join those he admires. But if he is continually denied, this is the stuff of revolution.

"The upcoming campaign of nineteen thirty-six will decide whether we will continue to make real progress against fear and depression, or whether we will go back to the old ways of doing business. We are in a race against time; whether we can get our disadvantaged into better living conditions before they are led despite themselves to violent acts.

"Now, I see many of my own sex in this audience. To you I say: Making a house a home in trying times like these is still the greatest gift any woman has in her power to give. I am a mother and a grandmother. To make a home with little means, under any and all conditions—this is our peculiar genius, and our glory. And with that I will leave you to return to yours, and thank you again for the warm welcome you have given me."

Inside the station house a refreshment table with tea and store-cookies bore all the hallmarks of having been hastily set up. As soon as she had finished they had ushered her off the windswept platform, thank the Lord, and straight back through the freight doors. She stood now in a makeshift receiving line with the portly man, whom she now understood was the mayor, and his little rotund wife, shaking hand after hand.

"Jennie Washko, and this is my little sister, Viola."

"How very nice to meet you, Jennie. Viola, you're such a beautiful little thing; you remind me of my own granddaughters. My! How excited we are today!"

"Mrs. Sy Rosen . . . Mr. Popovich . . . Mr. Nix . . . Miss Delite."

"How very nice to meet you. Thank you all for coming to greet me."

"Mrs. Cordelia Watkins, ma'am, chairman of the Women's Division of the Hemlock County Democratic Party."

"How wonderful to meet you at last, Cordelia. Will I be able to talk briefly with the committee this afternoon, before my train leaves, at four? And perhaps you could find me a stenographer so that I might do my column right after I meet with you."

Mrs. Roosevelt's eye moved ahead, evaluating the length of the line. A few feet away her eye caught that of a tall man with a twisted mouth, a Roosevelt and Garner button prominent in his overcoat lapel. He was smiling at her, hands thrust deep into the pockets of his overcoat. Then her attention was pulled back as a woman gushed eagerly, "My, Mrs. Roosevelt, you're the biggest thing we've had around here since Kate Smith came to town."

She laughed. "I'm one of her admirers too. I'm sure Kate drew a much bigger crowd than I did!"

"Oh, yes, there were people all the way down to the Holderlin works when she came in. When she sings 'When the Moon Comes over the Mountain,' you know, on the radio, it seems like she's singing it right to me; the moon comes up right over the hills here, too, you see—"

Five yards away now, Deatherage judged that he was well within range. It had started as a lark, an impulse, but as he contemplated it, it seemed more and more inevitable, predestined, that the pen of fate was already descending to write his name ineradicably on the pages of history. He contemplated the screams, the tumult, as he pulled the trigger for the last time and dropped the gun. He saw no reason why he could not escape in the ensuing chaos, if he moved quickly enough, while those around them were still in bewildered shock. Once back in his room he could alter his appearance, call for his car, and vanish. But even if he did not escape, he would be the hero of the larger portion of the upper classes. He might face the electric chair, like Bruno Hauptmann. But even that prospect seemed distant, and dread of it contemptible, compared to the enormous satisfaction of fame.

It would be the ultimate transformation.

He literally could not think of a reason not to do it and, glancing quickly around, he planned his movements. Three bullets for her, to be certain. The last two for Foster, who was armed. Then a dash to the left, down the platform steps, into the crowd, still packed, surging to and fro down along the tracks. Outside, the band was crashing into a swing tune. Those outside might not even hear the shots, or would confuse them with the bass thunder of the drums.

He stepped forward again, and the first doubt occurred to him.

It would all be very well to take advantage of an opportunity. But would he not be acting on a whim? The superior man did not act on impulse. He planned carefully, and executed his plans in utter detachment.

Gripping the handgun tightly, he wondered that he was not trembling. That he was not daunted. But all he felt was a delicious coldness.

The woman in front of him moved on, and he shuffled forward another pace. Eyes fixed on the tall woman in the black dress who eyed him for a moment, as if she suspected what was tumbling through his mind. He would have to decide quickly. The woman ahead of him stepped up, extended her hand to the President's wife. He heard her high-pitched singsong in reply.

Then there was no one ahead of him but her, and he stepped forward, the decision and the certainty coalescing suddenly in his brain.

"Mr. Pearl Deatherage, ma'am. One of your more fervent admirers."

Close up the man looked ill, drawn and with perspiration on his forehead. "How do you do. I'm so glad to see you. I see you were on our side in 'thirty-two. I *so* hope you will keep on working for us in 'thirty-six." She didn't let him get a firm grip on her hand. The trick was to draw them past even as you shook their fingers, always smiling. But he was lingering. He was fumbling in his pocket. She waited expectantly.

He drew out a clean folded handkerchief, and pressed it to his mouth. His eyes burned, fastened to hers. Then he inclined his head with a strange tense smile and moved on, toward the tea and cookies, and the next nervous excited face took his place.

"Mr. Angelo Picciacchia ... Miss Margaret Onuffer ... Master John Cummiskey."

"My, aren't you the little man."

"He's famous, Missus President. Been in the papers. This here is the boy who swallowed the harmonica."

A dark woman, Hebraic nose, inclined to embonpoint. "Mrs. Roosevelt, I'm Doris Golden. Rose Schneiderman introduced us at the Women's Trade Union League meeting in New York, before you moved to the White House."

"Oh, yes, I recall it quite distinctly. And what are you doing here, child?"

"Organizing for the CIO. You know about our strike. Will you visit our picketers?"

"How interesting, of course I will. Send a car round and I'll go there this afternoon."

Flashbulbs went off, and Golden jerked her head angrily to blur the pictures; of course, they'd be happy to get a photo of Mrs. R. talking to her, to smear them both. She moved on as the reporters closed in, yelling questions about her husband's promise to trim the federal payrolls by twenty-five percent, about her plans for the November campaign.

Deatherage leaned against a baggage cart, wondering at himself. He was not sure even yet why he had not done it. He'd been close enough to place the barrel against her belly. Close enough that he could have sent the second bullet into the ridiculous, braying, horse-toothed face.

But the superior man did not act upon a caprice. He acted based on rational calculation, passionless and detached, above emotion and sentiment. Nothing, not even his own enshrinement forever in history, could be undertaken on a momentary fancy.

Mouth compressed so that no one watching could have suspected that he was actually smiling to himself, he stood motionless, a silent somber figure in a gray felt hat, watching the motorcade move slowly off through the rutted, dirty snow.

Halvorsen was standing by the flaming barrel, stirring the ashes with a bar someone had found down by the rails, when the men on the road began to yell. "The bulls. The bulls!" He started to toss it aside, then realized an iron bar with the tip glowing red-hot might not be a bad weapon. Carrying it like a javelin, he ran up toward the street.

The cars came in a line, squad cars first, then behind them more vehicles with their lights on. The picketers stared, bewildered, then fell into a ragged line across the gate. Grim looks took their faces.

His jaw dropped when Chief Foster handed her out of the car. Around him some men muttered awed oaths. Others just said, "Jesus Christ, it's Eleanor."

Then he saw the photographers pile out, fitting bulbs into their cameras. "Grab your signs, boys," he yelled.

She didn't spend long at the gate. She had to meet with the district committee, and visit the CCC camp. She'd tried to reach the executives at Thunder, but they refused to meet

with her. All she could do was shake hands and talk briefly
with each man, and walk across the ruined ground where
they told her their camp had been. Their desperate sallow
faces, the furious tales of injustice made her both bitterly
angry and inexpressibly sad. She'd heard so many, in the
years since '29. Would it ever end? But the way their eyes
lit when they saw her made up for a little of it. She couldn't
bring them help, or jobs, or food, or help them settle their
strike. But she made the photographers shoot her shaking
hands with them, holding a mug of their watery coffee, sharing a doughnut. She told them how she'd never crossed a
picket line in her life, and how necessary what they were
doing was, and how she hoped they got everything they were
fighting for.

That afternoon the two officers stood in snow up to their
riding boots, observing the valley below. When the First
Lady's train began to move, the major lowered his field
glasses. A few paces away down the hill, his exec looked up
expectantly. "Now, sir?"

"Give it another minute . . . all right. Let's get them moving."

The captain lifted an arm. One by one engines started,
until with a clattering roar the whole hollow filled with the
snarl of motors. Then his arm dropped, and he broke into a
trot, following the commanding officer toward the waiting
motorcycles. A few seconds later the sidecars jerked into
motion, leading the file of drab-painted one-and-a-half-ton
Ford cargo trucks.

Seated across from each other on collapsible seats, men in
thick wool winter uniforms and puttees held their rifles upright between their knees as the column rumbled down into
the Allegheny valley.

As they rolled through Gasport the column split as planned
back in Pittsburgh, the first ten trucks and a reel truck turning
right onto Seward, the rear of the column and a covered
kitchen truck turning left. Snow-chains clanging and jan-
gling, they rolled slowly through the eastern part of town.

The Seward Avenue detachment slowed as they came abreast of Gate One. The picketers there watched them approach, faces going blank as they rolled slowly by. Then they swung up onto an empty patch of brushy ground overlooking the gate area. The southerly detachment rolled at fifteen miles an hour along the river, then pulled off Route Six opposite the Gower Avenue gate, the wheels grinding over ashes and shattered crockery and half-burned collapsed tents and smashed furniture down onto the pebbled slope beside the frozen river that had been the squatters' camp.

"Goddamned bastards," Golden muttered, looking at the paper in her hand. The sergeant waited, expression neutral.

"Is there an answer, ma'am?" he said at last.

She thrust it toward him, and Halvorsen read it over. It was some sort of military message form, printed carefully in pencil. Major Benedict Weaver III, Pennsylvania National Guard, respectfully requested to meet with the responsible officials of OWIU No. 178 and the executives of the Thunder Oil Company at 1500 hours 14 February in the lobby of the Grant House.

"That's three this afternoon, ma'am," said the trooper. Halvorsen squinted at him, a solid, florid-faced fellow, in not-too-well-fitting olive-drab wool, leggings, and blacked boots. The butt of a big revolver stuck out of a tan canvas holster. Beyond him the troops were setting up tents in neat lines. They looked like they were pitching camp for a long stay. On a little rise, dominating the gate area, a squad was stacking sandbags in a U.

"Where you from, soldier?" Golden asked him.

"Me? I'm from Swissvale, ma'am. Pittsburgh, not far from Frick Park . . ."

"I know it. Right across the river from Homestead. Correct?" He nodded. "Where was your dad on July sixth of 'ninety-two?"

"I know what you're talking about, but my folks lived in Ohio then."

"Well, what's the tip on this?" She waved the message.

"What are the boys saying? Whose side are they on?"

The guardsman's face closed. "We aren't on anybody's side, ma'am. We just want to get this over with so we can go back home. We ain't regular troops, you know. I got me a plumbing business that's losin' money right now. Though there's some of the boys don't mind getting back on army pay. But as far as whose side I'm on—I don't much give a damn, you want to know the truth."

Looking past him, Halvorsen saw the flared heavy barrel of a machine gun being lowered into position behind the sandbags. He cleared his throat, pointed it out wordlessly to Golden.

She ignored him, still speaking to the trooper. "I see. Well, please take this message back to your commander. We, the citizens and workers of Petroleum City, after suffering violence and abuse at the hands of the bosses, are glad to have the legal authority of the State here. Our president and the committee will attend the meeting and negotiate for an end to the strike in good faith."

The guardsman got it down in pencil, started to salute her, caught himself, and about-faced. They watched him stride across the snow toward the waiting staff car. "Okay, let's get the committee together and plan how we're going to approach this," she said.

"Did you see that machine gun?" he asked her.

"I saw it."

"Kind of changes things, havin' the army here—"

"It doesn't change a damn thing," she told him angrily. But they both knew it was not the truth.

Cavalry twill riding breeches, polished calfskin field boots, gold oak leaves, and a gleaming Sam Browne belt were revealed as Weyandt helped the officer remove his trench coat in the Thunder office. "Major Weaver," said Thunner, shaking his hand. "I am very pleased indeed to see you and your men here. I shall wire the governor my thanks. Scotch, I presume? Or would a dash of brandy be a better warmer-upper?"

"Thank you, sir; nothing at all would be most appropriate."

"I understand; duty status and all that. I would like first of all to say how much I respect the Tanbarks. I saw service myself, during the late unpleasantness in Europe. One Hundred and Ninth, Company D."

"Actually, sir, I'd heard that. Do you recall a Sergeant Major Selph? Preston Selph? He said to give you his best."

Thunner laughed. "Sergeant major, eh? I remember him as a rather slovenly private. I do indeed. Perhaps hot tea, then? Rudy, see to it. Come, let's sit down. My attorney, Ellis Hildebrandt. I believe you've already met Mr. Weyandt. And Mr. Pearl Deatherage, here to advise me on labor relations. Mr. Deatherage was with the Seventy-ninth in the Argonne Forest."

"Is that right, sir? I have some acquaintances from that outfit as well. What company were you with?"

A little to Thunner's surprise, Deatherage did not answer Weaver, did not offer any names. Simply shook hands with a thin-lipped smile. Thunner hesitated. Then said, a little more loudly: "Pearl?"

"Yes, Dan?"

"The major asked what company you were in."

Deatherage said, "I was not in the division for very long. His acquaintances most likely will not remember me."

Thunner studied him for a moment, frowning; then suddenly turned away, inviting the major to take a seat. They settled around the big conference table as he inquired about the route between Hemlock County and Pittsburgh. Major Weaver said it had been a difficult trip. They'd had to stop several times for the men to clear the roads of snow; the William Penn across the mountain at Cresson was closed tight. Thunner asked about fuel and oil consumption. Weaver said his unit consumed about one hundred fifty pounds of gas and oil every twenty-five miles. Thunner offered his firm's facilities for refueling, greasing, and maintenance of his vehicles, which Weaver accepted.

Finally the major cleared his throat, laying his cap carefully aside. "Well, to business. Sir, my unit has been activated under a general order from Governor Earle to restore and maintain the public tranquillity in Hemlock County, and, if possible, to help the responsible local authorities bring this unfortunate situation to a peaceful end. The Adjutant-General, Brigadier General Kerr, reached me by radiogram as we were convoying through Emporium to make sure my instructions were clear."

"What are your instructions?"

"You are the attorney here, sir?" the major asked Hildebrandt, who inclined his head. "I pass over for your perusal both General Kerr's message and a copy of Appendix G of Special Mobilization Plan A of the Pennsylvania National Guard. This governs our mission and our responsibilities to the civil authority. May I ask that you transmit it to the mayor as well?"

"We'll be happy to," said Thunner. "Ellis, see to that, please."

"Gentlemen, let me make clear at the outset that I am not here to take sides. We hold no brief for either party; although I cannot say I am in general an admirer of the elements that gather together under the name of organized labor. In my civilian profession, I am a sales executive with the H. J. Heinz Company. But you can understand the delicacy of my position. It is not a pleasant prospect, this facing of men who are fighting for their jobs; but I will carry out my duty. I do not wish to come in here like General MacArthur on his white horse, scattering the Bonus Marchers. The Guard must be an impartial observer."

Thunner said that he quite understood how difficult the major's mission was, and that he would endeavor not to increase his burdens in this regard. Then, leaning back, tapping his fingers lightly together, he reviewed for Weaver the history of the strike and his attempts to placate his employees. He dwelled on his successive offers of raises and safety commissions. Hildebrandt interjected a word about trespass and other violations of local law, which the police force, not wishing to invite further trouble, had chosen to let pass without notice. Thunner passed from this to the recent episodes of violence, including the sabotage of the pipeline, the mass attack on the refinery, and ended with the shooting of Eli Gant, an outrage which the local police had not yet solved. The major listened with a serious air, chin propped on his fist.

"But I have not given up my hope that we may yet bring matters to a peaceful conclusion. Our final attempt at settlement you may find a bit unorthodox. That is, I have agreed to stake the outcome of our disagreement upon a sporting contest."

"I beg your pardon?" said Deatherage. "Dan, I haven't been—"

Weaver blinked. "I'm sorry, sir, I didn't quite follow that either."

Thunner said, not even looking at Deatherage, "Have you ever indulged in pugilism, Major?"

"Boxing? A bit of it. In my salad days."

"I've decided to arrange a sort of smoker, actually more of a trial by combat, between a representative of the company and another for the strikers. The terms are to be as follows. If our side is victorious, the dispute is over and the men go back to work, at the increased wage rates we have discussed, of course. And there is to be no further talk of a union."

Deatherage stood. "I don't believe this is a good idea, Dan. I heard Rudy discussing it with Earl Vansittart. I must confess, I thought it was a joke. Don't tell me you're proceeding with this ludicrous suggestion."

Thunner looked up at him. "Mr. Deatherage: Sit down, please. You forget your place."

Deatherage said coldly, "My place is to advise you, sir, and this idea of a boxing match is tantamount to farce. It is not the way of a serious businessman to wager the conduct of his affairs on the outcome of a bet."

"I assure you, I am serious and the arrangements are being made. Right, Rudy?"

"Yes, sir."

"Dan, this is just not the act of a reasonable man. You are

counting on some notion of honor. These people have none, they have no—"

"*Sit down*, Mr. Deatherage," said Thunner, regarding him with a face of iron. "I am quite willing to believe you have no idea of sport—and perhaps no idea of honor as well. Since you have been the first to mention the word. In fact, I am beginning to suspect that many things you have told me are subject to doubt. No, sir! We will discuss this later, in private. Sit *down*, I said!"

Deatherage frowned, then subsided into his chair, shaking his head.

Weaver said, "It does seem rather like tempting the gods. And if the union fighter wins?"

"I daresay we needn't worry about that. I've seen them both box, and our chap is worlds beyond theirs. But in the unlikely event that he does, I've agreed on a sum of money to augment their war chest. That will make no difference in the ultimate outcome. I have no doubt we will end in possession of the field." Thunner paused. "At the same time, I'm not anxious to extend the work outage. I am sure you understand me, as a fellow businessman, when I say that no one makes a profit during an unpleasantness of this sort."

"Quite so. Yet your adviser here is correct; it is not the usual manner of settling these sorts of disputes. You're the commander here, though, as far as I am concerned. I will leave the manner in which you conduct your negotiations up to you. When is this—event?"

"It is set for Wednesday night, in the garage at our works."

"Well, sir, I think we understand each other. The only remaining question I have is, What if your fighter triumphs, yet your workers refuse to come back in?"

"Rudy?" Thunner twisted around in his chair.

Weyandt withdrew a piece of paper from his briefcase and placed it before the major. "What's this?" Hildebrandt asked, leaning forward to adjust his spectacles.

"The injunction ending the strike."

"Indeed. May I see it?"

"Just a minute, sir." The major read the paper. Then passed it over.

As the company attorney read, his eyebrows contracted. "Dan, someone's advised you incorrectly. This is not a legal instrument in this day and age."

"I'm afraid Judge Wiesel opines otherwise," said Weyandt. "All workers will return to work or be ruled in contempt of court. This constitutes the authority. The major here will provide the force. One way or another, as of next Wednesday night, this strike is over."

Thunner broke the silence that succeeded that statement by asking quietly if anyone would care for one for the road. At that the major stirred. He tucked his cap under his arm and stood. "Well, gentlemen, if you will accompany me, we can just make our meeting."

"Meeting?"

"The three-o'clock conference with the strikers."

"I don't believe it is necessary," Thunner said easily to the major. "I believe that now everything is well arranged and in sound hands."

"Very well, sir. Are there any further questions for me, gentlemen?"

Pearl Deatherage slowly put up his hand. "Sir?" said the major.

"Let me inquire, Major, as to whether your troops could benefit from the use of a firing range tomorrow."

The committee members sat waiting from a quarter till three until half past, but no one from Thunder showed up. Across from them in the lobby the officers waited, too, faces impassive. At last the major entered, alone, and the other soldiers rose hastily.

"Is Mr. Thunner on his way?" Golden asked him.

"The company representatives are not attending this meeting," the major told her coldly. "Therefore it will not be held. You people are free to go."

"You can't send troopers down there to drag 'em in here? The way you'd have dragged us in, if we hadn't shown?"

"We don't 'drag' citizens anywhere. If they decline to attend a conference, we have no further recourse. But I do have a request of you. Mr.—Melnichak? Lieutenant Clay has reported that your people are attempting to influence my men away from their duty. Tell your strikers to stay clear of them or I'll have to forbid any contact. Do you understand me?"

Golden said, "And I have a request for *you*, Major. Your field kitchen. Whatever sort of stew your cooks are making, it smells awfully good. Can we ask you for one meal a day—not for us, but for children under eight? They are the real victims of this lockout. Some are quite literally starving—"

"That's not possible. Those are government rations, and closely accounted for," the major told them. "And now I will bid you good day."

"Well, what now?" Melnichak asked her as she stood with her hands on her hips looking after the guardsmen.

"What now? What the hell do you mean, 'what now'?"

"I don't know. I just thought you might have had some last trick up your sleeve."

"I don't have any more tricks," she said, feeling suddenly weary. She dropped her hands, then lifted them again to rub her face, suddenly overwhelmed by the realization they were at the end of their rope. But she could not say that aloud, could not even say it to herself.

Stan said, "Well, I guess it's all gonna be riding on you, Red. Anybody got any Bugler on him? I'm out."

Pearson had a few grains in the bottom of his sack. They rolled one apiece, there in the lobby of the hotel, and lit them thoughtfully.

Twenty-eight

Jennie was coming out of the five-and-dime, head bent beneath a driving wind, when she almost collided with him. She couldn't speak at first, then stammered, "Hello, Bill," as he stood startled and uneasy on the shoveled sidewalk in front of Ballard's. He looked thinner and paler. His coat wasn't the same one he'd worn before; it was cheap and ragged. She wanted to touch him, but didn't dare. He cleared his throat and when he turned his head to spit his eyes left hers. She spoke quickly, to keep him from walking off.

"Where you living these days? You still down at Mrs. Ludtke's?"

"No, I had to move out of there. Sort of bunking it catch-as-catch-can right now."

"Is your car running all right?"

"Oh, I wouldn't take it on no long trips, but it's running." Halvorsen rammed his hands into the thin-worn pockets of the pawnshop coat. He felt guilty just facing her. Jennie'd never let him touch her. Just those unforgettable kisses, that night on the Ferris wheel at Hecla Park . . .

"I been following the strike in the paper. It don't sound too good, does it?"

"We're givin' it the best we can. I was glad when your pop finally came out with us."

"Uh-huh. He said first it was no good fighting the company; that it would always win. But we all talked to him, and said us kids'd work extra hard; and finally he went back out again."

Halvorsen shifted his plug glumly and spat again. He was wondering how Washko could have done it at all, how he could have worked even for a day for the man who'd killed his son. He was beginning to see what the old man had meant, there under the grape arbor. About things changing, when you had a family. But at the same time, it seemed like a fella had to draw a line someplace.

"Yeah, you just got to give it the best you can. How's them stockings going? Those cardin' machines still giving you trouble?"

She tucked her gloved hands quickly under her arms and said they didn't hurt as much. She rubbed them with Cornhusker's Lotion every night and it helped.

A soldier, one of the guardsmen from out of town, shouldered past them on the sidewalk. Halvorsen clenched his fists and stared after him, then controlled himself. "Uh, hey, look. There's a big colored show on tonight. The Cotton Club Revue." He didn't remember until after he said it that he was flat busted, he didn't have a sou to take her to something like that. It would cost fifty cents each, at least.

"I don't think that's the kind of show I'd want to go to."

"You mean, your parents would let you go to."

She cried, "Do you think that's the only reason I don't do certain things, Bill? That somebody don't let me? Don't you ever think it's because it's just wrong?"

"Don't get mad, Jen. I just don't see how goin' to a show can be bad—"

"I didn't say it was. Certain kinds are all right."

"Well, there's a Claire Trevor movie."

She shook her head, scuffing her boot on the pavement

and inspecting the toe. He looked at her downcast face, half
wanting to go on talking to her, half wanting to say forget
it and walk away. She was nothing like Golden. Not that
he'd want to be married to Doris, or have kids with her.
She'd made it pretty plain she wouldn't put up with that. She
was too dedicated to her damn movement . . . older than
him . . . and he knew he wouldn't trust her out of his sight,
not after what she'd said about sex. "Like blowing your
nose." That had a pretty unpleasant ring to it when you
thought about it. He noticed Jennie looking at him funny and
coughed and said, "Well, hey, where you headed now? Goin'
home? Can I walk along with you?"

"I guess," she said, and turned back toward her house. And
after a few hundred feet in silence she started talking again,
about her little sister, and how excited she'd been about
meeting Mrs. Roosevelt, and how they'd gone to the Carnegie and gotten her a book about her; how now Vi wanted
to be the wife of a president and go around doing good deeds
when she grew up. "Ain't that the nuts?" she said, laughing.
"And she's only seven. Where she gets these ideas. She'll
just work in the stocking mill, like me an' Ma."

"I didn't know your Ma was working."

"She had to go back, with Pa out. So now she's down in
the packaging. It ain't so bad in there, that's where they put
the older ladies and the kids."

They passed the turn to her street and he was just as glad;
he didn't want to go into the stuffy dark house and have to
talk to her parents, her sisters and brothers. He remembered
the night Joseph Washko had sat him down out back and
given him whiskey and milk and asked him about his plans.
And he'd had this glorious future in his head, marrying Jennie and going to engineering college. He spat into the snow,
smiling bitterly. What a sap he'd been.

"What you gonna do after the strike's over, Bill?" she
asked him, breaking in on his reverie. He kicked at a ridge
of frozen slush and gravel and blew out white cold-smoke.

"I don't know. Depends on if we win, or not."

"I guess if you win, you go back to bein' a foreman?"

"I guess. Maybe."

"And if you lose?"

"I'll be on my own then," he told her. "Probably have to leave town. I don't think Bryner'd take me back on again; he does too much business with Thunder. It'll pretty much take me out of circulation around here. Might be able to get a job out West, Oklahoma or Texas. They need oilmen out there."

"That'd be awful. To make you leave your hometown. But you're still gonna win, aren't you?"

"I don't think so, Jen. It's really getting me down. But I don't think we're gonna."

She said hesitantly, blushing and looking away, "I been thinking. That Claire Trevor movie. Maybe we could go to that. If you still wanted to."

He brushed snow off her shoulders, and made himself smile down at her. "I messed up, Jen. I forgot, when I asked you that, I forgot we got a meeting tonight. A union meeting."

"Oh. That's too bad."

He'd been meaning to say this and so far it had just stuck in his craw. Now he decided there wasn't any good way of saying it; or any better time than now. So he took a deep breath and mumbled quickly, as if telling her fast would slip it by her somehow, "Uh, Jen? I got to come clean with you. I been seein' another girl."

She turned quick as a flash and he found himself confronted by something he'd never seen before: a wrathful Jennie. "Oh, you have. Well, thanks for being so *honest* with me."

"Look, you already told me you weren't goin' to have anything more to do with me. That I was a cake eater, an' a Protestant, and we were too different—"

"So you go out and start going around with somebody else. And I just have to wait."

He stared at her open-mouthed as she raged on, calling him names he'd never thought she knew. Finally he managed a weak, "Gee, Jennie. I didn't know. . . ."

"You knew." Her face was closed now, nostrils pinched white. "Are you still seeing her? Who is it? Are you going to marry her?"

"Uh—no, I don't think we're gonna do anything like that. It wasn't exactly like that—"

"What *was* it like, Bill? Was it because I wouldn't do what you wanted? And she would? Was it one of those girls in the houses across the river?"

He looked away, shaken; how had she known about Fischer Town? No, she couldn't have; it was just a lucky shot. For a moment the hostile silence lay between them like a snow-filled ravine. Finally he said, "It wasn't anything like that. And actually I don't think I'm gonna be seein' her again. It was just one of those things. And if you hadn't given me the brush-off it probably wouldn't a happened at all."

"Can I believe that?"

"I ain't in the habit of lyin'."

She studied him for a moment more, and he swallowed before he could stop himself and damn near choked on tobacco juice. But she just turned again and walked on. He hastened his steps, jumping over a discarded tire lying by the road, getting rid of the plug as he caught up with her.

"So you're going to a meeting tonight. Or was that some kind of white lie, to not make me feel bad you're seeing her?"

"No, it's a union meeting."

"Can I go?"

"Can you go? Gee, I don't know."

"There are women there, aren't there?"

"Yeah, some, but it ain't exactly a social event, Jen. There's guys use pretty rough language at these things. They ain't supposed to, but they do."

"Will Miss Golden be there?"

He glanced at her sideways. "Uh—I suppose so. She's just about always at the meetings, yeah."

"Is it true she's a Jewess? And a socialist, like they say?"

"I don't know. I guess so."

She took a breath and asked the question she'd wanted to ask for weeks now. Knowing she probably wouldn't get an answer, but knowing that not getting an answer was an answer, too. "Is it her, Bill? The one you're sweet on?"

"Who—her? Good grief, Jen. She's kind of hard-boiled, if you know what I mean. I don't like women that thinks they're the same as a man." He wished she'd get off the subject; he was skating right along the edge of the truth, but didn't want to change it himself because it would seem like he was avoiding it.

To his relief she said, "Well, do you think anybody would mind if I went? I think it'd be awful interesting to see the workers settling things themselves. There's some girls down at the stocking plant, they won't let us talk union, but there's girls who go around whispering about it. If Mrs. Kohler finds out she'll fire them sure. I know they had a big hosiery strike in Philly not so long ago. Do you think I could come with you? I wouldn't make any trouble."

They got to the end of the cleared sidewalks, out where they turned to ashlittered snow-heaped berms and past that snow-covered fields and beyond that scattered farmhouses and barns and beyond and above that just the charcoal prickle of forest as the hills dammed the pearly sky. He looked at her eager eyes and flaming cheeks and said, "Well—I guess, maybe. I ain't really supposed to, but. If you really want to, and you let your maw know so she ain't worried about you, then—well, I'd sort of like to take you."

She took his arm, feeling its hardness under the threadbare wool. And after a while he put it around her, steadying her, as they picked their way over the frozen ruts and banks along the downhill road; and neither of them said anything else; just walked along back toward town, together.

They couldn't meet at Cassidy's anymore. And the other businessmen who owned the halls and bars in town had given them notice that they weren't welcome. The Citizens' Committee wouldn't like it, they muttered. You guys know what I mean. I got nothing against the union, but a fella's got to make a living. A fella's got to get along. He'd thought about it for a while, and finally gone to the Warsaw Club on Farragut Street. It was dark inside and cramped, but one of the old guys there was family with Melnichak and after a lot of talking among themselves in Polish they told him they could have the upstairs room. Then they wanted ten bucks up front, to cover breakage and the lights, and he had to go around with them about that for a while before they reluctantly agreed to take whatever came in when the hat was passed. Which he knew wasn't going to be much, but he didn't tell them that.

He went by Mrs. Ludtke's, leaving Jennie waiting outside on the sidewalk as he went in. Ludtke's was a men's boardinghouse; it was as much as a girl's reputation was worth being seen going in there. The parlor was empty, the big radio's tubes dark, the lights off. The familiar smell of old sauerkraut hung in the air.

"Yeah, I got it," said Shotner. He looked suspicious, barely opening the door a crack. For a second Halvorsen wondered if he had somebody in there with him. Then had to smile at the thought. Dick Shotner? Not likely.

Shotner passed the Krag out. Halvorsen worked the bolt to make sure it wasn't loaded, then slung it over his shoulder. "You g-goin' hunting?" Shotner asked him, and this time Halvorsen caught the sweet whiskey smell.

"Uh, no. Just need to use it awhile, okay? Thanks for hangin' on to it for me."

"You want, I could maybe buy it off you." No question, the kid was drunk.

"I don't know, Dick. It was my dad's. Uh, hey, you all right?"

"'M'I all right? No, I'm not all right. I lost my job."

"Down at the battery plant? I didn't know they were laying off."

"They ain't. Mr. Baines called me in and fired me."

"Gee, I'm sorry about that," Halvorsen told him. "Look, I got to go. We'll talk later, okay? Take it easy on the hooch. That stuff ain't going to help you none."

"Like to kill the sonofabitch. Kill all the damn sonsa-bitches."

"You're feelin' chesty, ain't ya? Look, you want to come down the Alpine tomorrow, there's some guys that know other guys in the office, there at Thunder. Maybe they can hook you up."

"You kidding? You guys are on strike."

Halvorsen told him they probably wouldn't be much longer, the next couple days would wrap it up one way or the other. He said he had to go, and Shotner closed the door.

He and Jennie got to the hall at six. The old guys downstairs didn't give him or his rifle a second glance, but they eyed her doubtfully. He left the gun behind the bar and went upstairs. He made sure the folding chairs were set up and the gas heater was lit to take the chill off. She insisted on going to the corner store for something to eat. He said they couldn't pay her back, but she said she wanted to bring something so he let her go.

Golden and Pearson arrived, climbing the creaky stairs together. She inspected the room, then, for some reason, tapped the walls. She seemed satisfied and sat in the front row as the door jangled again and again downstairs and a slow thunder of climbing footsteps signaled that the struggling masses were arriving.

Stealing a surreptitious glance at her hard, determined face, he was struck again by the difference between her and Jennie. They were night and day, experience and innocence, and he couldn't say which one he really wanted; or, rather, he wanted them both, in different ways, for different things. Just like they wanted different things out of him.

But that would all just have to wait.

Melnichak came in and started complaining right away that the room was too small: Halvorsen flashed back that it was the best they'd get; they were lucky they weren't meeting out in the goddamn woods.

Jennie came back from Pishko's with a big quarter bag of cheap sugar cookies and started laying them out. Some of the guys slipped them into their pockets. For their kids, Halvorsen figured. Shit, did he really want to tie himself down with a family? From a couple things Doris had let slip, he didn't think she could have any. But look at the Washkos, all those kids underfoot. That was probably what he'd get with Jennie. Catholics dropped another kid every time they turned around, everybody knew that.

Jennie busied herself with the cookies, but she kept one eye on the plumpish woman who talked in a loud voice to an intent circle of men. She looked old and her shoes were scuffed and worn. She obviously didn't take care of herself and when she laughed it was a bray, mouth wide open and her chest shaking so you could tell even across the room that she wasn't wearing a girdle.

She was the one Bill was mixed up with. Jennie had no doubt about that at all, and no doubt that the woman had let him do exactly what he wanted to her. She kept looking over toward her, and once their eyes met. But Golden didn't smile or acknowledge her existence in any way. Jennie couldn't tell if she'd been cut or if the other woman's mind was just somewhere else. She felt out of place, too young and a little silly. Resolving to herself that she would not let this happen, she quietly finished setting out the treats and found herself a seat in back.

Halvorsen had brought a young girl along. She was fussing with refreshments at a side table. Doris didn't care; if it was to test her or make her angry it wasn't going to work. There were more important fish to fry tonight.

She'd heard it through the grapevine, that some of the wives had decided enough was enough and it was time to call things off and send the men back to work. Not that she didn't sympathize. But sympathy won nothing, and giving in won nothing. Even if she was the only one left, she'd go down fighting.

At seven Stan Melnichak slammed his fist on the table to call the meeting to order. She sat with her arms crossed and watched them, the workers, a scattering of wives in back.

"The treasurer's report, well, we'll pass on that because as you all know we are stony broke. All right, who wants to talk first?" An arm shot up instantly from the seated crowd.

"Jack."

A stocky man in working greens, looking truculent. "It's time to quit, Stan."

"Sit down and shut up!" someone called.

"You go back, we'll stay out."

Melnichak cut off the bickering with a sledgehammer blow on the tabletop. "Just can it, when one of the brothers is on his feet! We don't shout nobody down, hear me? Go on, Bert, get it off your chest."

"I ain't got nothing else to say. Just that we gave it a hell of a good try. I don't know if you heard, Nick's little Mabel died today. Died of neglect, the damn doctor said. Like there was somethin' we done wrong. Thunner's goin' to pay in hell, but he's tied the can on us and it's time to throw in the towel and just go on back to work." He sat, and outcries and yells welled again, filling the little upstairs room.

"Steve, you wanna talk? You got your hand up, or are you pickin' your nose?"

Popovich lumbered to his feet, slow and massive, and stood until the noise faded enough for him to say, "I think he's right. A yard bull with a club, that's one thing. Now they got a machine gun at the gate. I ain't eager to mix it up with the army."

Golden sat watching, letting a faint smile play across her lips. Doing her best to project a confidence she did not feel. She would speak. But it was not yet time.

"Who else got somethin' to say? Somebody from in back."

Several women started talking at once, and the loudest overrode the others and said they had to go back; the company had won and all they were doing now was being hardheaded stubborn. She didn't mind being hungry herself, but it was the children crying that tore at your heart. "And the goddamned county relief, excuse my French, they won't give you a dime or a box of crackers. Say if you walked out of a job, there's no place on the welfare for you. Well, I'm sick of beggin' from my family, and goin' cold, and it's just time to say we lost and try to make the best of it before Thunner puts all of our men on the list and they don't never get a place again."

Melnichak said quietly to the others at the table, "We got to take a vote. Put it to 'em about Red fighting Thunner's pug and all."

"What if they say, go back right now? There's some folks here really got their steam up."

"Then we go back, I guess. That's democratic. Doris, whatta you think?"

"And not show of hands, either."

She didn't respond, though they kept glancing at her.

It was time to speak.

The gathering quieted as she got to her feet; but not completely, the way they had when she first came to town. A rustle of whispering kept on in the back of the hall. She cleared her throat and began in a matter-of-fact voice.

"I understand how you folks feel. After holding out so long, and suffering so much, it's natural to start to doubt. First of all, I want to say that as an organizer, and before that as a worker, I've been through dozens of these things. There is only one way to victory in a work action. That is to stick together. If we stick tight enough, long enough, there is no way we cannot win. If we only stay together, we will win in the end no matter how powerful the bosses are.

"But if they can split us up, if we lose faith in one another—then we lose, even if we should win on paper.

"The question before us tonight is not really whether to continue. And certainly not whether to risk everything on some circus-sideshow boxing bout! History tells us we have no choice but to continue this struggle, as long as bosses are bosses and workers are workers. This is about more than maintaining a wage, or a forty-hour week, or even safe working conditions."

She leaned forward, looking into tired, hungry eyes fastened on hers with a gleaming expression she was not sure how to interpret; whether they were expectant, or suspicious, or withholding judgment. But it did not seem that they were listening in the same way they had listened to her in the past.

"This strike is to answer one question: whether you as working people have control of your destiny, or whether you and your children and your children's children will serve as wage slaves for a financial dictatorship that will destroy our natural resources, debase your soul and your pride, and finally wreck everything you hold dear.

"All around us the workers are rising to a new consciousness. A puppet government attempts to appease them with bread and make-work. Vigilante groups and paid thugs are like a steel band around the decaying staves of the capitalist barrel. But beneath the steel it is crumbling away."

She took a deep breath and straightened, searching herself for the conviction she had to hold out to them.

"The one message I must get across to you is that no matter how much they take from us as individuals, when we march as one, we cannot be defeated. Labor has been assaulted with dynamite, enjoined by courts, beaten by thugs, charged by the police, bayoneted by the army, hung by the vigilantes, lied about by the press, milked by politicians, denounced by priests, stolen from by grafters, infested by spies, betrayed by traitors, and sold out by its leaders. But always it has risen again, nearer the goal, and striven on, bloodied but always gaining strength. Until today it is the only creative power left in the shell of a decaying society, and its mission of liberating the workers of the world is as certain of success as the rising of the sun tomorrow morning.

"Our personal suffering, yours and mine, shrinks to insignificance in the sweep of history! Today, in nineteen thirty-six, is America's last chance at revolution. If we can't make one in the midst of a depression, we will never achieve one on our soil. The plutocrats will divert the people with wars and token concessions, and we will never build a society that is fair to the worker. But if we can, then the golden age will dawn of true democracy and progress. And you, the proletarian vanguard, will be leaders in that dawn—"

Someone threw a cookie. It arched through the smoky air and hit her, and she stopped speaking, she was so taken aback. A shocked silence; then someone sniggered.

"She's not from here. Who the hell says we got to listen to her?"

"No more speeches."

"I fought them goons for my job, not no revolution."

"She's a goddamned Communist. Just like they always said."

Uncertain laughter, growing louder. She bit her lip, staring around. Brushed slowly, without thinking, at where the crumbs clung to her skirt. They would content themselves with the crumbs the bosses let them have. But at least, then, the children would eat . . . She shook her head, finding her mouth suddenly empty of words. Not because her head and heart were empty, but because they were too full of striving voices for one single voice to speak.

Halvorsen jumped to his feet. "Who's the yellow sonofabitch threw that? Come on, get up." He stared around, fists doubled, as Golden sank slowly back into her seat. No one responded.

"All right, then you better listen to me, 'cause I got somethin' to say. Wednesday I'm going to stand up and fight. You all heard about it. I know how fast the grapevine works. It's us going back, against two large for the strike fund. What I want is to have you folks behind me when I get in that ring. That's all I'm askin' for. Hold out till then, and back me up when I lace on those gloves. If I win, we'll be in a lot better shape with that two thousand. And if I don't— well, it's up to every man jack what he does then."

Melnichak announced that they'd write down their votes. Either *Back W.T.* or *Give up now*. Halvorsen had to admire the way he phrased it. Frank Latimer went downstairs for pencils, and they tore up the grocery bag from Pishko's for paper. The room went quiet, the pencils scratching.

The final vote went 97 to 52 to hold out till the boxing match. The meeting broke not long afterward, and there wasn't the usual lingering around to shoot the bull. Everyone left immediately, disappearing back into a bitter blowing night. He walked Jennie home, watched her up to her porch. When she turned to wave good-bye he was already gone, and the road lay empty and glistening under the cold light of the moon.

Twenty-nine

The last of the late afternoon light had ebbed away, sucked back into the wintry sky and the dark hills. A fitful wind laden with flaky snow blustered and ebbed down the valley, as if alternately resigned to and then enraged by its imprisonment. Here and there on the dark slopes wavered yellow stars, flickering and dimming, but never quite going out; the flare-offs from still-producing wells, hoarding crude against the day it would move again.

Feeling stiff as some B-movie monster, Halvorsen got out of DeSantis's auto. Carefully, because the snow was shellac-slick where many other tires had already passed. DeSantis hadn't let him drive; had insisted on calling for him at the Alpine, where he'd spent a fitful afternoon sprawled on the floor in the back room, trying to nap but not succeeding. Remembering all too vividly a hard-muscled chest, covered with the blue phantasmagoria of old tattoo; slicked-back patent-leather hair above a broken nose; an aggressive, angry head that looked like it had been machined out of nickel steel.

Jack McKee, the heavyweight champ of Thunner's stable. The man he had to beat. Or the strike would be over, and with it, everything he'd worked for since he was a kid carrying a pail of sludge paraffin in the wintry dawn.

Back when he'd starting training, Guertin had told him it was normal to feel butterflies before a tough match or a big crowd. It wasn't fear, just stage fright. He took a couple deep breaths standing there on the slick ground, head bent under the whispering snow, and it sank back.

"You feelin' okay, Red?"

"Uh-huh." Shotner and Melnichak, appearing from the icy dark with a squeaking crunch of footsteps.

"We gonna have our boys there?"

"We're all behind you, Kid, and you're gonna chloroform this sonofabitch."

Trudging toward the black loom of the garage, he didn't feel like the Nitro Kid. He didn't feel like any master blaster, or boss driller. He felt like a scared child.

Father Guertin had acted as the go-between, since the company still refused to deal with the committee. He'd arranged an open-ended bout, to go to a knockdown. There wouldn't be any judges, though there'd be a ref; actually, the same fella who'd ref'd when Halvorsen had taken on Gigliotta over in Chapman.

Sudden brilliant balls of light exploded ahead, and he caught his breath.

They were the old arc lights, set high above the Gower Avenue gate. At the same time the gate lights came on, and the united brilliance created shapes from the hitherto unformed darkness of the world; dozens, scores, of bent shadows striding steadily along behind the obscuring screen of snow. A dark mass resolved itself into a company of uniforms as he neared: gray Thunder plant protection, blue city cops. The two groups stood carefully separated, but they all held their nightsticks the same way, gripped in both hands, held at groin level parallel to the ground. Their features were cast in shadow by the downflung light, and it was as if the workers passed in between ranks of visageless figures, straggling through the gate in an irregular, unsteady, clotted stream that nonetheless marched inexorably onward into the darkened recesses of the plant. He tugged his cloth cap down over his eyes, figuring that shadow and snow would mask him, too. Hands thrust deep into his jacket, he followed the rest.

Past the office, the brick angularity of the labs, windows black, past the low long shed of the power building. Then another glare of light, painful and revealing in the vast gloom of the mountains and the sky.

The garage was lit as brightly as a theater. A shoal of automobiles was parked along Thunder Avenue and drawn up close to Still Three and the towers and equipment at the south end of the refining line. Through the electricitybright night another stream of hastening, faceless figures tided toward him, and yet a third from Gate Three. He thought fleetingly that here was their chance, that they could occupy the plant the way they'd tried to in the face of thugs and police, facing gas and steam hoses and leveled guns. Now, like a Trojan horse, they were within. Then he saw the line of Deatherage's goons watching them enter; and the browncoated state troopers, rifles slung over their parkas, who surveyed the intersection of the three internal avenues from atop a jerry-built tower of planks and pierced steel.

He pushed through the crowd near the door and saw faces turn toward him, saw recognition ripple over the packed multitude within. Caught a glimpse of cavernous space, the ring erected like a gibbet or a guillotine, an instrument of execution; of blinding lights overhead, the echoing din of hundreds of snared voices. A foreman with a strained scarlet face, yelling at a startled worker: "Put that Christly thing out, in here," while beyond rose the haze of hundreds of cigarettes.

He was jerked back suddenly, and found a wizened apevisage a foot below his eyes. "Kid. Kid! Not in there. Foller me."

He trailed Picciacchia's crablike limp around to a rear door guarded by two Thunder bulls whose bellies strained their coats. They fondled their revolvers as he approached. "This here is Kid Nitro," said Picciacchia.

"What, this beanpole's gonna put 'em up with **Jack McKee?**"

"He's gonna get his boots laced good."

"Don't answer them," the trainer said out of the side of his mouth, and they pushed past into a dim cold oil-smelling cavern.

As his eyes adapted he saw it was a parts room in back of where the Thunder lease vehicles and trucks were serviced. A bulb burned saffron dim above racks of tools, and the smells of grease and gasoline were suffocating. He followed the trainer's crooked lurch down aisles walled with replacement driveshafts, blocks, brake-drums, all wrapped tightly in translucent greased paper like a nightmarish collection of severed limbs. The next, smaller room showed every sign of being hastily cleared out and curtained off. He looked around for McKee, but saw no sign of the other fighter.

Picciacchia set to work. Halvorsen stepped out of pants, stripped off his union suit. The cold goosefleshed his bare skin. He sucked oily air as the icy curved aluminum of the groin-cup closed around his balls. "Lift your feet," said the old man, and he presented them like an obedient horse for the smooth-soled boxing shoes. An echoing murmur; voices on the far side of a partition, too distant to make out words. A light shirt, welcome in the cold air, and then he shrugged on the robe and belted it and hopped up where Picciacchia slapped the edge of a paint-spattered workbench.

The curtain parted, and DeSantis came in, smelling of talcum powder and hairoil and looking anxious. "Jeez, W.T., I lost you there for a minute. Didn't know where you went."

"I'm gettin' dressed out, Len."

"I see that, I see that. Well, how you feeling? Feeling good?"

"What's the odds out there?" he asked quietly.

Fatso looked away, up at the shadowed girder-webbed nave. "Twenty to one," he said at last.

"Twenty to one? How about with our guys?"

"Those *is* from our guys. Hell, Red, they ain't got that much to show. That's probably what's keepin' the numbers where they are. Anybody got a buck or two, he's savin' his plunging for the last minute. Waitin' for the odds."

"Uh-huh. Hope you got a piece of that, Len."

"I took all I could afford, W.T. You know whose side I'm on, goddamn it."

"Other hand," snapped the trainer. Halvorsen put one taped hand down on a pipe-vise to steady himself and held up the other. Picciacchia taped like a surgeon, chimpanzee lips pressed into a vanishing line. "That too tight? Between your fingers, there?"

"Yeah. That's too—"

"You want it tight. Want it to give you some support."

DeSantis pulled out his flask, started to offer it, then changed his mind and sucked at it noisily himself. As he was heeling the cork back in, the curtain parted and Lew Pearson came in. "Grand Central Station," said DeSantis. "Maybe I better get on out there. Well, best a luck, pal."

"Len. Wait. I want you in my corner. Help Angie out. Okay? In case anything happens."

DeSantis squinted at him. After a moment he said, "You got it, buddy." Then the curtains danced and he was gone.

Picciacchia told him to bend his head back and open his mouth, and smeared petroleum jelly over his lips, then inside them, so they wouldn't split as easy under a blow. He put another big dab on his nose and rubbed it in, then two more on his eyebrows. The slicker your face was, the less power came off the other guy's glove. Pearson just watched, not saying a word, and Halvorsen was just as glad; he wasn't feeling too much in the mood for light conversation. Finally the trainer stepped back and said, "Okay, you can start warmin' up." He hopped down and started flipping the jump rope.

Picciacchia jetted tobacco juice into the corner and said, "Now remember, this ain't no dancehall exhibition. This here is a grudge fight, to a finish. Oney way it's over is one a you, you or McKee, is goin' out of that ring feetfirst."

Guertin pushed through the curtain. The priest was wearing a dark overcoat. A gray muffler hid his Roman collar. A dead cigar bobbed in his teeth as he looked Halvorsen up and down. "He ready?"

"He's primed, Father."

"What's he weigh?"

"I didn't weigh him. It don't matter, this ain't a rules fight—"

"Find a scale. I want them both weighed before anybody climbs in the ring."

Halvorsen didn't see why that should matter, to the priest or to anyone else, but the trainer went obediently off in search of a scale. He finished jumping rope and started to shadow-box. Guertin pulled up a crate, passed a match across the cigar, puffed a couple of times, squinting at him through his painful mask as he danced and jabbed.

"I got to tell you this, Kid. My advice? Is not to go in that ring tonight. The weight difference alone, nobody'll think the worse of you. Anybody who knows the game, that is."

"How the h—how the heck can I not go in, Father? We got folks' jobs riding on this. Whether the kids are goin' to keep eating—"

"Then keep it short. If he lands a good one and you happen to go down, my advice is, stay down. Don't make Jack McKee mad, Kid. I seen him turn men into something, their faces—venison sausage looked better."

Halvorsen studied the great Hindenburg head. "Look, I don't get it. If you didn't think I could win this, why'd you set us up? I thought you figured I had a chance."

"What I want above all is to bring this strike to an end without any more bloodshed," Guertin rumbled. "You know, the ancient Hebrews used to choose a scapegoat, and send it out into the wilderness with the sins of the people laid on it. So that one would die, instead of the tribe. I wondered if perhaps you could be that symbol, sacrificed for them all; and, being that, bring peace."

Halvorsen stood silent, striking his taped hands together

with a faint clapping that echoed beneath the iron roof. Finally he said, "There's one thing wrong with that figuring, Father."

"What's that?"

"I'm gonna take this sonofabitch to camp."

Picciacchia came back, saying he'd found a shipping scale out on the main floor of the garage. The fighters could weigh in there. It wouldn't be totally accurate, but it would at least show the difference.

Guertin stood. He held out a hand. "Okay, Kid. If you want to try for it, best of luck. You're not going to outpunch Jack McKee, so remember the ringcraft I taught you. Boxing's a science. It's not two palookas mauling each other. Feel him out the first round, change your style, then go in to fight. Remember, he's a counterpuncher. Don't believe anything till you feel it land. Whatever happens, my prayers are with you."

"Go to hell," Halvorsen said, suddenly nauseated at the hypocrisy, sick, too, of his own fear. He pushed past the priest, following the trainer out toward where the crowd-roar grew, a continuous long rumble like a nitro shot deep underground roaring up toward where it would break loose.

The garage was a wall of smoke and light so dense he could barely see the pit of faces behind it. He followed Picciacchia, floating, hardly feeling his own feet. Men surged toward him, jostling, mouths open but soundless in the din.

Another curtain parted, and the crowd shot to its feet, the roar now suddenly becoming a contained, echoless solidity that filled every cubic inch of metal-roofed space. Men danced on the bleachers, cupped hands to their mouths as they howled and stamped and chanted. Smoke and whiskey-tang and beer and sweat mingled with the oil reek that came off the black concrete floor.

He stepped up on the scales. The weights clicked back and forth, shuttling in shrinking increments till the only number possible of all numbers here on this night was revealed in the little square nickel window. The doc jerked his thumb over his shoulder. He jumped down and turned and followed the trainer, who was pushing guys out of the way, between the bleachers and through a little narrow path or gauntlet made by the standing spectators as they eased aside, looking at him with curiosity, with hope, with hatred. Christ, they were all mixed together, the scabs and the thugs and the union boys.

Up the steps to the canvas, ducking under the ropes, and he stood and here he was, still feeling detached, as if he were watching a movie, as if he wasn't really here in front of hundreds of men about to get the crap beat out of him. And to try to do the same to another man. He raised his fists as the handler worked his gloves on, then hoisted his feet as Picciacchia rosined the soles. He remembered the codgers at Doherty's talking around the stoves about Pete Maher and John L. Sullivan and Jake Kilrain in the old days of bare-knuckle fighting. And they'd gone forty, sixty rounds. He couldn't even imagine fighting like that. This would be bad enough, but he'd just have to stick.

A stir, a mutter building to thunderous cheers interspersed with boos and yells of challenge. Turning, bouncing on his toes, he saw the crowd parting like the Red Sea.

Bare-chested, gray woollen robe draped like a cape, Sailor Jack McKee looked impressive and murderous. His shoulders looked like they'd been poured in a Pittsburgh steel mill. His hard, fleshless face was closed like a safe, the thin lips and elongated, almost Chinese lids stretched over his skull without expression. Only the ice-green eyes flashed, passing over the crowd with a mirthless sparkle of contempt. A step behind, wearing a sealed smile that seemed as much a part of his haberdashery as suit and tie and felt hat, Dan Thunner gripped his champion's upper arm as they worked their way down the corridor of bodies toward the ring.

Behind them was Father Guertin, and with him Deatherage, matching Thunner in gray suit and gray coat and fedora with the brim pulled down like Edward G. Robinson wore it.

"Forget about them. Stay loose; it's cold in here," said the

Italian-accented voice in his ear. He tore his eyes from them and bent, stretching his ham muscles, then began jogging back and forth in his half of the ring, tossing practice jabs and hooks.

Opposite him McKee swung up through the ropes. The gray cape caught, dragging off those smooth-muscled shoulders, and the fighter shrugged it off and let it go, stepping out under the hot glare of the big wire-caged Mogul industrial lights that blazed down focused from the distant roof, that blazed up reflected from a new spotless canvas floor as if from a field of fresh snow. The crowd-roar was like casing tongs squeezing his skull. He saw green flashing in the front row, a lot of cash changing hands. With four, five hundred men crowded into the shed and ten below zero outside, the bosses and foremen and the thugs from Phillie were flashing rolls of the new silver certificates as they placed their bets.

There was enough there for a payroll, and he saw other eyes than his squint as they watched it pass. Well, if he won, they'd be two thousand to the good. Enough to hold out till spring. Even better, he'd cock a snook at Thunner and Deatherage.

The unexpected crash of a band, and after a startled instant the assemblage surged to their feet, a wave of men taking off their hats to display naked scalps, bald heads, spiky cowlicks, combed-down hair. He stood from his stool, saw McKee, across the ring from him, lift a glove in salute. He moved his lips too, though he couldn't think of the words. He knew them; he just couldn't remember them at the moment.

"... and the ho-ome of the brave."

The band crashed to a halt and abruptly, without warning, there was Thunner, swinging a long leg between the ropes and ducking and then rising to tower upright before them all in the center of the canvas, as if he were the referee and judge beside and apart from the diminutive man who stood natty in black trousers and a glowing white shirt and bow tie and God-help-us sleeve garters just like 1890. And the silence filled the hall like a gas, only then letting through the rattle of a fine-grained sleet on the roof, and every man leaned forward as he sat or swayed forward as he stood. Yet still Thunner waited, head cocked, hands locked behind him like a teacher waiting for the class to quiet.

When they did he said, "Welcome back to Thunder, men."

He raised his hand at the swell of boos and shouts. "I know, I know. You're still out. Well, I've got an announcement to make.

"I agreed to this bout with the idea it would get things straight between us. You've made your point and I've made mine. I will never give up control of this company. But if there's something you feel so strongly about that you'll make the sacrifices you've made . . . well, it got me to thinking.

"Our original deal was: If Red here puts my man on the canvas, you get two grand. If Sailor Jack puts the Kid down, you come back to work.

"Here's what I want to say: I thought about this all last night, and my conclusion is, that's not a fair bet."

A startled and astonished rustle; then another, rising swell of outraged noise, the stamping of feet on wood and concrete, fists thrust above a tumult of caps. Thunner raised his hands high, and it ebbed again, at least to the point where they could make him out above the surf-swell of grumbling and threats.

"I thought about it, and I came to the conclusion that you laboring men are risking a lot more here than I am. And as a sportsman, and as an American—and we are all Americans here; I didn't see a man who didn't stand for the national anthem—I don't find that fair.

"So here is my proposal: that, as I said before, if Mr. Fightin' Jack McKee wins this bout tonight, you will all come back to work on the terms I published in the *Deputy-Republican*, join the Thunder Employee Representation Plan, and drop this whole business of an outside union forever.

"But if Kid Nitro Halvorsen here wins this fight, I hereby

give you my word, I will recognize Local 178 of the Oil
Workers International Union as the bargaining agent hence-
forth for its members, in any and all dealings with the Thunder Oil Company. And you know that whatever else you
think of me, I mean what I say, and when I give my word,
that word is good."

Past him Halvorsen, impressed despite himself, saw
Deatherage's face drain white; saw the turmoil and confusion
in the front row of the bleachers; Weyandt, Goerdeler,
Wheeler in his gray overcoat and belted revolver, uniform
cap in his lap, all sitting bolt upright, bemusement and surprise and something not far from rage in their faces. Only
Etterlin, the plant engineer, looked pleased. And he realized
it wasn't faked or false, that Thunner hadn't told any of them.
He'd made this decision on his own.

Then, with a sinking feeling, he realized what it meant:
that it was all up to him, the outcome of the strike, everything
they'd sacrificed and gone hungry for; it was all going to be
riding on him. He saw the eyes below swing toward him,
sharpening as they realized it too.

Trying to keep his emotions from his face, he began
bouncing on his toes, tossing punches at the insubstantial air.

She was pretty sure she was the only woman in this whole
vast garage. Not that it bothered her. She'd been the only
woman in mine shafts and tire factories, union halls and hobo
camps. But the raw seethe around her now made her turn up
the collar of the borrowed man's overcoat and pull her cloth
worker's cap over her eyes. Beside her Latimer danced on
the balls of his feet, freckled cheeks flushed, red hair tousled.

When Thunner swung himself up into the ring her eyes
had narrowed. But when he delivered his bombshell—when
she felt it explode among the workers around her, most of
them standing, the scabs and bosses had taken the seats in
the bleachers before the proles had been allowed in, didn't
it figure—her fists clenched in her pockets. Goddamn him!
First the jingoistic anthem; now the man-to-man appeal of
the fight, the square bet, all the ancient Anglo-Saxon bullshit.

While all the while he had them exactly where he wanted them.

Halvorsen didn't have a chance.

But maybe that was good. Maybe she could work with that. Work the crowd, start the murmur from mouth to mouth that it was all a trick, the bosses were playing them for suckers again to walk out now. They might go for that.

She was turning to Latimer, formulating the words in her mind, when that same strange equivocation she'd felt at the upstairs meeting caught her breath half-drawn. They didn't have it in them to keep on. They'd already lost, they had nothing, nothing; all she could do now was prolong their torment. She knew it was part of a larger plan. She knew their sacrifice would be another step on the road to the ultimate and eternal victory. But was it possible to work for their triumph and not cry for them as suffering beings? Halvorsen, close above her in the shabby house across the river, in the one stolen moment they had ever shared or ever would, she knowing it was foolish and selfish and wrong but doing it nonetheless, and him asking his ludicrous simple question: How could you care about the masses unless you cared about them all one by one?

She stood unknowing, lips parted; then she closed them slowly.

Fists rammed into her pockets, she stood silent amid the cheering, shouting men as high above her two figures bathed in burning light came forward to touch fists tentatively as the referee said a few inaudible words; then went back to their corners, turned, and regarded each other.

Until a bell clanged, echoing from the steel and concrete and quivering away into an expectant and breathless hush.

Halvorsen moved out deliberately, keeping his guard up. The couple times he'd been McKee fight he'd been impressed not only by his power, but also by his ringcraft. He was no carcass, no side of beef like Kelly. The slightest error by his opponent drew a lightninglike riposte. That was how he'd

put down Harry Greb, according to Picciacchia. Waited till
he neglected his defense, then tossed an overhand right with
the speed of a striking cobra that caught the champion behind
his ear, knocking him to the canvas. Greb had gotten up after
a startled two-count and proceeded to end the fight, but for
that moment McKee had been in the running as light heavyweight champ of the world.

Opposite him McKee cycled slowly forward, drifting
dreamlike closer. His taped gloves circled lazily. Halvorsen
kept his gaze on the garishly tattooed chest instead. When
the first jab probed he knocked it aside, resisted the temp-
tation to lunge, and backpedaled warily, circling to the left.

He wasn't sure how he was going to win this. He wasn't
sure there *was* a way to win this. Twenty-to-one odds meant
the crowd expected McKee to button his lip and send him
home wrapped in canvas with a stitch through his nose.
Punched silly, or with a cracked skull. He'd seen the ex-
fighters at Doherty's, with their shaking hands and shuffling
walk, talking like their tongues were tied in a knot.

But he still didn't like Thunner's magnanimous offer. It
wasn't the way the guy operated. He couldn't help thinking
it was a setup of some kind, though he wasn't sure how, and
this wasn't the time to try to figure it out.

McKee kept moving in. They measured each other with a
few extended jabs. Halvorsen figured he had maybe an inch
reach on the man.

Then things started, faster than he expected. The ex-gob
feinted, then abruptly laid a pinpoint combination on him that
he reacted too slowly to to stop. Those granite muscles powered fists like a derrick hammer. He counterpunched, but
McKee parried and slammed him again in the face with short
jabbing blows that didn't carry full power but that still jarred
his skull. He hunched over and connected solid to the body,
worked in two uppercuts to McKee's ribs while the other
concentrated on his head. He felt the skin over his eyes tear,
ripping under the impact of the heavy fists.

They clinched, broke instantly, and recovered. Circled,
close as a waltz, then exchanged another savage flurry. The

pace was terrific. Too fast and too hard. He felt something warm and wet soaking his eyebrows, and blinked, tossing his head back.

The bell clanged and he retreated cautiously, eyes still nailed to McKee, till the other dropped his guard and turned and jogged back toward his corner.

DeSantis had stripped off his jacket and was climbing through the ropes, ready to go to work. "Christ, Red," he said, mopping at the cut on Halvorsen's forehead, the towel dripping blood onto the pristine canvas. "Forget this. It ain't worth it. This son of a bitch is gonna hang you out to dry."

Bowed on the stool, sucking air, he didn't answer. He was squinting at the man opposite him, the one bouncing on the ropes as he yelled down to somebody in the crowd. "Tiltcher head back," Picciacchia: "Tiltcher *head*," and he obeyed, and something came down and the hornet-sting of it on his forehead penetrated even the fighting numbness.

Staring up into the light; and welling up at the edge of sight a moving bowl of open-mouthed faces stretching out into darkness. Never look at the crowd, Guertin had told him. Look out over it; but just this once he did, blinking out at them through the chalky haze of tobacco smoke and the smell of cigars and cheap Monongahela whiskey and the out-of-focus blurriness that came from taking five punches to the head in less than a minute. The corrugated metal ceiling reverberated with many-lunged clamor. Then Picciacchia pushed his head forward, and he shook sweat out of his eyes like a wet dog, snorting the smoky air in and out. Goddamn it, there was Guertin, squatting in the opposite corner, explaining something to a stony-faced McKee. Should have goddamn known, should have expected it, but outrage and betrayal closed his throat.

"Take a sip—spit it out." He spewed the fluid into the bucket Picciacchia held out, coming close to vomiting, then tilted back his head again as DeSantis pressed something cool and sticky to his eyebrows. "Ten seconds," someone said.

A hand gripped his ankle. He looked down, to see a bony

old man holding his foot. He saw it was the timekeeper, and nodded. The fellow glanced at McKee, then at a big old railroad ticker cupped in one hand; and pulled a lanyard.

The sound of the bell brought them both rushing out for the second round like bulls. They collided in the center of the ring, trading combinations with a fierce intensity that shut out everything else: the faces and the pain, shut out the shattering impacts of McKee's heavy fists. Head down, he hooked like a pile driver, then found himself swinging at the air. The other fighter had slipped away.

He followed, and they remeasured each other, floating back and forth, each seeking the other's cadence and rhythm, the scuff of shoe leather on canvas light as the sigh of leaves settling to the forest floor. He was surprised to see that he was the same height as McKee. He'd thought the other was taller. Indigo-inked designs writhed across his opponent's shoulders and chest, disappearing down his flanks into the black Everlast shorts. Dragons and ships and women, all blurred and runny like smeared blueberry-stain. Above them, behind neverstill, snake-swaying fists, the ice-green orbs tracked him, squinting a quarter of a second before McKee came in, feinting a right, then throwing a left and a right hook. Halvorsen caught the hook, surprising himself, and answered with a jab, then a right that glanced off McKee's turned cheek. That squint—did that mean he was about to attack or about to feint? Time was ticking on. He had to figure it, had to figure some way past that ever-ready defense without getting tied up.

Without warning or even apparently setting himself McKee tore through his guard with a one-two like slushed lightning, sucked him low with a combination to the trunk, and hooked again in a looping punch that even as he went down in the dazzling flash he knew he should have expected. The canvas leaped up and slammed him in the face like white ice into the *Titanic*. He tried to rise, then fell back whooping in air stinking of rosin and new cotton. Take the count. Take the break. McKee's shoes danced impatiently a yard away, then retreated as the ref motioned him back. The crowd-sound climbed to an earthquake roar that vibrated the plank framework under his cheek.

At eight he shoved up again, not cutting it too close, and when McKee came in sagged back against the ropes. Halvorsen let him close in. He took a punch, then unleashed an all-the-way-from-his-toes right from close range that snagged the other fighter on the point of the chin and sent him backward, shock icing his gaze even colder. He followed it with a rushing attack, a right, then the left again, but not leaving his feet like he just had, just implacably moving in and in and taking what he got back because he knew now he could handle what McKee was giving out and deal it back in the same fast brutal rhythm of punch, counterpunch, feint, and dance. He was grinning even as his head slammed back and he rocked on the ropes again, then slipped and came back off bludgeoning with a left, left, right hook to the ribs.

The heady, burning delight of the fight laced his veins like liquor, and he let it show, let the tight smile pull back his lips. McKee saw, and his eyes slitted with cunning and hate and the same brutal joy as they faced each other, two strong and utterly determined men each measuring himself against the other.

The next two rounds flashed by, running together in his mind then the way they always did when he remembered them afterward. Him and McKee head to head, working on each other's ribs. Probing like swordsmen for an instant's hesitation, a split-second's opening. He busted the other man's lip. Blood dripped from his mouth. McKee's fists tore into his eyes, started the bleeder gushing again. Picciacchia retaped it, forty seconds' rest—"Hold still. Bite. Get your breath"—and he went back into the ring.

Around them the crowd had grown silent. At first they'd cheered them on, each faction yelling as its champion landed a blow. When he or McKee stopped a punch or was knocked down, men mimed uppercuts, yelling bloodthirsty oaths from the bleachers. But gradually as the icy air warmed with the reek of wet wool and cigar smoke, the electric glare spilling down remorselessly over them all only concentrated like a burning-glass above the white square where two men strove at close quarters, they quieted. Suspecting perhaps that something larger was happening here than they'd ever witnessed before.

Thunner sat hunched over on the bottom row of the bleachers, fingers locked together or gently tapping one fist into an open hand. He was so close he felt the spray of sweat and saliva when a blow found the face of one of the fighters. He heard the thud of taped knuckles on bone and flesh, the involuntary grunts as a glove found its mark, the scuffle of leather. He smelled the sweat and effort of the men a few feet above him.

Beside him Pearl Deatherage touched his mouth with a folded square of cambric. His lips were clamped shut, and he sat turned slightly away from the man beside him.

The fool was risking everything. Yet even as he thought this, he was beginning to see that although it was not something he himself would have thought of, and though it was irritating that Thunner's offer of recognition if Halvorsen won seemed to have been unplanned, spur of the moment, the man's instincts were sound. He knew his audience. He'd touched exactly the right chords. These were oilmen. They might look like factory workers but they weren't making shoes or steel. They understood the role of luck; they were gamblers, too.

It was tough to judge it, when to twist it off and say you couldn't wring anything more out of the situation. Maybe that time was approaching. Thunner seemed displeased with him. He wasn't sharing his plans. But it wasn't here yet, regardless of what Thunner thought, because no matter what happened here tonight, he had one more piece of business to carry though. A bigger and more profitable one than anything Hemlock County had seen yet.

A faint smile glistening on his lips, Deatherage tapped them slowly with the the spotless square of cloth.

*   *   *

Pressed into the side of the bleachers by an inexorable wall of flesh, feeling the wood dig painfully into his side, Dick Shotner stared without flinching at the face of his father and his nemesis.

He wasn't twenty yards away. Even with his weak eyes he could see him perfectly. Could see the lined downturned mouth, the canny pouched eyes beneath the brim of his gray hat. He couldn't tell what he was thinking, and he didn't care. Loathing filled his mouth with the taste of bile.

He wished he had kept Halvorsen's rifle.

Round five, the bell. Halvorsen heaved himself up onto watery legs, forced himself out again across the acres of white space where the icy green eyes floated, daring him to come close enough to destroy him.

He'd grabbed a bigger cat than he could swing, that was all. McKee moved too fast and was too strong to put down. He weaved or slipped or parried every punch. Then out of nowhere a counterpunch or a right cross knocked his head back, and behind it came a straight that like as not he stopped with his teeth. He tried to figure when the guy was drawing him, but McKee was too smart to signal. Like Guertin said, you never knew what you were getting till it landed. The pace had slowed from those early rounds, though. McKee was saving it, holding back his attack. Giving his boss a show? Pulling his punches, to make it look harder than it was?

The son of a bitch. Helpless, raging, he kept trying to land a glove. But it was as if McKee had measured himself and tailored an envelope of air that was all his futile expiring blows found to punish.

Before the seventh round he sat dully watching McKee bouncing on the ropes, grinning down at a blowzy blonde making Clara Bow lips up at him from beside the timekeeper.

"Whasshould I do, Angie?"

"You're doin' all right."

"What do you say?"

"He's a tough nut but he'll crack. Don't talk, get your breath." The seconds were ticking away. He pumped his lungs like bellows on dying embers, sucked half a mouthful of water from the pail DeSantis held to his lips. It was all on him. Christ, he hated that son of a bitch. Look at him jumping around. He was lighter than McKee. He was younger, too. But every time McKee hit him solid he felt like his head would fly off his shoulders, and the roar of the crowd pulsed in his ears and he couldn't think. His legs felt like hot iron.

"Time," the old man whispered soundlessly, and clanged the bell. Halvorsen doubled his bleeding, puffy fists and heaved himself to his feet.

He forgot himself in round ten. He'd lost track by then, the only way he knew the round was the placard that a man held aloft just before the bell rang, walking it around the ring, then ducking away through the ropes as the ref trotted out.

Forgot himself, because he suddenly couldn't recall who or where he was, what he was doing beneath these merciless white-hot lights, impaled by hundreds of avid eyes staring from a dark that grew steadily gloomier and less penetrable, as if light itself were leaking from the world through the cold concrete floor and the iron walls that vibrated with each rattling gust of wind. He couldn't recall his name. Through it all his body raged, repudiating each blow or receiving it when his arms could no longer move to block. Once he forgot that he had to hit back, and circled locked in a defensive crouch, scuttling helplessly backward like a frightened crab.

The crowd began to howl, and he shook his head and recovered face to face with McKee's Vaseline-shining snarl. The rhythm. The rhythm. He weaved and slipped a right and ducked and moved in with a left jab to the body. Tucked his chin and followed it with a left hook and a straight right to the head.

But McKee wasn't there; he'd slipped outside and hooked up into his body so hard his breath puffed out with a explosive grunt. *Hook* and *hook* and Halvorsen was hooking too and they broke and circled till he slammed into the ropes behind him. He feinted left and slipped right and feinted a jab to the head, and followed it with a left hook, both of which McKee parried.

Somewhere in there they were clinching, entwined like lovers in the blood-smell and the slick, gritty feel of another man's skin and body hair. The ref pulled them apart and like he did every time they clinched, McKee used his weight, laying on Halvorsen's forearms, only this time as they broke McKee lifted his elbow on the off-side and smashed him in the face.

"Kid," said a voice sometime later.

He glanced to see the familiar face by his side, massive, solid, white-haired, engraved with a fine webbing around the eyes by years of pain like the counterfeiter-foiling complexity of a Treasury plate. Felt the rocklike pressure of the huge hands, knuckles parchmented with the pale delicate skin of the old boxer.

"Thanks for comin' over," he muttered through swollen, numb lips.

Guertin: "How's he holding out?"

"He's doing swell, Father."

"Kid?"

And faced with those eyes he had to tell the truth. Regardless of whose side he was on, he couldn't lie to this man. It would be like lying to God. He mumbled, "I ain't doing too good."

"Pull off his gloves for a second," Guertin murmured to the trainer.

"What? . . . What? Gee, Father . . ."

A gray rectangle appeared as if by prestidigitation. Halvorsen didn't understand, didn't even see where it had come from. He blinked. ". . . the hell's that?"

"A little indulgence, son. To help do the work of Providence, when Providence looks away. Hand me that tape, Angie." Guertin pulled Halvorsen's throbbing fist toward him.

Shielding it with his body, he began molding the soft sheet-lead over his knuckles.

He understood then, and jerked it away so violently he almost toppled off the stool. His face felt like a sponge; he could barely breathe, couldn't see. . . . "Goddamn it," he said hoarsely, "Let me be."

"It'll help, Kid."

"Hell with it, I ain't doing it. Put them gloves back on."

He weaved to his feet, making a vague, threatening pawing in their direction. DeSantis and Guertin stared up at him. Picciacchia's tiny eyes squinted nearly closed in his fist of a face, as if he were staring into the sun.

The bell blanged, and he lumbered around, forcing his wooden legs to carry him once again toward the man who waited, bobbing lightly, a confident smile on his hard face.

He was milling in close in round twelve, taking too many blows to the body, when he felt something crack in his side. The pain was immediate and intense, and he clinched up.

"Break, break!" yelled the ref in their ears. He grabbed blindly for McKee's arms, then broke. But he must have hurt McKee too because when they separated the other man was bent over, holding his stomach; and Halvorsen went back in unthinking with hate and pain and punched inside of McKee's hook from a semicrouch with a short straight left and right, and then came up with an inside uppercut at the same instant McKee unleashed a left hook, and connected so hard his arm jarred all the way down to the elbow. He felt the shock of it travel down the other fighter. McKee fell back, staggered into the ropes, and slumped slowly, glassy-eyed, to the canvas. The ref blocked him as he moved in, and Halvorsen stopped flat-footed, sucking air and lowering his guard as he watched the ref's arm come up slowly to start the count.

Too goddamn slowly. "One," said the ref, and raised his arm again. McKee began to blink, life returning to his eyes, but slowly, so slowly. . . .

"Goddamn!" he yelled, spitting out his mouth protector.

"Count the sonofabitch!" Around him the crowd was yelling so loud he couldn't hear himself. The ref's arm fell again, and rose with incredible deliberation.

It was a long count, two seconds for every second. At six somebody at ringside aimed a shaken-up beer into McKee's face, and started climbing up into the ring. Halvorsen lunged forward and kicked him back down between the ropes. At eight, in a pandemonium of screams and yells and thrown hats, McKee shook out his arms, braced himself on one knee, and came upright again.

The Sailor was discreet the rest of the round, fending him off, staying just outside of range. Halvorsen was glad of the respite.

At the bell he wheeled, gasping again with the pain in his side, and was plodding back to his corner when a terrific blow struck his ear. Eardrum ringing, he wheeled outraged to the ref, to find his hardened pushed-in face pointedly aimed away. Halvorsen shouted at him, but he said nothing, only jerked his thumb back to his seconds.

Someone rumbled open the garage doors, and from the freezing blackness beyond a fierce wind ripped off hats and cleared the smoky air. Welcome relief; he was rivered with sweat. Collapsing onto his stool, he rasped to Picciacchia, "Side hurts bad. Think he broke my ribs. The hell's this?"

"Rum an' orange juice. Shut up an' drink it. I saw somethin' happen. Saw him cuttin' you with his laces. Saw him cold-cock you after the bell, too. You made him mad, knockin' him down. Somebody bought the ref, for a count like that. Want I should throw in the towel?"

He coughed out the evil-tasting mix. "I can still fight. He's hurt, too."

"If you got a busted rib, he hits you there again, it'll drive them bone splinters right up into your heart." Picciacchia grabbed for a towel but Halvorsen shot out a hand. Holding the trainer's eye, he grated out, "I said no. Len, keep his hands off the towel. And gimme some water, goddammit."

"You bet," said DeSantis, looking scared. "But if he's right you might—" He caught Halvorsen's face then, and something in it made him stop speaking and close his mouth. He bent for water, and poured a cup into Halvorsen's tilted-back, opened mouth; drenched another over his sweat-streaming head and blow-reddened, effort-strained face.

McKee recovered fast. He came out aggressively for the thirteenth, feinting and jabbing and sidestepping. Halvorsen backed, not getting sucked into the feints. Then he realized McKee was talking to him. "Ya little shit," he said in the same flat, high-pitched, scratchy voice Guertin had. "That all ya got? Ya no boxer. Lie down, ya little shit."

McKee dropped his right, trying to sucker him into a left lead, but Halvorsen just kept circling away, sidestepping when he sensed the ropes behind him. His fatigued, battered brain was incapable of thinking now except in short fragments that only sometimes made sense. McKee trying to make him mad. Lose control. Thing to do, keep his head. They traded a couple of combinations, neither paying much attention to defense, then Halvorsen landed a right cross over one of McKee's lefts. McKee didn't wobble this time, just shook it off. "Ya don't hurt me, ya wet smack," he muttered. "Ya afraid a me, ya goddamn rubber baby. Ya goin' down, squarehead."

They were mixed in close, now, neither willing to give ground. Halvorsen had to protect his side and that made him clumsy. What if the trainer was right? Well, at least he'd die fighting.

He slipped to the outside on a left jab and left-hooked McKee's body, but got another jab that cocked his head back and rolled barely in time to miss a savage right. Break, circle, in again for another trade. This time McKee landed one in his side that spun red-flaming pinwheels before his eyes. Something was grinding where the blow had landed. He kept his face rigid, not telegraphing how much it hurt as they traded another combination, then clinched. As they broke McKee's hand lashed up. He jerked his chin back, just missing a backhand that would have broken his nose. He clobbered McKee too as they broke, and they sparred till the bell.

Back in his corner, Picciacchia looked anxious for the first time. Usually he was bland in a fight, not saying much, keeping his expression noncommittal. Now he kneaded Halvorsen's left side gently, muttering, "You feeling okay? You don't look good. Your face is all white."

He bobbed his head, not wasting breath he didn't have. A calmness was settling over him. A cold awareness he'd known before, handling the nitro when it spilled or when he started to slip on an icy plank.

"You gotta quit. Either that or you got to knock him out, Kid. A draw ain't gonna do nobody any good."

He stared straight ahead. One thing was right: couldn't take much more of this. Felt like he'd been in the ring for days. Time endless as a desert. But he knew it could only have been half an hour, including the breaks.

The bell. He came out crouching, unable to stand erect. If that meant he took uppercuts, too bad. Neck and shoulders stiff from the hammering. Couldn't move his head to slip a blow. His arms were trembling lead, the wraps and tape heavy as rocks on the ends of his arms.

McKee came out acting strange, wary. He carried his guard low, as if inviting him in. Blinking through a sudden burning in his eyes, Halvorsen saw an inhuman mask of blood and petroleum jelly, slicked-back hair and sweat-runneled chest. The sailing ship's decks were awash with blood. Dark bluish lumps grew on McKee's cheekbones. His mouth and nose were bleeding. But the brutal eyes still peered out from the wreckage, green and sharp as chipped lake-ice. As they closed the other fighter went into a fake-and-sidestep routine he'd used a couple of times before, then stepped in to sling a jab. It came in high and wiped his forehead, barely shaking him.

Halvorsen saw with cold alertness that McKee had drawn back his left shoulder a little to add force to the blow. He jabbed back, dropping his own right as if too tired to keep it aloft. McKee dropped an elbow and brushed it off, then circled in again. Fake and sidestep.

When the left jab flicked out again he rolled with it and

lashed out with a straight left, following instantly with a left hook. McKee saw the straight coming and weaved his head out of it, directly into the hook. Halvorsen took a step forward and smashed a right to the mouth over his dropped defense. McKee staggered into the ropes and he pursued, hammering in till the other lurched into a clinch. When the ref broke them he narrowly evaded a head-butt that would have cost him his front teeth. McKee laid another into his forehead. Blood and sweat stung his eyes like acid and he tossed his head back, trying to clear them. They were really starting to hurt.

Fourteen goddamn rounds. He didn't know how much longer he could keep this up. The butting and elbowing was getting worse. Each time the ref disregarded a foul, the Sailor got bolder. But now he knew that fast, tough Jack McKee wasn't no superman. If he'd gone down once, he'd go again.

"Get off your bicycle, ya yella faggot. Let's get this over with."

He didn't bother answering. They closed and hooked and the ref broke them up, held him off, yelling into his ear. Only with difficulty did he understand that the man was calling him for a low blow, warning him not to repeat it. He nodded, and the ref stepped back and he went in and threw a left hook off a left-jab lead and drove McKee back into the ropes. He followed him in and pounded him with weak, numb arms until they separated, facing each other. Halvorsen dug at whatever was in his eyes with the back of his glove as McKee shambled in, but just then the bell rang.

Back in his corner, his legs straight out and shaking like with the palsy as DeSantis and Picciacchia worked on him, he spat out the mouthpiece and said, blinking through a flood of tears, "I can't see. There's somethin' in my eyes."

"What are you talkin' about?"

"Tried to wipe it out, but it's gettin' worse."

"What's it feel like? Like it's burning?" He nodded. "That sonofabitch," said the trainer. "They used the potion on him. Keep massagin' his legs. I'm gonna go talk to this ref."

Picciacchia stood in the center of the ring, arguing heatedly with the official. The man in the white shirt stood with his arms folded. Finally he yelled, "You want to quit, quit. Is that it? There ain't no decisions here. Fight or cut bait."

The Italian came back, shoulders slumped. He said, "I tried. They got to the goddamned sonofabitch, that's all."

He had his head back, DeSantis was pouring water into his eyes, but it didn't help. It felt like they were on fire, deep inside. "What the hell you expect? He works for them," said Fatso.

"They put somethin' on his gloves, that's what they did. I seen it before. They call it the potion. You can't fight blind. What you wanna do?"

Halvorsen blinked. It was like being teargassed. Maybe it *was* tear gas. The world swam and blurred, and he had to keep squinching his eyes closed. "I can fight," he said.

"Don't be a sap. He'll Christly murder you."

He didn't think about it a lot, because he knew if he did, if he figured the odds and what he had to lose, he wouldn't go out there. But he knew one thing more, too: W. T. Halvorsen wasn't going to lose sitting on his can. If he had to go under, it'd be on his feet, fighting back.

The card walked around the ring with a big scrawled *15*. At the bell he heard the crowd quiet, as he squatted on his stool. Heard the scuff as McKee moved out.

"Just keep sittin' there," Picciacchia said into his ear, knotty little hands pressing down on his shoulders. "It ain't no shame to get beat this way. You put up a hell of a fight. Just keep sittin' there, and it'll all be over."

He wanted to listen. Every muscle-fiber told him he couldn't go out again. Every nerve screamed exhaustion. His bruised legs shook uncontrollably. But something rock-hard inside himself, something he hadn't known until that moment was really down there, told him different.

He could be knocked down. He could even be killed.

But the only way he could ever be defeated was by himself.

* * *

When he felt the Kid stir under his hands Picciacchia pressed down harder. It wasn't going to change anything. He'd known from the start this wasn't going anywhere. Just made sure of it, when he'd bent down, when everyone's eyes were on the center of the ring, and poured the little bottle from his pocket over the sponge DeSantis used to clean off the Kid's face between rounds.

The Kid had moxie. He had sand. But looking back over forty years in the ring and in the corner, Angie Picciacchia knew neither moxie nor sand never did you no good with a busted rib. These boys could go five, eight more rounds. Just a matter of time till McKee, knowing or not, rammed that edge of bone right up into Halvorsen's lungs, and he'd die coughing blood bright as the sunrise. Too bad about the strike and the union and all that, but that wasn't his lookout.

He figured he was saving the Kid's life. He didn't want any thanks for it. And he'd have done it even if Mr. Daniel Thunner himself hadn't had a talk with him about loyalty, and his responsibilities to his employer, and slipped him the hundred dollars just to help him remember, down at the gym that very afternoon.

When the crowd-sound was like the roar of a volcano, when he could feel it shaking the boards under his feet, he figured it was time.

He shrugged the hands off and got to his feet.

As he pushed his legs out into the ring once more the crowd-roar grew and grew. Now he had to judge it all by sound, and by the feel of canvas under his feet. Like ducking under at the swimming hole, everything blurred and wavery. A shadow shifted at the edge of his vision. He put up his guard and stepped forward behind a probing left jab. Instantly his head rocked back from a punch. He backed and lashed out with a straight right. Pain tore his elbow as it whiplashed in the empty air.

Hooks into his stomach, and he doubled, protecting his ribs. Then an uppercut rocked his brain. He staggered, groping for a body to clinch, but there was nothing around him, nothing but shapes and noise and burning light and the solid rising roar.

He knew it couldn't last long. Much as he might want to, McKee couldn't toy with him or the crowd would grasp that he couldn't see. The end would come suddenly, a haymaker he couldn't parry or slip or dodge.

He stared up helplessly into the burning light, raising his leaden arms once more like a blinded Samson.

When the ref's arm fell for the last time, a sigh like the first warning wind from a storm swept the garage. They stared at the crumpled form, at the sweat-streaming figure that stood above it. Whose fist was seized suddenly and jerked upward, the vaunting of victory.

Then somebody yelled, "Let's tear this place apart!" and the stampede began.

Golden was squeezed till she thought she'd burst, then suddenly the press eased and she was swept helplessly toward the open bay doors. For a moment all she could see was backs, hats, and raised arms, but she heard cries from in front, and the growl of engines. Fine white wires lit across the black sky. She recognized them after a moment as sleet, stinging down endlessly out of the dark. Then the current swept her near a stack of oil drums. She struggled free, clambering up onto them like a castaway onto a steep beach. Then pushed up the brim of her cap, surveying the whole brilliant-lit scene around her.

The milling gray throng was hemmed in on all sides by trucks. The bass rumble of the engines made a threatening counterpoint to the shrill cries of the hemmed-in crowd. Above them the arc-lights hissed showers of painful light down over the trampled snow, the hulks of cold equipment that walled the avenue inside the refinery. To her right, toward gates that she saw now were chained shut, a solid line three deep of army troops barriered the way out. Pressed back by the pointed glitter of fixed bayonets, the workers milled with raised fists beneath the falling sleet. She saw men kicking angrily at the snow, but beneath it was only asphalt, useless for defense. She had her .32, but it wouldn't help. The only thing it would bring on was a volley from those raised rifles, from the machine guns atop the armored cars and the rifles the state troopers pointed down from their tower perch. The men saw that, too. She saw fear take their faces as they realized how helpless they were.

She saw Melnichak below her and picked her way hastily down the pile of drums, almost slipped, and caught up to him from behind. He swung at her grasp. "They got us penned in like cattle!" he shouted. "But they can't shoot us all."

"Don't be too goddamn sure about that. This feels just like Homestead to me."

A massive hum, and crackle, and an amplified voice boomed out. "Thunder men! Calm down! Listen here."

They shaded their eyes to look up at an older fellow with a gray shaggy mustache, standing on the tower between two state police with rifles. He waited a few seconds while those below quieted down. Then he yelled out, "You boys had your fun?"

A ragged chorus of cries and insults rose from the swaying, steaming mass beneath. The troops glanced at each other, fingering their rifles.

"Those a you don't know me, I'm Otis Goerdeler, senior foreman of Number One.

"I told you hardheaded bastards when you first wanted to go out, a strike wasn't going to change nothing. It didn't work for me and it won't never work, because the company's too strong and they got everybody from the cops up to God on their side. And that's the God's truth, and I ain't even sayin' it's right, just it's the way it is and we got to live with it.

"Now, it's time to finish this up and get back to work. Mister Thunner can't give in, but he can give you a break, and I asked him to and he said okay. You can have your jobs back, every man jack of you except the agitators that stirred all this crap up in the first place. You know who I mean, and we don't need them in this town."

"Like Shorty?" somebody yelled up, and the men roared and pushed. The platform trembled, but Goerdeler leaned forward and yelled, "Bring them tables out here!"

Men came out of the fire station, by the office, carrying long wooden tables. Clerks came out, looking nervous, and took their places behind them, with the Thunder cops backing them up, hands on pistol butts and billy clubs.

"Here's the order. We are gonna set up a employee representation plan. You got safety beefs, pay beefs, you tell your employee rep and it goes up the chain from there. You men are goin' to line up now and sign up for this plan. Any man who signs up we're gonna forget you went on strike. Clean slate. Any lad who don't sign up tonight, that's it, you're never comin' back.

"So you can have your jobs back, but no union. And don't worry about the picketers. Take a look out the gate. There ain't nobody out there. If there's any left tomorrow, the troops got orders to escort you in."

She raised herself on tiptoe, but couldn't see anything. She muttered, "Stan, you see our boys out there?"

"I don't see 'em . . . but there's a lot of lights. Headlights, and what looks like torches."

"Torches?" she whispered.

Goerdeler pointed to the tables. "Line up and sign, or go out that gate and never come back again." The amplifier went *hisss* . . . *POCK* and went off. The foreman swung around and came rapidly down the ladder, hand over hand, and above him the troopers stared down at the throng.

"To hell with this. I'm signing up," shouted an ownerless voice. Melnichak answered it with a powerful bellow: "Stand fast! Nobody signs!" The men around them swayed, and a mutter rose.

"Stan, we can get them out of here. All they got to do is walk in one direction, we can push down that fence."

"They'll start shooting."

"I don't think so. It's a bluff. And like you said, they can't kill us all."

"Yeah, but now I'm thinking I don't want them to kill

anybody. Maybe Otis is right. I'm tired of this, Doris. It don't take nothing for me to stay out. They'll never take me back. But maybe for these others . . ."

She looked up at him and suddenly saw that he was defeated too; defeat was in his voice and his eyes. He looked hollow and old.

She grabbed their arms, pleaded with them. They wouldn't look in her face. Just one by one, tired and gaunt, plodded like resigned cattle toward the tables.

She shoved her way through the throng. A bull reached out to stop her, then hesitated as she pulled off her cap and shook out her hair. She looked back and Melnichak was behind her, and Latimer and a couple of the others. She stopped at the table and grabbed the wrist of the man who was bending forward over a card, wetting a pencil on his tongue. "Don't sign that, comrade. Don't give up now!"

"Move along, sister," said a cop.

"Let go o' me," said the man, giving her a poisonous look. He made a firm black scrawl on the card. "You Red bitch. Singin' about pie in the sky. That's what you're sellin', pie in the goddamn sky. You been playin' us from the goddamn start. I don't know what for, but I'm through bein' a sap."

She stood struck dumb. Started to open her mouth, and was astonished to see the looks of hatred from the men behind him. The obscene gestures, cupped hands—

The cop, at her back. "You best clear on out of here, Miz Golden. Sounds to me like these boys is had a belly full of you."

"Come on." Melnichak, grip closing on her elbow. "It's over. Let's go."

Shaking, she let them pull her away, let them half carry her toward the gate. The cops there leered and joked. One slid his billy club through a circled finger and thumb. She barely noticed, hearing only the jeers from behind her. From the ranks of the workers.

"Uh-oh," said Melnichak. "The Citizens' Committee."

She saw them then, the surging dark mass beyond the gate. Torches and lanterns swayed, and automobile headlights made shining cones on the snow. Some had masks. Others didn't bother. They waited in the snow, forming a rough gauntlet through which anyone emerging would have to pass.

Her knees sagged as her mind terror-flashed back to another torchlit night. A rope looped over a limb. The hood of a Model T. She turned, searching for the shelter of the gate, but a glance at the barrier of hostile faces and ready-held truncheons told her there would be no sanctuary there.

The sleet hissed as it fell, a steady low isolating sibilance that surrounded them all.

From the whispering dark two figures stepped out. One was a squat hulk of a man in a dark overcoat. The other was slighter, with a white silk scarf under his topcoat and an old-fashioned homburg setting off a weak-chinned face, a limp pallid mustache, startled youthful eyes that were somehow resolute, too.

"Don't be afraid. It's me, Guertin," the raspy voice said. "This here is young Reverend Sloan. Figured you might need an escort tonight. I'll take the front, Hiram. In case one of these yellow bastards takes it into his head to get rough. You follow them up, all right?"

"Thanks," she said, and she and Melnichak and the handful that were left, who had not signed, began walking.

Guertin led at first, but then, somehow, he vanished, lost in a swirl of sleet and dark figures. Spittle flew into her face. She kept her head up and kept slogging on, still hoping to make it to the river. Beyond that she had no idea where she was going. It was too late for the trolley to run, and they had no ride waiting. It was a mile back to strike headquarters. Well, she'd walked many a mile before. If only they could make it through this crowd. So far no one had actually touched her.

Between the walls of malevolent faces, cursed and reviled, head raised against the catcalls and spitting, she led the faithful who remained out from the burning city, into the outer darkness.

But then, as the last light from the gate area faded behind her, the mob surged in, the walls closed, and the gloved hands reached out. Suddenly she was alone, struggling in a black sea. Someone struck at her, but she parried it with her arm and ducked away. She glimpsed an opening, beyond it the distant star of a lighted window. She ran toward it, boots dragging in the deep snow, pushing and colliding with over-coated bodies. In the darkness and confusion they were be-laboring each other. For a moment she thought she might make it.

Then she saw the old man. Not Guertin, one of the strikers. She didn't know his name. Surrounded by the mob, hands locked over his head, he was being hammered to his knees by fists and sticks and clubs. A burly man took deliberate aim and kicked, shoeheel down on his spine, and he screamed horribly and toppled over onto the snow.

She tore her eyes from it with an effort of will, looking again toward the distant light. The final responsibility of a Party member was to escape, to fight again another time, and eventually to win. Two steps forward, one step back. It would come, as surely as the sunrise. She had to make herself as hard as steel.

Instead she screamed, "Stop it. *Stop it!*"

Staggering in the snow, she ran back toward the figures who were still raining blows on the unconscious man. She pulled at their arms, screaming into their faces to stop, to show some mercy.

Suddenly one wheeled, and the world cracked open on white fire beneath. She swayed, stunned, knees sagging away as he cocked the bat again. When he swung once more she fell, trying to scrabble away over the snow. Her clawed fingers dug into it, into the hard ice and sharp frozen-in gravel beneath, snapping away her fingernails.

"Who's that? Is that her?"

"That's the Red bitch, all right."

"Kill that goddamn whore!"

The sounds of blows, sodden in the winter air. Grunting and curses, a burst of laughter.

Till at last the mob backed away from a crumpled mass in the snow.

Then it surged back, stamping and kicking in frenzied abandonment and savage fury. A man picked up a cheap cloth cap from the snow. Put it on and danced a few steps, yelling, "Look at me, look at me, I'm Gurley Golden now." And the bitter wind blew in all their faces, lashing them with the icy stinging sleet.

Thirty

Halvorsen came to suddenly the next morning in a warm, damp, rumpled bed in a dark close place that smelled of mold and paste-wax and steam heat: a smell he recognized but a room that he did not. His face felt swollen and puffy. His chest was taped, and his hands were bound in damp towels. The wetness around him came from them, a moisture that for a moment he'd thought was blood. Through the walls an opera singer arpeggio'd from a distant radio. A faint, cold, bluish light seeped through an iced-over window carved with delicate scalloped filigrees of frost. In the same room with him, someone was snoring.

The remnants of a dream. Fists and brilliant light. The smell of cigar haze and oil. Blood on the snow.

Not a dream. Not a nightmare.

Real.

When he bed-creaked himself up, Shotner sat bolt upright, digging fists into his eyes. The lanky clerk was still in his rusty suit. The way it was rumpled up around his shoulders, Halvorsen guessed he'd slept in the chair.

"So y-you're up. How you feelin'?"

He said through thick lips, "Jeez, Dick. You didn't have to give me your bed."

"Somebody did. Keep quiet, now; Miz Ludtke don't know you're up here. Len and me carried you up last night. I'll go down and see if there's anything left from breakfast."

Shotner came back with cold scrambled eggs and bread and one of the heavy boardinghouse mugs. He tried, but he couldn't eat. His teeth hurt, his jaw hurt, the skin on the inside of his mouth was shredded. He just couldn't do it. The warm, strong boiled coffee went down easier, and he started to roll himself slowly out into the cold air.

Dick stopped him. "Just stay there, damn it. Sleep some more. It's only nine-thirty."

"I got to get down to the line—" He stopped, realizing that there wasn't any line anymore.

"Yeah." Shotner said, pouring him more coffee from his own cup. "There's sugar in this one, you oughta drink it. Now y-you're rememberin' huh? The lousy bastards had the army there when we come out, and the state police, an' the Citizens' Committee outside the gates laying for the guys who wouldn't sign to say they were giving up. Most all of them signed, though. They're starting the refinery up this morning. Oh, an' there's—there's some more bad news in the paper this morning. I'll leave it here; you can read it."

When he finished reading he lay back and stared at the cobwebbed ceiling. Trying not to think. Trying not to look back, because it hurt too much. But he couldn't shake the memory of one thing. Not her competence, or her hardness, or her casual, dismissive beauty in their one moment together. The one image he found himself remembering was the naked hurt in her eyes, the bewildered parted lips of a betrayed child, when a cookie had come arching from the back of a crowded room.

He was awakened by a scratch at the door. Then the knob eased around. He half raised himself on his elbow, glancing around quickly for Shotner. He wasn't there.

The door creaked open, and Jennie slipped in, in her old coat and work dress.

She looked scared, and well she might. "What the H you doing up here?" he whispered. "Jeez, Jennie, if anybody sees you—"

"There wasn't anybody in the parlor but Dick. He's watching out, in the hallway. I just had to see how you were." She started to shut the door, then hesitated; glanced at him; closed it firmly, and put on the latch.

He told her there was a chair under the breakfast things, but she came to the bed and felt his forehead. Her hand felt as cold and damp as the towels. "You look terrible," she said. "My dad told me you lost last night. He said you were hurt. He was hurt too; some men beat him up. I had to come and see."

He muttered, "I'm glad you did, but you better get out of here."

"I heard about . . . Miss Golden. I'm real sorry, Bill."

"So am I. Look, you better go. I mean it. Somebody sees you up here there'll be hell to pay."

"They'll think I'm a bad girl, I know. But God'll understand." She sat down beside him and started unwinding the towels. He closed his eyes and let her gentle hands minister to him.

And after a little while, felt her lips on his.

That was how Mrs. Ludtke found them, Jennie bent over him in the bed in the darkened room. She stood in the slammed-open door, immense washerwoman's arms crossed over her gigantic bosom, broad face red as flame and hair shooting out of the gray bun like she was electrified. "You get the hell out of my house," she told Jennie. "You too, Mr. Red Communist. I threw you out once already. And you take your queer friend along with you too this time. I got a respectable house here. I don't want to see any a you ten minutes from now."

Jennie had jumped up when the door banged. Her back was to him, but he could see her trembling.

"No," she whispered.

"What's that you say? You little hoor—"

"I said, no! I'm not leaving! You see he's hurt. I'm nursin' him! Now you get the—the *hell* out of our room!"

He blinked. He couldn't believe what he'd just heard: Jennie screaming at Mrs. Ludtke. Using the H-word. The landlady hesitated, eyes slitted, then wheeled her bulk nimbly as a bear threading a blackberry tangle. From the stairs she screamed back, "Oney reason I'm not callin' the cops right now is to protect my good name. Out before dinnertime! You too, Shotner! And I want paid triple for that room today."

Jennie left not long after, cheeks pale as candle wax, and Frank Latimer came up. Halvorsen wondered if he ought to start charging admission, he sure was a draw today. The kid stood looking him over for a couple of seconds, then said, "You sure's hell look like somethin' the cat dragged in."

"Feel like it. That son of a bitch McKee hits like a goddamn mule."

"Saw the fight. You done damn good, Red. I mean it."

"Not good enough."

"I got a feeling nothing would of been good enough to win that fight," Latimer said. "I heard one fella say we could of put Jack Dempsey himself up there and they woulda found some way to beat him."

Halvorsen remembered the burning in his eyes. "Gi' me a hand up, I got to piss like a racehorse."

When he came hobbling back down the hall, Latimer and Shotner were both sitting on the bed. When the door was closed Latimer said, "Red, I asked Dick to come in so the three of us could figure out what we're gonna do about this."

"What do you mean, what we're gonna do?"

"He means, we can't let *him* get away w-with this," Shotner explained, making strange writhing gestures with his forearms. "He's got to pay, for what he done to you fellas, and Miz Golden, and you, Bill, and for—and for everything."

Halvorsen looked at them for a long time in the darkened, too-hot room. They looked like kids, and suddenly—maybe

it was just the way he hurt whenever he blinked or moved—
he felt much older than they were. "What exactly you boys
got in mind?" he said at last.

"Not so *loud*," Shotner hissed. "These are real thin walls.
But Frank and I was talking."

"Let's hear it. Spit it out."

Latimer said, "I say we put him in a box."

"Count me out," Halvorsen told them. "I ain't gonna be
part of it. Too many damn people got hurt and killed in this
thing already. It's over. We lost. Rubbin' out Dan Thunner
ain't going to change nothing. Let's let those who can go
back, go back."

"We can't never go back," said Latimer excitedly. "You
can't, I can't, none of the real union sparkplugs can. We'll
never work a job in this state again."

"What about you?" Halvorsen asked Shotner. "You could
probably get a position over there now. They'll be hirin'
now."

"I'd never work there. I'd starve to death first. And anyway, I already asked."

"You put in at Thunder?"

"That's right, after they fired me at the battery plant. They
said they didn't need me."

"Jeez, Dick. You don't think your dad would—"

"He ain't my g-goddamned dad," Shotner said, but the
tightness in his long jaw and the way he blinked, like a
nightbird caught in the day, told Halvorsen different than
what his words said. "It don't matter. None of that matters.
Somebody's got to teach him a lesson. For beatin' us, and
killin' her. You know we're right."

He sighed. "Okay, tell me what you got in mind."

Squatting close to the bed, they told him.

The house stood lit above the town, and cars drove up beneath the porte cochere and to the front walk, and valets and
drivers stood waiting beyond the fieldstone wall, stamping
their feet and blowing on their hands. Despite the sleet the
day before, so heavy that houses had collapsed in Irish Hill

and the West End, the streets leading up here had been cleared and freshly ashed. Now only a few flakes drifted down.

The Sands, alight and alive. Its windows filled with swaying forms. Music seeped from the walls, and a fine woodsmoke lifted above the tall chimneys, hung in the moonless sky, then dropped slowly to layer itself along the hillside and the trees and the frozen motionless garden like a silent, pungent, glowing mist.

Thunner stood beside one of the fires, one hand thrown over an antique carved mantel set with the Victorian knickknacks his mother loved and collected. He held a brandy in the other as he talked earnestly with Conrad Kleiner and Henry Holderlin. Occasionally as he spoke, a trace of uneasiness or pain moved over his features, then was abolished with a straightening of the shoulders, a shrug. "So then I said to him, 'You take the Luger, Sergeant, but I have a little problem here. Perhaps you could help me out.' And he did." The men laughed, and Thunner grinned too, sharp and short, and turned away and began his roving through the great house.

Kerfoot Inskeep extended a hand. "I won't say congratulations, Daniel. Too many people hurt. Too much bad feeling sown. But I am very glad you won."

"Thanks, Kerfoot."

"Don't be too disturbed about the Golden woman. We'll deal with the situation. It's simply—"

"I don't want to talk about it, Kerfoot." Thunner smiled as best he could, but it felt like he was caught in barbed wire. Felt like the more he struggled, the more steel points buried themselves in his helpless flesh. "I know you'll deal with it. And I appreciate it. But I don't want to talk about it right now, all right?" He went on, not looking back at where the county chairman blinked thoughtfully.

"He's taking it hard," Inskeep said to Ward Van Etten. "I wonder if it's true, about the pension fund?"

"I shouldn't wonder."

"Still, we've got to keep him afloat. If Thunder went un-

der, it would be the end of the county. And he's really stuck
it out. We helped, but he deserves the credit."

They watched him standing by the window, looking out
into the snow.

The hollow was shrouded in night, and the road to it was
steep and slick. The sleet had frozen over deep snow, and
icy, rutted mud lay hard as cast steel beneath that.

He and Riddick and Shotner were crowded together in the
front seat of the Oakland. He was driving, keeping his eyes
and his attention on the narrow gap in the trees that created
itself continually out of the hazy soup of snow and fog and
darkness.

Much later, they reached the crest and began dropping,
chains clanking and grinding, into one of the most remote
hollows in the county.

The old maps called it Bone Hollow—no one knew why
anymore. But since the 1870s, the beginning of the long war
between Rockefeller and the local oil barons, no one had
known it by any other name than the one it bore now. It was
isolated and that was good; for now and then through all
those years a distant thunder from its direction had caused
heads to lift all through the western part of the county. The
next day a line or two in the local papers would give the
toll. Give names of men who would never be buried, for
their bodies had vanished in an instantaneous and painless
transubstantiation into the mindless atoms of earth and sky.
This was where it was brewed, the hell-stuff that cracked the
producing sand and brought light and movement to the
world; and that mishandled had snuffed out many a life so
fast that a man literally never knew that he had died.

Lurching from side to side, they made their way down
into Nitro Hollow.

Deatherage was standing at the bar, a large whiskey in his
hand. So they'd won. Won, if anything, almost too thoroughly. For that was not how the game was best played. Far

better to milk the cow a little at a time. He swallowed the last mouthful and was skating the glass across to the colored man when he spotted Thunner by the window. He grabbed the refilled tumbler and headed over to him at the same time Weyandt approached them from the billiard room.

"Evening, Daniel."

"Mr. Deatherage."

He caught the coldness in the owner's tone. He took a sip, trying to peer through the window to see what Thunner was looking at. Only the valley, spread out below in a carpet of twinkling lights. "You sound angry, Dan. Or disappointed. But you know, this will pass."

"Will it?"

"Always has. I've done a lot of these. The scab forms fast. Golden wasn't anything to anybody around here. Pretty body, but—"

"You're talking about her body?" said Weyandt, as if he couldn't believe his ears.

"I had a go at her once," Deatherage said, winking. "Years ago, when she was younger. I've had better . . . but she's gone, it's history now, and 'history' means it's already half forgotten and doesn't matter anymore. Keep the pressure on the foremen and you'll see, everybody will work twice as hard. Make them feel your eye on them. You have the membership lists, from the minutes. Winnow them out ruthlessly. Start with the oldest; that cuts your pension expenses down the road."

"You always give such good advice," said Thunner contemptuously. "Tell me one thing. Were you ever really in France? Were you ever in the service at all?"

"I believe you already know the answer. Or you would not have asked the question."

"You lying son of a bitch. Pretending you saw battle, shamming you were wounded—"

"No, sir; I pretended *nothing*. Your conclusions were the work of your own mind. And as for my disfigurement, I most assuredly did receive it in battle. From the boots of a gang of union enforcers in a meatpackers' strike." Deatherage's upper lip lifted. "Do I detect reproach? How strange. That you hired me to conduct espionage and strikebreaking, yet are outraged at what you term my duplicity. I admit to being something of the chameleon, Mr. Thunner. And if you require a villain, to set your mind at ease as to your own virtue, I have no objection to serving as such. Whatever you wish to blame on me, feel perfectly free."

Weyandt said, "You're responsible for the worst of it. Why *not* blame it on you?"

"The tame pup speaks!"

"You're drunk."

"And will become much more so; and with good reason." He swilled another mouthful of Thunner's scotch, and laughed. Took out an Old Gold and lit it.

"This whole thing would have been settled in a month without you."

"And you'd have the CIO sucking your blood from then on. Come now, gentlemen; do you really think that this is over?"

"They've come back to work," said Thunner. "What else is there?"

"You, sir, are a very naive man."

"Stop talking in riddles. It's finished. At last. Prepare your bill and I will pay it. As soon as you are out of my town."

"You will soon see very clearly what I mean, and what I am capable of, and how much you need me," said Deatherage. He and Thunner stared at each other.

Weyandt said, "Sir, regarding what he was telling you just now, wholesale discharges and so forth: I don't think that would be wise, if we really want labor peace in this valley."

"What would you do, Rudy?"

"What Abe Lincoln said after the war, how to treat the Confederacy. 'Let 'em up easy,' he said. That's what I'd do. Discharge the ringleaders, of course. That goes without saying. But keep the pay hike. Put some workers on the safety committee. Then ten years from now, they'll be telling your new hires: 'Stay with Dan. We tried it the other way and it didn't work. Learn from us.' "

The two men argued. Thunner stood between them, swaying slightly, eyes unfocused. Behind them in the window, wavering plumes of flame streamed up from the towers.

The Bryner Torpedo Company's works were dark and the woods around the sheds were thick, but Halvorsen had come here twice a day when he'd been a shooter, and he wheeled the coupe past it and into a sharp turn that pointed the headlights at a back door. He left the engine running and got out. He clapped his gloves together. Yeah, he was a little nervous.

"No guard?" said Shotner. He stared as Halvorsen put his shoulder to the door and rumbled it back. "No lock?"

"What for? Nobody in his right mind would want to steal this stuff. See those trees?"

Shotner turned. He studied the woods. "The little ones?"

"No, the big ones, on the ground."

"The ones lying down?"

"Yeah. Notice how they're all lying in the same direction? All the way up the hill? That's why they put these sheds so far apart. And why they build 'em so cheap."

"Cheez," said Shotner, comprehension dawning as he stared out at them.

The "stuff" was in wooden boxes filled with straw. He sniffed the heady smell and his heart started to pound. The chill dankness made him shiver. The others followed him in, but stopped just inside the door.

"Gee, I just got this instant headache," said Latimer.

"That's the nitroglycerin. Don't touch any unless you can't help it." He bent, looking along the floor toward the door.

"You might want to give me a little breathing room," he told them. Shotner swallowed. They sauntered away, toward the woods.

Halvorsen walked the route from the boxes to the car, making sure there weren't any holes or trip hazards under the snow; then started carrying straw. He lined the trunk six inches deep with straw and put more around the sides. Then he began moving the nitro. He carried two cans at a time, placing his boots slowly and cautiously, and swinging them

up and in and settling the square soldered cans carefully vertical, packing the straw in around and between them, like
packing eggs. Eight cans filled the little car's trunk. He debated putting some in the back seat, but decided not to push
his luck. He put his shoulder to the door, then spat into the
snow.

"You guys can come back now," he yelled.

Twin bashful shadows re-emerged from the night. Latimer
looked at the trunk. "How much you get?"

"There's ten quarts of nitro in each of those cans there."

"That enough?"

"Eighty quarts is enough to level the whole goddamn
downtown, you place it right," he told them. He unfolded a
blanket and drew it over the cans, then lowered the trunk lid
carefully and lashed it down. "So: Where's it go?"

They looked at each other. "We ain't decided yet," Shotner
told him. "But we got a couple ideas."

He eyed them narrowly, then sighed.

The house was sheltered by old maples, planted as a wind-
break many years before. Cherry and apple and pear trees
were spectral stripped shadows out back. Its glassless windows stared out blindly. The fields were bare, covered with
snow. Saplings stood here and there, vanguards of the returning forest.

He looked out over them for a long time.

"This where you grew up, huh?" said Latimer.

Halvorsen shook himself and turned around on the sagging
porch. He shoved the door open with his boot and flicked
flame out of the Zippo.

Guttering yellow light pulled out of blackness a glass-
strewn floor, peeling wallpaper. The winter wind blew un-
impeded through the empty windows. The roof had begun to
collapse, and the floorboards sagged, water-rotted, in the
middle of the main room. A door stood ajar. He moved carefully through it, holding the miniature torch aloft, to find
himself in an abandoned bedroom. A bed, a dusty dresser.
He looked at the dress draped over it.

"Somebody's been in here, looking for what they can find."

"Hobos."

Halvorsen found a lamp in the pantry and filled it out of a rusty can. When he twisted the wick up, the buttery light showed him a hand pump, an iron pot, a litter of crazed crockery whose faded patterns tugged at obscure places in his brain. He remembered taking baths in here in a tin tub. How cold the air would be when he stood up and poured the last of the stove-heated water over his head, then hurried shivering back into his longies. Before the 'flu came, back when his ma and pa were alive—

He said harshly, "We'll put it in here. In the kitchen."

Neither of them offered to help. He carried the cans in and put them on the floor in the icy-cold pantry, where nobody could kick them over by accident. He dragged a broken-backed chair over and looked on top of the pantry shelf. The hobos hadn't found the bottle. He held it up to the lamplight. Then went out to where Latimer and Shotner were building a fire in the stove, feeding in broken furniture and boards from where the roof was coming down.

"Don't burn that," he said sharply. "Go out back, look under the house. That's where we keep the firewood."

"Okay, we got the stuff," Latimer told him. "Now where we gonna use it? The refinery?"

Shotner said, "No. *His* house. The big one. The Sands."

"I told you, I ain't going for murder," said Halvorsen. "Same goes for the refinery. Guys on shift there all night. Too much gas around." He swallowed, remembering the smell in the Washkos' parlor.

"Someplace the bosses put their heads together, then," said Shotner, his narrow face lit by hate in the flicker from the stove. "I got it. The Petroleum Club."

"You are a real firebrand all of a sudden, ain't you?" Halvorsen asked him.

Latimer spilled the last of the home-stilled pear brandy into his teacup. "How 'bout the Thunder office, where he goes during the day. Or, hey—how about City Hall?"

Shotner: "They're just his stooges. I say hit *him*."

But the redheaded kid's mention of the office had triggered something in Halvorsen's mind. He searched for it.

"The Thunder Building," he said at last. "The new one they're putting up downtown."

They mulled it over. The stove began to smoke and he leaned over without thinking about it, like he had a million times when he was a kid, and fixed the damper. Then he told them quietly that was it, and that was the only way he'd be part of it. Blow up the big new building. There was nobody there, no one would be hurt, but no one would ever forget it.

"Okay, leave it to us," Shotner said.

"Leave it to you? Don't make me laugh, Dick. You'd get about ten feet with this stuff and trip. They'd never find a piece big enough to bury."

"When?" said Latimer, swaying slightly in his chair.

"Sunday. Early. Nobody's downtown then. Nobody's working." He took one sip of the brandy, then set it down. His eyes filled suddenly with tears. It smelled just like his father.

"What we gonna do till then?"

"Do what we always do. Then early in the morning I'll rig a squib, and we'll drive it down and put it in the building. Put it on the ground floor. Wipe it out."

"I'll stay here tonight, if that's okay," said Shotner. "That old bitch, she threw us out; I ain't got noplace else to go."

Thirty-one

Sunday morning, so early that night still covered the streets as they rolled the last few hundred yards, lights doused, and eased to a stop behind the construction site. Halvorsen, looking out, remembered when this wasteland of ploughed-up soil had been the Harriman boiler factory. They'd gone belly-up after the Crash, and Thunner, so he'd heard, had bought the site for pennies on the dollar and erected the grandiose monument to himself that loomed between them and the black sky, a square, towering darkness that seemed higher somehow than the hills.

He set the handbrake and climbed out. Shotner got out too, and Latimer. They stood together, shivering and pulling their coats together at the collar. Then Latimer said, "Gotta walk the dog, boys. Be right back."

"Don't freeze it off."

While Frank was gone Halvorsen pulled a half-plug out of his pocket, unwrapped the paper, and tucked it into his cheek. Then he unlocked the trunk and lifted the blanket and let it drop to the snow. He fingered the wire bails of the cans beneath it. Realizing only now how chancy it was going to be, to set eighty quarts of soup in a place he didn't know and couldn't see. For a moment he was tempted just to stack it here, against the fence. Even thirty yards away, this much nitro would take down all the glass and probably most of the outer walls. But then he thought about Doris, and spat on the ground. Thunner was lucky he wasn't setting this at his house.

He was lifting the first can out when he became aware of a dark figure walking toward him, across the shattered, desolate land. He tensed, thinking it might be a cop. The figure stopped, looking around. Then came on again.

"Who the h-hell's that?" whispered Shotner.

"I don't know. Keep quiet."

"Bill-ee," a voice crooned. "Billy Hal-wor-sen."

Halvorsen straightened, glancing around; slid the can back down into its nest among the others; eased down the trunk lid, covering what lay beneath, and went forward.

When he reached the waiting figure it was in the darkness away from any light. An arm was flung over his back, and the smell of cheap rye bathed his face, cutting the chill winter wind.

"Mr. Washko. What you doing out here this time of night?"

"Come to see you, Bill-ee. To tell you they know."

Halvorsen turned aside to spit, giving himself a second to gather his wits. "Who's 'they'? What do they know?"

"Every'ting you do, Bill-ee." Washko muttered, glancing around. "You know, you heard of comp'ny spies. You know how I know?"

"No. Maybe you better go home, get some sleep—"

"Because I'm one too." Something glinted, and Halvorsen took it as Washko pressed it into his hand.

"What the hell's this?" It was hard and round. Almost like a quarter, but bigger.

"Nineteen nineteen," Washko said, and a pride and a terror lingered in his hushed voice. "I was in Monessen."

"The steel strike."

Washko ducked his head again and then suddenly the words tumbled out, jumbled, as if they'd been corked in too long.

"Yeah, Monessen. I work in the number-two wire mill there, a wire drawer. I draw wire on the four blocks. Thirteen hours a day, and you go in an hour ahead of time to set up. We thought, after the war, we thought, we need an organization. So we strike Pittsburgh Steel. They called us dagos, and hunkies, and wops, and Bolshewiks. And they had the coal and iron police—we called them Cossacks."

"I heard of them," Halvorsen said.

"They'd ride up on the sidewalk and club us and the kids and women. Them horses was trained to fight. They'd grab you just like a mad dog. That's where I get this scar, on my face. One of them horses, on Ninth Avenue. We stayed out, and we stayed out, but we lost. They blackball me, and I got to leave and change my name. They take my job, my house, my name . . ." He breathed harshly for a moment, head turned away. Then laughed bitterly. "That goddamned Shannon. He tells me, go out with strikers: Be a goddamn spy, or I lose my job when goddamn strike over. So I spy for them. Sure. An' I ain't the only one. But me, I come tell you, so you know." He stopped speaking, yet his breath sawed on, harsh and loud. "They beat me one too goddamn many times. The bastards. Sonsabitches."

"What's this?" Halvorsen asked him, turning the object over in his fingers.

"That's the sign. So you recognize each man the other. See? The mark. On the woman."

Halvorsen examined the silver dollar by the flame from his Zippo. Apparently Washko was referring to a deep scratch that cut across the neck of the Walking Liberty. "What about it?"

"That's their mark. It means you vun of t'er goddamn finks. You find who got these, you find who else ratting on you."

He stared at it a moment longer, then handed it back. Finding it all hard to believe, but knowing this man didn't go around making up stories just to amuse himself. "Thanks," he said.

"You not such a bad boy. Jennie, she still like you . . . maybe I just getting old . . . aw, sonofabitch." Washko glanced down the street, then hastily walked off.

Halvorsen looked after him. Sucked the dark juice together in his cheek, and spat, slowly and thoughtfully. Then took a deep breath, and turned back to the job at hand.

Latimer was standing with Shotner by the coupe when he came back. Halvorsen studied them, wondering now exactly what Washko had meant when he said: "They know." He asked Latimer quietly, "Where'd you go just now, Frank?"

"I told you, to water a tree. Who was that? The guy you were talkin' to?"

"Nobody. Let's get in there before somebody else comes along."

They picked their way across the torn-up earth and down concrete steps into a basement entrance that as yet lacked a door. Shotner's flashlight showed them a half-installed boiler, stacks of cast-iron pipe, tool chests. The room smelled of fresh concrete and grease. Snipped-off scraps of electrical wire littered the floor. He bent and picked up a length, coiling it around his knuckles. Then kept on, through the boiler room and back into the basement as the dark closed down solid. The sound of their steps scraped and echoed away down an echoing black corridor.

He decided this would be far enough. No point lugging the stuff any farther than he had to.

But first he had to find out if Washko was talking through his bottle.

He swung suddenly on the two of them. "All right, boys, caps off."

Shotner stared at him. "What are you talking about, Red?"

"You heard me. Caps off. Put 'em on the floor here. Then empty your pockets into 'em."

They stared at him as he tapped his fist into his palm,

waiting. Finally Shotner plugged his hand into his pockets. Reluctantly, Latimer followed suit.

When the silver gleamed in the flashlight Halvorsen said, "Hold it. Let's see that."

"What, that? That's my hole money."

"Uh-huh. Give it here."

He held it close to his eyes, then suddenly reached out, spinning Latimer around. As the kid protested he wrapped the copper wire around his wrists, then twisted the free ends around a water pipe.

"Red, what's going on? What are you doing?"

"He's working for Thunder, Dick. I just got the tip."

"*He's* working for Thunder?"

"Yeah. A paid fink."

"Hey, I never—what the hell kind of setup is this? You got the wrong guy. You ain't gonna leave me down here, are you, Red?"

"Only for a little while." Halvorsen turned to Shotner. "Come on, we need that flashlight now. He'll be fine here in the dark for a while."

"Goddamn it. Don't leave me down here!"

"You brought it on yourself," Halvorsen told him. "Maybe it'll loosen your tongue. Think about it."

The cold ammonia smell of the nitro rose up into his face as he lifted the trunk open again. His heart accelerated, thudding in his chest. He stripped off his gloves, hissing through his teeth as the icy air bit his unprotected fingers, and tucked them into his jacket. He spat, then handed the flashlight to Shotner. "Hold it on the ground a couple of yards in front of my feet."

"What, turn it on out here? What if somebody sees us?"

"I ain't doing this in the dark, Dick. Just hold it for me, all right?"

He grasped two of the wire bails and tugged, wincing at a stab from his broken rib. He was taped up tight, but it still hurt when he lifted his arms. The tin cylinders came up smoothly, popping faintly as the bails took their weight. He could hear the nitro gurgling slowly inside. He pivoted, swinging them carefully over the lip of the trunk. Instead of setting them down he shrugged, balancing them like a Dutch milkmaid her heavy pails; and turned.

He pondered what the old man had said as his boots went crunch, crunch, over the loose gravel and brick shards and over it all the fine granular snow like sugar, so cold and dry it squeaked as he moved across it. Shotner kept the yellow spot of the light just ahead of his boots, picking out irregularities in the ground. He maneuvered cautiously around a depression, up a little rise, then stepped over snow-covered beams, carefully testing each foothold before he trusted his weight to it. Finally he reached the stairs, and went carefully and slowly down into the black maw of the basement.

Their breathing echoed hoarse and loud in the empty cold darkness. The light-beam lit the pallid clouds of their puffed-out breath. It flicked ahead down the corridor, but found no end but blackness. He followed the passage, a central aisle apparently, for maybe fifty paces, then lowered the two cans down with infinite gentleness to rest next to the rough-cast concrete of a support pier.

Bent over like that, he suddenly sensed the building's mass above him, the immense crushing burden of all those stories of brick and stone and steel like a physical weight on his back. It made sweat break under his arms. He told himself again that if he tripped it wouldn't hurt, but the thought didn't seem to help much. Whether it hurt or not, he'd still be dead. So instead he concentrated on memorizing the path as he headed back out, so that he wouldn't be helpless if the flashlight went out.

He repeated the trip, then took a breather leaning against the Oakland, stretching and shaking the tension out of his bunched, strained shoulders. His rib hurt like hell now, but he was halfway done. Four more cans, set the squib, and he could vamoose out of here. He wondered how Washko had found out about Latimer. Then he wondered if somehow it was a plant, if Deatherage was playing them all for saps. Spreading doubt. Making them think Frank was a rat, when he wasn't. But then how to explain the coin? How else to explain the ambush at the east gate; how they'd known everything, outmaneuvered and snookered the workers time after time? Goddamn them. Goddamn them all to hell.

He sucked air, forcing himself toward calm. It didn't do to get hot around this stuff. That made you careless. When he was cool again he grabbed the next couple of cans.

Sweat was soaking his union suit when he set down the last two tins of nitro. He'd left them sitting in the snow, outside, while he got into his machine and started the engine. He'd backed up, racking the gearshift, and gunned forward again. He did this several times, till his tire tracks were obliterated in a mush of muddy snow. Then pulled out onto a back street and headed uphill, parking several blocks away and trotting back. It would be light pretty soon. When the dawn came he didn't want the Oakland around, like a billboard shouting that W. T. Halvorsen was on the premises.

Now he lowered them carefully into place beside the others and put his hands to his back and stretched. The combination of nitro and tension was giving him a pounding headache.

Shotner's light was growing dim, but it showed them the silvery ranks, nestled tight against the concrete. Eighty quarts. Halvorsen reached into his back pocket and pulled out the hard cylinder he'd carried back there the whole time.

"Hey. You gonna let me loose pretty soon, right, Red?" Latimer said from the darkness.

Halvorsen examined the squib, not answering. The cap was thrust deep into the dynamite, the waxed paper folded neatly back in on it and taped. He'd cut the fuse for ten minutes. Bending, he worked the stick down amid the clustered cans.

"Goddamn! What are you gonna do?" said the kid, and this time his voice broke. Halvorsen felt bad; it wasn't so pleasant having to terrify somebody whom only minutes before he'd thought of as a pal. On the other hand, if he *was* a rat, he deserved the scare.

He stood, slapping construction grit off his pants. "You ready to talk?"

"Sure. Whatever you want me to say. What do you want me to say?"

"Just the truth, Frank. Like, where you really from?"

"I'm from Warren. Warren, Ohio. It's true, I ain't an oil-man. I worked coal."

"Who are you workin' for now? See, I already know you're a sonofabitchin' stool. But who are you rattin' for?"

After a long minute the kid said, "I been jobbing for Deatherage. For two years now. On and off. He needs some-thin' done, he calls me, I come and do it. It ain't personal, Red. I like you guys. It's just business."

Shotner was staring bug-eyed, his big head swaying like a blossom on a stalk. "Why, you mean you been selling us out all along?" he said. "For *money?* I say, leave him here. L-light that thing and walk out."

"Take it easy, Dick. We ain't gonna do that."

"What are we gonna do, then?"

He was opening his mouth to answer when a brilliant beam transfixed the three of them, bursting out from the black impenetrable depth of the inner basement. He whirled, arm jerking up to shield his eyes.

"Leave those hands up, gentlemen," said Pearl Deatherage. He emerged from behind the light as a rifle-holding shadow. "Thanks for the call, Walter. Hope I didn't get here too late."

"Walter?" said Halvorsen.

"No sir, they were just snapping their clackers; they didn't hurt me yet. But I sure am glad to see you."

He wriggled around the pipe, presenting his bound wrists, but Deatherage turned coolly away and addressed Halvorsen. In the light of Shotner's electric lantern, dim though it was getting, Halvorsen saw that the strikebreaker was in his gray overcoat, his gray fedora. The rifle was a lever-action, a .44 by the look of the bore.

"Kid, sorry to see you here. I admired your spunk in the ring. But since you were not content to lose there, you're about to lose very big indeed. This gentleman I don't believe I know?"

"That's Shotner," Latimer put in. "I mentioned him in my reports."

"That's right, you did." Deatherage examined him with interest, like a mounted specimen. "The one who believes he's related to Mr. Thunner. Don't see much resemblance, myself."

"It's t-true," Shotner spat. "He treated my mother shamefully. I went to see him, he said to me—"

"—that you were no son of his. I know that. And then later you went to him again, and told him you could help him, give him information; but you never did, nothing of any use."

"Wait. Wait—"

"And then you were fired, and came to him for a job, and he told you again he had no use for you. Yes, I know all that, but I don't really find it very interesting," said Deatherage, half smiling. "Though I daresay your friend here does."

And for a moment there was silence in the tunnel beneath the city. Broken only when Halvorsen turned his head and spat his chew out into the darkness. "That true, Dick?" he said quietly. "You, too?"

"I never told them nothing, W.T. I was just trying to . . . trying to make him see that I could be some good. It wasn't for money. It wasn't like that."

Deatherage cleared his throat. "Well. To answer the question you were posing when I joined the conversation: Mr. Latimer, as you know him, has been one of my most useful and loyal employees for several years now. He is one of the finest confidential operatives in the union-breaking business. But he was only one of my resources. I have local sources, and professionals . . . Mr. Thunner's been reading the minutes of your meetings since you got your charter. How? Oh, you'll enjoy this. When you post the copy of your minutes, to the Oil Workers International Union headquarters? One of the employees in their filing department mails us back the carbon."

Halvorsen stood rooted, head pounding, the underground cold gradually invading his heart. Washko. Latimer. Shotner. A clerk at the OWIU. And no doubt, more yet unnamed. He'd thought of them all as brothers, marching shoulder to shoulder toward a new dawn. Instead they'd been riddled from top to bottom with stools. Finks. Informers. He tried to collect himself; if the gun muzzle dropped or wavered, he'd better be ready to spring. But Deatherage looked too cool to be tricked or conned. He held the rifle compass-steady, aimed right at his belly.

"So what are you doing here?" Halvorsen asked him.

"Oh, just gathering evidence. Though it looks like we have about all we'll need." With his free hand the agency man roved what Halvorsen saw now was some kind of miner's light over the cans of explosive. "Here's what I'm thinking. Two things I could do. I could take you fellas down to the police station, turn you over to the local bluesuits. Which may not be very pleasant for you; and after which you can expect to burn for it, I should think. Or I can arrange matters such that you won't feel any pain at all."

"Say, Mr. Deatherage, if you could see fit to untie me here—"

"In a moment, lad. I'm trying to make a decision, if you don't mind. Things seem to be quieting down here in Hemlock County. The strike's settled. Mr. Thunner's going to go easy on his boys. Yessir, everything's going to be swell again and you and I can go home and never come back. But if this building were to go up in smoke . . ."

Halvorsen stared at the agent. He wasn't sure he understood what he'd just heard. "Wait a minute. I thought Thunner hired you to help beat us. And now he's won. So why would you want to—"

Latimer said, "Mr. Deatherage don't need to tell you nothing, Halvorsen."

"You've sure changed your tune," Halvorsen told him. "Now that I think of it, you were the one pushing this whole bomb thing from the get-go, getting back at the company and all. What about that, Deatherage? What are the police going to say when they find out it was Latimer put us up to this? Hell, he wanted to blow up City Hall."

"You stole the nitro. You carried it down here. Walter's what we call an agent provocateur, in the trade. He's on the side of truth and justice, boys. You're the Red anarchists. I don't think it's going to take a jury too long to figure that one." Deatherage set the lantern down, groping in his pocket for something while still holding the rifle on them. "But the more I think about it, it might be better just to let you go ahead with your plans. Yeah, Walter—no reflection on your efforts, but it just might be better to let them go ahead. Of course, everything might not turn out the way they anticipated. There might be an accident."

Latimer struggled, cursing under his breath. "Whatever you want, Mr. D. Say, how about getting this goddamned wire off? It's cuttin' into my wrists something awful."

"Turn around," said Deatherage, and Halvorsen saw what he had taken from his coat: a set of handcuffs. He stood still, immobilized not just by the pointed rifle, but by a sudden chilling realization.

Deatherage wasn't here to stop them. He had no interest in peace. He wanted the violence and hatred to keep on.

And what better way than to chain them down here, light off the nitro, and let them go up along with Thunner's cherished building?

He was getting himself set to take the bullet when from beside him Shotner said, "You ain't going to put those things on me."

"You're one of the plotters, Mr. Shotner. I'm afraid that's exactly what I'm going to do."

Instead, startling them all, Shotner jumped, awkward long arms darting suddenly for the agency man's throat.

Taken by surprise, Deatherage crashed backward. The lamp smashed over on the concrete, flashed with one dazzling instant of brilliance, and went out. Halvorsen ducked away, stumbling back into what smelled like a coal pit. Suddenly he was in utter darkness, listening to men yelling and a clatter and then a deafening bang as a shot and then another rang off the concrete walls, followed by a scream. He crouched, lips drawn back as he waited helplessly for someone to trip over the nitro.

When silence succeeded he slowly stood in the utter blackness beneath the earth. Put out his hand slowly, realizing only then that he had no light. He'd left his Zippo sitting on top of one of the cans, handy to the capped and fused dynamite.

"Halvorsen?"

No mistaking that calm, icy voice. But it didn't sound weakened, or hurt. But someone had screamed. Had one of those bullets hit Shotner? Or Latimer? No way to tell; he couldn't call out without giving Deatherage a bead on him. If the others were smart they wouldn't answer anyway.

He took a step forward in the dark, hand extended; then another. Keeping his boot soles hunting-quiet, making no noise at all, though his heart was slamming away like a Buffalo engine, thundering so hard red figures writhed before his staring eyes. Until something earth-cold and rock-rough kissed his fingertips. He followed the wall, one silent, searching step at a time.

"Halvorsen. Come out now and I'll take you down to the station. My word on it."

He'd had no idea the basement was this vast. But considering the scale of the building above . . . he'd gone down in a coal mine once outside Brockway; his uncle had taken him down just to show him what it was like. This was like it, only there wasn't any bugdust or black damp, and the ceiling was high enough that he could stand erect. Actually, this was a lot better than a coal mine.

Or would have been if Deatherage hadn't been down here too, with a gun.

He reached the far side of the room at last and fingered out an opening and thrust his leg through it. Climbed up and through, very slowly, and let himself down silently inch by inch on the far side. Good, one wall between them.

Then his foot hit something metal that spun away in a clatter, and he heard quick steps behind him and threw himself down as a tongue of yellow flame flashed out, blinding and deafening. The heavy slug cracked into something hard, and fragments of shattered rock or brick stung his face and skittered away through the darkness. He crouched, air fluttering in and out of his throat. Christ, he had to get a grip. Had to think, or he'd be gunned down right here.

He couldn't go back to the alley entrance. Deatherage was between him and that exit. But there had to be some other way out. The builders were still moving in equipment; there had to be accesses from these subfloors to the upper part of the building. Stairwells, service accesses, airshafts, elevator wells. It would be easier in daylight—he'd be able to see light from above and follow it—but they still had to be there. He just had to find one.

Before Deatherage found him.

He was moving again, creeping away, when he heard a click and then a fizzing snap, and light flickered faraway somewhere in the black.

"How long did you cut this fuse for?" The agency man's voice boomed through the echoing catacomb, through the lime-smelling cold air. "Not long, looks like. Come on in, Halvorsen."

Christ, he couldn't have. That would be the height of stupidity. Or of icy bravery. Thugs were supposed to be cowards, and probably a lot of them were, but he had to admit he hadn't seen any yellow streak in Deatherage. He wished he knew if Dick was still down here, if he was still alive. He might have been weak, he might have tried to please his dad, but at least he hadn't done it for money. He decided he had very little to lose and yelled, "Dick. Dick! You okay?"

"He can't answer you."

"If you killed him you'll pay for it!"

The cold voice drifted through the darkness, spooky as the Shadow's hollow laugh. "I don't think you'll be making me answer for anything, Kid. Come out now and I'll let the cops deal with you. Last chance, here."

"Nuts to you, you murdering sonofabitch."

He waited till he heard the hollow echoing chuckle again, then edged out into what seemed to be a corridor. The agency man had come from this direction. So it had to lead to an exit somewhere; and Deatherage obviously felt he could find it without a lot of groping around, or he wouldn't have lit the fuse. He'd wait till he passed, then follow him out. Shotner wasn't answering. He might be hurt, or even dead. The only remaining question was what had happened to Latimer.

At the moment he thought this, his hand met something smooth and long and cold, leaning against the wall. He traced its length in the dark. It was iron, four or five feet long and satisfyingly heavy. Some sort of tamper or reamer, left behind by the construction workers. He lifted it silently and drifted down the hallway.

Behind him rapid steps crunched. He flattened himself against concrete, then thought again and stepped out square into the center of the passage. Gripping the bar, he squinted into the blind darkness as the footsteps paced closer. When they reached him, he swung with all his might.

Deatherage heard the *whish* of parting air, and realized at the same moment that someone was standing directly in front of him. The instinctively raised rifle caught the violent blow full on the stock, knocking it from his hands. He bent instantly for it but his hands found only rough concrete, scraps of paper, sharp bits of wire or nails.

A second hiss passed over his head, and he launched himself beneath it, toward where its wielder must be standing.

He crashed into another body, and got in two quick punches before one landed in return, to the side of his head, that jarred him so hard he reeled away. Iron clanged on concrete. He raised his fists, but another blow came out of the dark to his chest so hard he gasped for breath.

He broke free and ran, slammed blindly into a wall, then felt his way along it, trying to orient himself. He'd been

walking toward the stairwell. Was this the way back? If he
guessed wrong he'd be trapped down here. He heard the
other man panting, not far away in the dark. His shoe ground
on something and he tensed. Had to stay quiet.

Then he remembered, and plunged his hand into his coat.

When his fingers closed around the butt of the revolver he
breathed out, relieved. But only for a moment. He didn't
know a lot about nitroglycerin, but there'd been a hell of a
lot of it there. Enough to bring the whole building down on
their heads. And *he* had lit the fuse.

Sweating in the cold, he slid forward, fingers searching for
some clue, some escape.

Halvorsen stood panting in the dark, unable to hear where
Deatherage had gone. He'd missed with the bar, and damn
near blacked out, his side hurt so much when he swung. But
he'd connected with two solid punches. His knuckles felt like
they'd been fractured. He'd have sore hands again tomorrow,
along with the busted rib.

Assuming he was alive.

Think, he told himself. Then he heard, off behind him, the
faint sputter and crackle of burning powder.

He wheeled instantly and ran.

As he approached he saw fine sparks spitting from the end,
smelled the sulfur stink of safety fuse. The sparks showed
him his lighter, too, sitting right where Deatherage must have
left it. Reaching over the cans, he pulled the dynamite free,
pinched the cotton sheath tight above the cap, and yanked it
out. He tossed the still-burning fuse off into the dark, heaved
the dynamite in the opposite direction. He was breathing out
in relief when he heard a moan.

He flicked flame from the lighter on the first pull, and held
it aloft. Its feeble illumination lit two crumpled bodies.

When he bent to touch Shotner's face, the flesh felt slack,
ice-cold. Yet the boy shuddered beneath his fingers. Halvorsen pulled his coat apart, ran his free hand along his ribs. He
didn't feel anything out of place, no warm, slick stickiness

of blood. Then he saw it, running down the back of the clerk's head.

Latimer was on his back, eyes open. The flame Halvorsen held over them danced back, a miniature reflection from motionless pupils. He didn't need to investigate the massive hole in the redhead's chest. One at least of the big .44 slugs had found a home.

He stood looking down for an endless time, knowing that this was the moment when he had to decide. Because he could leave now. Go out the back entrance, crank up the coupe, and clear out for California or the far West. Change his name. Change his past, like old Washko had when his strike failed. Forget all this and let the years cover it, let the dust drift down over it. Forget that a man called Deatherage had ever lived. Forget that a man named Thunner had paid him to spy on and beat and kill his friends. At least he'd be alive.

Yeah. He could do that.

Instead he clicked the lighter slowly shut, letting the cover snap closed on the flame and all light. Lifting his head, he walked steadily, hands extended, back into the darkness.

A hundred feet ahead of him, Deatherage found the stairwell at last, an empty opening to his left. The toe of his shoe slammed into a riser. His palm found the rough, unfinished wood of a handrail. Feeling relieved, gripping the revolver in his left hand, he climbed as rapidly as he could, less cautious now about the grinding sounds his soles made on the steps, about the hurried panting that echoed from the close walls of the stairwell. He had to get out. The seconds were ticking away. There, a suspicion of light above . . . he rounded a corner and it was marginally less black, and he went up one more flight and came out through a side room into the immense lofty emptiness of the central lobby.

The great mosaic was a smoothness beneath his feet. In the faint light that filtered through the entrance doors from the street all he could discern was shadows, some darker than the rest. Turning occasionally to point the revolver back at them, he stumbled across the open space toward the exit, mopping sweat from his face with a damp wad of handkerchief. Why was he limping? He didn't recall where, perhaps in the brief struggle in the corridor, but somehow he'd twisted his ankle. He succeeded in tangling himself in some sort of netting that had been left lying on the floor, and spent almost a minute trying to kick free of it, in gradually increasing anger, and then near-panic, before he no longer felt it dragging at his feet.

When he raised his eyes the silhouette of a man stood between him and the great arched entrance.

Halvorsen stood waiting, hands loose, as the shadowy figure neared him across the open floor. It stopped once, fighting with something at its feet. He heard harsh sharp breathing, the throat-tearing bark of a smoker's cough. Then it lifted its head, and he cocked his fists and said, "You'll have to come through me, Deatherage."

He noticed the gun only when the flash of it lit the great hall.

The crack echoed through the vast enclosure, setting a thousand echoes clapping like an applauding crowd. He felt the bullet pull at his hand as he spun and ran. The nearest cover was a great column. As he reached it the revolver banged again, and he ducked behind it and clung to the curving smoothness, cursing whatever it had been, lust for vengeance or foolish pride or both, that had made him come after the man after escaping him once. Now he was right back in the soup. Whatever he got this time, he deserved it.

Quick hurried steps, one shoe scraping; the agency man was wounded or hurt, but still coming for him. He looked around desperately and saw a ladder leading upward. It wouldn't buy him much time, but it was all he could see to do. He sprinted toward it, gasping as his broken rib tore at his side. Then began pulling himself upward, toward the lofty dark arch of the dome.

*　　*　　*

Deep beneath them, in the utter gloom of the basement, Dick Shotner opened his eyes.

He stared unseeing and nearly unthinking for some time before he remembered where he was, and what had happened. The struggle. The shot, so terrifyingly loud and close to his face he'd jerked backward involuntarily. To lose his balance, his skull slamming back as he went down against something hard and sharp; and that was the last thing he remembered.

Now he sat up. Hesitated; then called, not too loud, "Bill? You there?"

The words traveled away from him and came back only in his own voice, folded on itself by unseen angles and rooms all around him. His hands groped out across concrete. They met something smooth and cold. His fingers explored it before he realized, the hairs on the back of his neck stirring and lifting at the knowledge, that it was one of the metal containers that held concentrated destruction. He drew back his hand hastily. Then, fascinated, extended it again; flicked lightly with a fingernail, shuddering anew at the dull ping of liquid-filled metal.

He recalled himself and rolled over and tried to get to his feet. His head throbbed and swam like the one time he'd drunk wine, and had thrown up and chipped a front tooth on a sink. He sagged back to hands and knees, fighting the urge to throw up. When it subsided a bit he began crawling, not knowing where, not really toward any goal; knowing only that he could not, should not, remain where he was.

Some time later he dragged himself across a long hard object on the floor. He started to push it out of his way, then recognized its shape and pulled it to him.

Kneeling in the dark, he pushed the lever down. The empty shell pinged away into the dark. He pulled the lever up, and smoothly and with a faint click and scrape a live cartridge slipped into the rifle's chamber.

He was climbing as hard as he could, as hard as his ribs and labored breathing would let him, up into the shadows, like a fleeing spider. Behind him he heard something more ominous than he could have made up in a nightmare: He heard nothing at all.

When he looked back, he saw Deatherage hoisting himself up onto the ladder behind him. Halvorsen understood. Looking up from below, he would be only black against black. His enemy had decided not to waste bullets. Instead he would follow, till he was close enough not to miss. He'd have done the same thing if he'd been the hunter.

Instead of the hunted.

He wheezed cold air through a dust-filled mouth and figured he only had a couple more minutes to live. Still he couldn't see how he could have done anything else. It was the only way he'd ever have paid off for Doris, and Shorty, and all the others. The little girl, Mabel, coughing her lungs out in bloody chunks in a heatless shack. The poor son-of-a-bitching colored man, what had his name been, yeah, Gant, who'd died riding in a truck. A scab, but a man. And the cops had dug a slug out of him.

A .44 slug.

Behind him Deatherage struggled upward, pulling himself from the ladder onto a narrow, swaying, plank catwalk. Workers had been using it to finish the ceiling. It rose toward the uttermost pitch of the dome, where the great electrolier glittered faintly. His breath sawed in his throat. He peered ahead, but couldn't yet see the man he had to kill. A few more feet. Or, if he could hear him, maybe that would be good enough to shoot at.

He yelled, "Why'd you come back, Halvorsen? You could have made it out."

"I got somethin' against you, mister."

No good; he couldn't tell where the words came from; like a whispering chamber, the immense cupped dome played tricks with sound. He yelled, "Nothing's worth your life."

"Guess you and I see that different."

"I was doing my job. That's all. And you boys lost. You're dying for nothing. You still won't surrender?"

"I ain't comin' down to have you shoot me, if that's what

you mean," Halvorsen yelled. Clinging to the suspension
ropes, on the last and highest plank, a few feet farther up.
He was past fear now. Just icy cold, like in the last minutes
in the ring. The last minutes, when every point counted and
the decision was up for grabs. "This here's a grudge fight,
mister."

"Seems like you got a grudge against the world, friend.
All you radicals do."

"Maybe so," Halvorsen said, struggling to see it clear;
somehow it seemed important just now, here at the end, to
see it clear. "But I got a special one for you."

He swallowed. "See, it ain't Thunner so much. He's a
sonofabitch but I can see his side; he's fightin' for somethin'
that's his, that he and his family built, somethin' that's part
of him and he's part of. He don't give, and you got to respect
that. Even if he's on the other side.

"But you're different. That's what I can't figure, and I
can't let go of. All this between us and the company, it ain't
nothing to you. But you come in here and make your mess,
and get men killed, and coin your dollar from it. I figure
we'd have settled this whole thing in a couple weeks at the
outside, if you hadn't come in here. That's what I can't forget
about."

"Don't be so goddamn holy," Deatherage said, pulling
himself up another yard. Now he was standing on the scaffolding itself. It was narrow and swaying; there wasn't any
handrail or safety line. Just black air, seventy or eighty feet
of it straight down to the stone floor. "How about the Red
bitch? Walt told me you were sweet on her. But don't forget,
she was here before I was. Want to know who really kept
you from settling? She was the professional agitator. The
Communist. She was the snake in Eden, here, my friend."

"Sure, but what'd she make out of it? She never made
anything. 'Cause we ain't got nothing. So what'd she get out
of it?"

Deatherage lost interest in the conversation, because he
saw him then, an irregular shadow a few yards above him.
Crammed back into some sort of capital or decoration, too

dim to see exactly what; but unmistakably a human shape. He raised the revolver, took careful aim. Or as careful as he could, the way the scaffolding was swaying, a dangerous pendulum high above the mosaic floor.

"So long, Halvorsen."

A voice said in response, "Somethin' you forgot."

"What?"

Reaching into his coat pocket, Halvorsen mimed taking out a pocket watch. Looking at it. Drawling, "You forgot we only got thirty seconds left till this whole damn shebang goes sky high."

Deatherage froze, hand actually cramping closed on the swaying ropes. It was true. He'd forgotten the sputtering fuse, a hundred feet below them. Deep beneath concrete and brick and mosaic, but the crazed bomber opposite him was right. That much explosive would tear through the fabric of the building like tissue paper. Thirty seconds . . . a swift image of himself sprinting through the door, running across the street—

He began to back down the scaffolding, making it sway even more in his haste, in his nervous, frantic clumsiness. So that all Halvorsen had to do was take the already opened Case knife, whetstoned like he always kept it to shaving keenness, and saw it with three swift strokes through the suspension rope. He saw with the last slash the upturned face below him, and ducked back as the last shot cracked past.

With a ripping sound the last fibers gave way. The pale open-mouthed face turned downward; turned upward; then sank swiftly away, and disappeared from his sight.

The gray suit jacket was flung open as the body sprawled across the great mural of Progress, as if hugging the stream-lined trains, the soaring aeroplanes above the magic city. Halvorsen bent over it for a moment, then straightened.

Deatherage would never break another strike. Never pay another spy. Never take another organizer for a ride. His delicate long fingers lay relaxed at last, outstretched across the cold tesserae as if yearning for something forever beyond their grasp.

He was standing there when he heard the sirens.

When he peered out the lobby doors he saw the headlights coming down Main from the direction of City Hall. The first royal blue of dawn glowed over Candler Hill. He started for the stairwell down, then remembered the terrifying moments lost in the lightless darkness. Instead he ducked out the front, as the headlights bobbed closer, and broke into a painful lurching run for two blocks, till he felt safely distant. Then leaned into an alley and panted, eyes closed, holding his side. He felt weak as water.

When he felt a little better he went into the Star Lunch. It was open early, or perhaps late. The smell of beer and grease and cigarette smoke was dead and stale in the close, over-heated air. The very ordinariness of it seemed spooky and weird, as if the men sitting in the booths and at the counters and the women hustling dishes back and forth knew every-thing and were only acting as if nothing out of the ordinary had happened this early winter morning in Pennsylvania. Then, suddenly voracious, he slid into a booth and ordered eggs and ham and home fries.

Gradually he realized he'd killed a man. A man who might have deserved killing; but still, that he was a murderer in the eyes of the law.

Funny, it didn't seem to affect his appetite.

Some time later some of the customers left their seats and booths and gathered at the doorway in front, looking out. "What's goin' on?" he asked the waitress when she came back to warm up his joe.

"I don't know. Something about somebody shooting."

He got up, carrying the heavy mug, and took it to the front. The men, machinists from Holderlin, apparently, were peer-ing out, discussing the shots they'd just heard. One said it was a high-powered rifle, sure. Then a kid ran by on the sidewalk. "What's happenin', boy?" one fellow yelled. The kid turned, still running, and shouted back, "Some guy's holed up in that new Thunder building. He's shootin' back at the cops. Says he won't come out."

Halvorsen's grip weakened on the mug. He set it down by the ruins of someone else's farm breakfast and rubbed his face, feeling the prickly bristle of stubble.

It had to be Shotner.

He'd left him there, thinking he was dead; but he wasn't. That was the only possibility. With that hole in his chest, it couldn't be Latimer. And he'd lifted Deatherage's head, felt the jellylike sliding of bone in a smashed skull. It had to be Shotner.

The only one left who knew he was involved in the bombing.

He pushed past the men, getting some dirty looks, but the expression on his face must have dissuaded any protest. Halfway down the block he realized he'd left his coat in the diner, but he didn't go back despite the wintry air.

He was looking at the squad cars drawn up across the square, at the cops who stood behind them, revolvers drawn, facing the building. An occasional shot boomed out, sounding strange and frightening in the empty street. Looking up, he saw that shades were drawn in the apartments over the small businesses around the square, the dentists' offices and drugstores and the five-and-dime.

"Drift, brother," said a cop. Halvorsen recognized his face, but didn't recall his name. He was fumbling with a gas mask, trying to shorten the rubber straps.

"What's going on?"

"Scram, I said. Some nut with a huntin' rifle inside the building there."

"What are you gonna do?"

"Gonna rush him in a minute. Fire some tear gas in there, then rush him."

"I might be able to talk him out," said Halvorsen. "I think I know who it is."

"Nuts to that," said the officer. "We're through treatin' these Reds with kid gloves. Chief Foster says we're goin' in. There's the gas." A double pop, and smoky trails arched out from the cars to smash through the lobby windows.

"I wouldn't go in there," Halvorsen said. "It's pretty confusing. You'd need lights—"

"I told you to get the hell out of here," said the cop, giving him a shove. He jerked his fists up, but the officer was already running toward the entrance, fumbling to pull the mask down over his face.

Halvorsen watched, hands closing and opening as they disappeared into the lobby. If he was going, he had to go now. Just get in the coupe and go. When they found the nitro, they'd know someone else had been involved. Not to mention the two bodies. Shotner would break and tell them, sooner or later. Once they got him down in that cellar under City Hall, with the rats.

But he didn't go. He just stood there, watching the building in the pearly heatless light of the winter dawn.

The cops stumbled out, jerking their masks up as they cleared the lobby. "Nobody in there," they yelled. "He must of gone back in the building somewhere—"

That suddenly, he knew. Knew what Shotner would do, and how impossible, how suicidal it would be to try to stop him. But still he started forward, yelling "No!"

He was running toward the building when it seemed to bulge. A fraction of a second later a solid invisible wall hit him like a truck.

Where the building had been was suddenly a dusty-gray column of smoke and dust. Beams and bricks suddenly appeared in midair. He looked helplessly skyward as several tumble-arched toward him, then fell and smashed themselves apart on either side of where he crouched, hands locked over his turtled head, on the snowy pavement. The thud echoed back from the surrounding hills.

The smoke and dust blew clear, and for a moment the upper floors of the building seemed undamaged; seemed to stand still; bearing on the great escutcheons the legend THUNDER lifted forever, like a shouted protest from the oppressed earth to the gray, unfeeling sky.

Then they began to crumble, sucking in and downward

with a ground-shaking roar that went on and on. When it stopped, the air seemed still to quiver, as if it had transmitted something too overwhelming for it to bear.

A huge brownish red plume of smoke and dust hung over the heart of the town; then moved slowly off downwind.

A cop picked himself up off the snow. He looked at Halvorsen and said shakily, "The sonofabitch blew himself up. He blew himself up with the whole goddamn building. I just come out of there. Did you see me just come out of there?"

He nodded, suddenly feeling cold, and not just because he was lying coatless in the snow. He pushed himself up and brushed his shirt off with stinging hands, watching as the police began moving aimlessly about in front of the immense smoking heap of bricks and glass and I-beams. Flames were licking up here and there within it. All the windows were smashed around the square. He couldn't quite believe it, but the building was gone. It left a hole in the sky.

He couldn't think what to do next. Shuddering, he plunged his hands into his pockets. Not too much later, he headed back to the Star for his coat.

Thirty-two

Thunner was sitting in the inner office, staring into the flames, when Weyandt came in. He stood for a moment watching his employer. Then cleared his throat.

Thunner started, bringing an angry face into view. "What is it?"

"Mr. Vansittart's on the line. You didn't pick up in here, so I did. They're about to start the product flow."

"Tell him to go ahead." He sat before the fireplace, drumming his fingers; then got up suddenly, and went down the hall.

The air was crisp and chill but the snow-filled valley was full of morning light. He and the office staff stood outside on the cleared pavement. Passersby saw them and looked away. Thunner looked off over their heads, over the cast-iron cornices and false-fronted roofs of the old downtown, toward the smokestacks that streamed up black plumes into the clear sky beyond them.

A shrillness began, seemingly far off, then building and building; till the high steam-shrieking scream echoed through the valley, like some ancient creature imprisoned and tormented. It ended, but almost immediately built again, then again, ebbing and rising until suddenly it cut off so abruptly it left the ear aching with emptiness and loss. Then the echoes came rolling back from the hills, ringing first astonishingly close and then more and more distant in the cold winter air. Six long blasts of the whistle.

Number One was back in production.

Still Thunner lingered, eyes lowered now to the main street.

A little later a roar of engines thundered down the storefronts. A column of huge, slow-moving trucks followed. Troopers stared out from the back, gripping Springfields. The Guard was moving out. The people on the street watched, neither cheering nor reviling. Just watching them go.

He stood till they were out of sight, till the moment broke and was past and gone, part of time and history now; till the passersby scuffed by once more, faces hidden from the relentless wind, and his coatless staff began to shiver around him. Still he lingered, eyes distant. He did not turn, to look toward the still-smoking heap of rubble and brick and broken girders that were all that was left of the edifice he had reared to the heavens.

He would rebuild. He had promised himself that as he stood before the wreckage. Not as grandly. His resources were not infinite. But he would rebuild, and it would stand into the future, symbol of his will and justification for his life.

The strike was over. But it had nearly ruined him. He had to make sure it would never happen again.

At last he shook himself, drew a last deep breath of the clean air, and went back inside.

"Rudy," he said to the secretary, "Where's Ellis?"

"I believe Mr. Hildebrandt's in his office, sir."

"Ask him to step in, please."

When the balding company attorney came in, Thunner indicated for Weyandt to shut the door. They stood waiting as their employer settled himself at the massive desk.

"I want a list," he said.

Hildebrandt pursed his lips. "Of course, Dan. A list of what?"

"I think you know 'of what.' I'm talking about a discharge list. Not only that. A blacklist."

"You understand that sort of thing is quite illegal these days. As well, I think, as unnecessary."

"I agree with Ellis, sir," said Weyandt. "I still think we ought to be magnanimous. I think it'll pay off better in the long run."

"Oh?" said Thunner. "Go down the street, Rudy, and see how being magnanimous pays off. Thank God the construction company carried insurance. If we'd have taken delivery before that bomb went off, we'd be ruined."

Weyandt didn't respond, just looked at the attorney and raised his eyebrows. Thunner took out a sheet of paper. "Now. Here I have the list of Thunner employees who went out. And here a roster of the union membership, committee members, officers, and so forth, with remarks as to their activity and attitudes toward the company. I did not approve of his methods, but Mr. Deatherage did a thorough job. I would like to have the two of you go through these and make me a recommendation as to which employees we will no longer require."

Silence, except for the slow chuckle of the seasoned oak as it burned, the faint roar of the wind in the chimney.

"That would be participating in a felony. I don't believe I can do that for you, Dan," said Hildebrandt.

Thunner studied him. "You can't execute my wishes?"

"I suppose I could. But I don't believe I will."

"Then perhaps Thunder Oil would be better off without you."

"I have been thinking that myself, sir." Hildebrandt folded his spectacles with dignity, slipped them back into his vest pocket. "My resignation will be on your desk this afternoon. Good day."

Thunner watched him go, taken aback at having what had really been a bluff called. But there were plenty of lawyers in the world. He asked Weyandt, "How about it? You deserting too?"

The young man smiled. "Not me, Mr. Thunner. You'll have to carry me out of this company feetfirst."

"Good man."

"I'll take care of the dismissals, sir. But maybe you'd better mark the list yourself."

Thunner regarded him for a moment; then uncapped his fountain pen and bent forward, lips tightening.

Some of the names he knew; many he didn't. In his father's day, Colonel Charles Thunner had known every man he employed by sight and handshake. The works were too extensive now, but still he was acquainted with many of them, could put faces to many names, recognized their families. He was not doing something he enjoyed, or felt proud of. But he steeled himself and went slowly and conscientiously down the roster, putting a single letter after each name: R for retain; D for immediate discharge; B for discharge and blacklist throughout the Pennsylvania oil fields.

He was nearing the end when a tap came on the door. Weyandt went to it immediately, looking displeased, but his face changed to a smile of welcome as a dark-haired woman in a veil and furs stepped in. Behind her trotted a little girl.

Leola said, "Hello, Rudy. Forgive me for interrupting, Dan; I thought we would stop in for a moment before we go to the club. I'll send Ainslee back with Miss Verre, in the car. But she wouldn't give me a moment's peace. She has something for you."

"Mama, don't *tell* him." The little girl's face began to crumple.

"All right, all right, don't *cry*. You see what I mean. Go on, then, child. He's your father, don't be afraid."

"I made it," the little girl said. He took it; it was a cut-out picture of a man, colored with crayons.

"Well, what's this, honey?"

"It's you."

"Why have I got a saw on my head?"

"Silly. That's a crown."

"And is this you? Beside me? And you're a princess, I see. Is this your horse? What's his name?"

Face lowered, she muttered something he didn't quite catch. He chuckled as if he had heard it, though, and patted her head. Then he went back to his task. She dawdled, looking on. He came to Halvorsen's name, hesitated, then struck it through savagely. This was his return for helping a promising young man, hiring him on, training him, putting him in the ring.

"That's the letter B," she said, and he started, looking down at her again.

"Why, that's right, honey. I didn't know you could read."

"I know the letters. What are you doing, Daddy?" she asked, laying her head on her shoulder and regarding him with serious eyes.

"Making sure the company's safe, honey." He finished the paper and folded it, slid it into an envelope, sealed it. He handed it to Weyandt. "Have it typed up by someone you trust. Original to head of Personnel, marked Return. Carbon copies of the B list to the heads of the other corporations. Put the original in my safe when it comes back to the office." But she still watched him and he turned to face her.

"Honey, there's nothing more important than the company. It's what gives us everything we've got, and makes us everything we are. Someday you'll have a little brother. And he'll run our company, and maybe you'll help him, and it will belong to him and you."

"Why can't I run it?" the little girl said, eyes dark and thoughtful, fixed on his.

He chuckled. "Well, that isn't the way we do it, Princess. But tell you what, we'll go down later today and I'll give you another little tour. All right? Would you like that?"

He reached down, and the little girl smiled, the tears forgotten as her tall and wonderful father lifted her up above the world; up to where it was warm and high and made you laugh half in fun and half in terror. And she looked down from near the ceiling at their faces, her mother, smiling, and her father's friend, and the old room, and Grandpa's pictures, and the fire; and resolved to herself then, in that moment, that she would always remember this, and always love them, and always make them proud.

THE
AFTERIMAGE

He saw the soldiers ahead, deployed across the square, as soon as they turned onto Grant Street.

It was a gray cold morning in the Smoky City. He and Jennie had gotten up at five, long before dawn, and had coffee and doughnuts at a counter on Market and Fifth. Keeping it to ten cents apiece; they were traveling on what he'd sold the Oakland for, and what she'd saved from the stocking factory, and they had a long way to go before they could earn more. Harv Mulholland had warned them to get to court early if they wanted to see anything. He said one way or another, it probably wouldn't take long.

Halvorsen found a place at the curb for the Indian and put a penny in the meter. "Careful," he said. He put his hand under her thigh to help her down off the bike. She flinched, then blushed, holding his hand tight.

Last night had been their first together, in a second-class rooming house down on the Point. Father Guertin had married them yesterday morning in a hasty ceremony, and they'd climbed on the cycle as soon as they left the church and headed for Pittsburgh. He'd ridden the whole day with her arms around him from behind and everything they owned on their backs; and that night they knew each other for the first time.

On their first married day together a throat-stinging haze lay close over the Golden Triangle, tanning the air itself with the haze from Homestead and Turtle Creek. The cobblestones were slick with river muck, dank and clotted like old blood. The desk clerk who'd checked them in as Mr. and Mrs. Halvorsen told them that two weeks ago his desk had been under water. The three rivers had crested at the Point at over forty-six feet, and the only way about the Triangle was by canoe or rowboat. Now debris and mud lay everywhere. He stopped for a minute, sucking in the poisoned air.

"You feelin' all right?" she said.

He shook himself. "Yeah. Let's go. That must be the courthouse, there."

The massive granite building was as gray as the Depression. A line of brown-uniformed National Guardsmen in doughboy helmets surrounded it, bayoneted rifles holding back a sullen-looking crowd. He asked a guy what was going on and he said, "We're strikin' the friggin' mills. Steel Workers Organizing Committee."

"Good luck, brother. I'm in oil myself." He tipped his cap.

"Just watch yourself on the street. Them goddamn Silver Shirts are out lookin' for people ta beat on today."

They climbed broad granite steps toward brass doors. Two burly state cops in Sam Brownes and riding boots stared them down as they approached, campaign hats shading lifeless eyes. But they said nothing, let them pass, and the revolving doors hissed around, wrapping them in close, oppressive steam heat.

At the far end of a marble corridor he caught the hefty

suit-filling bulk of Harvey Mulholland, fedora covering his early bald patch. Stan Melnichak, in a work shirt and a cloth cap and a leather jacket. A dapper fellow in a raccoon overcoat and a Trotsky beard: the lawyer from the CIO. He and Jennie walked toward them across the green-and-white tile floor. He wished he had a chew. His mouth was dry. He sensed the hovering presence of Justice.

They stood waiting for a few minutes, then a tall door opened. "Our turn," said Mulholland, straightening. "Remember now, no spoutin' off in here, it just hurts us. We got to depend on the law to make this right."

The courtroom was smaller than he expected, the ceiling lower. There wasn't much of an audience. Mainly just three state troopers standing against the walls, and an empty bench, flanked by the flags of the United States and of Pennsylvania. The floor was bare scarred wood, old and scuffed white by generations of shoes. The radiators clanked and murmured to themselves like impatient spectators.

"This is it?" he muttered to Melnichak. "There's no jury or anything?"

"Right now it's a lawsuit," said Mulholland. "We're here to get it to trial. Quiet down now, here comes Scholtens."

"All stand. Oyez, oyez, oyez. The Federal District Court for the Western District of Pennsylvania is now in session."

A scrawny little old man with pince-nez like Woodrow Wilson's dragged his feet across the floor. He fumbled his way into his seat, adjusting his spectacles as the clerk told everyone to sit, then slid several documents in front of him. The judge pored over them for a long time with a cunning, sly expression. Then in a high thin voice he said without looking up, "The Congress of Industrial Organization and Oil Workers International Union Local Number One Hundred Seventy-Eight, versus the Thunder Oil Company, Daniel Thunner, et al., is dismissed due to failure to state a cause of action." He rose instantly. Everyone else surged to their feet, too. Halvorsen rose with them, gaping as the judge left the room in a swirl of black skirts.

The two attorneys, expressions grim, were picking up their unopened briefcases. He said to Mulholland, "What—what the hell was that? He didn't say anything about them killing Shorty, or Doris, or that scab—about shooting us down, and gassing people—"

"And he isn't going to. Those would be state charges, anyway. Failure to state a cause of action means even if what we claimed was true, we can't get any relief from the court. We don't have a right to organize, and nothing we say's going to change that."

"This is the law?"

"The slave-labor law the Fricks and Mellons bought." Mulholland looked like he was about to spit. "It'll change someday. And then we'll remake the world. But till then, brothers, I'm afraid we're at the end of this road."

He stood trembling, seeing again the faces of dead friends; of dying children; the pinched, pasty faces of starving and hopeless men.

Then through his anger and shame he felt a hand seeking his. He looked down into Jennie's gentle, questioning eyes. "We still going, Bill?"

He swallowed, understanding all that was past now; that his life had changed, and left so much and so many behind. That it would never be the same again.

"Yeah, I guess we'd better," he said.

The Indian was where they'd left it, Jennie's suitcase and his hunting pack and his dad's old Krag still lashed on behind. He stood for a moment, contemplating it; then raised his eyes.

To the high long shadows that lay behind the smoke of the steel mills and the mists of a rainy April; the everlasting mountains, already green with the first buds and early grass of spring. It didn't seem possible that he'd never see them again. That he could live without their silent presence, or ever feel at home. Well, maybe someday they could come

back. Someday, when all that had happened this year was
past and gone and maybe not forgotten, but at least not so
red raw that just to think of it made him grind his teeth
together till his jaw hurt.

"You ready to go?" he asked her.

"I'm your wife now, Billy."

"That blacklist reaches a long way. I'm just hopin' it don't
reach out to Texas. Gonna be a hell of a rough ride on this
bone-shaker." He hesitated. "I don't know if we'll ever get
that little house you wanted—"

"It don't matter. As long as we're together, I'll be happy,"
she said, and the trust and love in her face made him look
away. Made the sadness and anger fade, replaced by something he hadn't felt in a long time. Something that lies and
betrayal and violence had come close to crushing out. But
now he felt it stirring, like a nearly crushed seed, trampled
down, beaten, defeated, all but destroyed; but that nonetheless felt and responded to the suspicion or hint or even just
the bare possibility, of spring.

Like Mulholland had said, someday things would change.
Justice would triumph, and the truth could be spoken, and
men would do what was right. This wasn't the end of anybody's struggle. And maybe the fight wouldn't never end;
maybe it was part of what the world was and what men were,
for some reason they none of them were privy to or were
smart enough to understand. Until then, they'd have to settle
for what they had: for being young, and free, and loving each
other.

But one damn thing he'd learned, from Doris, and Shorty,
and Stan, and all the other men and women he'd stood shoulder to shoulder with. One thing he could take away and hold
on to. That wherever he saw a picket line, he knew a line he
wasn't going to cross; and as long as there was a barricade,
he knew which side he was on; and as long as somebody
was hungry, and another fella had more than he'd ever need,
he knew which of the two he was going to stand with.

He kicked the old cycle into roaring life and threw his leg
over it, then held out his hand. She slid on behind him, pull-

ing her dress down as she straddled it. The engine howled
as he fed it gas, shuddering on the mud-slicked cobblestones,
and he groped behind him to squeeze her hand once, tight,
close, before he kicked it into gear.